Strike A Match 3
Endangered Nation

Frank Tayell

Dedicated to Ruth & Ollie

Published by Frank Tayell
Copyright 2017
All rights reserved

All people, places, and (especially) events are fictional.

ISBN-13: 978-1979127691
ISBN-10: 1979127697

Other titles:

Post-Apocalyptic Detective Novels
Strike a Match 1. Serious Crimes
Strike a Match 2. Counterfeit Conspiracy
Strike a Match 3: Endangered Nation
Work. Rest. Repeat.

Surviving The Evacuation/Here We Stand
Book 1: London
Book 2: Wasteland
Zombies vs The Living Dead
Book 3: Family
Book 4: Unsafe Haven
Book 5: Reunion
Book 6: Harvest
Book 7: Home
Here We Stand 1: Infected & 2: Divided
Book 8: Anglesey
Book 9: Ireland
Book 10: The Last Candidate
Book 11: Search and Rescue

For more information, visit:
http://blog.franktayell.com
www.facebook.com/FrankTayell

Prologue - Refugees
17th September 2028, Channel Tunnel Refugee Camp, Kent
Nine Years After The Blackout

"Did you think we'd ever see so many people again?" Hassan Hafiz asked.

Saleema Hafiz smiled as she turned her eyes from their young daughter to the refugee camp built a few miles from the Folkestone entrance to the Channel Tunnel. "I didn't think there were this many people left in the entire world," she said.

The two parents sat at a sun-bleached, bird-pecked picnic table at the top of a grass-covered embankment. At the bottom of the slope, grass turned to a weed-dotted expanse of tarmac, marking the beginning of a monstrous vehicle park. The few trucks and lorries that had been abandoned there after the nuclear holocaust, nine years and one month ago, had been pushed to one side, left to rust in peace. In their place was a sprawling refugee camp. A forest of worn tents and corrugated lean-tos sprouted around each of the battered pre-Blackout buildings. Those temporary restrooms and restaurants, customs offices and cells had been built in preparation for congestion and delays that the nuclear war meant had never come. Some of those buildings had been re-purposed, others repaired, but all were full of those escaping the hunger and horror of the continental wasteland.

"There are more people coming through the Channel Tunnel," Hassan said. "Do you see?"

"I do," Saleema said. Like themselves, those new refugees would have endured a thirty-mile walk from Calais made in near pitch-darkness. It had taken their small family a day and a half to make that nightmare journey. There were no trains through the Channel Tunnel, not anymore, but there were trains in Britain. The smoke-billowing locomotive to the west of the camp was a sight even more wondrous than that of so many people.

"We'll be on that train soon," Saleema murmured. "On a train, Hassan. A train!"

"In three days, two hours, ten minutes, give or take," he said. An old reflex had him reach into a pocket to retrieve his phone to check that he had the correct time, but he had no phone, nor a watch, and nor did she. Neither had anything but each other, the clothes on their backs, and their daughter, Sameen. Their daughter had fared slightly better, having managed to bring a stuffed bear with her all the way from the compound. The ribbon was still around the bear's neck, but a fire had singed all but four letters from it: R, U, T, H. The young girl still clutched that bear in an iron-grip that rarely slackened even when she was asleep. Now, the bear trailed through the wild grass as the girl tugged daisies, mayweed, and dandelions from the soil.

"Three more days and three more nights in that tent," Saleema said. "At least it's not too cold."

"It's almost pleasant," Hassan said. "Remember August? Who knew that mountains got so hot in the summer?"

Saleema smiled, but said nothing. Before the Blackout, Hassan had spent his days in a temperature-controlled lab, his nights in an air-conditioned apartment. He had an encyclopaedic knowledge of anything binary, but a minuscule one of the world beyond.

The train sounded its whistle. Startled, Sameen dropped her flowers.

"Wave, dear, wave," Saleema said. "The train's going. Wave them goodbye."

Hesitantly, glancing more at her parents than the locomotive, the girl did.

"When we leave, we'll have been here ten days," Saleema said. "And thanks to Sameen, we're getting priority travel. That tells us a lot about how many people they were expecting."

"They thought it would be five hundred a week," Hassan said. "It's four hundred arriving each day, with a margin of error of plus or minus thirteen. That's in a camp with a maximum capacity of ten thousand, but which now has twelve thousand, two hundred and ninety-seven living here. Not counting those people coming through the Tunnel right now."

"You asked?" Saleema was surprised. Hassan wasn't exactly anti-social, but he'd not had much experience in socialising before they'd met ten years ago. That had been one year before the Blackout. There hadn't been much chance to socialise since.

"No," Hassan said. "When I was helping wash up, I counted the bowls. I crosschecked those against the latrines' storage capacity and the frequency with which they're emptied. It's a simple enough calculation."

"You know," she said, smiling, "if you'd asked, I'm sure someone would have told you."

"It's safer not to ask," Hassan said.

"This isn't the compound," she said. "No, it really isn't. I met some people from Ukraine at the clinic," she added. "Or Sameen did. She's good at meeting people."

"Ukraine? Where?"

"Kovalyn," Saleema said. "Well, no, they came from a place near Kovalyn which I couldn't begin to pronounce. It was a village on the eastern banks of the Dnieper River, in the shadow of an old water treatment plant."

"That's about two and a half thousand kilometres away," Hassan said.

"We travelled further," Saleema said. "Though they travelled for longer. They left in February. Their village depended on winter wheat, but the winter came early, and the snow came soon after. By January, it was clear that they were only going to have enough for half of their village. They drew lots to see who'd leave."

"Well, that doesn't make sense," Hassan said. "That would only leave them with half the labour to grow the food this year. By now, another half will have left. The remainder will leave next spring."

"Probably," Saleema said. "There were three hundred in that village. One hundred and thirty-eight left. Nineteen made it here."

"Oh. What route did they take?"

"South, at first," she said. "Towards the Black Sea. Something… something happened, but I'm not sure what. They turned around and went north. They ended up in the ruins of Hamburg before they found a convoy heading to Britain."

"They went south at first? Hadn't they heard of how Britain was recovering?" Hassan asked.

"No," Saleema said. "Not in their village. No convoy had reached it. They heard rumours from a few trappers as they travelled, but they weren't looking to come so far. They wanted a season of labour where they could earn food to take back to their village. It was around the time they reached the Danube that they knew they'd never see their home again. There were other people in the clinic with similar stories. Forced to flee by hunger, or the weather, or by bandits. And some of those bandits came from neighbouring villages where the harvest had already failed."

"That's similar to what we heard on that convoy," Hassan said. "And it has to be a similar story all across the world."

It was nine years and one month since the digital viruses were unleashed. They'd infected every circuit and motor that was on a network. Gates were unlocked, sluices were opened, motors overheated, and engines were shut down. Dams emptied, ferries sunk, planes fell out of the sky, and power stations failed. Batteries overheated and laptops and phones caught fire. Those fires spread to tables and desks, to rooms and roofs, and cities burned. No fire engines worked, no hydrants had the pressure to put out the flames. There were no ambulances to take the injured for treatment, and no electricity in the hospitals to provide it. The police had done what they could, supplemented by scratch military units and civilian volunteers. There was little that they could do. There was little anyone could do. So someone had done the unthinkable. Nuclear missiles had been launched. The electromagnetic pulse destroyed the electronic circuitry that the viruses had infected, but the fireballs and fallout destroyed civilisation. That first winter had been long. The second had been longer. Billions had died. But Britain, somehow, had survived better than most. Rumours of that had even spread to the underground compound. When it became clear to Saleema that they had to flee if their daughter was ever to have a life of her own, there was only one logical destination.

They had stolen an APC, slipped away in the dead of night, and made nearly five hundred miles across ruined roads before they ran out of fuel. Over the next week, they managed another fifty miles before they ran out of food. They would have died if they hadn't stumbled across the convoy. It had come from Britain, and was on a survey mission searching for communities of survivors. They'd found a few, though none large enough to even be called a village. The Hafiz family had been found room in the back of a wagon, and the rest of their journey was easy, though long.

Sameen ran up, a posy of partially crushed flowering weeds in her hand, the bear still clutched in the other. She thrust the flowers towards Saleema.

"They're beautiful, my sweet," Saleema said. "Just as beautiful as you. Now, why don't you find some for Daddy? But don't run too far," she added as their daughter rushed off along the overgrown embankment.

"Do you think she'll ever talk?" Hassan asked.

"There are doctors in the city," Saleema said. "Psychiatrists, too. She'll be fine when there is a little normality in her life."

Sameen had been born in the underground compound, and hadn't seen the sky until they'd escaped. She'd never spoken, though she occasionally mumbled in her sleep. The girl clearly understood what she heard, but simply didn't want to talk. As to why and what that meant, Saleema had no idea, and nor did any of the other coders and scientists who had grown to call the compound home.

Saleema had met Hassan ten years ago, one year before the Blackout, at a small conference that was being used as a recruitment fair by the man who would become their employer. Out of the hundreds who'd attended, she and Hassan were the only two who were offered a job. The salary was ridiculous, three times that which a post-doc fellow should be able to command. They'd both said yes. Hassan specialised in algorithms associated with pattern recognition, Saleema on more esoteric code to differentiate the moral from the immoral, but everyone was working towards one goal: to create the world's first truly intelligent artificial life. Saleema hadn't considered what that life would be used for.

Their work wasn't complete when the Blackout occurred, but it took years before she learned their creations had a part in that horror. Saleema had learned the truth of what had happened, and what she and Hassan had been involved in, shortly after Sameen was born. She and her new-born were in the compound's medical room. As Sameen slept, and Saleema rested her eyes, she heard her employer talking with Mr Emmitt in the corridor beyond.

What she'd heard hadn't made sense at first. Other people across the world had been working towards the same goal of creating artificial life. When it became clear that someone was going to beat them to it, a collection of digital viruses had been released. They were Frankenstein creations, abominations based on the research that she and Hassan, and all the others, had been working on. Those viruses had gone rogue, replicating, mutating, and rewriting their own code in a bid to survive. That was how the world had died. That was *why* the world had died. Simply so a vain man wouldn't be beaten to success.

Even knowing the truth, she and Hassan couldn't leave, not with an infant daughter and no known refuge. Days became weeks, and those turned to years. Mr Emmitt had gone out and come back, and so had other teams. News reached them of the horrors of the outside world, along with whispers that Britain had survived.

It turned out that those whispers had been wishful exaggeration. Britain had steam trains and coal power plants. It had a few hospitals and schools, but it was only a dim Victorian shadow of its former self.

"Why do they call the capital city Twynham, do you think?" Hassan asked.

"I'm not sure," Saleema said. "It's where Bournemouth used to be, I think. That's a seaside town."

"One and three-quarter million people here in Britain," he said. "It's not quite what we thought. I heard there's at least ten million in America."

"How would we cross the Atlantic?" Saleema asked.

"They have ships," Hassan said. "I asked. They send food and medicine across the Atlantic. We could buy passage."

"With what money?" she asked, plucking at her threadbare coat. "Besides, we want to stay hidden, and the best place to do that is surrounded by other refugees. That means Twynham. In America, how many people do you think come from thousands of miles away? We'd be too conspicuous."

"No one's looking for us," Hassan said. "But if they are, then distance is our best ally."

"We'll see," Saleema said. "But let's see what Twynham is like first."

Sameen ran over with another fistful of partially crushed flowers. Hassan took them and smiled. "Thank you, precious."

"They have schools in Twynham," Saleema said. "Schools with lots of other children."

Sameen tilted her head to one side, and gave her mother a quizzical look. Then she smiled.

"Maybe it won't be so bad," Hassan said.

"Maybe not," Saleema agreed. "But we've three days to go before we leave. Shall we go and see what's for lunch?"

Sameen took Saleema's hand, then held out her stuffed bear towards Hassan. He laughed, and took its grubby paw. Laughing, the family headed back towards the camp.

It took a minute before Saleema noticed the figure walking towards them. He didn't look like a refugee, or like one of the people from Twynham. His swagger was almost familiar. The man drew nearer and she saw his face. It was criss-crossed with scars. She stopped. Hassan did the same.

"What is it?" he asked. His face turned ashen as he saw the man walking towards them.

"Mr Emmitt," Saleema murmured. Sameen edged behind her mother's leg. Saleema looked around for help, for somewhere to hide, but it was too late. They had run for months, for thousands of miles, and yet they had been found.

Mr Emmitt stopped ten yards from them. His face moved in what might have been a smile, but as the scars moved, it only made his grimace even more sinister. He crouched down and addressed their daughter.

"Hello, Sameen," he said. "I've been looking for you."

"How did you find us?" Hassan asked.

"Where else would you go?" Mr Emmitt said, straightening. "What do you think of England? You never saw it before the Blackout, did you? Personally, I think this is an improvement."

"Why are you here?" Saleema asked. "We're not going back."

"You left with something that belongs to our employer," Mr Emmitt said. "I'm here to retrieve it."

"We didn't take anything," Hassan said.

"If it wasn't for us," Mr Emmitt said, "you would be dead. You would both have died during the nuclear holocaust. Instead, you are alive. You had a child. Oh, yes, you took something. You signed a contract, one that promised our employer everything you produced during the time of your service. *Everything*. Including her. Breach of contract is a serious matter."

"Contracts? You can't be serious," Hassan said. "Look around you. Look at this place. What contract is worth anything?"

"No," Mr Emmitt said. "You look around. Look down there. Refugee camps and clinics, trains and farms. The world is returning to where it was. Slowly, perhaps, but it is returning. In ten years, we'll have restored everything that was lost. When your daughter has children of her own, they will have computers and networks and *she* shall control them. Her grandchildren will control the world. The Blackout was a blip, a delay that will become a footnote in history."

"You're deluded," Hassan said.

Mr Emmitt shrugged. "We can discuss this on our journey."

"We're not going back with you," Saleema said. "And you can't make us. There are soldiers down there. You're right, there *is* a government. We'll tell them everything about you."

"And will you tell them about your own part in the end of the world?" Mr Emmitt asked.

"We didn't know," Hassan said.

"Yes," Saleema said. "Yes, we *will* tell them. We'll tell them everything. Whatever they do to us, Sameen will be safe."

Mr Emmitt sighed. "Why do people have to make everything so complicated?" He reached into his inside pocket and took out a small black case. He opened it, and extracted an injector-pen. He held it to his own neck, and pressed the plunger. He winced. "A choice, then," he said as he put the pen back into the case and took out a small glass vial. He dropped it to the ground and crushed it beneath his boot.

"What was that?" Hassan asked.

"It's remarkable how some people used to make a living," Mr Emmitt said. "You two spent your lives developing code. I spent mine fixing problems, but there are some who toiled away refining the worst viruses known to mankind. What's remarkable is how many of those viruses survived the Blackout. Take that one, for example. It can survive in temperatures from fifty degrees below to a hundred above boiling. It will remain viable in the air for up to three hours, after which it will die unless it's found a nice set of lungs in which to make its home." He glanced at the young girl hugging her father's leg. "I'll spare you the details. Suffice to say, it won't be pleasant." He put the case back into his pocket. Licked his finger, then held it up, testing the wind. "Ah, I think it might well spread to the camp. That's a pity. Still, there are plenty of refugees in Britain. I don't think they'll miss a few thousand more. They certainly won't miss you two. As you might have gathered, I have the antidote. You have about twenty-four hours in which it will be effective." He glanced down again at Sameen. "She *is* coming back with me. I'll leave you two to choose for yourself. There is a pub two miles up the road behind you. It's called the Five Bells. I will be there tonight. Tomorrow morning, I shall leave. Make your choice." He gave another evil smile, and walked away.

Hassan and Saleema stayed motionless until he had disappeared beyond the embankment.

"What do we do?" Hassan asked.

"He was lying," Saleema said. "Of course he was lying. There aren't any chemical-weapon stores left in the world, and they certainly didn't have any in the compound. No, he just wants to get us away from the soldiers down there."

"Then what do we do? Tell them?"

"No. Take Sameen," she said. "Meet me on the railway tracks, at that spot beyond the platform where there's that big tree. The one we saw two days ago, remember? I'll be there soon."

"Where are you going?"

"To get supplies for our trip," she said. "That's right, dear, we're going on a trip. A long trip. You're right, Hassan, Britain wasn't far enough away. Go. Quick now, I'll be there in an under an hour."

Saleema jogged away before Hassan could ask any more questions. They would only be a variation on where they were going and how they would get there, and she didn't have an answer. Maybe they could find a way onto a ship heading for America, or maybe they'd disappear into the English wasteland. For now, they had to get away from Mr Emmitt. He'd been correct in that Britain had been their only logical destination, but now they were here, would he really be able to find them again? She turned her mind away from that question, because the answer was too depressing. Instead, she focused on their immediate needs. Water was easy, and available to all at the pump-house by the old customs shed. Food was more difficult as it was stored inside what had been a small restaurant for lorry drivers. When she saw Martin Lowell was guarding the food-store, she realised it wouldn't be that difficult at all. The young man couldn't be more than a day over eighteen and was probably at least a year younger. Chronically embarrassed and far too trusting, that he was on guard duty spoke to how overstretched the staff in the refugee camp were. She coughed as she approached, then smiled as he looked at her.

"Hello, Martin. There's a problem in the clinic," she said. "We've a baby who won't take his mother's breast. We need to get some nutrients into him. Since there isn't any formula, we're going to try a powdered potato soup. We need a few boxes."

"Oh, right, of course," the young man said, stepping aside.

"Thanks," she said, went in, and grabbed a few of the boxes from the shelf. They were new-made cardboard, completely absent of logo or design. That they contained powdered potato was inked on the packet with a smudgy stamp.

"Thanks," she said, giving him another smile as she walked out.

The boxes weren't much, and Sameen wouldn't like it, but the potatoes were fortified with all of the nutrients a person needed. It would be enough to see them through the next two days. That should be all they needed. A plan was forming, a way for them to get away and be rid of Mr Emmitt forever.

She took a breath, but it caught in the back of her throat. She coughed, and found it hard to stop. She wasn't the only one walking with a hand raised to her mouth, coughing, spluttering. That wasn't Mr Emmitt, she told herself. Many of the refugees arrived sick. That was why she and her family had to sleep in a tent. The warmer, drier buildings were given over to those who were ill.

Her foot hit a guy-rope, and she stumbled. Focus, she told herself as she coughed again. She had to focus. Get to the railway. Get away from the Channel Tunnel.

She stumbled again, but then was beyond the tents. The air seemed fresher, the sky brighter as she hurried towards the railway line.

Hassan and Sameen were waiting. There was no sign of anyone else.

"I got powdered—" She coughed. "Powdered potato. Let's go."

"Are you all right?" Hassan asked.

"I'm fine," Saleema said.

"Have you considered that Mr Emmitt might expect us to run?" Hassan asked.

"I have," Saleema said. "But that doesn't mean we shouldn't. Too much introspection can only lead to inaction." That was something her father had often said. She coughed.

"Maybe we should go back," Hassan said. "Get you to the doctors."

"Hassan, be sensible," she said. "He wants Sameen, doesn't he? Even if he found a deadly virus, he wouldn't unleash it because that would hurt her, aside that it would kill thousands of others." Even as she said it, a seed of doubt began to grow. Mr Emmitt was a sadist and a murderer. She had seen him kill twice in the compound, and was sure he'd done far worse out in the wilderness.

"You're right, of course you are," Hassan said. "Where now? There won't be a train until tomorrow."

"Not from Folkestone," she said. "They have a naval base in Dover, which they supply by train. We just have to follow these tracks until it joins the railway line from Dover."

"And then, what? We jump—" He coughed. "It's nothing. I swallowed a fly, that's all. So we just jump onto the train?"

"They're steam trains, so they have to stop for water," Saleema said. "That's where we board. We follow the tracks until we get to a watering-stop. We wait for a train, and then we sneak aboard. We'll go to Twynham first, but then we'll get a boat to America. We'll disappear into the wide plains. We'll build a cabin somewhere among the sage." She stumbled.

"We should go back," Hassan said. He coughed.

"No, let's stop. Just for a minute," Saleema said. "Just a few minutes so I can catch my breath. Not here, somewhere quiet in case he's followed us. Over there, that bridge."

It was an old stone bridge, fallen into disrepair and disuse long before the Blackout. Saleema leaned against the crumbling balustrade, sucking in air. It was so hard to breathe, so hard to focus. She leaned forward. The ancient stone gave, and before she could catch herself, she slipped and skidded down the embankment and into the dry riverbed.

"Mama!" Sameen called, running after her.

Before Saleema could rejoice that their daughter had finally spoken, her breath caught, and she began hacking, coughing. She was unable to stop, even when Sameen slipped on the moss-covered stones and tumbled down the muddy incline. Hassan was hot on her heels, skidding after her, picking their daughter up seconds after she landed in a heap.

"Are you… are you okay?" Saleema managed to wheeze.

Sameen said nothing. Hassan carefully put her down, then sat on the dry leaves. They wouldn't stay dry for long. A raindrop fell on the back of Saleema's neck. Then another. A soft patter of large drops fell from a grey sky that promised there were far more to come.

"We… we have to… to go back," Saleema said. "To the pub. The… The Five Bells."

"No," Hassan said. "No, we… we…" But his words were lost in a hacking cough.

"We do," Saleema said. Her knees and elbows screamed in agony as she pushed herself to her feet. "Come on, Sameen."

Their daughter stood and took her mother's hand.

"This way," Saleema said, and led her daughter along the dry riverbed, back towards the Channel Tunnel. Hassan pulled himself up, and followed.

"He really… he really did it," Hassan said. "He poisoned us."

"He poisoned the entire camp," Saleema said. "Just to… just to get us back."

"Why?" Hassan said.

Saleema looked at her daughter, then back at Hassan. She thought she knew the answer, but she would never say it, not to him. Her foot hit a root, she tripped, fell.

Hassan reached down, but there was barely any strength to his grip. She managed to get back to her feet.

"The rain's getting heavier. We should stop," Saleema said. "Rest. For a few minutes."

"I don't think we have time," Hassan said.

"We do. He said we had until tomorrow morning," Saleema said. Ahead was a delivery truck. From the gouges in the side of the embankment, someone hadn't realised the riverbed was there until it was too late. From the moss growing on the tyres, it had been there for years. The rain grew harder, pounding on the metal, echoing loudly in her skull. She thought it was the rain. Saleema pushed herself past the truck. The cold metal against her skin was like ice and then fire. She reached the cab, the door was open, but only a few inches.

"Here," she said. "We'll rest here for a few minutes. Just until the rain stops."

"A few minutes," Hassan said. "No longer."

The three of them climbed inside. The rain pounded on the fractured windscreen, but the cab was dry. Sameen began to cry.

"Hush," Saleema said. "Hush. It's okay. It's going to be okay."

"She… she dropped her bear," Hassan said. "It's… it's outside."

"Here, look at this," Saleema said. She pulled the leather-bound photo-album out of her bag. It was small, but she had few pictures of her life before the Blackout. There weren't many taken since, but there was one, taken just before they fled the compound. It was just the three of them, mother, father, and daughter, standing between two artificial plants. Looking at the picture had seemed to comfort their daughter during their long trek to Britain. Saleema held the photo-album out, but it fell from her fingers to land in the footwell.

Sameen cried, and that cry turned to a cough.

"I'll... I'll get her bear," Hassan said. But he didn't move

Chapter 1 - Hot Pursuit
5th November 2039, Edinburgh

Captain Henry Mitchell ducked just before the metal box flew over his head. The box hit the row of rusting shelves and, as Mitchell reached out to grab Pollock's arm, the shelves collapsed. The detective leaped back, and the murderer ran towards the rear of the ruined supermarket.

"Why do they always run?" Mitchell muttered, as Pollock pushed his way through the rotting rubber doors that led to the supermarket's storeroom.

Mitchell took out his flashlight, turned it on, and scanned the ground for his truncheon. His wasn't one of the standard-issue torches with their fragile filament bulbs, but an old-world LED light, barely larger than his palm but with a beam that could stretch for a hundred yards. It was excellent as a light, but useless as a cudgel, and Mitchell was determined not to use his sidearm. He wanted Pollock alive.

The truncheon lay on top of a decayed sign where only the words *Must End Soon* hadn't yet been consumed by iridescent black mould. Mitchell grabbed his nightstick, clambered over the fallen shelves, and headed after Pollock. As he reached the broken door, he heard a rattle of chains from deep inside the stockroom.

Mitchell grinned. "I locked the door!" he yelled. "There's no escape that way. There's no escape anywhere. Your description has gone to every ship in every harbour. You won't get out of Britain. Just accept it, Pollock, I caught you. Surrender." He paused, waiting, listening. After such a long chase, Mitchell doubted the man would give up so easily. He was right.

He heard a sound. A terrifyingly familiar click of a magazine being slotted into place. Mitchell dived sideways just before a cloud of bullets shredded the rotten door. As lead ricocheted off shelves and freezers, Mitchell squirmed across the dirt-strewn floor until he was behind a cracked pillar supporting the partially collapsed ceiling. He clipped the truncheon back onto his belt, turned off his flashlight, and drew his sidearm. It wasn't a government-issue revolver, but an old world nine-millimetre so familiar it felt like an extension of his hand.

The detective weighed up his options. There were two ways out of the supermarket, but both were from the main part of the store. There was the customer entrance, partially blocked by the rusting remains of an ambulance, or there was the hole in the roof above the frozen-food aisle. It was beneath that hole that Pollock had set his bivouac. From the brief glimpse Mitchell had caught before he was seen, Pollock wasn't the first to camp in the ruined supermarket. In fact, Mitchell suspected it was the remains of the previous fires that had inspired Pollock to take shelter here.

The smoke from that fire had been visible for two miles. As everyone knew that the monks in Edinburgh Castle offered shelter to all weary travellers, he'd surmised Pollock might have started the fire. Mitchell arrived at the supermarket three hours previously, climbed onto the roof, confirmed he'd found his quarry, then crept around to the rear and secured the exit in the loading dock. That the murderer hadn't noticed him spoke to how Pollock truly wasn't cut out for the life of a fugitive. More immediately, it meant the desperate man's only escape was through Mitchell. He slid the safety off his pistol.

"Just surrender," he called out.

"You surrender," Pollock replied. "You know what this is?" There was another rat-a-tat and a corresponding thud and ping as bullets ripped through the doors.

"Why don't you come out here so I can see it better," Mitchell called back, easing himself lower.

Pollock was stupid, but not that stupid. "It's an AK-47. Do you know what that is?"

"Of course I do," Mitchell said. "Did Emmitt give it to you?"

"I didn't work for him," Pollock said.

"Who *did* you work for?" Mitchell replied.

Three weeks ago, after Emmitt's arrest, Captain Henry Mitchell had scoured through the evidence left in Longfield's home, Commissioner Wallace's office, and in Emmitt's lair in the New Forest. None of them had left anything so useful as an alphabetical list of their co-conspirators, but Mitchell was a detective. A *good* detective. He'd devoted the last twenty years of his life to mastering the craft. One by one, he'd identified the co-conspirators, their confederates, and the criminals they'd employed as muscle. Arrests had been made, and though not every arrest had led to a confession, enough had. Mitchell had rolled up almost the entire organisation in a matter of five days and six sleepless nights. *Almost* the entire organisation. Some had run, and Mitchell had given chase. Pollock was one of the last to be caught.

"We've arrested everyone else," Mitchell called. "Give it up, Pollock. There's no escape. Your only chance—" Bullets sprayed through the decayed door, arcing upwards so that the last three slammed into the ceiling. Dust, grit, and brittle plastic rained down around him. "It's got a bit of a kick, hasn't it," Mitchell said. "Is that the first time you've ever fired a Kalashnikov?"

Many of the refugees who arrived in Britain had fought their way through a European wilderness that had become home to bandits, pirates, and worse. Those who made it often arrived armed, though rarely with much ammunition. In an attempt to neutralise the potential danger, the government had produced a hunting rifle of a calibre larger than that old-world weapon. Rounds were only issued to those with hunting or farming licences. Replacement cartridges were heavily taxed. Rather than discouraging firearms, that had only encouraged the black market. Emmitt had supplied his confederates with assault rifles but those had been old-world British Army SA80s that fired the NATO round, a different calibre from the AK-47.

"Did Emmitt give you that rifle?" Mitchell asked again.

"I've never heard that name before," Pollock replied. "I was just out hunting, that's all."

"Hunting? In Edinburgh? I know the stories say it's a wild city, but I don't think a judge is going to buy that. Why did you do it?"

"Do what?" Pollock replied.

"Why did you kill Jameson?"

"I didn't."

Mitchell moved an inch closer to the door. "Jameson was Emmitt's spotter during his assassination attempt on the prime minister. He was arrested, and since then, has said next to nothing. Four days ago, it was decided to transfer him to a work detail in Cornwall. He was moved back to a holding cell in Police House. At three in the morning, you entered the building, ostensibly looking for files that had been taken from your department. At three-twenty, you left. At half past four, the guard looked in on Jameson and found he'd been shot. Through the bars. Not with an AK-47, I'll add, but with a round from a government-issue revolver."

"So? I didn't do it," Pollock said. "I... I was only in the building because I wanted to get all my paperwork in order before my holiday."

"Your hunting holiday, here in Scotland, in the shadow of Edinburgh Castle? A place taken over by monks who follow a strict code of non-violence towards animals?"

"That's why I'm not staying at the castle," Pollock said. "And... and I only shot at you because I thought you were a bandit. That's all. You should have announced yourself, not come charging down the roof at me."

"Now that I have announced myself, why don't you throw your gun out?" Mitchell said. There was no reply from Pollock. Mitchell sighed. "You're an interesting man, Pollock. Technically you hold the rank of captain in the police, but in reality, you're a clerk. You work in central government, keeping tabs on all the police personnel files. The rank is a courtesy, a way to ensure you don't get bullied or blackmailed into handing over information you shouldn't. You took the rank to heart, though. You even had a uniform made. *Made*, I should add, not issued."

"A captain *is* a captain," Pollock said. "I had every right to wear that uniform."

"Not really," Mitchell said. "Commissioner Wallace got you the job, but since you weren't on the police payroll, I didn't think to look at you when we were searching for his cronies in the force. More fool me. But you want to know why I'm here? Why I followed you?"

"Why?" Pollock said.

"We knew that Wallace had corrupted dozens of officers," Mitchell said. "Some worked for him for money. Others thought that, when he became prime minister, he'd reward them with promotions, power, and prestige. When I pushed, when I dug, when I drew the truth out, I found that though that might have been *why* they continued working for him, the reason they began was blackmail. Longfield was the clue there. She liked to blackmail. She even recorded herself threatening some of my colleagues. Threatening to let their secrets be known to the world. For some it was gambling or an affair, for others it was something achingly more personal. Longfield's video recordings were the leverage she and Wallace needed, but how did she learn about them in the first place? That was you, Pollock. The civil service clerk who was responsible for keeping personnel files secret. That's how you helped them. And then you killed Jameson. You murdered a prisoner in custody."

"I didn't," Pollock said.

"You might have dared to wear a uniform you had made," Mitchell said, "but you didn't carry a revolver. You knew that would be going too far. The gun was inside your briefcase. You attached a sheath-silencer that you had in your left trouser pocket. Jameson was asleep. You tapped the gun against the bars to wake him, and then you fired. Three times, though only two bullets hit. Unfortunately, one hit his heart. He died."

"None of that happened," Pollock said. "You've got no proof."

"I've got video," Mitchell said. "After the counterfeiter, Josh Turnbull, was murdered in custody, I installed some cameras in the cells. Oh, I know, that's old-world tech. It can't be used in the trial, but I don't need to use it. Based solely on the guard having seen you in Police House, and then your failure to arrive at work the next morning, we got a warrant to search your home. I saw how you lived, Pollock, and it's far beyond your means. You've got a wine cellar, for Pete's sake."

"I recovered all those bottles myself," Pollock said. "I found them out in the wasteland. That's bona-fide salvage."

"And the steak?" Mitchell asked. "Did you salvage that, too? It would cost me two months' salary to buy all of that meat."

"That's... I... I hunted that," Pollock said. "Wild cows, out on Salisbury Plain."

"You kept it in a *freezer*!" Mitchell said. "Your electricity bill alone is more than your salary, and that's not counting how much it cost you to have a freezer restored. You shouldn't have run. You shouldn't have shot at me. But if we're going to talk about the things you shouldn't have done, then we'll start with killing Jameson. Even so, even now, there's a deal waiting for you. Wallace died in his study back in September. The torturer, Eve, died in a ruined church. Longfield killed herself in her home. Fairmont, the assistant to the American ambassador, died in the New Forest. A few minutes after that, we arrested Emmitt. Who's left? Who told you to kill Jameson? Give me a name, Pollock. Give me a name."

There was no reply, but there was a soft rasp as of boot heels scuffing the ground as Pollock shifted position. The doors were ten feet from Mitchell. Beyond that were another five feet to where Pollock was concealed. The rasping came again. Maybe a little more than five feet. Was that too far?

"How about this," Mitchell said. "How about I guess a name. Adamovitch, yes? It was Longfield's under-butler. Go on, tell me I'm right." There was no reply. "Then tell me I'm wrong. Look, Pollock, this is obviously going to end with either you or me dead. In which case, what harm is there in telling me? It was Adamovitch, wasn't it?"

"Maybe," Pollock said. "Maybe it was. So what? Does it matter?"

Mitchell relaxed. Adamovitch was the last piece of the puzzle. With Longfield dead, Emmitt in jail, and their organisation in tatters, there was a boss-shaped hole in the criminal tapestry of Twynham. The butler was trying to fill it. Importantly, thankfully, that meant that Pollock and Adamovitch were the last. There were hired thugs and rented muscle, of course, but those were a dime-a-dozen down on the docks. They would vie against one another to fill the power-vacuum left by the conspirators, but they were petty criminals with petty dreams who'd be as easy to catch as Pollock.

Mitchell slid his pistol back into its holster and unclipped his truncheon. He swapped it to his left hand and gripped the LED flashlight in his right.

"Frederick Charles Pollock," Mitchell said. "I'm arresting you for murder. You don't have to say anything, but anything you say will be taken down and may be used against you. Should you fail to say something that you—"

There was a short burst of gunfire that abruptly ended as the magazine was finally emptied. In a flash, Mitchell flicked on the torch and pitched it into the stockroom. As the light tumbled and spun, Mitchell followed it. Just before the light struck the wall, Mitchell spotted Pollock. The murderer was crouched behind an overturned desk. His hands were awkwardly working the gun's mechanism, but his eyes were on the spinning light. Mitchell dived forward, swinging the truncheon up, knocking the assault rifle from the man's hands. Mitchell twisted his wrist, turning the truncheon so that it was at ninety degrees to his arm just before he slammed into Pollock's chest. The man fell back as Mitchell grabbed Pollock's right arm. Pollock kicked out, but Mitchell used the man's own momentum to spin him around, down, and onto his back. He pushed the truncheon under one elbow and then another.

"Like I was saying," he said as he cuffed the man's wrists. "You're under arrest."

He searched the man's pockets and retrieved two spare magazines for the rifle. They went into a drawstring bag. Mitchell collected his light, and then picked up the AK-47.

"Where did you get this rifle?" Mitchell asked.

"I've had it for years. Got it off a refugee."

"I don't think so. It looks new. Or newly out of storage, anyway. Did it come from Emmitt?"

Pollock shook his head.

"Was that a no? Or was that a not-going-to-answer?" Mitchell asked. He slung the rifle over his shoulder. He would have preferred if it was an SA80 like the weapons Emmitt had given to the crooks in Windward

Square. They had ostensibly been hired to commit a robbery, though in reality they were a distraction, there to be caught to facilitate the rescue of Fairmont, the assistant to the American ambassador. The ammunition given to those dupes in Windward Square had been duds, but the rifles had all come from an old British Army storehouse. An AK-47 was far more troubling, particularly one that looked as if it had been in storage for the past twenty years.

"All right," Mitchell said. "Let's try a different question. Where were you going?"

Pollock shook his head.

"On your feet," Mitchell said, pulling Pollock up. "You know what I heard? Adamovitch boarded a boat to Maine five days ago."

Pollock gave a short, derisive snort.

Mitchell smiled, and pushed Pollock towards the door. That snort of derision confirmed a hunch he'd been developing. Adamovitch was a weasel, in temperament, in looks, and in intelligence. He would know that there was no chance he'd be able to stow aboard a transatlantic cargo ship. That witness from the quayside tavern had been either mistaken or lying. The question, then, was whether Adamovitch was in Scotland, or somewhere far closer to Twynham.

Just before Mitchell had jumped down through the gap in the ceiling, Pollock had hung a saucepan over the fire. The contents had boiled dry, adding the scent of burned potatoes and herbs to the damp and decay pervading the ruined supermarket. Next to the battered office chair Pollock had been sitting on was his haversack. Mitchell pushed Pollock into the chair, and opened the bag.

"Potatoes, herbs, water, and… what's this?" He took out a manila folder. "This is Riley's personnel file. Why do you have this?"

"Look at it, and you'll see," Pollock said.

"Oh, that creeping worm of doubt that feeds a hatching suspicion," Mitchell said.

"What?" Pollock said.

"You should read more," Mitchell said. "I saw those books you had in your house. Row upon row of classics. You had the complete collection of hundreds of authors, but not one spine was cracked. Don't worry, you'll get the chance to read in prison." He threw the folder onto the fire.

"You're not going to look? You're not curious?" Pollock asked.

Mitchell ignored him. Anna Riley had been a young girl when he'd rescued her. He'd adopted her soon after, and, a decade after that, she'd followed him into the police force. He knew her far better than any words in a file.

"On your feet, Pollock, time for you to face justice."

He kicked ash onto the fire, and then marched the murderer out of the supermarket.

Edinburgh hadn't been officially re-occupied, but the castle-turned-monastery had become a popular destination. Not quite as a holiday, nor as a pilgrimage, but for people who wanted to see proof that a world existed beyond the mines of Wales or the rooftops of Twynham. Due to the increased demand, the Railway Company had re-opened the station, and there was talk of formally re-occupying the city. That would remain as talk until the separatists in Leicester, who called themselves the Kingdom of Albion, had been brought back into the fold. The new Prime Minister, Phillip Atherton, had taken over the peace talks himself, and was threatening to start war talks if an agreement wasn't reached soon. That wasn't Mitchell's problem.

He marched Pollock away from the supermarket and down towards the railway. It was a cold but pleasant evening. Night had settled, but the sky was clear, the stars bright. He didn't need his torch, but kept it shining on the ground in front of Pollock. He didn't want the man to trip and claim he was pushed. It was almost over. Adamovitch was the last one left, and then all the conspirators and their confederates would be caught or dead. There would be other criminals and other crimes, of course, but they weren't Henry Mitchell's problem. Once Adamovitch was arrested, Mitchell would be free. He wouldn't retire, not exactly, because copper now flowed in his veins. After twenty years, it was time for his life to become his own. *Once* Adamovitch was arrested, and there weren't many places for him to hide. Yes, it was almost over.

Mitchell was almost in a good mood when he reached the station. He cuffed Pollock to one of the benches, walked over to the signal box, unlocked it with a key he kept around his neck, and changed the pattern of lights, signalling that the next passing train should stop.

"Can't we wait inside?" Pollock asked.

"It's a nice night," Mitchell said.

"It's freezing," Pollock moaned.

"Not yet, it isn't," Mitchell said. "There's that crisp dryness to the air that tells me snow's on the way. Can't you taste it?"

"Snow? And you're going to leave me out here."

"Enjoy it," Mitchell said. "This might be the last night sky you ever see. The coal train from Wales will be coming through at eight minutes to midnight. From then until your dying day, you'll be indoors at night. No, enjoy the air. Enjoy this last moment under the stars."

But the train that arrived wasn't carrying coal. It wasn't even a steam train, but a diesel locomotive, pulling a smartly decorated carriage and a flat bed with a crane and small fuel tank.

Mitchell had never seen the locomotive before, and hadn't seen a working diesel engine since before the Blackout, but he knew the carriage, and knew who would be driving the train.

The door to the locomotive opened, and Rebecca Cavendish peered down.

"Hello, Henry. Did you get your man?"

"Always, Rebecca."

"And you always do." She smiled, but it was a more close-lipped expression than he was used to seeing on his old friend.

"What's wrong?" he asked.

"Climb up and I'll tell you. Rehnquist, get the prisoner on board."

A broad-shouldered, tapered-waisted bull of a guard in the green livery of the Railway Police jumped down. They were called police, though their role was halfway between train conductor and soldier. After the Blackout, the trains had been the lifeline linking the disparate communities in Wales,

England, and Scotland. The land between had been riddled with bandits. Most had now been subdued, but a solitary train or remote station was a tempting target for those who preferred to steal what others worked to attain.

Mitchell gave Rehnquist the key to the cuffs, let him take custody of the prisoner, and climbed up into the locomotive's cab.

In many ways Rebecca Cavendish *was* the Railway Company. She'd been a train enthusiast on a heritage railway before the Blackout, and had brought a dozen steam locomotives south soon after the bombs had fallen. She, and those engines, had become a crucial part of the country's survival. Cavendish's legs had been crushed during an icy winter when they were laying new track on old roads. That hadn't even slowed the woman down. Her body might have been confined to a wheelchair but her mind had soared. She'd created an intricate network of railways that linked the towns and villages, the mines and farms, and so the country had been kept whole rather than collapsing into a thousand different kingdoms.

"That's Pollock?" Cavendish asked as the prisoner was hauled aboard the carriage.

"That's him," Mitchell said. "He confirmed that Adamovitch was the one behind Jameson's murder, and that Adamovitch is still in Britain."

"I'll pass word up and down the line," Cavendish said. "Do you still want it kept quiet?"

"For now," Mitchell said. "At least, I want it to stay out of the newspaper. I don't want Adamovitch to know we're on his trail."

"My people will keep it close," Cavendish said, "but if I can't give them a name or a picture, I can't guarantee he won't slip by them."

"Give me a few more days," Mitchell said. "There a few more leads to follow." He looked around. "This is a diesel locomotive, Rebecca."

"Ah, the great detective at work," Cavendish said, as she pulled a lever, pressed a button, and the train began to move.

Mitchell smiled. "Where did you find it?"

"It was abandoned near Carnoustie," she said. "I've had people restoring it this last year."

"Where did you get the fuel?" Mitchell asked. "Was it from the new wells they've opened in America?"

"Hardly," Cavendish said. "I will *not* be beholden to them. No, it's the first batch of biodiesel from Truro. This was meant to be a test run for the train. If it could make it from the outskirts of Dundee all the way to Twynham, we'd have called both the locomotive and the fuel a working success. The plan was to use the diesel engines to take supplies through the Channel Tunnel. It would be safer, and cleaner, than running steam engines and the fans needed to keep the air clear. Things have changed. I take you haven't heard?"

"Heard what?" Mitchell asked.

"There was an attack on the garrison in Calais this afternoon," Cavendish said.

"Bandits?"

"This wasn't a simple band of outlaws," Cavendish said. "This was an army. At least two-thousand strong."

"Two thousand? Are you sure? Are you serious? Where did they come from?"

"Not from France," she said. "But more than that, I don't know. I got word four hours and…" She pulled out a battered watch. "Four hours and eighteen minutes ago. The message was in code, and so it was brief. All trials of this locomotive are over, and we are to collect the Marine garrison from Penrith and bring them south to Dover with all haste."

"It's that bad?" Mitchell asked. "It must be if they're bringing down the Pennines garrison."

"It's not good, Henry," she said. "But the Marines are holding the line. The Channel Tunnel won't be breached."

"I sent Ruth to Dover," Mitchell said. "I thought she'd be safe there, surrounded by the Royal Navy."

"She will be," Cavendish said. "Those bandits won't get through the Channel Tunnel. In a few days, they'll all be dead. No, focus on finding Adamovitch. Do you think he might still be in Scotland? Perhaps Pollock was trying to meet with him."

"Possibly," Mitchell said. His mind turned to Ruth Deering, newly transferred to Dover, a city now on the front line. "You better drop us off at the first town we reach," he said. "I need to have a proper word with Pollock, and if Adamovitch is in Scotland, I don't want to have to travel all the way back here."

And once Adamovitch was caught, then Ruth would truly be safe. He could have her transferred far from Dover, and then, finally, his job would be done.

Chapter 2 - The Dover Constabulary
10th November, Dover

"Close the door, you're letting the heat out," Police Sergeant Elspeth Kettering said.

"I thought I heard thunder," Ruth Deering said as she shut the door to the Dover police station. "But it was only artillery fire from Calais."

"Well, it won't go on for much longer," Kettering said, shuffling through the day's paperwork. "Give it another few days, and they'll have flushed those pirates back into the forests of France."

"You said that yesterday," Ruth said. "You said it last week. In fact, you've said it every evening since those pirates attacked the garrison ten days ago."

"I must be right, then," Kettering said. "You forgot to sign the interview log."

Following the arrest and trial of Emmitt, Ruth had been promoted to constable. Like all new constables, she'd been given a choice of assignment. She'd asked to be assigned to the Serious Crimes Unit in the hope that would see it reopened. It hadn't. Instead, she'd been sent to Dover.

Ruth walked over to the polished oak counter and signed the interview log.

"That was a good collar," Kettering said. "Jonah Craddock, caught with his hand in the coat pocket of a master tailor."

"If Craddock had thought to look around before he tried to rob her," Ruth said, "or if she hadn't been so absorbed in the delivery, it would never have happened."

"Then Craddock would only have gone on to rob someone else," Kettering said. "And that might have been better for him. The cloth that tailor was unloading was for Marines' uniforms."

"I thought they made them in Scotland," Ruth said.

"Do you wear the same uniform every day?" Kettering asked.

"Well, yes," Ruth said.

"I meant you've got a spare, don't you? There's no laundry in Calais, but there's plenty of mud, plenty of jagged rocks and splinters of metal to rip and tear cloth. The Marines can't fight naked, and if the uniforms don't get repaired, they might have to."

"No laundry," Ruth murmured. "I never thought of that."

"War isn't just about shooting bullets," Kettering said.

"Then it is a war?" Ruth asked.

"It's the closest to one that I've heard of in the last twenty years," Kettering said.

"The newspaper hasn't printed much," Ruth said.

"No, I suppose they don't want to worry people," Kettering murmured. "Not that I agree with the notion. If they don't print this story, then it makes me wonder what other stories they're not telling us."

"Me, too," Ruth said. "Before I caught Craddock, I was patrolling the dockside. There were two old sailors with three arms and two eyes between them, playing chess by the chandler's yard."

"Matherson and Bramble," Kettering said, automatically. "Matherson lost his arm and an eye in… let's see… sixteen years ago, March 2023. They'd stuck a steam locomotive onto an old rubbish barge and were calling it a paddle steamer, right up until it blew up about a mile from shore. Bramble saved Matherson's life. Now, Bramble lost his eye when he was part of an expedition down the Nile. He says it was plucked out by a golden dagger looted from one of the pharaohs' tombs, but you should always take an old sailor's stories with as many grains of salt as they've got flowing through their veins."

Before Ruth's arrival in Dover, Elspeth Kettering had been the city's only police officer. She'd fallen into the job shortly after the Blackout. While a few constables had come and quickly gone in the years since, the sergeant had remained. Kettering was the very definition of a local plod. She knew who lived behind which doors, as well as many of the secrets hidden behind their curtains.

"Bramble and Matherson," Ruth said. "They were saying how this wasn't going to be over any time soon."

"And why did they think that?" Kettering asked.

"Well, they said, that for the last twenty years, the Navy's not done more than ferry expeditions along the coast. The only real action they've seen is to sink a few wooden sailing boats coming out of the pirate enclaves along the Mediterranean."

"I wouldn't let any of the Marines hear you say that."

"I wasn't going to," Ruth said. "But they all talk as if they've got the same kind of ships they had before the Blackout, you know, the kind with missiles and helicopter decks. Not… not…"

"Not floating artillery platforms?" Kettering said. "Well, maybe, but I'd say that since we can hear the artillery from here when the wind is in the right direction, the Navy's guns are more than powerful enough to knock the pirates loose."

Dover was the home-harbour for the Channel fleet that patrolled the western European and North African coasts. It was a Navy city, but there were close to fifteen thousand civilians living inside Dover's walls. Some tended the herds of dairy and beef cattle that kept the sailors fed. Others worked in the shipyard, the chandlers, or the steelworks. Then there were the shopkeepers, the telegraph operators, messengers, and railway workers, the teachers, doctors, and all the others needed to keep the engine of civilisation ticking along. Technically, all those civilians were subject to the same laws as in every other city. Sergeant Kettering, and latterly Ruth Deering, were there to enforce them. In practice, there were few crimes, and even fewer since the assault on Calais had begun. Those crimes that did occur were usually taken over by the military police, and at seven p.m. every evening, the M.Ps took over policing the city until seven a.m. the next day.

The door opened, the bell jangled, and CPO Mordechai Rubenstein came in.

"Smells like snow," the chief said, pushing the door to. "Busy day?"

"You're early, Chief," Kettering said.

"What's a few minutes between friends," Rubenstein said. "Do you have anyone for me?"

"Only the one," Sergeant Kettering said. "Jonah Craddock. Caught picking the pocket of Carol Crane, master tailor."

"I know her," Rubenstein said. "She's got the contract for the officers' dress uniforms. Talk about picking the wrong pocket."

Ruth smiled at the chief's weak joke. It was part of their ritual. Each night, at seven p.m., the police cells would be emptied, and the prisoners taken to Dover Castle. In the morning, they would be taken before the judge and there given the chance to volunteer before they decided how to plead.

Rubenstein signed his name at the bottom of the transfer sheet. Kettering signed hers, and Ruth fetched the prisoner.

"Mr Craddock, a pleasure to meet you," Rubenstein said. "You've a choice of twelve months or five years. Twelve months clearing rubble, or five years of sea air with money in your pocket and food in your gut. Something for you to think about. Evening to you, officers." He marched the prisoner out of the station.

"Twenty minutes," Kettering said. "And then we're officially off duty."

Ruth went back to the desk to finish the paperwork.

Dover was different to Twynham. *Very* different. The pickpocket was the highlight of the week. There had been a few drunk and disorderlies, a lost cat, and, since the fifth of November, a spate of invasion-scares that had all come to naught. In short, and aside from the battle raging thirty miles away in France, life was blissfully uneventful. Ruth was almost enjoying it.

"Anything to watch out for tonight, Sarge?" Ruth asked as she signed her name on the last piece of the day's paperwork.

"Mrs Gunderlee's cat may have gone missing," Kettering said as she took her scarf from the hat stand.

"Again?" Ruth asked.

"It's a cat," Kettering said. "And I said *may*. Mrs Gunderlee was kind enough to give us advance warning. At some point around dawn, she'll hammer on the door to let us know that the cat has safely returned, as it has done every night for the last six months. Otherwise, it should be quiet. Do you have any plans?"

"I do," Ruth said. "I've plans for a good book and an early night."

"Oh, come now," Kettering said. "You're too young to waste your evenings away indoors. Eloise and some of her friends are going to the old theatre tonight. They're showing *North by Northwest*. You should go with them. It's a good film."

Eloise was the sergeant's eldest daughter. She was about Ruth's age, was coming to the end of her apprenticeship in the city's small coal power station, and was considering enlisting in the Navy.

Dover, situated on the southeastern tip of Kent, the most southeastern county of England, was a city isolated and alone from the rest of the country. For years after the Blackout, Kent had been subject to raids from offshore pirates, making it unsafe for anyone to live out in the wilds. There were a few farms, of course, but the herds and farmers came into the towns at night. Folkestone was home to the garrison around the entrance to the Channel Tunnel, and the railway company maintained a few water-and-coal stops, but otherwise few people had made their home east of Hastings. Subsequently, Dover had its own small power plant, water treatment facility, and tall walls ringing the city.

"Tell her thank you for the offer," Ruth said. "But I'm really looking forward to my book."

"There will be people there," Kettering said. "People your own age."

Ruth smiled, but didn't reply. In many ways, the sergeant was much like Ruth's own mother, at least after seven p.m., but Ruth wasn't looking for friends. Not now, not after the last two months.

"How many movies have they approved now?" Ruth asked.

"*North by Northwest* is the thirtieth," Kettering said. "The lawyers still say that unless it can be proven that all of the rights-holders died in the Blackout, the film can't be shown. Reading between the lines of that newspaper piece, the judge was a real fan of Alfred Hitchcock, otherwise the exception wouldn't have been made."

"If it's only the thirtieth film, then it'll be on for a while," Ruth said. "I'll see it closer to Christmas."

"If you're sure," Kettering said, in a tone that suggested that she disagreed. She pulled on her long coat. "Five minutes to seven. The military police will be on duty soon. I tell you what, why don't you—" But before she could finish, the door opened, and a sailor ran in. She wasn't in uniform, but a sodden PT kit.

"You've... you've... you've got to come," the sailor panted.

"Where?" Kettering asked.

"We were... were coming back from our run," the sailor said. "A woman flagged us down. A landlady. She found a body. One of her tenants. He's killed himself."

Chapter 3 - A Lonely Life
Dover

The carved-oak street sign said that it was New Hope Road. Whitewashed graffiti had turned the *New* into *No*, and Ruth thought the artist had the right of it. Even though it was silent now, the small-arms range was situated in the scrub between the back of the houses and the city's northern wall. The wall was easy to spot. Electric-searchlights had been installed every twenty metres, and their beams now pierced the dark Kent countryside beyond.

Ruth had visited the firing range, though she'd stuck to the target range rather then joining the Marines in the battle-drill exercises conducted in the bullet-pocked buildings. Even watching from the instructor's observation platform, the noise had been intense. It was a constant barrage of bullet and shell that, she'd been told, was partly caused by an old-world sound system. That had been granted an exemption from the technology ban on the grounds no one told the Royal Navy what to do in Dover. What the sound must be like for the people who lived in this street, Ruth could only imagine. From the look of the houses, the residents had no option to move elsewhere.

The old-world houses had been subdivided again and again. The nearest had the number 2F painted on the old metal garage doors, and that looked like the roomiest of the properties visible. Wood smoke and burned cabbage barely masked the smell of the outdoor toilets, yet there were no To-Let signs. There was no law requiring people to live inside the walls. There was no need. The last pirate raid, eighteen months ago, had resulted in the brutal death and mutilation of a family of dairy farmers and their entire herd. Even with Calais now blockaded, bombarded, and slowly being reduced to rubble, no one would risk going outside the walls after dark. Right now, they were staying inside their rented rooms, though threadbare curtains twitched as Ruth and Sergeant Kettering followed the sailor down the road.

The victim's house was almost at the very end of the street, clearly identifiable by the sailor standing at ease in the doorway, and the other sailor who stood by the gate next to an irate woman in a bright pink overcoat.

Look at the shoes, Ruth thought. That was one of Mister Mitchell's first lessons. Always begin with the shoes, and this woman's were distinctly out of place. They were of that old-world shiny black plastic that almost looked like leather. Expensive, though not as expensive as having a new pair made. Showy, too, particularly on a street like this. The coat was heavy, even for this frosty November evening, but there was no hat on the woman's head because that might have disturbed her big-haired 'do.

The house outside of which she and the sailor stood had a whitewashed door. So did the houses either side and two of those opposite. Ruth pegged the woman as the landlady. The house was small, a three-bedroom that had been split into four judging by the numbers on the letterbox by the gate. However much the tenants were paying, it was far too much. Moss spilled from the blocked gutter until it met the ivy growing upward, strategically planted so that it would hide the gaping crack in the wall. Two of the front windows were broken. A third had been boarded up at least a year before. Ruth upgraded her first impression of the middle-aged landlady to slumlord.

The sailor by the gate snapped his heels together and his hand to his forehead.

"At ease," Kettering said sternly.

"Ah, *finally*," the middle-aged woman said, in an accent that was English and overly prim. "Now you're here, you can tell them to let me go. *And* I want to press charges for being illegally detained."

"Just a minute, ma'am," Kettering said and turned to the sailor. "What's going on?"

"Well, I can tell you that," the landlady said. "Mr Wilson's dead. Shot himself. I flagged these sailors down, and now they won't let me go home."

"And you are?" Kettering asked.

"Mrs Dempsey," the woman said. "I'm the owner of these properties."

"Of the five with the whitewashed doors?" Kettering asked.

"That's right," Dempsey said. "And four cottages by the seafront. I'm a—"

"And what time did you find the body?" Kettering interrupted.

"At six o'clock," Dempsey said. "When I should've been having my dinner. It'll be ruined now."

Sergeant Kettering made a show of taking out her watch, checking the time, and marking it down in her notebook. "Does Mr Wilson have a first name?"

"Noah, I think. Maybe Norman."

"I see. And why were you going to speak to Mr Wilson?" Kettering asked.

"I wasn't," Dempsey said, "but his employer sent a messenger to me. He'd not shown up for work. They were worried. Worried he'd run off, I expect."

"And you were, too?" Kettering asked. "Is that why you came to check? You were worried he'd done a moonlight flit?"

"It has been known to happen," Dempsey said.

Not in Dover, Ruth thought. Not when the gates were locked from dusk until dawn.

"Where did he work?" Kettering asked.

"Sprocket and Sprung," Dempsey said. "For nineteen years, according to his employer when I asked for a reference. Now, can I go?"

"Just a few minutes more, ma'am," Kettering said. "How long has he been renting the room?"

"Four months. His contract is for a year, mind you."

"I see," Kettering said. She turned to the sailor. "And who are you?"

"Lovett, seaman, first class," the sailor snapped. "Off the *Dauntless*. We were on a training run. When we were hailed, I went into the cabin— I mean room, confirmed that the deceased was… um…" The sailor faltered. "Was deceased." He finished. "I've left Williams guarding the room, and sent Merrick to alert you."

"Did you touch the body?"

"No, ma'am," Lovett said.

"What about you?" the sergeant asked Mrs Dempsey.

"I didn't touch anything," Dempsey said. "Didn't even turn the light off, though I expect I'll be the one picking up the bill. How long is this going to take?"

"We'll go and see," Kettering said. "Constable?"

Ruth fell into step behind the sergeant, and they went into the house. The slumlord might have left the light on in the victim's room, but there was no light in the hallway. Kettering tried the switch by the door, but nothing happened.

"No bulb," Kettering said. "That tells you a lot."

So did the smell of damp pervading the property. It was worse than outside. Another sailor stood by the open door at the end of the hall. She wasn't quite ramrod-straight, but stiffened as Kettering and Ruth approached.

"Did you touch anything?" the sergeant asked.

"No, ma'am," the sailor said.

Kettering took one look through the door then turned to her. "You know where the coroner is? Good. Off you go, sailor."

The sailor left.

"All right, Deering," Kettering said. "Take a look, and apply some of that famous detectoring that Mister Mitchell taught you."

Ruth pulled on her gloves as she stepped into the doorway. The room's light might have been on, but the bulb was dim. She took out her torch. It was an old-world LED, a gift from Riley, and offered a far stronger beam than Kettering's standard-issue, two-foot-long club of a lamp. Ruth could almost hear the sergeant's nostrils flaring at this flagrant use of taboo technology, and then dismissed it as she examined the scene.

"The victim is male," Ruth said. "Around fifty years old, maybe fifty-five. He's bearded, but that's been trimmed not styled. It's the same with the hair on his head. He probably cut it himself. He's dressed in a dark suit, slightly threadbare but clean. There's a knitted jumper under the jacket, but no tie. He's not wearing shoes. He's lying on the bed, his right hand is on his chest. His left is hanging over the side of the bed, nearest to the door. There's blood on the wall behind the bed, and on the sheets and his clothes. Death was from a bullet to the brain."

"Oh, so you're the coroner now, are you?" Kettering asked.

"Fine. The victim was shot—"

"Victim?" Kettering prompted.

"Deceased," Ruth said. "The man was shot in the head. There's a gun lying on the ground near his outstretched left hand. It's a revolver." She took a step across the otherwise empty and clean floor. "A government-issue revolver. Looks clean. There's no blood splatter on it." She peered at the man's wound.

"How many cartridges in the gun?" Kettering asked.

Ruth cracked the weapon open. "Six. It was fully loaded." She emptied the rounds into her hand. "Only one has been fired." She put the casings into a brown paper evidence bag, and then put the gun back where it had lain.

"Interesting," Kettering said. "Each bullet would cost a day's pay. If he was keeping one for himself, for whom did he buy the other five? His ration card's on the table. His first name *is* Noah."

"Did you know him, Sarge?" Ruth asked. "The landlady said he'd been in Dover for nineteen years."

"I've seen him around," Kettering said. "But I didn't *know* him. He never crossed my path, which means he never broke a law. Not until now."

"Suicide isn't a crime," Ruth said.

"Unauthorised possession of a firearm is," Kettering said. "And as you pointed out, that's a government-issue revolver. What else can you tell me about the scene?"

"It's a large room," Ruth said. "But I think it was the only one he had. The bed takes up about half the space. Next to the bed is a chair. On the other side is a cabinet, and next to that, against the exterior wall, is a stove with a ramshackle chimney. Next to it are floor-to-ceiling curtains. I assume they're covering a window, and that means the stove's chimney leads directly outside. Against the other wall is a table on which are some paints, mostly blues and greens. Next to that is an empty easel. There are six finished paintings. Three are on the floor, propped against the wall. The other three are hanging on the wall opposite the bed. Everything is tidy, more or less. There's no carpet, but there are rugs, and they look relatively clean. I guess the stove was for heating and cooking."

"Not many possessions for nineteen years in Dover," Kettering said. She crossed to the curtains and pulled them back an inch. "These are sliding doors. There's an outhouse in the garden. Not that you can really call it a garden. It's a dumping ground for rubbish. I can see some of the ruins they use for live-fire exercises. If the man was shot during the daytime, then it's possible no one heard it over the gunfire from the firing range. One saucepan, one mug, I don't think he entertained."

"Where did he wash?" Ruth asked.

"The bathroom will be upstairs," Kettering said. "Though, considering there's an outhouse, I'd say that it probably doesn't work. He would have done his best with hot water from a saucepan and the public washhouses."

"It's a grim way to live," Ruth said.

"It is," Kettering said. She crossed to the fabric wardrobe, and rifled through the clothes. "Ah, I've found the bullet. It's in the wall, about level with the man's head. We'll need pliers to extract it." She turned to the paintings. "Those are good. *Very* good."

"They are," Ruth said.

All were seascapes. The three hanging on the wall formed a triptych portraying a day in the life of a sailor. The first showed a fishing boat hauling in a net during a storm. The middle painting had the ship arriving in port. The third portrayed a shadowy figure standing next to a picturesque cottage while the boat was now safely anchored in the harbour.

"Do you think that man is looking towards his boat?" Ruth asked.

"I think he's looking towards the gathering storm clouds," Kettering asked. "But a better question is whether the man in the paintings is Mr Wilson. You notice that he hasn't painted the man's face. He left that part of the canvas blank."

"Perhaps he hadn't finished it," Ruth said.

"Then why hang the picture on the wall?" Kettering replied.

Ruth bent, and examined the three pictures on the floor. There were no faces in those pictures, either. One showed a dozen Royal Navy ships sailing into the distance. Another showed Dover's cliffs, the sea below empty of ships, but festooned with gulls the same shade as the white chalk cliffs. The third was another fishing boat at sea. It looked similar to the ship in the three paintings hanging on the wall, and she wondered if that painting had originally been part of the sequence.

"He was good," Ruth said. "Really good. I'd have paid for one of these."

"I'd say he was good enough that you shouldn't have been able to afford one of them," Kettering said.

"So why was he living here?" Ruth asked.

"That's the wrong question," Kettering said.

"What's the right one?"

"Well, there's two, actually," Kettering said. "And the second is linked to the first, and that first is why was this man murdered."

"He *was* murdered, then?" Ruth asked.

"You tell me."

Ruth looked again at the victim. That had been her first instinct in seeing the corpse, that this was a victim of someone else rather than just his own despair. The advice of Henry Mitchell came to her.

"He's not wearing any shoes," she said. "He's got rugs on the floor. Nice ones, too. Nicer than the furnishings in the rest of the room, and they're clean, but I wouldn't want to walk barefoot out into the hallway. His shoes are by the back door. They're worn, but like the suit, they're clean. He paid attention to his appearance, though not to style."

"And how does that prove he was murdered?" Kettering prompted.

"Okay." Ruth tried to visualise the scene before the man died. "The shoes are by the back door because that's the door by which he entered and left. He didn't use the front door. Well, why would he? There's no bulb in the hallway, so it would be easier coming and going via the back, making use of natural light."

"Good point, but that's not it," Kettering said. "Try again."

"If he was a victim, then someone came in. They got him to lie down. They... they sat in the chair while he lay on the bed. They fired from the chair, and left the gun. They ran, probably back the way they'd come."

"You're deducing the events based on the supposition he was murdered," Kettering said. "Now *I* know he was murdered, but *how* do I know that?"

"You saw a footprint outside?" Ruth guessed.

Kettering sighed theatrically. "Mister Mitchell will be very upset."

"The angle of the gun?" Ruth said. "The way it's fallen? The— The gun's clean! Someone cleaned the gun. There's no blood or brain splatter on the gun, but there is on the wall."

"A dead man doesn't clean up after himself," Kettering said. "That was the clue. The paintings were the hint. Look at them. They're all of the sea. There's no suicide note, but that's not uncommon. I've attended a fair number of suicides in my time. Not as many now as there were a few years ago, but people usually die in a spot that has some personal meaning to them. Sometimes opportunity will override that. If he'd slit his wrists in a bathtub, I'd understand, but he shot himself. He liked the sea. That's the common feature in the paintings, so why didn't he shoot himself on the cliffs?"

"Because he didn't shoot himself."

"Precisely," Kettering said. "Confirmation is on the sleeve of his jacket. The gun is meant to have fallen from his left hand. On the painter's smocks hanging in the cupboard, the paint is all on the right sleeve." The sergeant held up a sleeve of white cotton. "The left sleeve is almost immaculate. The man was very definitely uni-dextrous."

"That's cheating," Ruth said. "How was I meant to know that?"

"I never said you couldn't look in the wardrobe," Kettering said. "We know this man was murdered. We know the method. Any ideas about motive?"

Ruth hadn't, but she took the hint, and examined the room again. "There's a paint pallet on the table-top, but no canvas on the easel. Maybe

Mr Wilson was killed for the picture. Maybe he painted something that the killer didn't want him to. Like their face."

"Or someone else's face. Or maybe not," Kettering said. "Maybe Mr Wilson simply didn't like what he'd painted and threw it out. We have a starting point, the beginning of a list of questions, and I've a few for that landlady. Dust the gun for prints, do the same for the easel, and the glass doors. Then sketch the scene. You know the routine."

Ruth took out her notepad, but as soon as Kettering was outside, she took out her tablet. The small square of plastic and glass had been a going-away gift from Isaac. She wasn't sure if the gift was meant as an apology. Considering what she knew of Isaac, probably not. Not that she knew much about him. The man mostly lived out in the wasteland and outside of the law, but before the Blackout, he'd been her adoptive-mother's assistant. The tablet had come loaded with music, books, and even a few old TV shows. Other than the encyclopaedia, Ruth was most taken with the light. The entire screen could be turned into a lamp bright enough to read her favourite paperbacks. The tablet also had a camera. As she had to keep the tablet concealed, the only opportunity to take a photograph had been inside her rooms above the police station. Since nothing in there changed except her meals, and she saw no point in taking pictures of those, she'd not made much use of it. Here, though, the camera could save her an hour of awkward and inaccurate sketching. With one ear listening in case the sergeant returned, she snapped photographs from every angle.

Fifteen years ago, the bodies of five women had been found in the cellar of a house in Parkstone. There had been few clues and less evidence. Ultimately, the killer had been caught because a barman had overheard him boasting about the crime. The barman had recorded the conversation, and that had been used as evidence to arrest, charge, and bring the killer to trial.

The defence had argued that, since no one knew which devices the AIs had infected, no one knew which devices might have been compromised and so whether any data stored on them could be trusted. The prosecution had brought forward a dozen experts who attested that *they* knew, but it wasn't enough for the judge. The charges had been dismissed. The killer had been set free. As much as any crime can be said to have a happy ending, this one did. A police officer had followed the killer. He had stalked him, watching his every move, knowing that the man would kill again. Before the murderer could strike, he was arrested, knife in hand. However, the precedent had been set. Old-world technology could be contested in court. As no officer wanted another guilty suspect released on a technicality, technology wasn't used. Ruth wouldn't use it in this case. She'd have to submit sketches of the crime scene with her report, but she would rather draw them in the comfort of her apartment than in the grim surroundings of Mr Wilson's room.

She bent down, aiming the tablet under the bed. By the light of the flash, she saw something near the wall. She fished it out. It was a sketchbook, open to a page on which sea and cliffs had been drawn in pencil and charcoal. In the bottom-right-hand corner was an odd smudge of blue-grey paint. It puzzled her until she thought about where the sketchbook was, and where it would have been. She checked the victim's socks. On the left sock was a slight smudge of blue-grey paint.

"You kicked it under the bed," she said. "So… yes, you would have been walking by it. You kicked the sketchpad under the bed in the hope that the killer wouldn't see it. Why? What didn't you want the killer to see?" She flicked through the pages. Some were filled with drawings of the same section of cliffs, other pages had a view of the sea from the cliff tops. A page near the front had a near-perfect sketch of a Roman galley. At the back was a drawing of a three-masted tall-ship that reminded Ruth of the oil paintings of Nelson's fleet festooning the Naval headquarters in Dover Castle.

She turned back to the page with the smudged paint, looked at Mr Wilson's sock, then at the floor, and finally at the curtained doors.

"If the killer had come to the front door, you would have put your shoes on to go out into the hall. You didn't put your shoes on, so the killer came to the back door. Was it locked? Did they knock? You opened it, and then walked back into the room, presumably backward because you had a gun in your face. As you walked towards the bed, you kicked the sketchbook underneath. You were told to lie down. Hmm. You thought the sketchbook was important. Did the killer? Presumably not as important as the painting. There's paint on your sock, and paint on this page, but since all the drawings were done in charcoal, the paint came from something you were working on at the time." She checked the six pictures, but all were dry. "And the killer took that painting with them."

She glanced up at the light, then at the curtains covering the double-wide glass doors.

"You had the curtains open, didn't you? Of course you did. That's the only possible reason you stayed in a place like this. You wanted the natural light. The killer shut the curtains so your body wouldn't be seen by anyone going to use the latrines outside."

She dusted the curtain rail, and then the wall. There were plenty of prints, but Ruth doubted they belonged to the killer. Someone who'd had the foresight to wipe down the gun would have remembered to clean their prints from anything they'd touched.

She continued her search, taking an occasional photograph, but the only other notable find was the painting at the back of the wardrobe. Ruth doubted it had anything to do with the crime.

It was a painting of a woman and two children in a park. From the plane flying overhead, it was of the world before the Blackout. A woman stood a few feet from a boy who was pushing a slightly younger girl on a swing. Though all three figures were facing the artist, and though the smallest details on the clothing had been picked out, right down to the tear in the girl's jeans, they had no faces. Instead, there were three blank sections of canvas without even sketch marks underneath.

"Was this your family?" she asked.

Mr Wilson didn't answer.

The coroner, Dr Olivia Long, arrived ten minutes later dressed in full military uniform. Like the mayor and many other members of Dover's civilian administration, Dr Long was in the naval reserve and took full advantage of that to attend the officer's mess with its un-rationed menus.

"Just one?" Dr Long asked, gesturing at the corpse.

"Yes, Doctor," Ruth said. "One poor man, murdered for no good reason."

"Murder?" Long peered at the corpse, then the hand, then knelt and examined the wound. "Almost certainly. The angle looks wrong for it to have been self-inflicted. I'll have confirmation for you by tomorrow morning. Your sergeant wants you."

Kettering was outside, alone. "Did you find anything?" she asked.

"There's a painting in the wardrobe," Ruth said. "It was wrapped in a sheet, hidden at the back. It's of a woman and two children playing in a park before the Blackout. I think it was his family. They didn't have faces."

"Maybe Mr Wilson didn't like painting faces," Kettering said. "Or perhaps he just couldn't bring himself to do it. He lived alone, so I think we can guess what happened to his loved ones."

"You sent the landlady home?" Ruth asked.

"She didn't have much to say. I got a little more out of Mr Wilson's neighbours, but only after they were sure that Mrs Dempsey was no longer within earshot. When this case is closed, I'm going to open an investigation into her. She is not a good person. That being said, this *is* a good place for a murder. That house on the left is rented by a group of inshore fisher-folk. They wake at three, return fourteen hours later, eat, sleep, and wake to do it again. On the other side, there are two families with young children. The parents work on the docks. They're too exhausted to notice anything. In Mr Wilson's house, the top-floor rooms are currently vacant. Two cobblers paid a deposit and a month's rent in advance, but never came to take up occupancy. Their tenancy started on the sixth."

"The day after the attack on Calais?" Ruth asked.

"Right. They were going to open a shop here, and I think we can guess why they didn't. The ground-floor room has been rented by a naval officer who wanted a billet on shore for *entertaining*. As his ship set off for Africa a week ago, he won't make much of a witness, at least, not to this crime. I think he'll be persuaded to take the stand against Mrs Dempsey just as soon as I've worked out what to charge her with. As to Mr Wilson, though, no one heard or saw anything yesterday. Around here, they make a point of not seeing things."

"What do we do now?" Ruth asked.

"You tell me," Kettering said.

"Well, Mrs Dempsey was alerted that something was wrong by Mr Wilson's employer. I suppose we go there."

"No," Kettering said. "First we send word to the castle and find out if the Navy want to take over. I'm sure they can find a reason to claim jurisdiction. On the off-chance they don't, tomorrow will be a long day, so go home and get some sleep."

The police station was dark, cold, and haunted by the ghosts of old prisoners. On every previous night, that had made Ruth hurry upstairs and shut the door to the apartment. After the squalor of Mr Wilson's home, and knowing that the rest of the houses on that street would be much the same, she saw her accommodation with a clearer eye.

The old police station had burned down during the chaotic three days before the nuclear bombs had brought an end to the AIs and to the old civilisation. The building in which the police were now housed had been a provincial bank before the Blackout. The strong room had become the cells. The offices upstairs had become a small apartment. Ruth's bedroom was smaller than Mr Wilson's room, but it was *just* a bedroom. It had a table as well as the bed, but along the corridor was a small kitchen, complete with a sofa and a patched leather chair. At the other end of the corridor was a locker-room with a gravity-fed shower and two separate toilet cubicles. It wasn't as spacious as Ruth's old house on the edge of the refugee camp where she'd grown up, but it was pleasant. Homely, though not quite a home, because Kettering lived with her family in a house three doors down. There were throw pillows on the sofa, a rug on the floor, and four framed illustrations that had been rescued from a battered copy of *The Final Problem*. A teapot and almost-matching cups and saucers were on the shelves, though pride of place went to the mug with the hand-painted message *World's Greatest Detective*. That had been a gift to Kettering from one of her children. The sergeant had been Dover's police officer for nineteen years. During that time, the city had gone through four mayors, two admirals, and a dozen constables, but Elspeth Kettering had remained the one constant. The apartment had become Kettering's office so as to keep her work from spilling over into her real life. Ruth appreciated those homely touches. It helped remind her that though the rooms were above a police station, there was more to life than crime.

"The only downside is that there's no kettle," she said.

There *was* a stove. She struck a match, and held it to the kindling, wistfully remembering the little cabin that the Serious Crimes Unit had occupied in the yard of Police House in Twynham. Mister Mitchell had wired an illicit plug that powered an electric kettle. That had kept them in as much hot water as they could ever need. That memory brought back others, of times with Maggie in their home on the edge of the resettlement camp, of her childhood when everything had seemed so much simpler. Join the police force and see some of the world, that had been her plan. Well, she'd joined the force, and she'd travelled far from Twynham, and finally realised that, though her surroundings might change, she wouldn't.

Searching for the Folkestone refugee camp had been a mistake, yet it was one that she'd had to make. Maggie had found Ruth there, wandering between the tents, able to speak only one word of English: five. Maggie had adopted her, and Ruth hadn't thought much about the camp since, not until she had been leaving Twynham. She'd asked Maggie where the camp had been. Folkestone was only a few miles from Dover, and the camp only a few miles further than that, close to the garrisoned entrance to the Channel Tunnel. On her first free day, Ruth had gone to see it for herself, but there was nothing left of the camp. Two giant cairns stood either side of a field that had become the mass grave for those who'd died. Moss and ivy were now intertwined around the small plaque, and the only words still readable were 'lest we forget'.

Ruth shivered at the memory, and took out the tablet, swiping through the photographs she'd taken of Mr Wilson's room.

"It really wasn't a great way to live," she said, speaking aloud to drown out the grim memory. "But you were a good painter, so why did you choose to live there? Was it for the daylight, or was it that you really didn't care where you laid your head?" She settled on the picture of the family without faces. "That's it, isn't it? You just didn't care."

She set the tablet on the table, and while she waited for the fire to take, she sketched the crime scene.

Chapter 4 - Bacon
11th November, Dover

"Only three arrests last night," Ruth said, putting the charge sheet down in front of the judge. "All drunk and disorderly with criminal damage. One took the fine, one took enlistment, the other's pleading not guilty. Or he was, half an hour ago. He might change his tune when he sobers up."

That was the disadvantage of living above the police station. Each morning, she was woken by the military police with the charge sheets of the previous night's civilian arrests.

"Gruel," Judge Clancy Beauregard said. "These are the depths to which I have sunk, gruel. Unsalted, unsweetened, unspiced. As my meal, so is my life."

Ruth hadn't been there to see the judge's fall from grace, but she'd read about it in the newspaper. Everyone had, and not just in Britain. The story had even been reprinted in the paper in Maine. Before the Blackout, Beauregard had been a lawyer in Florida. He was one of the many cruise ship passengers miraculously lucky to run ashore on the southern English coast. Through charm as much as diligent application of their post-apocalyptic law, he'd risen through the ranks of the judiciary to become the senior justice in Dover.

Two months ago, Beauregard's wife of eight years had demanded a divorce. She'd done it halfway through an opera being performed by the Royal Navy's dramatic society, and in the presence of the Admiral of the Fleet. She'd demanded it so loudly the performance had stopped. In a way, that was a blessing, as the judge had then had a heart attack. Quick intervention by a naval surgeon had saved his life, but he was now single and on a very restricted diet.

"Chin up, sir," Ruth said. "I heard that there's going to be some nutmeg in the shops for Christmas. Not the real thing, I guess, but something from the chemical works in Twynham. Still, it'll make a change."

The judge turned a baleful eye on Ruth. She retreated to Kettering's table.

"I wouldn't want to be in his courtroom this morning," Ruth said, though quietly enough that she wouldn't be overheard. "Sleep well?"

"Hardly at all," Kettering said. "I've ordered for you."

"Porridge?"

"What else? The Navy don't want this case."

"They don't?" Ruth asked.

"The victim's employers have a Navy contract, so the military could claim jurisdiction if they wanted. It's Calais." Kettering leaned forward. "They brought another eight bodies back last night. That makes twenty-nine dead in the last ten days, plus another thirty-three in that first assault. I don't know how many have been injured, but nor do I know how many of the pirates are left. They sent more Marines to Calais this morning, so it has to be a good number." She leaned back. "That makes it our case, at least for now. I went to Mr Wilson's place of employment last night."

"They were open?" Ruth asked.

"Not for customers, but they offer a twenty-four-hour repair-or-replace service. That's how Mr Wilson earned his crust. Apparently he was a dab hand with a soldering iron. Pan, pot, or mangle, he could affix a new handle twice as fast as anyone else."

"Ah." Ruth frowned. "He can't have earned much, then. The National Store sells old-world frying pans for a pittance."

"Which not everyone can afford," Kettering said. "Besides, that was the problem with the old world. We were too busy throwing out that which could be repaired. But you have a point, Mr Wilson didn't earn very much. Certainly not as much as he could have as a painter."

"Do you think the motive for his murder is workplace jealousy?" Ruth asked.

"It's unlikely," Kettering said. "Everyone who was there seemed upset at the news. Wilson had been working there since a few years after the Blackout, but he kept to himself. He'd show his face at company socials, but would leave as soon as it was polite. His work with a soldering iron wasn't his only source of income. He sold a few of his paintings to his co-workers. By all accounts, he earned more than he needed for that cheap room."

"So what did he spend his money on?"

"Trackers and private detectives," Kettering said. "It's a sad story, but which of them aren't? He and his family were on a car ferry, on their way back from Calais when the Blackout occurred. The AIs hacked into the ship's system and opened the cargo doors. Wilson got his wife and two children onto a lifeboat. There was no room for him. When the ship sank, he ended up in the sea. Mr Wilson was saved by a fishing boat, and was brought here to Dover. The lifeboat never made it to shore. A month later, as he was walking the cliffs, he saw the lifeboat that his wife and kids were in. No sign of them, of course. He spent his entire life since looking for them. If you ask me, I'd say that lifeboat he found wasn't the one his family had taken. It probably wasn't even from the same ship. The man just didn't want to let go."

"That *is* sad," Ruth said. "And he's worked at Sprocket and Sprung ever since?"

"More or less," Kettering said. "Sometimes he would disappear for a day or a month, chasing some impossible lead in Scotland or Wales. Painting was Mr Watanabe's idea. It was something he suggested to Wilson about ten years ago, something to take his mind off his family. It didn't work, but it turns out Wilson was as good with a brush as he was with a soldering iron."

"Who's Mr Watanabe?"

"One of the co-founders of Sprocket and Sprung," Kettering said. "There are two, Mr Watanabe and Mrs Illyakov. It was Mr Watanabe's sixty-fifth birthday two weeks ago. Mr Wilson painted him a seascape of eleventh-century Japanese fishermen."

"He finished the painting two weeks ago?" Ruth asked.

"He gave it to Mr Watanabe two weeks ago," Kettering said. "He must have finished it some time before then."

"Then he must have been working on something new," Ruth said.

"More than that, he'd switched shifts," Kettering said. "Mr Wilson wanted to catch the dawn light for his current work, so didn't come into work until two p.m."

"Then if he was shot as he was getting ready for work, it was around lunchtime?" Ruth said.

"Yep," Kettering said. "The people he worked with knew that, and if one of them wanted to shoot him, I'm sure they'd have done it somewhere more secluded, like wherever he was painting this picture. Not in a residential street in the middle of the day."

"Then it was probably someone who didn't think he'd be at home?" Ruth asked.

"I'm not sure," Kettering said. "The murderer didn't know whether the man was right or left-handed, so no time was spent planning the crime. It's possible that they followed Mr Wilson home, heard the roar from the firing range, and decided to take advantage of it to cover the sound of the fatal shot. On the other hand, they might have planned to commit the crime there *because* of the firing range. There's too little evidence to tell."

"But you have a theory?"

The waiter walked over, bringing them their breakfast. He placed a bowl of steaming porridge in front of Ruth, and a paper-wrapped package in front of Kettering.

"What's that?" Ruth asked, though she could guess from the smell.

"My lunch," Kettering said.

"That's *bacon*," Ruth said a little too loudly. The judge looked up, his nostrils flaring.

Kettering placed a proprietorial hand on the packet.

"I haven't had bacon since… since last Christmas, I think," Ruth said. "We were fattening one in Twynham at the refugee centre, but that was closed and Mum moved out just before I was transferred here. I don't know what happened to the pig, but I doubt I'll see a slice of it."

"Then I know what to give you as a present this year," Kettering said.

"Why is it your lunch?" Ruth asked. "More importantly, why can't I have one?"

53

"Because I was in the club that was fattening the pig," Kettering said. "One pound a month this has cost me. A joint for Christmas Day, some rashers, and a few chops to tide me over until then. You're welcome to share the joint, but not the bacon. And not a word about it to my girls. There's a reason they cooked it for me here. As to why it's my lunch, speaking to his employers did give me one solid lead. Last week, Mr Wilson went to Hastings. He'd seen an article in an old copy of the newspaper about two cousins. One worked in a Welsh mine, the other was an orderly at the hospital in Hastings. Do you know about the hospital? It's an odd place. You know how a lot of cruise ships came ashore just after the Blackout."

"With mostly Americans on board, like the judge?"

"Precisely. A cruise was an expensive holiday. The kind of thing you'd have to earn serious money to afford. Like money from being a lawyer, or a doctor. Those doctors all grouped together to set up a research hospital in Hastings where the old knowledge wouldn't be lost. Anyway, these two cousins; both had thought the other had died in the Blackout until the miner was in an accident. She needed an operation on her spine, and the only place that could attempt it was in Hastings. That's where she went, and thus the two cousins were reunited. Mr Wilson went to Hastings to see if his family were there."

"Because of that article?" Ruth asked.

"Yes, he led a sad, small life. He painted. He worked. He slept, and desperately dreamed that his family were still alive. He didn't socialise, not even with his colleagues though he'd known some of them for nearly two decades. He had no friends, and it doesn't look as if the killer knew him. In which case, it's most likely that he was killed because he was in the wrong place at the wrong time. As he was in Hastings last week, I think that might be the place. There was some trouble with smugglers there a few years ago. Your Mister Mitchell was involved in that case. I'm going to see if someone has started that business up again."

"I've never been to Hastings," Ruth said.

"And you won't be going there today," Kettering said. "I'll catch a train in an hour, and I'll get the goods train back this evening. Speak to the coroner, and then go back to his employer. Get some formal statements written up. Ask about Hastings, but also about the trackers that Wilson employed to find his family. If I don't find anything at the hospital, that might be our best lead. Perhaps one of these so-called detectives thought Wilson had more money than he did, and came to Dover to shake him down. Get some names." Kettering picked up the brown paper package. "And eat your porridge before it gets hard."

Chapter 5 - A Good Employee
Dover

"He was a good employee," Mrs Illyakov said in a tone that suggested it was the highest honour she could bestow. "A good painter, too."

"I can see you appreciated his artwork," Ruth said. Illyakov's office had nine paintings on the rear wall, positioned so that the person sitting behind the desk could view them.

Mrs Illyakov, the owner of Sprocket and Sprung, was five-foot-one, a few years past fifty, and had a thin, angular face. Her clothing was fashionable and cleverly tailored to make her look petite, though there was a slight stretch to the fabric betraying broad shoulders and wide arms. There was no wedding ring on her finger, nor any trace of a spouse or family in the office, yet the sign on her door read 'Mrs'. In fact, other than the paintings, there were no personal touches in Mrs Illyakov's office at all. It was entirely functional, right down to the floor-to-ceiling glass door that gave her a view of the workshop.

"Did I appreciate his art? Yes and no," Mrs Illyakov said. "Mr Wilson had a natural talent, but he didn't know it, nor how accomplished he could become with further application. I purchased his paintings because someone had to give Noah the price for his paints. They were expensive. A lot were mixed for him personally. He would often abandon a picture because the sea wasn't the correct shade of blue."

Ruth stood, and walked over to the wall. The paintings were, again, all seascapes of one kind or another, though Dover's white cliffs featured prominently in each.

"You bought them from him? For how much?" Ruth asked.

"That would depend on how much paint he needed," Mrs Illyakov said. "Sometimes he'd give a picture to a colleague. Sometimes he would bring one in and leave it by the bin, there for anyone to take." She gave an expansive shrug. "I'm not surprised he killed himself. He was holding onto his old life too tightly. He wouldn't let go, so it was inevitable that, when he accepted his family were dead, he would decide to join them."

Ruth nodded. She'd kept their supposition that Mr Wilson was murdered to herself. "What can you tell me about his family?"

"Nothing that I didn't tell your sergeant," she said. "They died during the Blackout. Noah refused to accept it."

"Do you know what painting he was working on?" Ruth asked.

"It was a search for a new world," Mrs Illyakov said. "That was all he'd say."

"How long did it take him to complete a picture?" Ruth asked.

"A few weeks if he was happy with it. Longer if he decided he didn't like the shape of a cloud. Artists," she added.

"Was he acting differently of late?" Ruth asked. "Did anything happen that could have caused an abrupt change in his mood?"

"Other than his trip to Hastings? No."

"Did he talk about what he found there?"

"Not to me," Mrs Illyakov said.

Ruth had already interviewed most of the other employees and found they had less to tell her than Mr Wilson's boss.

"What about the detectives he hired to find his family, did he ever talk about them?" Ruth asked.

"He hasn't used any for a year," Mrs Illyakov said. "He was a sad man who led a sad life, which, sadly, has come to a premature end."

"Yes, I suppose you're right. Thank you for your time."

"If you find anything, do please let us know," Mrs Illyakov said. "I'll have Mr Watanabe show you out." She pressed a button on her desk. A bell jangled above the door. "Don't worry," Mrs Illyakov added. "It's entirely mechanical. The button is attached to a wire, which, in turn, connects to the bell. The only technology we have here is that which is licensed by the government."

Ruth gave a smile that didn't stretch further than her mouth.

"I do not think he killed himself," Mr Watanabe said, as he walked Ruth back through the maze of shelves.

"No?" Ruth asked. "Why not?"

"He and I were the same," Mr Watanabe said. "Stranded here without our families. We talked of them often. He would never have given up his search."

"You were stranded here?" Ruth asked.

"I was stranded in England," Mr Watanabe said. "Ten thousand miles from my home in Shimoda. Mr Wilson was stranded in time, and with each day, only got further from his destination. No, he would not have killed himself."

"Do you know what he was working on when he died?" Ruth asked.

"The pump mechanism for an industrial pressure hose they use in the dockyard. The Navy's approach has been to patch and mend, but after twenty years, the pump is more patch than mechanism. He had to strip it down to its constituent parts and then rebuild it."

"Sorry, I meant do you know what he was painting?" Ruth said.

"Ah, he told me that it was Julius Caesar's arrival in Britain," Mr Watanabe said. "It wasn't intended to be a historically accurate piece, but representative of how we, as a species, had arrived in a new country though without ever having moved in space."

"Oh, that's fascinating," Ruth said, though she wasn't entirely sure she understood what Mr Watanabe meant.

"I truly thought he was on the road to recovery," Mr Watanabe said.

"Do you know where he was getting his inspiration?"

"It was a section of cliffs to the west of the city," Mr Watanabe said. "Somewhere not too far from the main road, though I'm not sure precisely where. It was one of his favourite spots. It's where he painted the picture for me."

"He painted your portrait?" Ruth asked.

"Oh no, he didn't do faces. I meant he painted a picture he gave to me for my birthday. Fishermen from my home country, landing on a beach. He put in a cherry tree in full blossom despite it being too close to the salt-laden sea. He liked beaches. He said that picture was his masterwork. I took it to the castle. They have an art historian there who cares for the exhibits. She offered me a year's salary for the picture."

"Really?"

"I wouldn't sell it," Mr Watanabe said. "I certainly won't now."

Ruth paused by a bank of floor-to-ceiling shelves. According to the neatly stencilled labels, they contained nuts, bolts, and washers.

"Mr Wilson painted those, as well," Watanabe said. "The labels. Each is hand-painted, but each is as identical as if it were printed."

Ruth glanced at them, then back at Watanabe. "Weren't you a co-owner of this business?"

Mr Watanabe smiled. "Originally. But it is a long way to Japan. You see, I might have been stranded in England, but I always planned to return. I used this business to buy the goodwill of sailors and their captains. Goodwill can only get you so far. I sold my half of the business to Mrs Illyakov so that I could purchase passage on the first ship that went to Japan."

"You went home?"

"Home? I don't know if I would call it that. When a swallow flies south in the winter, does it say it is returning home, or leaving it? I returned to Japan. My old home was gone. My family were dead."

"I'm sorry," Ruth said. "Were there any survivors?"

"Oh, yes. Some, but no one that I knew." He gave a thin smile. "I returned to a place I once called home, but having returned, I wished I hadn't. Each culture on this planet had a myth that recounted the dangers of that very act. I should have heeded them."

Ruth thought of her own recent trip to the refugee camp. "And what is it that you do here? I thought you repaired pots and pans."

"Ah, no. Well, yes, we do. We perform repairs for the Navy. We make barrels for breweries. We craft tools for the farmers and fisher-folk. Most of all, we give people *time*." He gestured at the odd assortment of household items on the workbenches against the exterior wall of the room. A children's pushchair with a broken wheel was on the nearest. On the one behind was a pedal-powered sewing machine. The bench by the window had the more familiar workings of a clock.

"Time?" she asked.

"They called them labour-saving devices. Truly, they saved people time wasted on grinding chores so they could spend it with those they loved. Yes, that is what we do. We repair what is brought in. If it can't be repaired, we will fashion a replacement within twenty-four hours. Even with Mr Wilson's death, we must hold ourselves to that. Our word is our bond. It is important above all else."

"I know what you mean," Ruth said.

"Then you'll find who killed Mr Wilson?" he asked. "You give me your word?"

Ruth had spoken automatically, but she couldn't say no. "Of course," she said, and instantly regretted it.

As she walked down Castle Street, Ruth regretted it even more. Before she'd met with Mrs Illyakov, she'd spoken to the other staff. They'd all seemed upset at the loss of Mr Wilson. It was possible that they were just very good actors and there was some petty motive of revenge at the heart of this sad story, but Ruth didn't think so. Mr Wilson was the proverbial golden egg. Unless she'd completely misunderstood, he'd given away his paintings to anyone who asked for them and for however much they felt like paying. From what Mr Watanabe had said, those paintings were genuinely valuable. If money was the motivation, then someone would have kidnapped Mr Wilson, secreted him in a remote house with paints and canvas, and promises that the best detectives in the country were being hired to search for his family. Killing him meant no more pictures, and no more rainy-day funds for his co-workers.

No, aside from the fact that they all appeared to have liked Mr Wilson, his co-workers only had a motive to keep him alive. If Mrs Illyakov was correct, Mr Wilson hadn't hired a tracker in the last year. Thus, it was unlikely that a so-called detective was behind the murder. In short, she'd exhausted the list of obvious suspects.

She paused by a window to the National Store. Large posters announced the arrival of cinnamon, mace, vanilla, nutmeg, and cloves. Like the Satz! brand of powdered tea, they were manufactured at the chemical works in Twynham. Like the tea, they were available off-ration this Christmas. The newspaper had carried a vivid debate in the letters column about the health impact of these 'unnatural' spices. Ruth hadn't followed the debate, and was reasonably certain that the letter writers hadn't either. She was simply happy that, though her diet might remain as unvaried as ever, there would be a little more variety in the flavour.

In the plate glass, she caught the reflection of a figure. Male, bearded, head bowed, back bent, at least middle aged, possibly older. His clothes were well-mended, fourth-hand, and black except where they were coated in the earthy tones of mud. Only his boots looked relatively new and recently cleaned. His hands were deep in his pockets and his coat was wrapped tight around his throat. She'd seen him before, that morning, near the police station. She'd dismissed him as a tramp who'd come to the city looking for work and a warm bed for the winter. Now she wondered if he was following her.

Without looking around, she set off, heading down the street until she reached a butcher's. Pretending to read the sign extolling customers to order their Christmas chicken before it was too late, she looked for the tramp in the shop's window. The man was gone.

"No gunshot residue on his hands, and the trajectory is wrong. No, he didn't shoot himself," Dr Long said.

The coroner's laboratory was in the grounds of the castle, though not in the fortress itself. The small Naval hospital had once been a museum. After the Blackout, during the chaos of those early days when the world was crumbling, the castle had become a focal point for local and ship-borne survivors. Most had required medical care beyond that which the under-supplied, over-worked doctors and nurses could provide. The museum had been used as a morgue until graves could be dug. Now the castle had become the Royal Navy's command centre for all operations in the pirate-infested European waters. A few small rooms were given over to the city's civilian administration, with the coroner given an office beneath the hospital.

"But the gunshot killed him?" Ruth asked.

"Absolutely," the doctor said. "I've sketches over there for your file. The angle was wrong for it to be self-inflicted. The gun was held about three feet from the man's head, and fired almost level. The trajectory took the bullet through the left temporal bone, exiting through the parietal bone on the right-hand-side of his head. I'm recording this as a murder."

Mr Wilson's body was covered with a sheet, and for that Ruth was glad. She'd seen more dead people than she could easily remember in the last three months.

"Was there anything else?" Ruth asked.

"Not especially," Dr Long said. "The victim was malnourished, but clean. There were no restraint marks around his wrists or ankles, and no signs of a struggle. Of course, if the killer had a gun, that's not surprising. Did he paint the pictures that were in his room?"

"Yes, he was an artist," Ruth said.

"A good one," the coroner said. "I think I've heard of him. There was talk of a man who could paint the sea so vividly you could almost smell the salt."

"Talk? What kind of talk?" Ruth asked.

"In the officer's mess, usually whenever discussion of how a sailor might spend their pay came up."

"And you think it was Mr Wilson?" Ruth asked.

"Ah, I'm giving the wrong impression. It wasn't a great secret, I was just never that interested. I can ask around to confirm it."

"That would be helpful, thank you," Ruth said.

"The murder wasn't done by a sailor, though," the coroner added.

"How can you be sure?"

"Because if a sailor wanted to stage a suicide, they wouldn't do it on dry land."

There was a welcome chill to the air, an icy breeze that helped clear the laboratory's chemical smell from Ruth's mind. Mr Wilson had been murdered, but she'd already known that. She didn't suspect any of his co-workers, and that left the list of suspects frustratingly blank.

There were two obvious leads. Hastings was one. The other was that the clue lay in the missing painting. If Mr Wilson had seen something, or someone, and added that to the picture, then it was possible that was why he was killed. It was a long shot, far less likely than Hastings, but a stroll along the cliffs would confirm it. If nothing else, it would clear her mind, and that would be preferable to spending the day patrolling the docks.

There was a bakery on the other side of the road. Since she was going for a walk in the countryside, she decided that she might as well take her lunch with her. She stopped for a bicycle-powered cart to pass, tipped her hat to the driver, and, as she glanced around to see if there was any other traffic, saw the tramp who'd been following her. He stood in the narrow alleyway between a funeral home and a clockmaker's. She darted across the street. Her hand dropped to the revolver at her belt.

"Hoy!" a cyclist yelled. Ruth skipped out of the way. When she looked towards the alley, the figure was gone. Ruth ran into the alley's mouth. There was no one there, but there was a fresh boot-print in the mud.

Recent experience had caused her hand to drop to the revolver, training made her draw her truncheon. She eased down the dark alley, around the half-filled bins. There was a side door to the clockmaker's. It was locked. She kept going to the end of the alley and into the road beyond. There was no sign of the tramp.

That settled it. Someone *was* following her, and she'd rather they followed her out into the open country where there would be fewer places for them to hide.

Chapter 6 - The White Cliffs
Dover

"I think I know why you came here to paint," Ruth said.

She'd reached the end of the road, or at least the point where the old A20 stopped following the coast and turned inland. Smoke hung above Dover a mile and a half to the northeast. To the southwest lay the ruins of Folkestone. There was nothing in the town but a garrison of Marines guarding the entrance to the Channel Tunnel. Even the chain gangs on rubble-clearance had been evacuated following the attack on Calais. To the south, at the base of the chalk-white cliffs, lay the sea.

Ruth stood on a battered stretch of concrete that had once been either a lookout point or a small car park. There was such a thick carpet of struggling grass, straggly heather, and scrubby gorse it was impossible to tell which. The overgrowth stretched along the chalky cliffs eastward. To the west was a precipitous drop where the cliffs fell down to a sandy beach dotted with chalk-white stone. She'd inspected two sets of ruins and three lonely lookout points on her short walk from the city, but the smudges of paint at her feet confirmed that this was where Mr Wilson had come.

Ruth took out her tablet, swiped at the screen, and found the photographs of the crime scene. The chalk-white cliffs *might* have been the charcoal drawings in his sketchbook, and the drops of green-blue paint on the gravel *might* match the smears on the pallet. It was hard to be certain.

"But what are the odds two people were painting at this spot?"

She took a photograph of the paint, and another of the cliffs. She would compare those with the original evidence when she returned to the station. Then she put the tablet away, and took in the view.

The gate-captain had confirmed that Mr Wilson left the city every morning for the past two weeks except for the day he spent in Hastings. The names of those coming and going from the city weren't usually recorded, but Mr Wilson was always waiting for the gates to be opened.

Because of that, the gate-captain remembered the victim. He'd even tried striking up a conversation, but Mr Wilson had only mumbled monosyllabic replies while staring at the ground.

"But if Mr Wilson finished work after midnight, and was at the gate before dawn, he can't have slept for more than four hours."

That told her something about her victim, but not about the murderer.

A steel-hulled sailing ship, flying Britain's flag, was a quarter mile out to sea. A dozen fishing boats were trawling in its wake. She didn't think it was a sight like that which had got Mr Wilson killed. The beach at the base of the cliffs to the west was shallow enough for a craft to make landfall. She imagined raiding pirates coming ashore, and Mr Wilson sketching them. She pictured the raiders looking up, seeing the artist with his easel, and then chasing him back to the city. Except Mr Wilson would have warned the gate-captain. Even if he hadn't, while no record was kept of those coming in and out of the city during the day, a sentry would have noticed a pirate war band coming into Dover, and pirates wouldn't have stopped with only one murder. Besides, the steep cliffs would be nearly impossible to climb. No, the killer wasn't someone who'd spotted Mr Wilson from down on the beach.

"But who was it?"

She took a few more photographs, then glanced through the pictures she'd taken, pausing when she reached the family portrait.

"You didn't paint faces," she said. "Either you couldn't, or you chose not to. So even if you did see someone doing… doing something, you wouldn't have been able to paint a picture that identified them. That's why the sketchbook was left behind. Not because you kicked it under the bed, but because the killer tossed it aside after confirming you hadn't recorded anything incriminating. Not that it mattered. By then, it was too late. The murderer was in your… your room." She hesitated in calling it a home.

That left the question of why Mr Wilson's work-in-progress had been taken. As a trophy? Because the killer liked art? If the answer *was* in Dover rather than Hastings, it wouldn't be found on the cliffs. She turned to face the road. The *road*, the same road that Mr Wilson had walked up and down for thirteen days out of the last fourteen. The easel would have marked Mr Wilson as an artist. To a stranger, it was a reasonable assumption that such a person could faithfully draw someone's face.

"Why would the killer care?"

That was another unanswerable question to add to an increasingly long list. She left the cliffs, and headed back to the road.

Closer to the city, the fields were grazed by the beef and dairy herds that supplied the Royal Navy with fresh beef and hard cheese. The livestock was owned by the Navy, and was brought into the city every night. The drovers were on salary, paid a monthly wage to tend them. Ten years ago, the first civilian mayor of the city, as her first act in office, had claimed every scrap of land within walking distance of the city that the Navy and Railway Company hadn't. She'd had orchards planted, filling the abandoned fields with apples, pears, quinces, damsons, and any other fruiting tree that would grow in the slightly toxic soil. As the orchards didn't require constant maintenance, no farmers had to spend their days over a mile from the safety of the city's walls, and so no Marines were needed to protect them except during a few hectic weeks of a late summer harvest. In other words, there was no obvious reason for someone to come down this road so late in the year. Technically it linked Dover to Folkestone, but the Channel Tunnel garrison were supplied by rail. When Ruth had gone searching for the refugee camp in which Maggie had found her, she'd taken the train the ridiculously short distance to Folkestone, then walked from there. The Navy had a training run, but that took them in a gruelling loop to the north of the city.

Ruth paused by the rusting ruin of a wrecked lorry. The road *did* run from Dover to Folkestone. Her mind again turned to a raiding party. There were plenty of ruined buildings along the road, and far more inland. Any of those might be a useful lair in which to hide, but why, then, would someone come onto the road, and do it so often they were worried about Mr Wilson recognising them? It didn't add up, and that, she realised, was why Sergeant Kettering had gone to Hastings.

A robin landed on the twisted remains of the lorry's cab. Ruth watched the bird, but her eyes travelled to the vehicle. Something about it stirred an ancient memory. Inside the cab, grass sprouted in the footwell. Moss occupied the seats. Metal gleamed on the skeletal steering wheel where generations of birds had sharpened their beaks. The wing-mirror was still intact, though covered in a thick patina of dirt. Ruth wiped her finger across it. In the reflection, she saw the tramp who'd been following her in the city. He was two hundred yards down the road. She only caught a fleeting glimpse before he ducked behind a battered sign, but Ruth was sure it was him.

Nonchalantly, she turned around. Whistling an off-key tune, she made a show of inspecting the truck, then the road, and then the sea. She looked at everything but the sign behind which the tramp had hidden. She sauntered along the road until she was level with the lorry's rotting rear tyres. She released the button on her holster. She didn't draw her weapon, but kept her hand close to it as she took step after slow step. A hundred yards. Fifty. Thirty. She saw the sign's shadow on the grassy scrub, and how it appeared to have two extra, lumpy, supporting struts. Beyond the sign was nothing but grass and gorse. There was nowhere for the tramp to run. She drew her weapon.

"Police! Come out! Step out into the road, hands raised!" she barked. Slowly, the shadow moved. The tramp stepped out from behind the sign. He was smiling.

"Hello, Ruth," Captain Henry Mitchell said.

Chapter 7 - The Tramp
Dover

"Mister Mitchell?" Ruth asked.

"The one and the same," Mitchell said. "Would you mind lowering your weapon?"

"What happened to you?" Ruth asked, holstering her revolver. "I mean, why are you dressed like... like... like that?"

"Haven't you seen the paper? It's the latest fashion."

"You're undercover? Your disguise is... well, it's good. But why are you here?"

"That's a very long story," Mitchell said. "But unless I've missed my guess, the answer is the same one that's brought you out here."

"You mean Mr Wilson's suicide?" Ruth asked.

"Who's Mr Wilson? No, let's find somewhere with a little more cover. We don't want to be spotted."

Ruth followed the captain up a narrow rabbit-track and through thick gorse until they came to a hillock of tangled brambles. On second glance, Ruth realised they were growing out of the remains of an ancient automobile.

"That's a Rolls-Royce," Mitchell said. "Used to be a famous brand. World-famous. Even I'd heard of them, and my interest in cars was always more in keeping my old lemon on the road. But this will do. Hunker down and keep your eyes on the west. I'll watch the east."

"Who for?" Ruth asked. She sat, but then immediately stood and moved upwind of the captain. "Sorry, sir," she added. "You're a tad ripe."

"There's not much chance to wash out on the road. You have to make do with streams and water troughs, and a good farmer keeps too close an eye on their cattle for the latter to be a regular option. I did manage a bath after I saw Atherton last week."

"You saw the prime minister?"

"I did." Mitchell stretched out his leg, opened his jacket, and took out a flask. "Coffee? Not the real thing, I'm afraid. Just the ersatz kind, and it's cold."

"I'm fine," she said, easing a few more inches away from him.

"Then you begin with your tale," he said. "Why are you out here? Who's Mr Wilson?"

"An artist whose body was found in his lodgings yesterday. He worked at a repair shop in the town, but didn't show up for his shift. He was shot. It was staged to look like a suicide, but done by someone who didn't know he was right-handed. A painting was missing from his easel, and he was drawing his inspiration from a spot on the cliffs a little way up the road. That's why I came here, to see if the place would give me a hint as to what he might have seen. The only other real clue we've got is that he went to Hastings last week, looking for his family. He lost them in the Blackout, but he refused to accept they're dead. Sergeant Kettering went to Hastings, I came here. I've got some photographs." She handed her tablet to Mitchell.

"Ah, another one of Isaac's tablets. He missed his calling, that man. Should have been in product design. And if he had…" Mitchell trailed off as he swiped through the photographs.

"Why are you here if it's not about Mr Wilson?" Ruth asked.

"It might be," Mitchell said. "You know how I feel about coincidences, but this is the last place I'd thought I'd be. Literally. As to how I've ended up here, I've been tracking the associates of Longfield and Emmitt."

"Because of Jameson's murder?" Ruth asked.

"You heard of that?"

"It was in the papers," she said. "I mean, the man who helped Emmitt attempt to assassinate the PM died in custody. That had to be reported. They didn't say how it happened, though," she added.

"He was shot through the bars of his cell with a silenced revolver. The killer was a man named Pollock, a civil service clerk with responsibility for the police personnel files. He held a theoretical rank of captain so that he couldn't be browbeaten by line officers into revealing the secrets of their colleagues. He used that rank to gain access to the cells. I caught him up near Edinburgh on the fifth. That's what I've been doing these last few weeks. I've been hunting down the last members of the conspiracy. All those who helped Longfield, Emmitt, and Wallace. The kind of people who, now that there is a vacuum at the top of our nation's criminal pyramid, might attempt to fill it. And I'm almost done."

"I could have helped you," Ruth said.

Mitchell shrugged. "It's easier when you know any footsteps following you belong to unfriendly feet. Besides, a forty-year-old man wandering the countryside is a common enough sight in Britain. Eyes will fall off me as easily as apples from an overloaded cart. A young woman, though, would only get the wrong kind of attention." He relented. "Fine, yes, I wanted to do this alone. Riley was shot. You were abducted and tortured. I *needed* to do this alone. And I needed to make sure it was done, that they were all caught or dead."

Ruth let it go. "But *why* are you here? You're tracking someone?"

"A conspirator," Mitchell said. "He's the last serious threat to our society. He arranged for Jameson's murder and is the last surviving member of that group who might be able to rebuild Longfield's organisation."

"Who is it?" Ruth asked.

"Ivan Adamovitch."

"Adama— Wait, you mean Adams, the under-butler at Longfield Hall?"

"The very same," Mitchell said. "He and about ten other members of Longfield's personal staff disappeared before we could arrest them. There was a pursuit. We, ah…" His hand went to a slight tear in his jacket's sleeve. "We got nine of them. Adamovitch escaped. Pollock, the man who killed Jameson, confirmed that the murder was committed on Adamovitch's orders."

"There wasn't anything about *that* in the newspaper," Ruth said.

"No, we've been keeping it quiet. I wanted Adamovitch to think he was safe, but I was on verge of putting his picture in the newspaper before I learned that he might be near here. As I said, this really was the last place I expected him to be. You see, some jewellery went missing from

Longfield's mansion. Necklaces and earrings that once belonged to Jackie Kennedy."

"Who's she?"

"She was the wife of a U.S. president about eighty years ago," Mitchell said. "The jewellery was to be returned to America after they've held their reunification election. In terms of cash value on the streets of Twynham, they'd buy you a night in a relatively clean room. In America, sold to the right person, they'd buy an entirely new identity. Their absence made me think that's where Adamovitch was intending to go. The trail I found seemed to confirm it. Adamovitch planned to make use of Longfield's American contacts to start a new life across the Atlantic. Emmitt's arrest was printed in the newspaper, along with his sentence. Everyone knows that he's awaiting execution. It's no great leap to assume that he might share some names in order to save his neck. A paranoid butler might take that Emmitt's not been executed yet as proof he *has* shared something. Other than a few military-reinforced enclaves along the European and African coasts, there's nowhere to flee other than America."

"But you think Adamovitch came to Dover instead? Why?" Ruth asked. "This is on the wrong side of Britain. The only big ships in the harbour belong to the Royal Navy. With the blockade of Calais, not even fishing boats are venturing far without an escort."

"Precisely," Mitchell said. "Like I said, I didn't think he'd come here. Not originally, but it seems he left a false trail."

"Wait, hang on," Ruth said, as the penny finally dropped. "Do you mean that sending me to Dover was your idea? It was your way of keeping me out of danger?"

"More or less," Mitchell said. "I won't apologise. It was either this or sending you to live with Isaac, but that would have meant you'd have to leave the police force."

Ruth turned her eyes to the road. A month ago, she'd have replied immediately, accusing Mitchell of... she wasn't sure, but she'd learned better since. "Dover is basically one large barracks," she said instead. "You can't throw a stick without hitting the military police. Why would he come here?"

"Presumably because Europe is his real destination," Mitchell said. "There hasn't been much about the siege of Calais in the press, so it's possible that he wasn't aware that no ships were leaving. As to why Europe, well, the answer to that lies in how much he knows. To be more precise, in how much Longfield knew. Some of her companies supplied the Royal Navy. She had a stake in the munitions business. It's possible that she'd gathered information on our ships, their weaknesses, and their disposition. That kind of information would be invaluable to the warlords and bandits of the European heartland."

"Like those in Calais?" Ruth asked.

"Exactly," Mitchell said. "From the reports I've read, this information wouldn't buy Adamovitch a new life. He'd be thrown in a cell and tortured until every last drop of knowledge had been bled from him. Those are evil people in Calais, but maybe he doesn't know that, or maybe he thinks that a dance with the devil is better than the hangman's jig."

"And that necklace, that was just a way of throwing you off the scent?"

"Either that or a way of proving that he is who he says he is."

"How do you know he came to Dover?" Ruth asked.

"Mostly thanks to Rebecca Cavendish," Mitchell said. "She's had people listening for rumours, and there have been a lot of those of late. Do you know what time of day Mr Wilson was killed?"

"Mr— Oh, well, he was one of the first to leave the city in the morning. The gate-captain remembered him waiting for the gates to be opened. He returned around midday, and started his shift at two. He was never late."

"And he was painting in the same spot each day?"

"I think so," Ruth said. "For the last two weeks."

"Then he was killed because he saw someone."

"That's what I thought," Ruth said. "Do you think it was Adamovitch? He saw Mr Wilson as a painter who could perfectly re-create his face. You said you were keeping his picture out of the paper, but it would have been printed soon, right? Adamovitch would have thought so, and he would have worried that a painter would be the kind of person who'd remember having seen it."

"That sounds plausible," Mitchell said. He rubbed his legs, but kept his eyes on the road. "The question we must ask ourselves is why was Adamovitch on this road? Was he going into Dover? Why? For food, or to make contact with someone, and is that someone connected to Calais? We won't know the answer until we've found him."

"You waited until *after* you saw the prime minister before you had a bath?" Ruth asked.

"I didn't want to have to wash twice," Mitchell said. "Now, tell me more about Mr Wilson."

She filled him in on the crime scene, and on Sprocket and Sprung. He told her about Pollock and the criminals he'd arrested. Minutes became an hour, and then two, but there was no sign of anyone on the road.

"Do you have any food on you?" Mitchell asked.

"Sorry, no."

"Then it's time to go looking for him," Mitchell said. "I make it five minutes past two, yes? If someone was coming down this road everyday at the same time, they didn't do it today. I expect that the murder of Mr Wilson changed their plans. They must be in some abandoned house somewhere, though within walking distance of Dover. Is your gun loaded?"

"Always," Ruth said. Even so, she double-checked.

Chapter 8 - Smoke, Wood and Gun
Dover

"How's Sergeant Kettering?" Mitchell asked as they followed the road away from Dover.

"Fine," Ruth said, scanning the muddy puddles for footprints. "Do you know her?"

"I know a lot of people," Mitchell said. "How's her family?"

"Well, I suppose," Ruth said.

"You're enjoying Dover?" he asked, and then gave a loud sniff.

"It's been a lot quieter than Twynham," she said. "At least it was up until yesterday. The Navy deal with most of the crimes. There's a lot more paperwork, though. That seems to be about ninety percent of what I do."

"And that's another problem that needs to be solved," he said.

"The paperwork?"

"No, the Navy. And the railroad, the telegraph people, the chemical works. We're a collection of petty fiefdoms gathered under the umbrella of an ancient democracy, but we are not democratic, not yet. We call our representatives members of parliament, but there's still no viable opposition. It makes me almost wish for the old days of political parties." He sniffed again.

"Do you have a cold?"

"Wood smoke," Mitchell said. "At this time of year, no one is going to spend their days hiding in a cabin without a fire." He sniffed. "Nothing."

They continued following the old road, passing a panel van that was more red rust than white paint.

"You don't think we're democratic?" she asked.

"Not really, not in the way people mean when they use that word. I thought we were heading in the right direction, but after the last couple of months, I'm not so sure. Each time I think the crisis is over, a new one rears its head. I suppose a quick glance at a history book would tell you that's always been the way, but there's little comfort in that."

"You mean the trouble in Calais?" she asked. "When the wind's coming from the east, you can hear the artillery, but there's not much about it in the papers. I had to ask the military police what's going on. I'm not sure how much to believe, or how much they know, but even if a tenth is true then it sounds worse than anything I could imagine."

"That sounds about right," Mitchell said. "The last time I traversed the wilds of Europe was just before we opened the Serious Crimes Unit. There were bandits and barbarians, of course, but they were a nuisance, not an army. There were small towns and growing villages, and they all wanted to know what crops would be most valuable to trade with Britain. There was hope. There were even a few refugees who left the safety of Britain to return to their old home. To put it in perspective, I'm talking about thousands of people where once there were millions, but for the first time in twenty years, I thought that maybe the world was putting itself back together. Then these pirates appeared."

"Do you know much about them?" she asked.

"A little. There were three groups; one came from the north, one from the south, one from the east. Their ideologies are so utterly conflicting that, when they met, they should have butchered each other. They didn't. Instead, they headed straight for Calais and the entrance to the Channel Tunnel."

"They were trying to invade?" Ruth asked.

"Possibly, I don't know," Mitchell said. "The Marine garrison in France held them back until reinforcements could arrive, but the majority of the Marines and Navy are now engaged on that front. A year ago, there was hope. Now? Now, I'm not so sure. Be glad you're a copper, though war will make bloody work for us all. Smoke. Do you smell it?"

Ruth sniffed. There was a faintly acrid tang to the air, though she couldn't see any smoke rising above the bare-branched fruit trees or the occasional lush conifer. She turned her gaze downward. The road was covered in a thin layer of rotting mulch with occasional tendrils bursting through the cracks close to the drainage ditch on the eastern edge of the road. It was there, in a patch of flooded dirt, that she saw it.

"Sir! A footprint! Someone came this way recently."

75

Mitchell paused, bent, and peered at it. "Size ten. A shoe rather than a boot. Do you see the intricate pattern of waves in the tread? I think I can name the cobbler who made that shoe. She has a shop in Pokesdown. Each pair is made to measure, and appears to have a plain style, but each tread has a unique pattern. You'd only know that someone was wearing them if you looked for the prints on a wet day. It's precisely the kind of footgear a pretentious butler might buy. Do you have your handcuffs?"

"Of course."

"Cuff me. I'll play a chicken-rustling tramp who graduated to stealing seed. I thought it was flour, and stashed it out in the woods. You caught me, and I'm now leading you to where I left my haul."

Ruth took out the cuffs, and looped them loosely over Mitchell's wrists. She didn't lock them. "I don't know that will buy us much time," she said.

"A few seconds is all we need," Mitchell said. "We want the man to come out of his lair with curiosity in his heart, not a gun in his hands. Speaking of which, keep yours holstered. He'll see us before we see him, so let's not look like a threat."

"Not much chance of that," Ruth said. "Adamovitch will recognise me as quickly as I will him."

"I don't think so," Mitchell said. "He'll just see a copper in uniform. Pull your cap low, and keep your head down."

If it hadn't been for the occasional ivy-covered sign, Ruth would have thought they were walking along a forester's track rather than what had once been a main road. After another two hundred yards, as the scent of wood smoke grew stronger, they came to a shallow stream that cut a five-foot-wide path straight across the road. On the far side, angling into the woods, were another three footprints, all with the same intricate tread.

"We're close," Mitchell said, though it took another five minutes before they reached the fire.

It had been set outside a house that was partially thatched and two-thirds ruined. The neat-packed straw covering the eastern third of the one-storey dwelling was the only part of the main building still standing. The rest, a newer extension, had collapsed along with the chimney. The fire had been set outside a double-garage. The imitation-wood doors had been raised. It appeared that was where the criminals lived. It was where they now sat, and there were three of them.

One was a massive man with a shaved head left bare on this cold autumn day. The second was small, wiry with a gymnast's frame. He wore a tight-fitting but threadbare jacket of faded red, and almost-matching hat and gloves. He looked like he was feeling the cold, and alternated his hands from the fire to under his armpits. The third man Ruth recognised immediately. It was Adamovitch. He wore the long, black overcoat that was a butler's winter-wear with a grey fedora pulled low over his ears.

A steaming saucepan hung over the fire, filling the air with a mixed aroma of rich game and bay leaves. More important was the assault rifle propped against the wall of the garage, ten feet from the skinny man.

"There might be more people inside the house. We've got to flush them out. Get ready to take cover," Mitchell whispered. Then, in a wild yell, he added "There! The seeds are under the fire. They're burning 'em!" Mitchell staggered into the clearing, his cuffed hands waving vigorously.

The three men stood.

"Sorry about this," Ruth said cheerfully, as she followed Mitchell into the clearing. "I'm pretty sure he's lying. I'm absolutely *certain* he's mad, but procedures have to be followed. You don't recognise him, do you?"

"Who are you?" the skinny man asked. His accent was English, from the north.

"Sorry," Ruth said again. "This man's a thief. He stole some seed stock that had been set aside for next year's planting. I think he ate it, but he says he stashed it around here."

"The fire!" Mitchell barked, angling towards the garage and the assault rifle. "It's under the fire!"

"Seed?" Adamovitch asked, he sounded suspicious. "No one plants anything around here. Who are you? Wait, are—"

Before he could finish, Mitchell let the handcuffs fall from his wrists.

"You're under arrest, Adamovitch," the captain said, drawing a pistol from under his coat.

The skinny man dived for the rifle, grabbed it, rolled, and was bringing it up before Ruth's weapon was free from the holster. Mitchell fired before Ruth could bring her weapon to bear. The skinny man crumpled. The large man grabbed the spit from the fire, and swung it around his head.

"Put it down!" Mitchell yelled.

The large man roared, and Adamovitch ran.

"Stop him!" Mitchell barked, but Ruth was already sprinting after the butler.

The large man threw the spit towards her, but Ruth jumped over it.

"I meant shoot him!" Mitchell said.

Ruth didn't, and she didn't turn around or reply.

Adamovitch ran into the ruin of the old cottage. Ruth knew better than to follow him inside. He wasn't going to ground. She ran around the edge of the building, reaching its rear in time to see the butler pulling himself through a broken window.

"Stop!" she barked, levelling her revolver.

He ducked inside, and out of sight.

Gun held tight in her hand, the barrel unwavering, Ruth edged towards the window. She passed a door filled with rubble, then a wide hole, then a broken trellis. The window was five feet away.

She heard bricks scrape against one another, but the sound came from behind. Ruth spun as Adamovitch launched himself through the wide hole, knocking her to the ground. She lost hold of the revolver, so punched and kicked at the butler until she could roll herself free. The revolver was on the ground, two feet away. Adamovitch was reaching for it. She dived forward, aiming her elbow at his side. She landed hard, and he winced, reflexively curling into a ball as she rolled to her feet, and grabbed her weapon.

She backed up a step, levelling her gun at the fallen man.

"I'll shoot you," she said. "I really will."

Adamovitch opened his mouth, then his expression changed. "I thought it was you," he said.

"You're under arrest," Ruth said.

78

"You were friends with Simon," he said. "You're the copper, aren't you?"

"What do you mean?" she asked.

"You're Simon's pet police officer," he said. "Oh yes, I know all about you."

"Like what?" she asked. She'd been in the academy with Simon Longfield. She'd thought he was a friend. In truth, he had spied on her for his mother, and so for Emmitt. Simon had been responsible for her abduction. In the end, they'd caught and confronted him, but they hadn't charged him. They'd handed him to Isaac. Ruth still wasn't sure what had happened to Simon. Sometimes she hoped he was alive, other times that he was dead. What she really wanted to know, what she'd not asked him, what she doubted Simon could answer, was *how* he could have betrayed her.

"What do you know?" she asked the butler.

Adamovitch smiled. "I'll tell you, but there's a price."

"Ruth?" Mitchell called.

"I've got him," she said. She stared into Adamovitch's eyes. "No," she said. "No deals. No bargains. There's no price I'm willing to pay, not for you."

Chapter 9 - Victory Pie
12th November, Dover to Twynham

"Here you go, victory pie," Mitchell said, handing Ruth a greaseproof-paper packet.

"It looks like a Cornish pasty," she said.

"It's both," Mitchell said. The train juddered as it reached the top of an incline. "It was something my father and I did after a game. We'd go out for a slice of pie. If we couldn't find pie, we'd get a hot dog, or ice cream. Once it was just root beer drunk in the parking lot of a gas station. It didn't matter what we had, we always called it victory pie."

"Oh." She unwrapped a corner and took a bite. "It's mostly meat. That's good. What sport did you play?"

"Baseball," Mitchell said. "But the games were my father's. He— He really knew how to pitch a ball." He smiled. "And this is a victory in every sense of the word. You arrested Adamovitch."

Ruth glanced back down the train towards the next carriage where Adamovitch and his large accomplice were under guard by officers of the railway police.

The previous day, leaving Mitchell to guard Adamovitch, his large accomplice, and the corpse of the skinny man, Ruth had run back to Dover. The Marines had been called out. The prisoners were escorted to the cells while the corpse was sent to the coroner. Mitchell and Ruth had conducted a preliminary examination of the scene, but night had come, and they'd left it under guard by a company of Marines. From the bandages and recent scars, most were walking-wounded from Calais now on light duties while they recovered. The investigation would be continued by officers from the Naval Intelligence Unit, with Sergeant Kettering observing as a representative of the civilian authority. Mitchell had insisted on taking the prisoners back to Twynham, but had had to send a telegram to Prime Minister Atherton before the admiral acquiesced.

"Yes, well done," Mitchell said. "You caught the last conspirator."

"It's your arrest, sir," Ruth said. "*You* should get the credit."

"They were your cuffs, so it's your collar," he said. "Your name will be on the report, and in the supporting documents. The paper will love it. With little change in Calais, this arrest represents news. Good news, too. They'll want a statement from you."

"They will?"

"Well, you got a mention in that article about Emmitt," he said. "They'll enjoy making you the hero, and I'd rather it was you than me. I'd like some anonymity in my retirement."

"You're retiring?" she asked.

"In a sense," Mitchell said. "Adamovitch was the last of the conspirators. Well, more or less. There are a few thugs and hired hands, but Weaver can find them."

"So you'll leave? And do what, go where?" The victory suddenly tasted bittersweet.

"The world is changing," Mitchell said. "Weaver was right about one thing, I'm not suited to the type of policing Britain needs. Once Calais is liberated, the real work will begin, and it won't be over nearly as quickly. We'll need to establish fortified settlements across the continent. We'll need farmers to till the soil, soldiers to protect them, and trains to connect them, but who will govern them? Are they to be enclaves of a new British Empire? Not if I can help it. We'll bring back democracy, we'll bring back civilisation. We'll do it properly this time. I only returned to the police to keep an eye on you. Perhaps I didn't do as good a job as I should have, but you don't need me watching your back anymore. No, it's good that your name goes in the paper. You deserve it."

"I'd rather stay anonymous, too," Ruth said.

"That's impossible," Mitchell said. "It's not just that it's important for people to know the civil power are busy keeping them safe while the military are engaged overseas; it's the paintings. When the newspapers report Mr Wilson's death and how that led us to Adamovitch, they'll mention his paintings. The journalists will see the picture we've taken into evidence, and they'll want to see those paintings you found in Mr Wilson's room. We haven't had much time to create art in the last two decades.

When people read about Mr Wilson's paintings, they'll *demand* to see them. The newspaper might risk printing high quality pictures, though I'm not too sure they will with the British election coming up in May. What's most likely is that those pictures will go on tour around the country."

"Really?"

"After Adamovitch's trial is over," Mitchell said. "People will want to see the pictures, particularly Mr Wilson's last piece. After all, it's a *very* good painting."

They'd found the picture in the garage in which Adamovitch and the other two had been sleeping. It was indisputably Mr Wilson's work, and almost certainly the picture he'd been working on when he'd been murdered. The painting was unfinished, but it depicted a sweeping section of chalky cliffs near where Ruth had found the droplets of paints. In the shallows was a crashed plane. On the cliffs was the pencilled outline of a steam train. In real life, there was no crashed plane on that section of beach, nor did the railway come that close to the coast, but that, she thought, was the point of the painting. Floundering a few hundred yards from the shore, Mr Wilson had drawn a wrecked car-ferry. Pulled up onto the beach was a battered lifeboat. Next to it, standing among the chalk boulders, were a woman and two children. Where the ferry was still a charcoal outline, the three people had been completed, including their faces. They were obviously Mr Wilson's family.

"Do you think that the picture meant Mr Wilson had accepted that his family were dead?" Ruth asked.

"It's hard to say. That trip he made to Hastings would suggest he hadn't," Mitchell said. "You know what I think the story *should* be? That the trip to Hastings made him finally accept they were gone. That he wasn't originally going to include his family in the picture, but when he returned he added them. That's why their faces are clearly visible. He'd finally come to peace with their fate."

"That's a good story," Ruth said, "but one with such a sad end."

She stared out of the window at the trees rolling by. There seemed to be a lot of trees in Kent. Or perhaps they had crossed the border and were now in Sussex. From what she understood, the old county boundaries hadn't meant much in the old world, and meant even less now.

"The ammunition is strange, isn't it?" Ruth said. "I mean how they had so much, but only one rifle."

"About two thousand rounds, all the calibre for an AK-47. Those are common enough weapons, at least in Europe. The ammo looked like it had come straight out of some old-world storehouse. But yes, it's odd there were was only one rifle."

"Then the revolver with which Mr Wilson was shot was the skinny-man's only weapon?"

"I guess so," Mitchell said. "Which only begs more questions than it answers."

Though they finally did have some answers to Mr Wilson's murder. Two of the gate-sentries had recognised the skinny man, or at least they'd recognised his red jacket, hat, and gloves. He'd gone into Dover at least once a day. Confirming he'd followed Mr Wilson to his small flat was a task for Sergeant Kettering.

"Do you think they're smugglers?" Ruth asked.

"Almost certainly," Mitchell said. "But was Adamovitch there because he wanted to be smuggled out of Britain, or because the ammunition was being smuggled in? Longfield's, and Emmitt's, original plan was elaborate, but can be summarised as a bid to cause chaos. Perhaps Adamovitch thought to bring that plan to final fruition."

"Without rifles?" Ruth asked. "I don't like all the questions. I want to know why they murdered Mr Wilson."

"We'll get the answers when we're back in Twynham," Mitchell said. "After all, murder is a capital crime. I'm sure that one of the two prisoners will happily confess in order to save their neck. Anyway, that's not a problem for you. Enjoy a day off. Spend some time with your mother."

"Hmm," Ruth murmured, and took a bite out of the pasty to avoid saying anything else.

Just before they'd caught Emmitt, Ruth had learned that her mother, with Isaac's help, had been the person who'd created the first artificial consciousness. It was that creation that had precipitated the apocalypse, though it was caused by digital viruses unleashed by some unknown hand. Ruth didn't understand the difference, and hadn't asked for details. In fact, she hadn't really discussed it with her mother at all. She hadn't exactly run away from Twynham, but her departure had been deliberately rushed. Ruth had written letters while she was away, and her mother had replied with apologetic swiftness, but neither had mentioned anything of substance. They had avoided the past, both recent and distant, and talked about the weather, the food, the opening of a radio station in Twynham, and a cinema in Dover. Ruth had been dreading returning to Twynham for Christmas, but that return had come sooner than she'd expected, and now she wasn't at all sure she was ready for it.

"You look thoughtful," Mitchell said.

"You look odd," she said in return.

"You mean without the beard?" he asked, rubbing his recently shaved face.

"I meant without the uniform," she said. "When you were dressed as a tramp, I could accept that as a disguise. That suit, though, it's… well, it's weird."

"I thought I looked rather dapper," Mitchell said. With the Dover constabulary consisting entirely of women, Mitchell had gone to the nearest tailor for a new set of clothes. His dark charcoal suit had come off-the-rack, and was of the new-world design with more pockets than was common in pre-Blackout wear. "I thought I'd take advantage of the government picking up the bill," he said. "Besides, I needed a new suit. There's a carol concert at the American Embassy that I can't avoid attending. You won't be in town for that, I'm afraid. I think we can leave the evidence collection to the Royal Navy, but it's unfair leaving Sergeant Kettering with all of the paperwork. You'll have to catch the night train back to Dover tomorrow."

One night with her mother? Ruth thought she could manage that. She nibbled at the pasty. The wild woodland abruptly turned to fields. Then a paddock. Then a herd of cows that turned to watch the train pass.

"You sent me to Dover because you thought it would be safe," Ruth said.

"Yes."

"But there are other military towns."

"True."

"But you sent me to Dover because of its proximity to the refugee camp in which Maggie found me?"

"Yes. Yes, I did," Mitchell said.

"You knew I'd go?" she asked.

"I knew you'd want to visit it sooner not later, so I thought this would be an ideal opportunity for you to get it out of the way. You can start the new year as a new person, having made a clean break with the past."

"You knew I'd find nothing there?" Ruth asked.

"Yes," Mitchell said. "I went there myself on three occasions. The first was about a week after Maggie brought you back to Twynham. I went looking for clues as to who you might be. About two years after that, I went back again. It was about the same time of year, too, just after your birthday. Riley and I came over, do you remember? We brought a biscuit-cake. It was Riley's idea."

"I... not really. Sort of. That was Riley? She was wearing a green frock?"

"That was her dress phase. It didn't last long. She'd been stealing them from the National Store. Discovering that was what made me realise I had to spend more time with her, and that I needed to teach her how to be a good copper because she was a terrible thief."

"Ah." Ruth rolled the memory over in her mind. Now that Mitchell had given her a few details, they slotted into the snapshot she had, and she was no longer sure what was memory and what was overlay. "When was the third time? That you went back to the refugee camp, I mean?"

"That was about two years ago. I was tracking a serial killer. Caught him just outside of Versailles. France was different, then. There were a few farms. There was even a vineyard outside of Rouen. I'll admit that I delayed my return to spend a couple of nights there. The wine was interesting, though I don't have much to compare it to. But it was a nice setting, and there was a—" He stopped, and smiled. "There was a moment stolen in time," he said. "A few hours when I wasn't a police officer, but I was still a father, and I had to return. I was in a maudlin mood when I got back to Britain, thinking of what might have been. I took a detour past the refugee camp to remind myself of what *had* been, and the task that is before all of us. It was hard to find. Nature had reclaimed the site. I imagine it hasn't changed much in the last two years."

"No, it's pretty overgrown."

"No memories?" he asked.

"No, not really. I can sort of remember running through the tents. Before that, there's something about a bridge. I don't remember much else."

"Then it's best to let the memory be," Mitchell said. "The past is over. Adamovitch is the last piece of this puzzle. In a few weeks it'll be a new year and a time for new beginnings for all of us."

"Hmm. Maybe. I hope so." She took another bite of the pasty. "Did you go back to the vineyard?"

"I did," he said. "Before you joined the force and we opened the Serious Crimes Unit. I arrived too late. They'd burned it down, massacred everyone inside. I don't know if it was one of the groups that's now in Calais. It really doesn't matter."

Ruth had many more questions, but Mitchell's expression had grown dark. Now wasn't the time. She finished the pasty, and watched the fields roll by until the rocking motion of the train put her to sleep.

The jolting of the carriage woke her from it. She sat bolt upright. Her hand fell to her holster.

"Relax," Mitchell said. "We're home. In Twynham," he added.

"Oh. Right." She wiped sleep from her eyes. "What now?"

"We take the prisoners to Police House," Mitchell said. "Then I'm off to see Atherton while you go to see Maggie. Riley's got a sofa that's not too uncomfortable. You can sleep there tonight. Maybe you can take her for a walk tomorrow. She's not getting out of the house enough."

Ruth stood, grabbed her bag, and they made their way through to the compartment with the cells. The officers of the railway police already had the two prisoners in wrist and ankle chains.

"I think his name's Yanuck," the corporal said. "We heard them talking."

"Yanuck?" Mitchell said turning to the large man. "Mr Yanuck, nice to meet you. We have Longfield's records at Police House. They are surprisingly detailed. We'll find you in them. This is your chance to confess. If you do, you might save your neck."

Yanuck's eyes flickered towards Adamovitch. The butler scowled.

Mitchell smiled. "All right lads, here's how it's going to go. We're going to take you to Police House. You'll be booked for murder, smuggling, and conspiring to foment rebellion. Treason will probably be added to the charges, but it's the murder of Mr Wilson that means you'll swing. We have the painting, after all. When the jury sees that, you'll be convicted. Your only chance is to answer our questions about Longfield and that ammunition you had. And, of course, we only need one of you. Think on that as we walk to the station, because when we get there, we'll want some answers."

The corporal opened the door, and jumped down to the platform.

"Stand back," she called to the railway workers. "Stand back, prisoners coming through!"

Yanuck was pushed forward into the doorway. And then, his head exploded.

The man collapsed as Mitchell pushed Ruth back. The captain dived forward, knocking Adamovitch from his feet even as Yanuck's body fell down to the platform where screaming railway workers ran away in panic.

Ruth pushed herself to her knees and drew her revolver. When she got to the doorway, she could see nothing but the smuggler's corpse and people running away in scared confusion.

Chapter 10 - Number 10
Twynham

"A sniper? This is a bad business," Prime Minister Atherton said. "A bad business, indeed. Do you have any conclusions?"

"I have evidence," Mitchell said. "And that's leading me toward a hypothesis."

"Please, Mitchell, I'm not in the mood," Atherton said. "And this really isn't the time."

Though she was standing ramrod-straight, Ruth's eyes darted between Mitchell and the prime minister, trying to read into the subtext of their words. It was three hours since the shooting. The railway police, supplemented by a detachment of Marines, had searched the platforms' roofs and the top of the warehouses that lined that section of track. Nothing had been found during that preliminary investigation. The Marines had escorted Adamovitch to the courthouse jail, leaving Ruth and Mitchell to report in person to the PM. He had been in his study, working. The room was so dimly lit Ruth couldn't read any of the words on the papers and reports covering the ancient oak desk, though she thought the annotated map was one of France.

"It was the work of a professional," Mitchell said. "There was one shot, fired from at least three hundred yards, but probably further. The shot was fired the moment that Yanuck appeared in the doorway. The killer had to have known that Yanuck was on the train, but there was no way to know which platform we'd arrive at, and so which side of the train Yanuck would emerge from. About five minutes elapsed between the train arriving and the shot, so there wasn't much time to prepare. Hence, this was done by a professional."

"A message was sent from Dover?" Atherton asked. "And that message warned the sniper that Yanuck was on the train?"

"It had to be, yes, sir. From that, we know that Yanuck was the target," Mitchell said. "To make that shot, our sniper has to be good. Good enough that, if they'd waited until both Yanuck and Adamovitch had alighted from the train, they could have shot both of them."

"So the sniper works with or for Adamovitch," Atherton said. "Or knows that Adamovitch wouldn't talk. Does this mean Yanuck was the weak link? Who was he, anyway?"

"A smuggler," Mitchell said. "Possibly smuggling ammunition for Kalashnikovs."

"Two thousand rounds," Atherton said, he gestured at the papers on his desk. "Your report said as much. You don't know anything more?"

"Other than his name, not much," Mitchell said. "But I have a theory. At first, I thought Adamovitch was trying to get out of Britain. I was wrong. I think he planned to take over Longfield's operation. That shipment of ammunition had to be for her, part of her scheme to sow division and discord prior to the election. Whether Adamovitch intended to continue with that plan, or had come up with a new one, there's only one use to which those bullets could be put. My theory is that he went to Dover to win those smugglers over to his cause."

"Two thousand rounds is enough to start a civil war," Atherton said, "but it is *not* enough to win it." He picked up a sheet of paper. "Do you think there's a connection with the criminals in Calais?"

"Possibly," Mitchell said.

"They are the ones who would gain from chaos on the streets of Britain. Every Marine deployed guarding a grain silo or power station is one that can't fight in France."

"Um…" Ruth murmured.

"Yes?" Atherton asked. "You have something to add."

"Well… um…" Ruth swallowed. "It's that the attack on Calais was on the fifth, wasn't it? The fifth of November, and wasn't that the date Ned Ludd thought something big was going to happen. I mean, we thought that Ludd was just a dupe, a decoy, but maybe getting us to think that was part of Emmitt's plan."

Atherton glanced at Mitchell, and raised an eyebrow. Mitchell shrugged.

"Thank you, Constable," Atherton said. "We were aware of that, and I believe you are correct. The attack on Calais was arranged by Longfield, or by Emmitt, and scheduled for the fifth. Either they were planning something else for that night, or they wanted us to think they were. Regardless, their goal in choosing that particular date was to maximise terror. Unfortunately, knowing that doesn't help us. It took months for those bandits to reach Calais. The assault must have been arranged earlier this year if not before, and once arranged, it would have been impossible to call off."

"Oh. Right. Sorry," Ruth murmured.

"Was there anything else you wish to add?"

"Well, it's... it's just that I knew Adams. I mean Adamovitch. I mean... I don't mean I knew him," she added hurriedly. "It's just... um..."

Atherton sighed. "Yes, you knew Simon Longfield in the academy. I have read your file."

Ruth blinked. She hadn't realised that she *had* a file. "Adamovitch wasn't important," she said. "He oversaw people setting the tables for dinner, and made sure that the hunters kept the pantry full. I asked Simon what all the people working there did, you see. Adamovitch wouldn't have had much contact with Mrs Longfield. He spent most of his days polishing the silverware and dusting the plates. I don't think Mrs Longfield would have told him anything, so whatever he knows, he must have learned it by stealing a look at files and papers."

"Unfortunately that might include the design of the ships laying siege to Calais," Atherton said. "They are all of the new Nile Class. Longfield was involved in the board that designed them. As we are the sole sea-power, armour was reduced in favour of speed. There are weaknesses that could be exploited."

"But Adamovitch has been caught," Mitchell said.

"Indeed," Atherton said. He turned back to Ruth. "What is your impression of Dover, Constable?"

"Um... it's nice, I suppose. Like a small version of Twynham," Ruth said, confused by the apparent change of topic.

"It will not be secure until Calais is in friendly hands," Atherton said. "Calais won't be secure until we have outposts in Dunkirk, Boulogne-sur-Mer, Bethune." He drew a semi-circle with his finger on the map, then he drew a wider semi-circle. "To secure those, we must hold Ostend, Lille, Amiens, and Dieppe. Then, France, Belgium, The Netherlands." He pointed at the map. "Spain. Portugal. Germany. Europe. The World. The barbarians have held sway too long. To destroy them, we risk consuming all that we have created, and all that we will create for generations to come. Yet, if we stand idly by, they will still come. We can destroy the Channel Tunnel. We can isolate ourselves, protect ourselves with the Navy, but the pirates will take root. They will kill, convert, or co-opt the few survivors unfortunate enough not to have made it to this island refuge. The darkness will grow building in strength until, like a tidal wave, it will sweep over us. You won't have heard what happened in Athens?"

"No, sir," Ruth said.

"Few have. Five hundred souls were impaled alive in the ruins of the Parthenon. And do you know who they were, what they did to deserve such treatment? They were archaeologists, looking to preserve the old ruins against a time when civilisation might once again wish to look upon where it began. Find this sniper, Mitchell."

"Yes, sir," Mitchell said.

As she turned around, Ruth realised there were two portraits, one either side of the door. Both were men, one was balding with a moustache, dressed in a jacket, tie, and waistcoat. The other wore the clothes of two centuries before. She wasn't sure who the men were, but they were positioned to face Atherton, almost as if they were judging him.

"Well, how are we going to do that?" Ruth said when they were outside. There were more Marines on duty, with two on the rooftop opposite. "Find the sniper, I mean."

"We look for the evidence," Mitchell said. "You understand what the prime minister was saying?"

"That we have to find the shooter," Ruth said.

"No," Mitchell said. "He was saying that the war has begun. It was something his predecessor tried to avoid, but perhaps we can't any longer. Calais is just the beginning, but this particular struggle won't end in my lifetime, maybe not in yours. Yes, be glad you're a copper, but remember that police aren't soldiers." He shivered. "But we are coppers, and this is our case. Where would you look for the sniper?"

"In Dover," Ruth said. "Someone sent that message warning the sniper that Yanuck was on the train. If we find out who that was, then we'll know who we're chasing. I'll go back to the station and get the next train to Dover."

"No, you won't," Mitchell said. "You'll go and see your mother and get some sleep. I'll send a message to Kettering and ask her to find who sent the telegram from Dover. You can go back in the morning. Mid-morning."

"You're trying to keep me out of the way again," Ruth said.

Mitchell didn't reply.

Chapter 11 - Homeless at Home
Twynham

For as long as Ruth could properly remember until two days before she'd left for Dover, she and Maggie had lived in a large house on the outskirts of Twynham. The downstairs had been a schoolroom for children from the neighbouring refugee resettlement centre, and Maggie had been their teacher. Maggie had viewed the centre as counterproductive because few children stayed there more than a few weeks, and so had petitioned to have it shut it down. Surprisingly, the government had listened. Notification of the closure had arrived shortly before Riley had been shot, Emmitt had been caught, and Ruth had been transferred to Dover. As Maggie was out of a job, and as Riley required home-care in order to be discharged from the hospital, Maggie had moved into the sergeant's home.

The small cottage had been empty when Henry Mitchell had claimed it. He'd moved out a few years ago to give his adoptive daughter space. Ruth had visited the cottage a few times before she'd left for Dover, and not much had changed in the weeks since. The leaves had been raked, the roses cut back, and the gutters cleared. The only significant difference was a pig lying half-asleep inside a sty where the lawn had previously been.

"I know you," Ruth said. The porker gave her a baleful glare. "You were the one we had at the old house. Then there *will* be bacon at Christmas." Although Ruth wasn't sure she would be coming back to Twynham for it. She lingered by the sty, putting off the moment when she'd have to go inside.

There was plenty of light to see the pig. Mitchell had put the house on the electricity grid. Actually, Ruth suspected it was Isaac who'd done it, and that Mitchell had chosen the cottage because it was close to the substation.

Ruth rang the doorbell. A familiar American East-Coast accent tempered with two decades living in Twynham muttered a litany that grew in volume as it approached.

The door opened. "Ruth!" Maggie said, taking a step back in surprise. "What are you doing back?"

"Hi, Mum," Ruth said. "It's a long story."

"Is that Ruth?" Riley called. There was a clatter and then a thump as the sergeant rolled her wheelchair into the living room doorway before she managed to get it through to the hall. During the arrest of Mrs Longfield, Riley had taken a shotgun blast to the chest. A bulletproof vest had saved her life, but not her mobility. Ruth still wasn't sure whether the sergeant would ever recover full use of her legs.

"Hi, Sarge," Ruth said. "How are you feeling?"

"Is that blood on your uniform?" Riley asked.

"It's not mine," Ruth said.

"Then whose is it?" Maggie asked.

"Like I said, it's a long story."

"Shot in the train station?" Riley asked when Ruth had finished. "The telegraph office is key. Find the message, find the messenger, and then you'll find the sniper."

"That's what I said, and I said that I should go back to Dover to find who sent it," Ruth said. "But Mister Mitchell has benched me. I'm to go back tomorrow, but not even on the first train."

Riley smiled. "We don't need to go to Dover to find out who the message was for," she said. "We'll go to the telegraph office in the morning, find out what messages came from Dover and when they arrived. That will get us a description of the shooter."

"And I'm sure that's what Henry is doing right now," Maggie said. "There's no need for either of you to get involved in this."

"We *are* involved," Riley said. "We're police."

Maggie frowned, but didn't argue. That, Ruth thought, was a sign of growth.

As she was currently confined to the wheelchair, the dining room had been converted into Riley's bedroom. Maggie had taken Riley's old room. The other, smaller, bedroom was full of Mitchell's books and boxes. Ruth wasn't sure if he would go back to the room he had in a pub on the other side of town, or if he would sleep in the house, so she took the sofa.

It wasn't as comfortable as her bed in Dover. With Maggie snoring almost loud enough to make the windows rattle, it certainly wasn't quieter. The room was warm, though.

Ruth lay in the dark, staring at the ceiling, running through the events of the day, trying to find a pattern in the chaos.

"It's me," a familiar voice said.

Ruth opened her eyes, and sat up. The voice came from the hallway. And then came another.

"You should have rung the doorbell," Riley said.

"I didn't want to wake up the entire house." Now she was more awake, she recognised the voice of Captain Mitchell.

Ruth pushed herself to her feet and went out into the hall. Riley sat in her wheelchair, a sawn-off shotgun in her lap. Mitchell stood by the open door, a tired smile on his face.

"What's going on?" Ruth asked.

"I heard someone trying to break in," Riley said.

"I wasn't breaking in," Mitchell said as he closed the door. "I lost my keys when I fell in a bog in the Midlands. I was trying not to wake Riley because—"

"Henry?" Maggie asked, coming down the stairs. "What's going on? Anna, why are you holding that gun?"

"There's been another murder," Mitchell said. "Five of them, to be exact. I came for Ruth."

"Five murders? Who?" Ruth and Riley asked at the same time.

"Do you remember Ned Ludd?" Mitchell asked.

"The mad saboteur that Ruth caught," Riley said. "The telegraph was cut in five places. She stopped Ludd from cutting it in a sixth."

"Is he dead?" Ruth asked.

"No, he's fine," Mitchell said. "But you remember that house we found, the one that he and his group were using prior to the sabotage? There was evidence suggesting that, with Ludd, five others were there. They're the ones who are dead."

"It happened this evening?" Riley asked.

"No. About twenty-four hours ago," Mitchell said. "The bodies were discovered at around ten in the morning. The police were called. Weaver took charge of the case, but didn't draw the line between them and Ned Ludd until after she heard of Yanuck's assassination. She checked through the fingerprints you took from the house, Ruth, and then she called me. Now I'm here."

"And *why* are you here?" Maggie asked.

"Ruth collected evidence from the original crime scene," Mitchell said. "I need her to come and take a look."

"I'll come, too," Riley said.

"You won't," Maggie said.

"Actually," Mitchell said quickly. "It's a farm cottage about a mile outside the city. There's too much mud for that wheelchair. I'm sorry, Anna."

Riley stared at Mitchell for a long moment. "Fine. Then I'm going to the telegraph office. Ruth said that a message was sent from Dover."

"I've got Sergeant Kettering looking into it," Mitchell said.

"In Dover, so I'll look into it here. Either I'm a copper, or I'm not," Riley said. "And if I'm not, then why am I still here in Twynham?"

Ruth sensed she was witnessing the tail end of some long-running argument.

"All right," Mitchell said.

"I better get dressed," Maggie said.

"Why?"

"You're not going alone, Anna," Maggie said.

Chapter 12 - Five Bodies
13th November, Twynham

The crime scene was only a mile outside the city, but it took them half an hour to reach it. A thick frost had fallen during the night, turning the poorly repaired tarmac into a rink-slick road. Mitchell and Ruth stopped their bicycles next to a pair of police cadets. Ruth vaguely remembered them from the academy, but couldn't recall their names. Judging by their baleful glares, they clearly remembered her. Ruth was confused by the unwelcoming stares until she remembered that she was a constable, and they wouldn't reach that rank until December at the earliest.

"Watch our bikes," Mitchell said, leaning them against the hedge.

Ruth followed him under the rope, and into the crime scene.

The cottage was at the very edge of a working farm, built on a plot that had once been part of a field. Ringing the cottage was a lush hedge far younger than that which separated the field from the road. Entry to the cottage was through a three-foot-high wooden gate, and that was being guarded by a puce-faced cadet whose name Ruth *did* remember. Grace Harding, a quiet young woman who'd passed out during two consecutive anatomy classes.

"Why are there so many cadets?" she asked the captain. "Where are the police officers?"

"Didn't I tell you?" Mitchell said. "After Commissioner Wallace, then Longfield, then Pollock, a lot have been dismissed or sent to one of the new, and very isolated, radio-repeater stations. We don't know whom we can trust. The cadets are being rushed through their training because the alternative is relying solely on the military and railway police."

That shone a very different light on Mitchell's one-man mission to hunt down the last of the conspirators. It hadn't been out of pride, or a sense of his own brilliance, but because he no longer trusted anyone to help. But that light added a shadow to her being sent to the relatively quiet posting in Dover. Despite the murder of Wilson and capture of Adamovitch, that had been an indulgence the country couldn't afford.

"Hi, Grace," Ruth said, as they drew near the cadet. "Is it bad?"

The cadet nodded, swallowed, shook her head, and stepped aside.

Assistant Commissioner Weaver stood on the path that led from the road to the house.

"Mitchell, Deering," Weaver said by way of greeting. Dawn was barely breaking, but even by its sepulchral light, the assistant commissioner looked tired. "Have you been briefed?"

"Yes, ma'am," Ruth said, though it had been brief. "Inside the cottage are the murdered bodies of the five saboteurs who worked with Ned Ludd."

"That's my current theory," Weaver said. "Take a look, I want to know if you recognise anything or anyone. Mitchell, a word?"

As the captain went to speak to the assistant commissioner, Ruth walked up the path towards the house.

The cottage was a two-storey dwelling. The walls were covered in flaking milk-brown paint, but with red brick around the narrow windows and narrower door. The frames and door were painted a vivid green. Recently, too, judging by the sheen. As she stepped closer, she realised that the paint on the walls wasn't flaking but had been peeled back as if someone was preparing it to be re-plastered. The windows were clean, the gutters were clear, and the path had been swept from the gate all the way up to the front door, which was held open by the foot of the first corpse.

Ruth took out her notepad, using the act of writing as a lens with which to obscure the violence of the scene.

"The victim's female, twenty years old or thereabouts," she murmured as she scrawled a brief note in her pad. "Dressed in a rough-cut tunic and tubular trousers. Similar to the clothes Ned Ludd made for himself, though these are of a better cut. Rope sandals on her feet, not clogs like Ludd wore." She took another look at the body. "She was shot twice. Once in the stomach, once in the chest. The wounds are about six inches apart."

"I'd say the stomach wound was first," Mitchell said.

Ruth jumped. She hadn't realised the captain was behind her.

"From the way she's fallen," Mitchell continued, "the shooter was standing roughly where you are. The victim opened the door. The shots were fired from the hip. No casings, the killer must have picked them up, but I would guess at it being a handgun rather than a rifle. Do you recognise her?"

"No," Ruth said.

"Me neither," Mitchell said. "There are four others."

Ruth nodded, and carefully stepped over the dead woman. The front door led to an uncarpeted hall with three doors off it and a staircase leading up. The door to the left was open. Another body lay on the floor just inside the room.

"He was shot in the back," Ruth said, stepping over the corpse. "Two shots— no, three, I think. All close together. He's dressed like the first victim, in coarse but tailored cloth."

"They were limited by materials more than they were by their own skill," Mitchell said. "That looks like hemp. It's cheap and common enough, used in sailcloth and rope. We could get one of the labs at the university to do a fibre analysis. We might be able to trace it back to the store that sold it, but that would take weeks, and I'm not sure how it would help."

"He was shot in the back, so he heard the first woman being murdered," Ruth said. "Maybe he saw the killer. He started running, but didn't get far." She bent down and carefully moved some of the long, lank hair from the victim's face. "No, I don't know him."

The room had another door. It led to a dining room and two more victims. One lay slumped over the table, a bowl of spilled gruel underneath his fallen head. The other lay on the floor, her arm outstretched, almost as if she was reaching for something. The fifth and final victim had fallen in a heap by the back door.

"She almost made it outside," Ruth said.

"Weaver said the back door had been sealed. Wedges have been rammed into the frame," Mitchell said. "The killer did that before he knocked at the front door. He made sure they couldn't get out before he began. Hmm."

"What is it?" she asked.

"I'm not sure," he said. He turned around, taking in the small kitchen. "It's something on the edge of thought. Give me a moment, I want to look upstairs."

Ruth opened the cupboard under the sink, then the one above the counter by the window, but her gaze kept returning to the body by the back door.

"Why were you here?"

The victim didn't answer. The cupboards gave no clue, either. There were bowls and cups, though no two of the same design. There was a sack of flour, another of oats, and a third containing potatoes. The pantry's shelves were filled with wizened carrots, radishes, and a few onions. There was no sweetener, no powdered tea or coffee, no canned food, or anything else that had come from or passed through a factory. There was nothing except that which grew out of the ground.

She heard footsteps on the stairs. Mitchell came back into the kitchen.

"You don't recognise any of the victims?" he asked.

"No, sir. This happened while they were eating breakfast. That means the back door was sealed during the night, but the killer waited until they were all awake."

"Awake and likely to all be downstairs," Mitchell said. "I suppose, at night, there would be the risk of someone jumping out a window and escaping into the darkness. This way, he knew he'd get them all."

"Or her," Ruth said, remembering the woman who'd tortured her.

"No, I think it was him," Mitchell said. "Mrs Foster said the rent was paid by a man."

"Who's Mrs Foster?" she asked.

"The woman who runs the farm this cottage is built on. She discovered the bodies. So, they were killed at breakfast time. There are a couple of candles upstairs, but no electricity to the property."

"You wouldn't expect there to be, not if these five were anything like Ned Ludd."

"And you don't recognise any of them?"

"I only got a brief glimpse of three of them before they ran away and I arrested Ned Ludd," she said. "It could be any of them, or none."

"Hmm. Ned Ludd and three others were cutting a telegraph line in the woods. That spot was chosen because Simon Longfield knew you went along that track every day. You were meant to discover them sabotaging the telegraph. We don't know if you were meant to catch them, but when we found their lair, there was evidence of six people having lived there for a few nights."

"And it was far worse than this place," Ruth said. "I mean, this cottage is somewhere I'd want to live in. That place, I'd only want to run away from it. And that was key, wasn't it? I mean, that they ran away but Ned Ludd couldn't because he was wearing those wooden clogs he'd made for himself. They were students and employees of the university, weren't they?"

"Some people went missing from the university," Mitchell said. "We can ask someone from the vice-chancellor's office to try to identify these people, but no one there's been able to identify Ned Ludd. You stopped Ludd cutting that section of telegraph, but the line was cut in five other places and almost simultaneously. Up until now I've assumed that the other lines were cut by those followers of Emmitt who died during the confrontation in the New Forest. What I'm wondering is whether we're going to find five more houses like this one, each filled with the bodies of misguided saboteurs. Did you find anything else?"

"There's some vegetables in the cupboards, flour and oats, but no tea or sweetener or anything else that came from the chemical works."

"Interesting, but I'm more interested in the lights, or the lack thereof. At this time of year, it gets dark around four p.m., and with so few candles, they would have gone to bed early. That means they would have been up long before first light. No candles have burned down to the stub, so unless our killer blew them out, the murder took place around dawn, but the door was blocked in the middle of the night. To put that another way, the murder happened before we left Dover."

"Then you think this is connected? I mean, of course it's connected, but do you think this was the same person who shot Yanuck?"

"I hope so," Mitchell said. "Otherwise we have two assassins on the loose. Of course, it means that the warning message to the killer *wasn't* sent from Dover just before our train left, but the night before, a few hours after we'd arrested Adamovitch and the smuggler. Go and keep Weaver occupied. I want a moment to think."

Ruth found the assistant commissioner in conversation with a middle-aged woman. By her rubber boots, waxed hat, and much-repaired dungarees stained with every shade of mud, Ruth took her to be a farmer.

"Ah, Constable Deering," Weaver said. "This is Mrs Foster, the owner of this cottage, and the farm and fields either side."

"Ma'am," Ruth said.

"It's terrible, isn't it?" Mrs Foster said. "Do you know who did it?"

"Investigations are continuing," Weaver said. "The constable has some questions for you. Excuse me."

Weaver headed for the house, and Ruth had no way to stop her. Deciding that Weaver's feud with Mitchell wasn't her business, but that the murders were, she turned to the farmer.

"This must be a very trying time for you, ma'am," Ruth said, "but there are a few questions, and the answers will help us catch whoever did this."

"Of course. I'll help any way I can. They were such nice boys and girls. That's all they were really, children. Their whole lives were ahead of them. It's so cruel, so wicked."

Ruth nodded. "What time did you discover the bodies?"

"Yesterday morning. Around ten," Mrs Foster said. "That's when I brought them their milk. I did that everyday. It was included in the rent. Milk every day, bread and vegetables every other day, a sack of oats, wheat, and potatoes once every week. They were good tenants. Very good. I should have paid them for all the work they did."

"What kind of work?" Ruth asked.

"They cut back the brambles, cleared the lawn, repaired the roof, repainted the doors, and were about to start on the walls. The cottage was a tumbledown shell when they moved in. I wouldn't have rented it out except we were that desperate for money. It was a bad harvest. If it weren't for the fixed prices the government pays for the supplies they send out as food-aid, we'd have gone under."

"And how long have they been renting the cottage?" Ruth asked.

"They've been living here for about a month," Mrs Foster said. "But I've been renting it to Mr Squires since late September. The twentieth, I think. No, it was the twenty-first. I remember because that was the day I got a letter from Terry. My son, he's gone to the mines, you see."

"And who is Mr Squires?" Ruth asked.

"As I told the commissioner, I'm not too sure," Mrs Foster said. "He said he worked at the university. He paid in cash, up front, for six months."

"Can you describe him?"

"Oh, he was medium height. Five-ten, give or take. Maybe six foot. White. English, I think. About forty, maybe. Or maybe younger. Or... older, I suppose, although he wasn't old. He had a thick black beard, but I thought it looked dyed, though I don't know where he would get the dye from." Her hand went to her own greying hair. "He had a limp, I remember that. Not that it stopped him from walking. He walked to the farm, and left on foot. No horse, no bicycle. I thought that was odd. Then again, it was odd that he wanted to rent the cottage."

"What did he say he wanted it for?" Ruth asked.

"He said that his nephew was going to take the cottage for the winter. Him and some friends. They were hermits, Mr Squires said. He said they wanted to eschew the fripperies of modern life. He said let them see what a winter without electric light was like, and then they'd change their ways. I... well, he paid cash, and we needed the money. No one turned up for a month, and then, one day, I saw that they were here."

"And you began bringing them milk and bread?"

"Mr Squires came by that evening. He asked me to make sure they didn't starve. He said he'd check up on them. Mayhap he did, but I never saw him again."

"Do you have an address for Mr Squires?" Ruth asked. "Any way of contacting him?"

"No," Mrs Foster said. "I didn't think to ask. I'm ashamed of that, I really am. I should have asked, but he paid in cash and, as I say, we were desperate." She wrung her hands together in obvious distress. Ruth took her arm and led her along the path to the gate, and back out onto the road where the bodies weren't visible.

"Do you know which of the victims was his nephew," she asked.

"I don't, I'm sorry. They were polite when I brought them the food, but they took it at the gate. The only times we talked were when they'd ask for tools or paint. I offered them work in the farm. I mean, look at this place. You didn't see what it was like before, but they knew what hard work was, and they didn't mind. They didn't ask for payment, or even thanks."

"They didn't take you up on the offer of work?"

"No. No, but I think they would have done. There wasn't much else for them to do here. Whatever lesson Mr Squires wanted them to learn, they didn't need it. In another week or two, I'd have had them at the big house. I'd have had them in proper clothes before the first snow. Next year… next year…" She trailed off.

"Mr Squires told you they were hermits? Do you mean they were religious?" Ruth asked.

"I couldn't say," Mrs Foster said. "They said they wanted to live outside of the world. To live apart from it. I have sons," she added. "Two of them, and they went through a similar phase, though when they were a little younger. It was when they learned what the old world had been like, and understood that their own lives would never be as easy. No, just a few more weeks, and I'd have had them at the farm. They'd have been safe then."

Ruth nodded, though she disagreed. She suspected that if the saboteurs had been at the farm, then everyone there would have been killed as well.

"Thank you for your time," Ruth said. "You've been very helpful. We might have some more questions as the investigation progresses, but I think that's all for now. Oh, one last thing. The rent that Mr Squires paid, was it in twenty-pound notes?"

"I… yes, I think so," Mrs Foster said.

"The old notes?"

"Of course. This was before the currency was changed."

"I don't suppose you kept any of them?" Ruth asked.

"No. Is that important?"

"Not really. Thank you." Ruth went back to the cottage.

Mitchell and Weaver were in the kitchen. Both had their eyes on the door, though Ruth thought it was more that they were determinedly not looking at one another than staring at a clue.

"What did you learn from Mrs Foster," Mitchell asked.

"The cottage was rented by a Mr Squires who said he worked at the university and was the uncle of one of the victims," Ruth said. "Squires is white, has an English accent, a limp, a beard which might have been fake, and is between thirty and fifty years old. Either Mr Squires is the killer, or he's going to be the next victim, but we're not going to find him based on that."

"I got that name from Mrs Foster yesterday," Weaver said. "And then I took her to the university. There's no one working there called Squires. There are some with limps, and a few of those have beards, but she didn't recognise any of them. Well, why should she? A beard can be shaved, a limp faked."

"But why would someone rent a house and then kill them?" Ruth asked.

"So we could find them," Mitchell said. He pushed at the wedged-shut door. "Whether the killer was Mr Squires or not, he could have let them run. They wouldn't have come to the police, would they? No, he wanted us to find them and find them dead."

"But why were they here in the first place?" Ruth asked.

"So that they could die," Weaver said. "Perhaps the killer originally had other plans, but killing them was always reserved as an option. Within hours of Adamovitch's arrest, they were murdered and in a way that ensured their bodies would be found. What does he expect us to do next?"

Ruth shrugged. "Move Ned Ludd? Maybe he's the real target. He'd be able to give us a better description of Mr Squires, after all. Maybe he knows something else."

"Possibly," Weaver said. "This killer is cleaning up loose ends. The smuggler who brought ammunition and who knows what else into Britain, the saboteurs who cut the telegraph. That leaves Emmitt and Ned Ludd as the last threads hanging adrift."

"Not the last," Mitchell said. "There's Adamovitch, Pollock, and more than a dozen others that we've arrested over the last month."

"If the killer wanted them dead, there was more than enough time before they were in custody," Weaver said. "I think Deering has the right of it. These people died because they could identify the killer."

"Then that means it's not Mr Squires," Mitchell said. "If it was, he'd have killed Mrs Foster, too."

"A good point," Weaver said. She frowned. "I'll have her put into protective custody, just in case. Whatever is going on here, our hand is being forced. Whatever move we are expected to play next, I don't think we'll find the answer here."

"There's someone who could tell us," Mitchell said. "I think it's time we had a word with Emmitt."

Chapter 13 - Death Row
Twynham

"Ah, Henry, how are you?" Emmitt asked as Ruth and Mitchell walked into the courthouse jail's small interview room. The warder closed the door and turned the key, locking them inside with the mass murderer. "And Sameen as well. I hope you're well?"

"Don't—" Ruth began, and stopped, though a fraction too late.

Emmitt smiled. At least Ruth thought it was a smile. The criss-cross lines cut deep into his face made his expression hard to read. His hands were cuffed to the interview room table, his ankles shackled together. Mitchell sat down opposite him. Ruth stayed by the door, watching the prisoner as the prisoner watched her.

"Did you see your new neighbour?" Mitchell asked, gesturing towards the now-closed door. The interview room was in the lowest level of the courthouse, at one end of a corridor that had five small cells, a small shower room, a table and chair for the warder, and stairs leading up. Other than Emmitt, there was only one other prisoner.

"My new neighbour? You mean Mr Adams?" Emmitt said. "A new neighbour, but an old friend. I assume your presence is connected to his arrival. Unless you've finally agreed to my request?"

"What request," Ruth asked.

"Have you been keeping secrets from her, Henry?" Emmitt asked, his tone almost coy.

"He's been writing letters to you," Mitchell said to Ruth. "All his correspondence comes to me. I decide whether it's to be sent on, or whether doing that would be a threat to national security."

"What did the letters say?" Ruth asked.

"That I wanted to talk," Emmitt said. "And I don't know why you would hide the letters from her, except you do have a paternal instinct, don't you, Henry. Under your wing, you have two police officers to whom you act as father, yet you have no biological children. That's interesting, don't you think?"

"Not really," Mitchell said. "And I didn't come here for cod psychology."

"No, you came here to talk," Emmitt said. "Please, go ahead. Why not begin with what you're offering."

"I'm offering nothing," Mitchell said.

"That's not how an exchange works, Henry. I will happily tell you whatever you want to know, but I need something in return."

"Your sentence isn't up for negotiation," Mitchell said. "You're going to hang."

"The judge said as much," Emmitt said. "And yet, here I am."

"You might be able to file your appeals faster than the court can deny them," Mitchell said, "but they'll run out. Then you've nothing but the long drop ahead of you."

Emmitt smiled again. When he'd been sentenced, Ruth had assumed the execution would take place immediately. Now she understood how the man had remained so calm in the face of an unavoidable death. He'd planned for his arrest. He knew exactly which appeals to file, and in which order, and precisely how long it would take for each to be denied. And when one *was* denied, Emmitt had the next ready and waiting to be filed. Even so, Mitchell was right, it couldn't go on forever. The appeals would run out, and that meant…

"You have something to trade," Ruth said. "That's why you're so calm. You know something, and know we'll offer you your life to learn what it is. All of your appeals are just stalling tactics until the time's right."

"Really? That's what you think?" Emmitt asked. "I'm almost offended. No, I just have faith in the fairness of the British judicial system. The sea air suits you, Sameen. It's doing wonders for your complexion."

"Stop calling me—" She stopped. "How did you know I was in—" Again, she stopped. "Adamovitch talked."

"Not really, except to curse my name," Emmitt said. "But I can put two and two together. Ask your question, and then I will tell you my price for an answer."

"There's an assassin loose in Twynham," Mitchell said. "He murdered the five Luddites you had cutting telegraph wires. He shot a smuggler called Yanuck while he was in custody. This guy is clearing up loose ends, Emmitt, and that's how I'd describe you."

"Yanuck is dead?" Emmitt glanced at the door. The scars crinkled in what might have been a frown. "I see. Then Adamovitch was in Dover attempting to get passage to France?"

"Possibly," Mitchell said. "He's as tight-lipped as you are."

"Ah. Well, let me clear a few things up, though I'll ask for nothing in exchange. Yanuck was a smuggler. Sometimes of loot from the ruins of the old-world, but his bread and butter came from people."

"Smuggling people out of Britain?" Ruth asked.

"Into Britain," Emmitt said. "You might welcome survivors with open arms, but they do have to reach here first. Some might stumble across a convoy heading west. Others may find an old boat, or risk their lives paddling a homemade raft. The rest have to buy their passage through a continent rife with danger. That is where Yanuck came in. He didn't call himself a human trafficker, but that's what he was."

"How much did he charge?" Mitchell asked.

"Nothing up front," Emmitt said, "but everything later. It was rare someone coming from Europe would have anything of material worth. No, Yanuck would charge them once they were settled in Britain. That price *was* sometimes in cash. Sometimes it was a service. It might, to make up an example off the top of my head, involve a night watchman at the chemical works looking the other way so ink could be stolen."

"Ink for printing bank notes?" Mitchell asked.

"Do you really want me to spell it out for you, Henry?"

"Yanuck was essential to your schemes?" Mitchell asked.

"More or less," Emmitt said. "Though he didn't act under our orders." He turned to Ruth. "If it had been down to me, Sameen, I would have gutted him years ago. The world is better off without him in it."

"So you say *now*," Mitchell said. "What about the five saboteurs. The Luddites. They were just kids who were tricked into believing that a world without science was one without evil."

109

"Their deaths are unnecessary and unfortunate," Emmitt said. "How did it happen?"

Mitchell's eyes narrowed, as if he was weighing up how much to say. "They were in a house outside the city. During the night, the back door was sealed. At dawn, the killer knocked at the front. The victims were unable to escape. They were shot at close range. Yanuck was shot from five hundred yards. You should keep an eye on the rooftops the next time they let you outside for exercise."

"A sniper? That *is* interesting," Emmitt said. "And proof that this killer had nothing to do with me. If I'd had access to that kind of talent, I wouldn't have needed to attempt the assassination of the prime minister myself." He rubbed his arm where Ruth's bullet had broken the bone. "You work with the tools available, don't you, Henry? There is nothing I would like more than to help you solve this case. Unfortunately, there is nothing I can tell you that *would* help." He turned to Ruth. "I truly am sorry. Did you find the refugee camp, Sameen?"

"What about the other telegraph lines that were cut?" Ruth asked.

"What about them?" Emmitt replied.

"Are we going to find more houses filled with corpses?" Ruth asked.

"Ah, as to that, I couldn't say, though if history teaches us one thing it is that death is the only constant. If you mean will you find a house with more… more Luddites, no. You can rest easy on that score, Sameen."

"Stop calling me that," Ruth said, finally unable to stop herself.

"It's your name," Emmitt said. "What else should I call you?"

"Officer Deering," Ruth said.

"Yet you were first introduced to me as Sameen," he said. "So you *did* go to the refugee camp near Folkestone. You discovered, like so many before, that there is nothing there but ghosts. Did any speak to you?"

Ruth narrowed her eyes, but bit back a retort and the hundred questions she wanted to ask.

"The ghosts spoke to *me*," Emmitt said. "Years ago, I followed you there. Rather, I followed your parents. I was tasked with bringing you back home, you see. I arrived a few weeks too late. Disease had destroyed the camp. Thousands were dead. I assumed you were among them. Well, you know what they say about assumptions, and I can truly say that I've never been so glad to be proven wrong."

"Very good, very good indeed," Mitchell said. "You've taken what Simon Longfield told you, added a few guesses and a lot of vague hints, and come up with something that no one can disprove. What's your game? What do you hope these lies will gain you?"

"They're not lies, Henry. I speak only the truth. The five... Luddites, you called them? My pet saboteurs, is how I referred to them. They were being kept prisoner, I assume? Though not with chains, I suspect. No, they were being kept in place with words, yes?"

"Of course they were, and you know it," Mitchell said.

"I don't," Emmitt said. "They should have been released. They should have been instructed to flee northward and individually. They were just playing a game, but life is not a game. No, they would have been found and arrested. That was my plan. Your police department is small. The number of competent officers even smaller. Interviewing those five, then following the circular leads they gave you would have kept at least twenty of your best people far too busy to notice what was really going on."

"And what was that?" Ruth asked.

Emmitt smiled and raised his cuffed hands. The shackles clinked. "Oh, that hardly matters now. No, suffice it to say that killing the Luddites was never what I intended. If anything, it is counter-productive. Rather than having the nation concerned about an unknown number of saboteurs on the loose, their deaths will gain sympathy to the Luddite cause. That helps no one."

"The Luddite cause? That's your cause, you mean," Ruth said.

"Oh, it's hardly that, Sameen," he said.

"Have you heard about the attack on Calais?" Mitchell asked.

"A little," Emmitt said.

"It began on the fifth of November," Mitchell said.

"And?"

"Did you organise their assault?" Mitchell asked. "Did you arrange it?"

"I thought you came here to discuss Adamovitch," Emmitt said. "He knows nothing. He listened at keyholes, and he probably stole a few files, but he is not the real danger. Yanuck might have been, but I suspect it is this sniper who is your real threat. As to their identity, as I say, I don't know. If I did, I would not have been the one in that apartment building, looking down my sights at the prime minister."

"If your goal is different from the Luddites," Ruth said, "what is it you *do* want?"

"The same thing as Henry," Emmitt said. "We don't want to restore the world to its former blood-drenched glory. We want to build something better. We differ on our definitions of what that is, and in the lengths that we will go to in order to achieve it. As time has proven, we don't differ that much."

"Who do you work for?" Mitchell asked.

"I could ask you the same thing," Emmitt said. "Who do *you* work for? Is it still the professor?"

Mitchell frowned.

"She was your employer when we first met," Emmitt said. "You truly don't remember, do you? I confess, I didn't know you'd survived, either. No, and I can understand why you don't recognise me. It's the face, isn't it? I didn't always look like this. A mutual friend did this to my face when I was sent to recruit her. She finished the work that you began, Henry. Do you remember a hotel corridor on the night the world died? Do you remember a university basement? I do. I remember you."

For a moment, Mitchell said nothing, but his face had gone taut. "I'll speak to the judge," he finally said, "and see if we can get your execution moved up." He stood.

Ruth looked at Emmitt. There were many questions she wanted to ask. From his crooked, evil smile, the man knew it.

"Fresh air has never tasted so good," Mitchell said as he and Ruth blinked in the sunshine outside the courthouse. A group of prisoners were being loaded onto a horse-drawn wagon. From their hang-dog expressions and downcast eyes, they were being taken to begin their sentence. A little further along, near the smaller door at the building's far corner, a dark-haired woman came out alone and unguarded. She stared at the clouds as if disbelieving that she'd been set free.

"You can't believe anything Emmitt told you," Mitchell said.

"I know," Ruth said. "But that doesn't mean that some of it isn't true."

"Simon Longfield will have shared some things you told him, and Emmitt made up the rest. It sounds plausible, that's all."

"And the hotel? *Was* there a hotel?"

"I…" For a moment she thought he was going to fob her off. "Not here," he said. "Whether or not there's a single grain of truth in anything that Emmitt said, Ned Ludd is the next obvious target. If we're going to talk, let's do it where we can keep an eye on him."

"Is he still at Police House?" Ruth asked.

"No, they needed the cell. He's not competent to stand trial, and sending him to prison would do no one any good. He kicked up a storm when they tried to move him into a medical facility. Too many electric lights. We can't let him go, and since he has no home, he can't be placed under house arrest. I had him moved to Religion Road. It was one of the few places where he wouldn't need to be exposed to too much technology."

"How are you, Mr Ludd?" Ruth asked.

The man they only knew as Ned Ludd looked up from his rake. Ruth knew it was Ludd's rake because it was made of slender birch branches, recently cut and roughly trimmed. Ruth would have called it a broom, but he was using it to move leaves around the sundial in the convent's walled garden.

Ludd gave Ruth a thoughtful scowl. "I know you," he said. "They know you, too. They're watching. They're always watching. You know why? It's because of the secret. I know the secret. I won't tell. You shouldn't either. Understand?"

Ruth didn't. "I won't tell anyone," she said. "How are you?"

"They're watching," Ludd said. "They're always watching. Listening. Waiting."

"Do you remember a man called Mr Squires?" Ruth asked.

Ludd stopped moving and muttering. His eyes narrowed.

"He was the man who recruited you?" Ruth asked.

"I was recruited by Ned Ludd," Ludd said.

"But you know who Mr Squires is?" Ruth asked. "We need to find him. Do you know where he might be?"

"Watching," Ludd said. "Waiting. Listening." He swept the crude rake along the grass with renewed vigour.

Ruth smiled, and walked back to the picnic table where Captain Mitchell sat.

"Anything?" he asked.

"Sorry," she said. "Nothing coherent."

"I thought he might speak to you," he said. "Then again, he's not spoken to anyone else, so perhaps it was a vain hope."

There was a loud clatter from the roof of the convent. Ruth spun around, her hand dropping to her holstered revolver.

"It's fine," Mitchell said. "Relax. That's just one of the wardens." He peered upwards, and raised a hand. "Corporal Spinacre, I think. He's a Marine, sent home from Calais due to stopping a piece of shrapnel with his thigh."

"Then should he really be clambering across a roof?" Ruth asked.

"He went with Rabbi Cohen's expedition to Jerusalem a few years ago," Mitchell said by way of reply. "Now, that's a story worth telling."

"I'd rather you told me the one about Emmitt," Ruth said. "But will Ned Ludd really be safe here?"

"For now," Mitchell said. "Until I can think of somewhere better. I asked the mother superior to send for Mrs Zhang. Do you remember her? Isaac's associate who runs the funeral home. She'll provide close protection, but she'll also send for Kelly. Set a sniper to catch a sniper. Of course, that means Isaac will come with her, but the good and the bad often arrive together."

Worried he'd changed his mind about telling her, she went for the direct approach. "What did Emmitt mean about a hotel?"

"Yes, that's troubling," Mitchell said. "Not the hotel itself. That's immaterial. He was talking about the Blackout, about the day it began. Maggie, Isaac, and myself were there, but no one else was. No one except the people who came to kill us."

"You mean Emmitt was one of them?"

"Maybe. When we first met Emmitt at that tumbledown house where they were counterfeiting the notes, I thought I recognised him. I wasn't sure. It's the scars on his face, they make it hard to know what he looked like before. On the other hand, he's had the chance to kill us on more than one occasion, and yet he hasn't."

"There have been plenty of other times that he's tried," Ruth said. "What happened at the hotel?"

Mitchell looked from Ruth to Ned Ludd, then at the ground, and finally at the sky. "It's a story I try not to think about much these days, but I suppose you deserve to know."

Chapter 14 - The Blackout
August 2019, Russell Square, London

The eighteen-year-old Henry Mitchell stared in confusion at the computer screen on the hotel-room desk. "You created an artificial intelligence?" he asked. "You mean like the assistant on my cell-phone?"

"No," Isaac said, his eyes never leaving the younger man's. "Not like on your cell-phone. That's a narrow AI, good at completing the same task over and over. In the case of your phone, that's adding a conversational overlay to the results from a search engine. What we've created is more than simple Boolean algebra. It's the world's first artificial *consciousness*. It's alive, Henry."

"Can it talk?" Henry asked.

"Would you expect a baby to talk? You're still thinking like this is a virtual assistant. It can communicate, but we haven't added a voice component yet. Besides, giving it a voice would mean giving it a gender, and that's a philosophical debate too far for the professor."

"What does it do?"

"Do? Do?" Isaac half laughed, half growled in frustration. "This is *life*, Henry. Artificial life. A conscious being. Do you ask a human what they can do?"

Henry looked around the small room in the Russell Square Hotel, searching for something familiar with which to anchor himself. There was nothing at all familiar about the strange hotel on the wrong side of the Atlantic.

He crossed to the window. Outside, red buses, black cabs, and bicycle couriers crammed the narrow road. It reminded him of a movie. It reminded him of the establishing shot of *every* movie set in London he'd ever seen. Up until an hour ago, he'd thought that was funny. Up until an hour ago, he'd actually been enjoying himself in England.

The professor and her odd assistant had hired Henry Mitchell to be their bag-carrier. Since they'd arrived at the hotel, there had been nothing to carry, so he'd played the tourist. He'd visited the monuments and museums, been to The Globe, and had his first legal drink in a pub once frequented by Charles Dickens. It had been the break he'd needed, a way of finally dealing with the death of his father, his disastrous year at college, and the future ahead of him. That was up until an hour ago.

"This is big, isn't it?" Henry asked.

"There's nothing bigger," Isaac said. "It'll change everything. The personal computer came first, then the World Wide Web, then social media. Now it's this. It's going to change the world."

"How?" Henry asked. "I mean, what exactly will it change?"

"Everything," Isaac said. "Our understanding of what life is, what death is, and what it means to be human. I'm sure there'll be a few commercial applications, and those'll net us a few trillion dollars apiece, but it's the philosophical ramifications that will have the greater impact on society."

The glib way the man threw in that impossibly large number irritated Henry. Isaac wasn't more than a few years older than he, yet in that time he'd helped create… create… Henry still wasn't sure.

"So it's not an AI? What do you call that?" He pointed at the screen.

"I call that a laptop which I've used to access the University of London's email server," Isaac said. "It's not our creation."

"The university's email server, why?" Henry asked.

"Because we sent out a video demonstrating the consciousness about an hour ago. Think of it as a teaser, or a trailer, if you will. We sent copies to some of the more sensationally minded tabloids, but I also sent some to our… I won't call them peers, but they're academics at the university who are attending the conference. I want to find out how people react to our creation before we put on the feature presentation tomorrow."

"You're hacking a university? That's illegal."

"Now that, Henry, depends on how you define the law. I can think of a few intelligence agencies who, if they knew what we were about to announce, would seize every computer, drive, and scrap of paper we'd ever scrawled a note on. In five years time, me hacking into the university will simply be a nicely dramatic scene for the movie they'll make about my life."

"You mean we could be arrested?"

Isaac gave a weary sigh. "Of course, Henry. With every great leap forward, there is risk. One of the reasons we decided to make the announcement in London is that we'll be afforded similar legal protections as if we were home in America. At the same time, we're safely distant from the NSA and the other acronymic intelligence services. They will learn what we've done at the same time as the rest of the world. Then we will have the far greater protection that is only afforded to the successful scientist. As to the morality of what we're doing, and whether *any* government has a right to suppress it, let's leave that to future generations to discuss in ethics classes. This is the next step on a road walked by Pythagoras and Pingala, Newton and Einstein, Lovelace and Turing, Hopper and Berners-Lee. This is the next step, the ultimate step. Everything changes after today. Even the laws."

"And if it goes wrong, if it takes over, if it replaces us, what then?" Henry asked.

"You've seen too many movies," Isaac said. "If we can create an artificial consciousness, we can overlay it with the memories and experiences of the now-living. We can replicate the very essence of anyone. Even you. We can all live forever."

"As a few lines of code," Henry said. "What kind of life is that?"

"A better one than most people have now," Isaac said. "The robotics will catch up. And then… Think of all that's to come. We can go to the stars, all of us, because we will no longer have our frail bodies holding us back. It will be a brave new world, Henry."

"A dystopia with a paper-thin veneer?"

"Too many books, too," Isaac said. "Is anyone thrusting Soma down your throat?" He turned back to the keyboard, and tapped out a few lines. "Now, the professor and I don't want to deal with the press, but they will be clamouring for stories, so why don't you come up with some. I suggest you ask for an eight-figure advance for your first memoir. *High* eight figures. Why don't you go down to the bar, enjoy that it's legal for you to drink in London, and start working on the first chapter. I'll call you when it's time."

Time for what, Henry wanted to ask, but didn't. In truth, he could do with a little time to process what Isaac had said, and so better formulate the questions he needed to ask.

He opened the door, and stepped out into the hall. The hotel was old and musty. Little natural light penetrated the narrow corridors. Despite its name, the hotel was five confusingly irregular blocks from Russell Square. The location determined the price, and the location was worth it. It was on the edge of Bloomsbury, close to the British Museum and the University of London's dozens of colleges. Outside, every building had at least two small plaques pinned to the wall recording the names of famous dead residents. Poets, playwrights, politicians; everyone who was anyone had lived there once.

"Maybe I'll get a plaque," Henry murmured as he headed for the elevator. "No, definitely not." This was a holiday job, though he'd already decided to quit college. He'd applied and been accepted for the police academy. The rest of his life would be devoted to protecting the public and upholding the law. The trip to London had been his chance to see some of the world. He'd seen London, and he was glad. The entire city was like a museum. Like a museum, its contents had no place in his future. Henry wanted to get back home to America so he could begin his new life.

He pressed the button for the elevator. "Lift," he corrected himself. "When in London…"

The lights on the numbers above the door illuminated one-by-one. After a minute, the lift arrived. It wasn't empty. The professor stepped out.

"Ah, Mister Mitchell," she said in her schoolmarm voice. "And how are we this evening?"

Whatever Isaac and the professor had thought they'd created, and however badly their presentation went tomorrow, Henry had only been paid half the money in advance. The rest wasn't due until next week, and he'd need it to cover his next few months' rent. Though the corridor was deserted, talking about their secret project aloud wasn't going to endear him to the woman. "Fine, Professor. Isaac gave me the rest of the evening off."

"Yes, of course. Have fun," she said absently, and headed towards Isaac's room.

Henry stepped into the lift. The door began to close, but Henry shoved his hand out to stop it. The doors slid open. Henry didn't move.

Something else had just occurred to him. Isaac was hacking into the university's servers. Someone might notice. If they did, they'd call the cops. There would be an investigation. It might take a while, but they'd discover who was responsible. Actually, considering that it was the University of London, the security services might get involved, in which case it would be discovered quickly. It was unlikely that Henry would face any charges, but it might shred his chances of joining the police force back home.

"Damn."

He stepped back out into the corridor and let the door to the lift close.

"Elevator. It's a damned elevator."

He walked along the corridor, back towards Isaac's room. He'd have to tell Isaac to stop, and do it in front of the professor. He'd have to threaten to report it to the police. But what if Isaac didn't stop? Then he really would have to go to the police.

"Damn."

Along the corridor, three doors ahead, a man stepped out of his room. He was of average height, had a military buzz-cut, and tinted glasses over his eyes. His suit was a dull black, and so were his boots. They were so thickly padded that they distorted the otherwise razor-sharp crease in his trousers. He gave Henry, in jeans, blazer, and high-tops, barely a glance before walking down the corridor away from him.

Henry slowed his pace, not wanting an awkward confrontation in the hallway. He'd had enough of those since they arrived. Conversations always began with a variation of 'what brings you to London', and he'd not come up with anything that didn't make him sound like a teenager on a holiday.

The man took the corridor down which their rooms were on. That was annoying. Henry slowed his pace further. He'd thought he might be able to speak to the professor before she got inside.

Henry took the turning. He saw the professor at the door to Isaac's room. The man in black had sped up a little. That was odd. There was nothing down this corridor but the fire escape. That and their rooms.

The professor looked down the corridor. She saw the man. The man half turned, reaching for something in his back pocket. No. Not his back pocket. He had a holster at the small of his back. Acting without thinking, Henry ran at the man.

The man drew the gun, and was bringing it up and around when Henry dived into him, knocking the man sideways into the wall. The man spun around, recovering quickly from the blow. While Henry was still bringing his fists up, the man lashed out. His palm slammed into Henry's jaw. Henry rocked back, tasting blood, seeing stars. He reached out, grabbed the side of the man's head, and shoved him sideways. The man's head hit the corner of a brass light-fitment. He crumpled to the ground, unconscious. Henry hoped he was only unconscious.

Spitting blood, Henry staggered back a step, turning his head, trying to clear it. His foot stepped on something. He looked down. It was a semi-automatic nine-millimetre pistol fitted with a suppressor. He picked it up, flipped the safety on, and for want of anywhere else to put it, slid it into his waistband.

The professor stood, open mouthed, next to the door to Isaac's room.

"Call the—" Henry stopped, and spat again, clearing the blood from his mouth. "Call the police," he said to the professor. Gingerly, he leaned forward, reaching out to check the man's pulse. He half expected the man to spring to his feet. He didn't, but he was still alive. Henry checked the man's jacket. There was nothing in the pockets except two spare magazines. He put those into his own pocket and stood. What he'd been looking for, what he'd been half-hoping, half-dreading to find was a badge, but police didn't carry silenced pistols, assassins did.

"What are you really doing—" he began as he looked toward the professor, but she had already gone into Isaac's room. Leaving the assassin on the floor, Mitchell hurried inside.

The professor was loading external drives into her bag. Isaac still sat at the small table, his fingers dancing across the laptop's keyboard.

"Did you call the police?" Henry asked.

"Did you kill him?" Isaac replied, not taking his eyes off the screen.

"Kill him? Of course not. He's unconscious," Henry said. "Are the police on the way?"

"How much longer do you need, Isaac?" the professor asked, ignoring Henry.

"Two minutes. Three at the most," Isaac said.

"No, there's no time," the professor said. "There's no time at all. We need to leave, *now*. There's a fire escape at the end of the hallway. Mister Mitchell? The fire escape. We're leaving this hotel. It's not safe, not any more."

"Why not. What's going on?" Henry asked.

"Isaac!" the professor snapped. She turned back to Henry. "He was an assassin hired to kill us and destroy what we've created. If we wait for the police, more killers will come. They will shoot and we will die, along with an untold number of guests and staff in the hotel. No, we can't wait here. It will be safer for us to go directly to the authorities. There is a police station a block away. Isaac, now!"

"Fine!" Isaac snapped the laptop closed. "After you, Henry."

The assassin lay more or less where Henry had left him. He'd slumped to the floor, curling almost into a ball. The professor ran toward the fire escape, Isaac was close on her heels. Henry was halfway there when the professor pushed at the door. The fire alarm sounded, high-pitched and loud. Automatically, Henry turned around. The assassin was on his knees, a small gun in his hand. Of course the man would have had a back-up piece. And as Henry realised it, the assassin fired. The shot went wide, thudding into the ancient plasterwork.

The assassin fired again. Again the bullet went wide. The man shook his head, then raised his free hand to the gash where he'd hit his skull against the brass light-fitment. Henry took that as his chance, and sprinted for the fire door. He dived through and into the dark stairwell. A pair of bullets thudded into the closing door.

Dim emergency lamps on the underside of each landing illuminated the bare concrete stairs. Henry could hear the professor and Isaac running down them, already at least two flights below. He thought of going up, of hiding, of distancing himself from whatever madness he'd been thrust into. Again, thoughts of his future career came back to him. He couldn't run away, not now. He had to report what had happened, and since the professor wanted to go to the police station…

Henry ran down, taking the steps two at a time. One landing, then another. Above, he heard the door open. He heard footsteps following him. The footsteps below had stopped. A moment later, Henry reached the bottom. There was only a door in front of him. He pushed it open, and ran out into the brightly lit London night.

"You took your time," Isaac said. He had his phone in his hand. "It's this way," he said, pointing.

"How far?" Henry asked, glancing back at the door. "Because that man's following us."

Isaac started running, the professor followed. Henry fell in at the rear, uncertain what was going on, and what he'd become a part of. At least they were heading to the police station. This, whatever it was, would all be over— He heard the glass shatter before he heard the shot. He spun around. The assassin stood a few feet from the hotel, legs braced, gun held in both hands. A figure knocked into Henry as the assassin fired again. Henry hadn't noticed how many other people were about, but it was London, the streets were always thronged with tourists, students, locals, and commuters. Henry wasn't sure which category the young woman fell into, but the bullet meant for him took her in the throat. She collapsed, and that was when Henry realised that people were screaming, running in every direction, away from the gunman. Henry dropped to his knees, clamping his hand over the injured woman's neck, trying to hold in the blood. He couldn't. No one could. Her eyes met his. Blood bubbled up around his fingers. She went still.

Another shot. The bullet hit the window of a car, abandoned in the street when the shooting had begun. Henry looked towards the hotel. The man was walking towards him, gun raised.

The gun he'd taken from the assassin dug into Henry's back as he rolled sideways into the gutter and behind the car. He drew it, stood up, and let months of target practice take over.

Henry had tried to go to the batting cages after his father had died, but the memory was too raw, the place too full of missed opportunities. He'd never managed further than the parking lot. Instead, he'd spent night after night at the firing range, shooting his rage and frustration out on target after target, telling himself that he was training for the academy.

Henry had the man square in his sights, but as his finger curled on the trigger, the streetlights went out. Then the lights in the buildings either side went dark. There was the sound of yelling, of a distant crash of metal against metal. Then there was more screaming, this time coming from further away. Henry tried to spot the assassin, but couldn't. Instead, he backed away along the street, heading after Isaac and the professor.

Distance was hard to gauge in the mostly dark, screaming city. The only illumination came from a few dimly lit windows. Henry could no longer distinguish the pavement from the gutter. An arm grabbed his. He spun around, raising the gun.

"Woah! It's me!" Isaac said. "Did you get him?"

"No," Henry said. "Where's the police station? Where's the professor?"

Isaac had his phone in his hand, but the screen was dark. He had a headphone in his ear, and almost seemed to be listening. "We want to go this way," he said.

Despite the darkness, Isaac knew where he was going. He led Henry down a dark alley and into a pedestrianized square, cutting across to its far side where a figure stepped out from the shadows. It was the professor.

"What's happening?" Henry asked.

"Nothing good," the professor said. "But we can stop it."

"Not from here we can't," Isaac said. "Come."

He led them onward, down an alley between two towering buildings. Behind them, the lights suddenly went on. All of them. Not just the streetlights, but every light in every window of every hotel, office, and university building. Just as abruptly, the lights were extinguished.

"That's not good," Isaac muttered. He tapped Henry on the arm. "Put that away."

He looked down at his hand. It still held the gun. He looked up at Isaac as every light flashed back on. In the second that the street was lit up, he saw people. A few were hurrying along the street, but more were gathering in the doorways of buildings. Some looked as if they had come downstairs, others as if they were taking shelter there. All of them looked more baffled than scared. Henry slid the gun back into his waistband, and pulled the jacket over to cover it.

The police had to be on their way. They *had* to. He could hear sirens, though they weren't close. As Isaac led them down one street and then the next, Henry looked for a uniform, for a flashing blue light, but the only flashing lights came from the buildings around them.

"Down here," Isaac said, leading them into an open courtyard. To one side was a collection of massive pipes. On the other was a noticeboard dotted with flyers and leaflets.

"Where are we?" the professor asked.

"Among the university buildings," Isaac said. "That's Birkbeck behind us. SOAS is somewhere over there."

"Where do we want?" the professor asked.

"Senate House," Isaac said. "The university has a basement lab where they stream images for the British Museum. If someone in a museum in Tokyo wants to examine something from a British collection, it's brought there."

"They have the bandwidth?" the professor asked.

"I hope so," Isaac said.

"Then why have we stopped?" the professor asked.

"Because this is a good spot for an ambush," Isaac said. "Have you got that gun, Henry?"

"You want me to shoot that man?"

"If he's followed us, yes," Isaac said.

"You can't be serious," Henry said. "That's murder."

"He tried to kill us about twenty minutes ago," Isaac said.

"That doesn't make it all right."

"Look around you, Mister Mitchell," the professor said. "Listen to the screams."

Henry didn't draw the gun, but he did edge towards the side of the large pipes. The lights suddenly flicked on. A small group, about twenty-strong, had coalesced outside one of the university buildings. A few still fruitlessly swiped at dark-screened phones, but most were looking around. He wasn't sure for what, but he couldn't see the assassin.

"Who is he?" Henry asked.

"A killer," the professor said.

"Be more specific," Henry said.

"Isaac told you what we have done?" the professor asked.

"Created an artificial consciousness," Henry said.

"And do you know what that means?" the professor asked.

"Not really," Henry said. "Do I need to? What's going on with the streetlights? What's—"

"I can get you all the answers you need," Isaac said. "And most of the ones that *I* need, but not here. Let's— Damn." He pulled the earbud out of his ear. "The phone network's gone down. Now we really need to move, and hope he hasn't followed us."

Isaac led them to a stone granite building. It was securely locked.

"Keep watch," Isaac said, as he levered off the lock's panel.

Henry turned around, peering into the darkness. There were more sirens now, and more screams, but none seemed to be getting nearer.

"Done," Isaac said. "And ridiculously quickly. They call that state of the art, you know."

By the light of his smartphone, Isaac led them into the building and down into a sub-basement room. It had five rows of tiered seats, a little like a theatre. At the front was a large glass case. Above it, on a moveable and rotatable arm, was a boxy grey camera. At the side was a bank of screens. Isaac and the professor made a beeline for them. Mitchell sat in the front row of theatre-seats, and tried to process what had just happened. After a minute, he gave up.

"What's going on?" he asked.

"Later," Isaac said. He'd taken out his laptop and had plugged a cable into it. His fingers flew across the keys. The professor peered over his shoulder.

Henry knew her field was neuroscience. Isaac seemed to be some kind of hacker. Mitchell wondered how they'd met.

He took out his phone. There was no signal.

"Were you responsible for the streetlights flickering?" he asked.

"No," Isaac said.

"Who was?"

"Tell him," Isaac said. "Otherwise he's only going to keep talking."

The professor turned around. "Someone is trying to stop us demonstrating our artificial consciousness. It's possibly a government. It is more like to be some corporation."

"A company?" Henry asked. "Some tech company just hacked London's lighting system?"

"They think that whoever creates the first functional, truly artificial intelligence could patent the concept," the professor said. "They think whoever is first would own the market for long enough to become the sole global monopoly. Imagine a driverless car where there is a sentient being in control, but one that can react a million times faster than a human? Planes, shipping, satellites. Every missile could have a driver, every remote cannon an operator. That's what they think. Overnight, the value of their stock would go through the roof. Every country on Earth would throw money at them. They want to get rich, and they think this will ensure it, but only if they are first."

"They think? You mean they're wrong?" Henry asked.

"They've been watching the same movies you have," Isaac said. "That's why we beat them to it."

127

"It's a consciousness, a person, a being," the professor said. "It's code in the same way that you are chemical signals. It's like saying that, if you take two humans, and use them to make a third, that third human would be as proficient in any task that either of the first two had previously mastered."

Henry parsed that. It was an odd way of talking about parents and children. "Code doesn't need to be fed, right? It doesn't need to sleep?" he said.

"How can it be alive if it doesn't dream?" the professor said. "And though it is code, it requires energy to operate. This is not—"

"We've a problem," Isaac interrupted. "This has gone global."

"What has?" Henry asked.

Isaac turned around. "It's a virus," he said. "They've unleashed a virus. Strictly speaking, they've had millions of viruses embedded in thousands of different systems, and they've just been activated. The streetlights were the beginning, I don't know where it will end, but this is designed to keep the authorities distracted while they find us."

"You said it was global, why isn't it just London?" Henry asked.

"Because the best place to commit a murder is on a battlefield," the professor said. "No one ever notices another corpse. This is the same. In all of this chaos, no one will know who the real targets are."

"It's worse than that," Isaac said. "There's another virus, a self-replicating bot that's searching every networked computer for our creation. They want to destroy our child."

"It's not our child, Isaac. I've told you that before," the professor said.

"Well…" Henry hesitated. "Can you stop it? Can't you send your AI to… I don't know, to fight it?"

"Nope," Isaac said. "I told you, it doesn't work like in the movies."

"I wish you would tell me how it *does* work," Henry said. "What do we do?"

Isaac turned back to the laptop. "*You* do nothing. *I* save the world."

Henry paced back and forth until Isaac told him to stop. After that, he sat, watching the pair. The professor had taken out a tablet. Henry wondered if their artificial consciousness was on it. If not, it had to be in one of the bags they'd brought from the hotel. Isaac was right. What he knew came from movies, though he'd picked up a little more from the news. The stories of hacks where viruses had brought down IT systems, or made power station turbines spin so fast they blew up, or caused missiles to explode in their bunkers. He tried to sift through the memories as to which had come from his newsfeed, and which he'd seen on the big-screen.

"Okay, good news, bad news," Isaac said without taking his eyes from the laptop.

"What's the bad?" the professor asked.

"It's spreading. They've attacked the power stations. Primarily, I think, to give cover to their agents in London. The attacks on the rest of the world were a way of masking where their true interest lay. Air traffic control has gone. GPS, GLONASS, and Galileo are still okay, but they're getting into phones and personal computers, causing the batteries to overheat."

"Mine hasn't," Henry said.

"Of course not," Isaac said. "I gave it to you."

"What's the good news," the professor asked.

"I'm not sure I can kill it, but I think I can speak to the person doing this," Isaac said. "Or one of them. They've been selective in what's been attacked. It's like a road, and I just need to follow it. Of course, that leaves the question of in which direction we'll find the Emerald City, and who we'll find behind the curtain. This is going to take some time. Henry, this is a university. Universities have vending machines. Find me something to eat."

Henry was glad to leave the room. It was only when he was out in the dark corridor that he wondered if he should have checked it first, though it appeared empty. He took out the phone, and switched on the light.

He'd wanted to become a cop, so now it was time to consider the evidence. He knew that Isaac and the professor were up to something, and that there was a conference taking place in London at which they were due to speak. Isaac had said he'd been hacking into the university's email server, but had he? They'd talked about creating some kind of AI that wasn't really an artificial intelligence, but was any of that real? The phone was real, so was the gun in his waistband. There was blood on his hands, blood that belonged to that woman who had died on the sidewalk. That was undeniably real. The streetlights had flickered on and off. He'd heard cars crash, but who was behind it? Was it Isaac and the professor? They'd advertised for an assistant for an overseas trip, and hired Henry principally because he wouldn't understand what they were doing. But what *were* they doing? And what were they really doing in the university's sub-basement?

He walked down the dark corridor, shining the light on each door in turn. Which was more plausible, that this professor and her assistant had created a genuine artificial intelligence, or that this was some kind of heist? Considering the lone assassin, it was more likely they were robbing the mob than the Bank of England, but that meant Henry's only purpose on the trip was to be the fall guy.

The corridor branched. He scanned the light along the walls, looking for a sign that might indicate where he'd find the vending machines. Universities didn't signpost vending machines. Isaac had just wanted him out of the room. He tried the phone. There was no signal. He dialled 911 anyway, then remembered that it was 999, but the phone didn't work. A phone that Isaac had given him. He looked at it with a growing sense of gnawing suspicion. He needed to find a landline and call the police. Whatever was going on, that was the only sensible thing to do.

Checking the doors as he went, he continued down the corridor, following the arrow that pointed toward the lifts. If he couldn't find a working phone, he'd go upstairs, outside, and simply get away.

He tried a door. It was unlocked. He pushed it open, glanced along the corridor, and saw a shadow. He shone the light in that direction, blinding the three figures wearing night-vision goggles. As they ripped the devices from their faces, Henry froze. One, with a bandage wrapped around his head, was the assassin from earlier. The other two he didn't recognise. Both were men. All three carried compact submachine guns. A man with the bullet-shaped head recovered first, brought his weapon up, and pulled the trigger just as Henry dived into the room. Wood-chip and plaster sprayed over him as he rolled across the floor. He'd dropped the phone. It lay near the door. The light was still on, reflecting off the white-panelled ceiling.

He was in a seminar room with a table and desk at the front, and three rows of stackable chairs facing it. He crawled behind the desk and dragged the silenced pistol from his belt.

"This isn't your fight," a voice called out. The words were English, but the voice wasn't British, nor was it American. It was the kind of accent used by someone who'd learned the language as an adult, but hadn't quite mastered the inflection. "I know you're armed. Throw out my gun. Go home."

Henry weighed his chances. They weren't great. The desk was chipboard and veneer. It might slow a bullet, but it wouldn't stop it. There was no other cover in the room, no other escape. He wasn't sure how much help the professor and Isaac would be. Besides, the only way to reach them was through those three men.

He levelled the gun at the door. "Who are you? What's going on?"

"Ah, a very good question. You've got yourself caught up in a game that's bigger than nations. The fate of our species is in your hands. For all of us to survive, I need to know where your friends are. Take me to them, before it's too late."

"I—" Henry began. A shape appeared in the doorway. The bullet-headed man swung into the room. Henry fired, a reflexive three shots straight into the centre mass. The man fell as the second goon stepped into the doorway. He was shorter, his barrel aimed slightly higher. As the assassin pulled the trigger, and bullets flew inches above Henry's head, Henry fired two shots. The first took the man in the neck, the second missed, but the assassin collapsed.

Henry waited, watching the man bleed to death. He waited, expecting the last assassin to step into the gap. He waited, expecting a hail of gunfire that would mark his death. The assassin didn't appear. Henry blinked. He listened. There was no sound at all. The killer had gone. Of course he had, he'd gone to find Isaac and the professor.

Henry wanted to stay behind the desk forever, but he couldn't, so he stood, and took a step towards the two dead men. He heard something in the hallway just before the assassin stepped into the phone's pool of light. Henry had the gun raised. He pulled the trigger. It clicked, jammed. The assassin grinned. Henry dived forward, slamming his entire body into the man. There was a staccato rat-a-tat as the assassin's gun went off, a soft patter as the bullets thudded into the carpet. Henry roared, punching and kicking, shoving and jabbing, screaming and butting while the assassin tried to bring his gun to bear. Henry pushed his forearm against the assassin's throat. The man let go of his weapon, and jabbed his own hands into Henry's sides.

Henry screamed, as much in fear as pain, and punched his palm into the man's face. He felt the man's nose break. The assassin backed off a step, reaching for something inside his coat. As he did, Henry reached out, grabbed the man's bandaged-covered head, and slammed his face into the door. The glass window was reinforced with wire mesh. It cracked but didn't break. The man pushed himself back, but he was still trying to draw something from his coat. Henry slammed the man's face into the reinforced window again and again. The wooden frame split as the assassin's face was lacerated on the glass. The man finally gave up on his concealed weapon, and threw a wild punch. Henry ducked, and swept his leg out. The man stumbled, but didn't fall. Henry grabbed the back of the man's bandaged head, and brought it down onto his rising knee. The man collapsed.

Henry stepped back. The assassin's face was covered in small scars, a crisscross of bloody lines where the reinforced mesh had cut deep into his skin. Not checking to see if the man was dead, Henry grabbed the submachine gun from one goon, and then the next, and then took their ammunition and the night vision goggles, and then the jammed pistol. He was uncertain which way to go. Outside? And then where?

The assassin groaned. Henry aimed the submachine gun at the man. Self-defence was one thing, shooting a barely conscious man was something else. It was a line he couldn't cross.

132

There was a beeping noise. It came from the assassin's belt. It was an odd device, not quite a smart phone, not quite a sat-phone, but it was receiving an incoming call. Henry picked it up, and pressed the green button.

"Is it done?" a man asked. He sounded old, speaking in cultured English.

Henry didn't reply. He didn't breathe. He waited.

"Who's there?" the voice asked.

"It's done," Henry said, in his best impersonation of the assassin.

There was silence on the other end, and then a short bark of laughter before the call was disconnected.

Henry tried the number pad. The phone didn't work. He dropped it, and returned to Isaac and the professor.

"Where's the— What happened?" Isaac asked.

"That assassin," Henry said. "He came back. He wasn't alone. We need to go. Right now. What was it you said, that there's a road, and if you followed it, you would find them? Well they followed that road back to you."

"I got through to them," Isaac said. "To one of them, at least. I got a —"

"Later," Henry cut in. "This isn't the place, and we haven't got the time. We need to get out of here and find the authorities. Whatever this is, it's bigger than us."

"Agreed," the professor said. "It's a short walk from here to Thames House. MI5," she added.

"There's no other option?" Isaac asked.

"No," the professor said. "This… this is something beyond our ability to manage. It's time to admit defeat, before it is too late for us all."

Isaac led them through the building, heading in the opposite direction to that in which the assassins had come.

Outside Senate House, the city was dark. An orange glow was reflected off the clouds, but it didn't come from streetlights. As the smell of smoke spread through the air, they jogged down the road until they reached the junction.

"Which way's MI5?" Henry asked. There was a roar in the sky. A plane soared low, barely above the rooftops. A fraction of a second later, it crashed into the university building they were just in. A cloud of brick and dust, sound and flame erupted behind them as the building was destroyed.

"Strike a match," Isaac said, "and hope the world *doesn't* burn."

Chapter 15 - Twenty Years Later
13th November 2039, Twynham

"We didn't make it to Thames House," Captain Mitchell said. "At first, I thought that plane had been deliberately flown into Senate House. Perhaps it was, but as the night wore on, more planes dropped out of the sky. We took shelter, hoping that when dawn came and we could properly see the world around us, we'd gain a better understanding of what was going on and how to face it. By the time the sun rose, it was already too late. The virus had... mutated is the best word. It was clearly beyond its creator's control. Thames House was destroyed, along with so much else. Isaac saw what was going to happen. Saw, or read, or heard, because he spent half his time online and the other half searching for a connection. Before the networks went down for the last time, he sent a warning to some people on a government list. People with useful skills. People who — well, no, that's another story, and one that ended with us and a few thousand others sheltering in a deep-level underground station when the nuclear bombs went off above our heads. That's when the world ended." He shrugged.

"Oh." Ruth said. She turned to watch Ned Ludd, still painstakingly raking a lawn that had virtually no leaves on it. "I've a question."

"Yes?"

"Actually, I've got lots."

"Ask them," he said. "I'll answer."

"The assassin, that was Emmitt?"

"I think so."

"And the man you heard on the phone, that was his employer?" she asked.

"Maybe. Maybe his employer, maybe just someone co-ordinating the attacks."

"Who was he?" she asked. "Or them, or... well, who was behind it?"

"I don't know, but I've thought a lot it over the years. Someone who was rich, but money will only get you so far. Emmitt managed to get weapons into Britain, and if you don't know how difficult that used to be, ask Weaver. My theory is that he had the backing of a major government. I doubt they knew what he was actually doing, but they gave his people diplomatic cover. Precisely which government, I don't know."

"But they survived? I mean, are they still out there?"

"You're thinking about what Emmitt said about your parents?"

"Yes… no, not really," Ruth said. "I don't know."

Mitchell frowned. "Well, there's no way for Emmitt to have known about the hotel or the sub-basement without him being the assassin who tried to kill us. I suppose it's possible that Isaac or Maggie told someone, but… no, I think that assassin was Emmitt. In which case, he escaped from London. He would have returned to his employer and then, probably, he killed the man for causing a plane to crash into the building he was in."

"Except Emmitt was loyal, wasn't he?" Ruth asked. "I mean—" She stopped. "He still is, isn't he? He's loyal to someone, otherwise why is he risking his life to do any of this? From what he said, if he's to be believed, he thinks he's part of a cause. If he wasn't, if he was just a lone survivor, then having printed all that counterfeit currency, why didn't he buy himself a comfortable life, or a seat in parliament or, well, anything?"

"Yes, and that's what I'm now wondering. Up until today, I thought he was the man running the conspiracy. Perhaps for Longfield, perhaps for himself. Now, I'm not so sure. It's Calais. Everything else, from the counterfeiting to the sabotage could be viewed as a path to political power in Britain. Calais, though, is different. It has the effect of tying up our military resources, but it feels like it's part of something bigger."

"The assassination, too," Ruth said. "I mean, that wasn't just about killing the prime minister, that was about disrupting the relationship between Britain and the U.S."

"A good point," Mitchell said. "Then there is someone behind all of this who's playing a very long game. Perhaps it *is* Emmitt, but perhaps not. Perhaps Emmitt is working *for* someone, but more likely he's working *with* someone. Either way, he's a true believer in this cause, and there is no one more dangerous than that." His eyes went to Ned Ludd who'd finally stopped raking and was now watching a robin that had landed on the sundial.

"I've another question," Ruth said.

"I said I'd answer them all," Mitchell said.

"Do you think Isaac was working for... for him, whoever he was?" she asked.

"No. I did, at first. That would have been the simplest explanation. That he'd stolen some code and taken it to the professor to complete the work. But no, Maggie has known Isaac all her life. She vouched for him. And no, she wasn't working for them, either. On their own, driven by their own demons, those two created something utterly new under our pale sun. It would have changed the world. It *did* change the world, just not how they'd imagined it."

"I've got more questions, but I think I'll keep them for later. I suppose what I really want to know above all else is what do we do now? I mean, this changes everything, doesn't it?"

"It might do," Mitchell said. "Emmitt's old employer might be alive. He *might* be behind the assassin. Their lair, wherever it is, *might* be where the ammunition we found in Dover came from. It *might* mean that, when we catch this sniper, there'll be another waiting to pick up the gauntlet. Or it might not. I'm going to make no more assumptions, they'll only lead us into danger."

"What *are* you going to do?" she asked.

"Tonight, I'm going to warn Isaac. Tomorrow, I don't know. I might need to speak to Atherton and tell him what Emmitt said. That would involve telling him the truth about Isaac, and that will surely complicate matters."

"The prime minister doesn't know about Isaac?"

"Yes and no," Henry said. "Atherton knows what happened in the Tube station, and about Isaac leading us to the coast to find the ships with their supplies. The old PM knew, but I don't know what she told Atherton except that she didn't tell him everything. Isaac has been allowed some latitude because any jury would have been filled with people whose lives he saved. No one would have found him guilty, and thus he has been left alone. The proviso was that he didn't put himself in a position where he'd end up in court."

"I don't like all these secrets," Ruth said. "And I don't think they should have been kept in the first place, but I don't see how telling the prime minister would help now."

"Nor do I," Mitchell said, "but he is the prime minister. If I'm going to call myself a police officer, there are some laws that have to be followed."

"Well, fine, but it won't help us catch the sniper, will it?"

"Maybe it does," Mitchell said. "Emmitt could have told me who he was when we arrested him, or at any point since. This is the secret he's been holding back. This is why he knew he wouldn't be executed. *This* is his bargaining chip, and it's staked on a very weak hand." He stood. "I'll speak to Isaac. When Mrs Zhang arrives, go home. Get some rest. I'll see you in the morning." He left.

Ruth turned to face Ned Ludd, though she barely saw him. She replayed the captain's story. It was obvious that he'd not told her everything. He *had* told her about killing those two assassins, so she wondered what he'd left out.

It was only twenty minutes before Mrs Zhang arrived. She was dressed in a smart old-world suit but carrying a battered canvas bag that clinked as she put it on the table. She nodded to Ruth, turned a full circle, and surveyed rooftops and walls.

"He will be safe," she said. "Go. You will be safe, too."

There was a calm professionalism about the woman, one that begged more questions, but Ruth's brain had no space for them.

"Thank you. Goodbye, Mr Ludd," she called to the man.

He looked up from his rake, and frowned. "You're leaving?" he asked, and he sounded almost upset. "Then watch. Keep watching. Always watch, because *they* are watching you. Watch. Yes, keep watch, it is the only way to be safe."

Ruth smiled. "That was almost coherent. I think he's getting better."

She left Religion Road, and took a slow walk through the city. It wasn't that she was revisiting old haunts, as she'd seldom come into town while she lived in the refugee camp. During her brief time in the Serious Crimes Unit, the only places she'd visited had been full of death and violence, and there had been too much of that today. Instead, she wandered the roads almost at random until she found herself at the radio antenna on the cliffs of Southborne. The antenna itself was a tranquil monument amid a bustling hive of activity. Scores of builders swarmed over the apartment buildings, houses, and shops being redeveloped. The building in which Emmitt had attempted to assassinate the old prime minister and Ambassador Perez now had the Stars and Stripes flying from its roof. The absurdly long flagpole was dwarfed by the antenna, but the first thing any ship would see when approaching the harbour would be the American flag. She'd thought it strange that the U.S. embassy was moving to that particular building. Perhaps that was part of the reason why. Standing outside the embassy were a pair of U.S. Marines in their old-world dress-blues.

Ruth considered going inside, or at least seeing whether she would be let inside. Perhaps the ambassador would want to play another game of chess.

That idea sprang into her mind fully formed, and it was such an odd one, it made her stop in her tracks. She stared at the building, confused until she realised why the thought had come to her. She wanted someone to talk to. The ambassador wasn't a friend, but that was the problem. She knew so few people. She could hardly discuss what Mitchell had said with Isaac or Maggie. For the same reason, she couldn't discuss it with Mrs Zhang or Kelly. Aside from her feud with Mitchell, Weaver was an assistant commissioner. There was Riley, of course, but she was, in every way that mattered, Mitchell's daughter. And then there was Simon. He was the last person in whom Ruth had confided, and he'd betrayed her. No, there was no one with whom she could talk, though she desperately wanted to.

Feeling suddenly alone in the world, she went back to Riley's cottage.

Chapter 16 - Watching The World Burn
14th November, Twynham

Ruth couldn't sleep. A soft amber glow eased its way beneath the dining room door showing that Riley was still awake, but Ruth wasn't in the mood for conversation. When she'd returned to Riley's cottage, Ruth hadn't mentioned what Mitchell had told her about the Blackout. Instead, she'd let Maggie and Riley assume she was dwelling on the murder of the five Luddites. Ruth had said little during the evening, but Maggie had been more than happy to do most of the talking. She'd enthused over how she and Riley had spent the day sifting through telegram reports and interviewing messengers. To Ruth it had sounded tedious. Judging by Riley's expression, the sergeant had thought so, too. Maggie, though, had spoken as if it had been one of the most enjoyable working days of her life. It was puzzling, and even more so when taken with what little they discovered.

They'd learned that a message had been sent from Dover at just before seven p.m., approximately four hours after Adamovitch and Yanuck had been arrested. The message read: *No fish today. The boat has sunk. Catching the train tomorrow.* Maggie was certain there was a coded message hidden within the words. Riley thought it was simply a pre-arranged signal to indicate that Adamovitch had been arrested and would be on a train 'tomorrow'.

What was more illuminating, and how they had concluded this message was the signal to the sniper, was that the telegram had been sent to Wallace Fairmont, a composite of the names of two of the now-dead conspirators. No address had been given, and so the message had been pinned to the board outside the telegraph office. That was hardly rare since it was half the cost of having a telegram hand-delivered. As the board was prominently placed outside the telegram office, anyone could have read it, but one of the clerks had remembered seeing a bearded man with a limp lingering outside. It wasn't much to go on, and as clues went, it didn't take them very far. Nevertheless, Maggie had been genuinely excited at being involved in police work. Or perhaps it was trying to find the code hidden in the telegram. Maybe that reminded Maggie of her life before the Blackout.

The sofa squeaked as Ruth sat up. The past didn't matter. What mattered was catching the murderer before he struck again. The fire was burning low. She stood, crossed to the small basket filled with split logs, and placed one in the grate. There was a crackle of sparks, a soft whoosh as ash fell into the hearth, then a rocking of springs from the dining room. A moment later came the sound of wheels turning, the door opening, a gentle thud as Riley banged into the wall, and then the sergeant wheeled herself into the living room.

"What's keeping you up?" Riley asked.

"Emmitt," Ruth said, mostly truthfully.

"He can't be trusted," Riley said. "What did he say to you?"

"Some stuff about my family," Ruth said. "It's a long story."

"So tell me," Riley said, wheeling her chair close to the fire.

"It's nothing," Ruth said, feeling uncomfortable sharing it.

"Emmitt's got inside your head," Riley said. "Talking about it might get him out of there."

"I don't believe him," Ruth said. "But the thing is, I think he does. It's weird, but he actually seems to think I'm called Sameen, the daughter of someone he used to work with, or maybe for."

"Emmitt's lying," Riley said. "He learned a little about you from Simon Longfield, and now he's trying to sow confusion in your mind."

"But why, what does he gain?"

"The obvious answer? He wants help trying to escape," Riley said.

"He thinks that I might break him out of jail?" Ruth asked.

"He's awaiting execution," Riley said. "That's the definition of desperate, but maybe he wants your unwitting help. He'll tell you that the secret is in a box sealed with a combination lock. You'll be instructed to bring it to him."

"And inside is a gun?"

"Or a key," Riley said. "Or something less obvious but which will enable him to escape. Remember, he had his appeals worked out in advance, so he has to have a plan for when those appeals fail."

"Mister Mitchell thinks he's going to trade information for his release. Maybe information on who he really works for."

Riley shook her head. "They would never release him. He'd buy a few days, maybe a few weeks, but nothing he could say would win him his freedom."

Ruth stoked the fire. "I wish I knew."

"Knew what?" Riley asked.

"Everything," Ruth said. "Anything. Every time I think I'm getting close to an answer, another question comes along. It's not just Emmitt, it's... well, I just want some certainty in my life."

"You and me both," Riley said. "But there's no such thing. I was certain that I'd be a police officer, and that, having returned to the rank of sergeant, I'd be a captain by spring. I was certain I'd be married by this time next year."

"Married? I didn't know you were engaged."

"Precisely," Riley said. "Do you see a get-well card, the bunch of flowers? I haven't heard a word since I was shot. Certainty? No, all my certainties vanished in an instant of pain. I'm left with only the determination that I *will* walk again."

That put Ruth's own fears into sharp perspective. "I'm sorry," she said. "I've been going on. I should have made more time to ask you how you've been doing."

"Today is better than yesterday, and tomorrow will be better still," Riley said. "That's about as much certainty as I have right now. Are you going back to Dover tomorrow? Or today, I should say."

"I think so," Ruth said. "We don't have many leads. Adamovitch won't talk. Not to me, anyway, and I don't think Weaver will let me near him. Mrs Foster's description of Mr Squires is too vague to be of use."

"Though it's too big a coincidence for a man with a limp to have rented that cottage and to have picked up the message that came from Dover," Riley said.

"Maybe," Ruth said. "Sometimes coincidences do happen. Either way, the only solid lead we have is that someone sent that message from Dover. I don't know if there's anything I can do that Sergeant Kettering can't, but at least I'd feel useful."

"Agreed," Riley said decisively. "Come on, then." She wheeled the chair backward. It banged into the grate. "Damn. Push me into the kitchen. I'll make us some breakfast while you pack for us both."

"For both of us? You want to come to Dover?"

"The principal advantage of having the person who runs the railway in a wheelchair is that she made sure the trains and platforms were accessible," Riley said. "Give me a push, and do it quietly. I don't want to wake your mother. You'll have to tell me how you managed to live with her without going mad. Seriously, she's driving me crazy. I can't go a metre outside without her tagging along. I'd—"

There was a knock at the door. Riley had a gun in her hand before Ruth had turned her head. The knock turned to a loud hammering.

"Push me into the hall," Riley whispered. "Quietly!"

Ruth did, and only then remembered her own weapon was in the holster in the living room.

"Pull the door open, then stand flush against the wall," Riley whispered.

Ruth opened the door, stepping back as Riley levelled her gun, but it was a uniformed constable outside, one Ruth recognised from the courthouse.

"I've got a message," he said. "From Captain Mitchell. You're to come immediately."

"Where to?" Riley asked.

"The courthouse," the constable said. "It's on fire."

Ruth hadn't realised how many potholes there were in Twynham, but the wheels of Riley's chair managed to find each one. It took an age to push the sergeant through the night-time city, but the fire still blazed when they got to the courthouse. The three-storey red-brick building was engulfed. Smoke billowed up through the roof. Flames licked up the walls, then burst from a second-storey window, spraying glass onto the fire crew below. They didn't even pause as they changed the aim of their hoses, but even Ruth knew it was too late for those weak jets.

"There, Mister Mitchell," Riley said, pointing towards a solitary silhouette a little distance from the frantic fire crew.

Ruth wheeled Riley towards him. Mitchell glanced around, then turned his attention back to the blaze.

"Did everyone get out?" Riley asked.

"There are a few burns and other minor injuries," Mitchell said. He gestured to the group of grey-clad prisoners sat on the grass verge near the board where the day's judgements were usually displayed. "There's only two who aren't accounted for."

"Who?" Ruth asked.

"Adamovitch and Emmitt," Mitchell said.

"They escaped?" Ruth asked.

"No," Mitchell said. "The fire chief is certain that the blaze began on the floor that their cells were on. She's also certain the fire didn't begin close to the stairs. That's as far as she was willing to go. Literally and figuratively. The heat was too intense for her to get beyond the bottom step. Only two of the cells were occupied. Those belonging to Adamovitch and Emmitt."

"What about the warder on duty?" Riley asked.

"Abed Khan," Mitchell said. "He got a telegram at midnight, one that had to be signed for in person. He went upstairs, and was gone for less than ten minutes. When he returned, the blaze was well underway. He's been taken to the hospital with first-degree burns. He tried to get to the prisoners, but couldn't. He did say that there were flames coming from both Emmitt's and Adamovitch's cells."

"What was in the telegram?" Riley asked.

"The truth lies in the past," Mitchell said. "Sound familiar?"

"That was on the coins we found," Ruth said. "Commissioner Wallace had one, and so did the Ambassador's assistant. But I thought they were a lie, a joke that Emmitt dreamed up."

"Right, but that was what Emmitt told us. Can we believe it? I don't know. I think that message was for us. We're being taunted."

"Do you think the warder was involved?" Ruth asked.

"I doubt it," Mitchell said. "His brother-in-law is a judge, and he's training to be a solicitor in the spare time he doesn't spend working at the soup kitchen. The guards for those cells were chosen because they were dependable."

"And if he was involved, why send the telegram?" Riley said. "He was only gone for ten minutes?"

"If that," Mitchell said. "I thought the murderer would try to shoot Emmitt. We had more guards outside, and we kept the other cells empty. Only truly trustworthy officers were allowed near Emmitt. After Adamovitch was brought here, we had some of the trials moved just to limit the number of people in the building. It turns out that didn't matter because I didn't expect this."

"What do you mean?" Ruth asked.

"It happened too quickly," Mitchell said. "The blaze has taken and spread to the entire building. They must have hidden accelerant inside the walls or under the floors. That would have taken time. Months, maybe. Maybe longer than that. After all, if Emmitt was making plans in case he was incarcerated, then surely someone else might have made their own plans for that eventuality. All that was needed was the opportunity. With Adamovitch in the cells, too, that opportunity was too great to pass up."

"But how did it start?" Ruth asked. "Didn't any of the guards notice someone sneaking in?"

"That's the point," Mitchell said. "I think it was started remotely."

"How?" Ruth asked.

"There are plenty of old-world triggers if you know where to look," Mitchell said. "And the first place I'd look would be an armoury where you'd find ammunition and assault rifles. Failing that, there's more than enough raw materials if you know how to make one. A lot of people did. Emmitt and Adamovitch. The Luddites, and the smugglers. They're loose ends, and Emmitt was the loosest of them all. This sniper is cleaning house. The deaths of Wallace and Longfield have left a vacuum. Someone is trying to fill it, but knew they couldn't while Emmitt lived."

"But why not kill Adamovitch when he got off the train?" Ruth asked. "Why wait until tonight? Or why not wait until Yanuck was in one of the cells, too."

"If Yanuck hadn't been shot, he and Adamovitch would have been taken to Police House," Mitchell said. "But you raise a good question, why didn't the sniper kill Adamovitch at the train station. Why not kill him and Yanuck in Dover? And I'll give you another. Why were the Luddites killed, but Mrs Foster wasn't? Why has no attempt been made on Ned Ludd? Jameson was murdered, but his killer, Pollock, wasn't. Everything that has happened has been done for a reason, so what is the reasoning behind killing some, but leaving others alive?"

"Maybe it's not as complicated as that," Riley said. "Maybe it's just a matter of opportunity. After all, that fire will have destroyed a lot of records, a lot of evidence. Maybe that was the real goal."

"Not if the fire began in the cells," Mitchell said.

"Or maybe," Ruth said, "the fire is to ensure that people know there's *been* a fire, that Adamovitch and Emmitt are dead. I mean, there's no way this can be hushed up. If someone wanted to take over, it's not enough just killing Emmitt, you need everyone to know it, too."

"Maybe," Mitchell said, but in a tone that said he disagreed.

"Someone sent that telegram to the warder," Riley said. "And someone in Dover sent that telegram to the killer. The telegraph is the answer. We're narrowing in on them."

"But too late," Mitchell said.

It *was* too late. Ruth hadn't believed anything that Emmitt had said, but she'd wanted to. Now there would be no way to confirm the truth in his words, no way of learning if he really knew something of her parents.

"I'll see you later," Ruth said.

"Where are you going?" Mitchell asked.

"The railway station, eventually," Ruth said. "But there're a few hours until the first train. I want to clear my head."

"It might not be safe," Mitchell said.

"Sir, frankly, if whoever did this wanted us dead, they could have killed us tonight, or yesterday, or whenever. They don't want us dead. We're too useful. After all, we just gave them Adamovitch and Emmitt."

Ruth made her way through the thin crowd gathered near the police rope. She paused to stare at the faces, searching for a middle-aged man with a beard. She saw none, but beards could be shaved. With no destination in mind, she headed away from the inferno.

Her mind turned to the crime. Begin at the beginning, she thought, but where had it begun? Longfield's death, Emmitt's arrest, or Mr Wilson's murder? Mr Wilson… Thinking back on his crime scene, she realised how poorly it had been staged. The coroner had spotted it in an instant. So had Sergeant Kettering. Even Ruth had sensed something had been wrong before the sergeant had coaxed out specifically what. Therefore Mr Wilson had died in order to lay a trail that led to Adamovitch. It had guaranteed that Adamovitch and the smugglers had been on that train. The death of Yanuck had guaranteed that Adamovitch had been in the cells. And there he'd died with Emmitt, but why? Why did they have to die together?

"Excuse me, Officer," a wiry man leading a milk cart called out to her. "What's going on up there?"

"The courthouse is on fire," Ruth said. There didn't seem any point lying.

"A fire? How?" the man asked.

"Investigations are continuing," Ruth said, deciding the vague question deserved an equally vague answer.

"Are the roads closed?"

"Only around the courthouse," Ruth said.

"Typical," the man muttered. "And it would have to be on a delivery day." He clicked the reins and led the horse down a side road. His muttering kept up as he led the cart on a detour, but Ruth ignored the words, and watched the man walk. He didn't seem to be limping. She shrugged, and turned her mind back to the crime.

If the goal, or part of it, was to get Adamovitch into the courthouse jail, did that mean the butler had nothing to do with Mr Wilson's murder? She ran through the confrontation at the cottage again, stopping when she absently stepped into a puddle. She swore. Above, from an open window, came a loud tut-tutting, then a louder slam as the window was shut. Ruth glanced back towards the courthouse. She was at least a quarter mile away, at the edge of the more affluent part of the city. The reflected glow of the fire on the clouds was barely visible, but the acrid smell of the inferno was a thick blanket coating the city.

Why kill the five Luddites, but not the farmer, Mrs Foster? There was an obvious explanation. Mrs Foster had given a vague description of a bearded man with a limp. Beards were easy to grow and shave, a limp easy to affect. At some point, a bearded corpse would turn up in the morgue. When identified it would be discovered that the man had a limp. They would assume it was Mr Squires, and have no way to prove otherwise. Yes, that was *an* obvious explanation, but it didn't mean it was the correct one.

She shook the water from her foot, and continued on. Why kill Adamovitch in the cells rather than at the railway station? The only answer was that there was something else going on. Something that would tie together all the loose strands. She had no idea what it was.

She paused by a shop window with a display of Christmas ornaments. A row of Santa Clauses were identical to ones she'd seen in Dover, though the prices were twice what she'd have paid further east.

The sun was rising, casting enough light to distinguish between smoke and cloud. There were more people up and about now, and most were looking towards the inferno if not heading directly towards it. She headed in the opposite direction, vaguely angling towards the sea. She stopped as a shop assistant moved a sandwich board out onto the pavement. It advertised a 'Breakfast Special', and that only reminded Ruth of how long it had been since her last meal.

"Morning, Officer," the shopkeeper said. "Any idea what's going on?"

"Just a fire," Ruth said, and kept walking. Stopping for breakfast would only bring questions, and she had enough of those as it was. Her stomach offered a growl of protest. She glanced back at the shop, and as she did, caught the shadow of a figure moving into the lee of the alley. Ruth faced ahead, pretending she hadn't noticed.

She sauntered down the next turning, picking up her pace immediately after. There were no handy alleyways in which to hide, but there was a house with an overflowing and overly tall hedge. She snuck through the gate, and ducked down behind the mottled leaves. She waited… waited… waited… waited until the figure walked by at a brisk clip. It was a man wearing a dark tailored coat, a scarf wrapped around his neck, and a Panama hat pulled low over his ears. His left hand swung in time with his legs, but his right was buried deep in a pocket.

Ruth already had her hand on her holster. She drew the pistol as she bounded out of the front garden. She rammed the revolver into the man's back.

"Woah!" he exclaimed, turning around. In his hand was a tablet, not a gun, and on his face a mildly surprised, slightly amused, and very familiar smile. "You can put that away," Isaac said.

"Why do people keep following me?" Ruth said, holstering her gun. "I swear, the next time, I'll shoot first."

"It's not safe for anyone to be out on their own," Isaac said. "When Mrs Zhang called to say you'd been summoned, I thought I should follow. I thought we'd be safer together."

"Mrs Zhang? Isn't she watching Ned Ludd?"

"I've put Kelly on that," Isaac said. "I had Mrs Zhang watching you."

"Right. First Mitchell follows me, then Mrs Zhang, then you. Why not try talking next time?" she grumbled as she walked away from him. "Try saying, hi, Ruth." She stopped. "Except it wasn't Mitchell first, was it?" she asked turning to face a bemused Isaac. "You followed me before, didn't you?"

"Did I?"

"Weeks ago," she said. "I was following that barman."

"So?" Isaac asked.

"So that man had a limp," Ruth said. "The man who paid for the cottage in which we found the five Luddites had a limp."

"Mr Squires. Henry told me," Isaac said. "But as far as leads go, that's more than just tenuous."

"It's better than wandering the streets aimlessly. Do you know where the barman lives?"

"You want to question him?" Isaac asked. "This smacks of desperation."

"Then give me a better lead," Ruth said. "Give me something, anything. You said you know what's going on, then you know what's going to happen. This killer is going to strike again, and soon. All we're doing is collecting the bodies, waiting for the next to fall. Give me a lead, a clue, anything, or tell me where the barman lives."

"You know, you remind me more of Henry than you do your mother," he said. "But," he added, "I can't tell you the address. I don't know it." He looked up and down the street. A couple stood in their front garden, ostensibly examining a drainpipe but clearly eavesdropping. "Over here," Isaac said. He led her down the road and into an alley that abruptly ended at a neat pile of rubble.

A house had stood on the spot, but had collapsed. Over the years since, bricks and guttering, pipework and joists had been salvaged to repair the neighbourhood buildings. Those materials not yet needed had been neatly stacked behind a crude but sturdy fence.

"This will do," Isaac said. "Keep watch."

"Why?"

Isaac smiled, and took a tablet out of his pocket. He tapped at the screen, then held it up to the side of his face. Ruth frowned, and was again about to ask Isaac what he was doing, when Isaac spoke.

"Henry, I'm with Ruth. No, she's fine. I am too, by the way. Yes, yes, all right. No, it *is* urgent. She says you're looking for a man with a limp. The barman from The White Hart fits the bill. Yes, she thinks the man had a limp. Do you know where he lived? Right. No, of course not. Of course. Henry, I promised to keep her safe. You worry too much. It's not —" He stopped speaking and lowered the tablet from his ear. "He hung up," he said.

"That's a phone!" Ruth said. "You made a phone call!"

"No need to shout it so loud," Isaac said.

"When you said Mrs Zhang called you, that's what you meant, right?"

"The barman lives on Somerset Road," Isaac said, evading her question. "Henry's still at the courthouse. I don't think he'll have any trouble getting a judge to sign off on a warrant. He'll round up some police and go and pay the barman a visit."

"How do you have a working phone?" Ruth asked. "I mean… I mean… well, how?"

"The simple answer is the radio antenna," Isaac said. "I use that as a mast. It's why I was so keen for it to be built. As more radio antennas are built, I'll be able to co-opt them into my network, and so get coverage nationwide and then across the world. There's a little cafe near the church two streets from here. They do a wonderful line in pancakes. Why don't we go and have breakfast, and I can give you the longer answer?"

"Why haven't you handed this over to the government?"

"Because a man needs a hobby," Isaac said with a grin that was intended to be disarming, but only succeeded in riling Ruth more.

"Somerset Road. Fine." She turned her back on him and stormed out of the alley.

"No, hang on, wait," Isaac called, hurrying to keep up. "Henry's taking care of it. He's organising a posse."

Ruth ignored him. There had been too many secrets and lies, too many questions. It was time she had some answers.

Somerset Road was a mixture of grand homes split into flats long before the Blackout and semi-detached houses converted into apartments in the years since. Potholes in the road's surface had been repaired, but with a shoddy mix of cement and gravel. The gutters had been cleared, but the roofs hadn't been cleaned. There were electric streetlights at the junction, but the only illumination further down the road was from windows belonging to the earliest of risers. From the flickering, most of those lights were candles or stoves. A few of the front gardens had been dug over. Some of the others had sheds, and a few even had benches. Judging by the profusion of As and Bs on the front doors, most homes were subdivided into flats, but there were very few Cs or Ds. The street wasn't home to the affluent, but at the same time, the denizens weren't poor.

"Which one?" Ruth asked.

"Henry said to wait," Isaac said.

"Since when have you ever done what he told you to?" Ruth asked. "Tell me."

"Well, now you really do remind me of him," Isaac said.

Ruth drew her truncheon. "Tell me or I'll arrest you," she said. "I'll cuff you, march you to Police House, and charge you with responsibility for the end of the world. I'll tell everyone what you did."

Isaac weighed that up. "No," he said, "you won't. But since you're that determined, it's 19B. Are you sure about this?"

Ruth didn't reply, but walked along the street, marking off the houses until she came to number nineteen.

There were two padlocked sheds in the front garden, one for each of the two flats. Ruth tried the front door. It was locked. She turned around. Isaac was smiling.

Ruth stepped aside. "I bet you know how to pick a lock," she whispered.

"Henry really isn't going to be happy," Isaac said. He pulled a small leather case out of his pocket and extracted two oddly shaped needles. He bent over the lock. It clicked.

Ruth pushed past him, and into the house. There were two doors in the hallway, 19A and 19B. She let Isaac pick the lock. Beyond the door were stairs. She put her foot on the first. It creaked.

For a moment, she wondered *what* she was doing. Then she wondered precisely *why* she was doing it. And then she heard a louder creak from upstairs. The barman was awake. All doubt fled from her mind and she bounded up the stairs. There were three doorways at the top. The one immediately in front of the stairs led into a compact kitchen with a potbellied stove whose chimney exited through the wall next to the open window. The next door led into a small sitting room. Ruth had time to think that it was a spacious flat for a man who had to be earning less than she was when a figure appeared in the third doorway. The figure was male, dressed in black, but it wasn't the barman, because who would cover their face with a mask in their own home?

"Stop!" she roared, raising her hand.

Before she could bring her pistol to bear, Isaac dived into Ruth, knocking her into the living room. There was a roar of gunfire, and a bullet whined through the air, thudding into the hallway's wall. Isaac moved to the living room doorway. He drew a monstrous handgun from a holster under his arm.

"Sorry to trouble you," Isaac called out. "I think we've got the wrong house." He was about to swing around the doorframe when there was another shot. A bullet thudded into wooden bannister surrounding the stairs. Ruth drew her revolver.

"Get out of the way," she hissed.

Isaac ignored her. Instead of pointing his gun around the door and out into the hallway, he pressed it against the wall, just underneath the old light switch now covered in a dozen coats of paint. He fired. The entire wall shuddered as the bullet was propelled through the thin plaster. Even above the roar from the monstrous hand-cannon, Ruth heard the masked man swear. Ruth hoped it was in pain.

"Sorry about that," Isaac yelled, as he took a hurried step to the right. There were three shots from the masked man, all in quick succession. One hit the living room door's frame, one the wooden bannister, the third something metallic in the kitchen. Whoever the masked man was, he was a terrible shot.

Isaac pointed to the window at the back of the room and made a circling motion with his hands. Ruth thought he meant she should climb out the window and make her way around to the front of the house so as to pin the man down. Instead she bounded into the hall. There was another roar from Isaac's gun, followed by the sound of wood splitting as the partially deflected shot hit something inside the room. In the hallway, there was no sign of the masked man. Ruth dived into the bedroom, rolled across the floor, brought her gun up and around, but the man was gone. The window was open. She ran to it. The masked man had dropped down to the street. Ruth bounded back into the hall, jumping down the stairs two at a time.

"Get back! Get Inside!" she yelled at the dishevelled couple standing in the doorway to the ground floor flat.

Outside, she saw the masked man kick down the wooden gate that marked the alley between a pair of large semi-detacheds. Gun raised, ignoring the onlookers gathering in doorways and at windows, she followed.

The alley led to a rear garden covered in an obstacle course of foot-high beanpoles and fine netting that had slowed the masked man's progress. He was only halfway across.

"Police! Stop!" she yelled.

The man half turned around, and fired. The bullet went wide. Ruth raised her revolver, but the man dived forward as Ruth pulled the trigger. A fraction of a second after her bullet hit the fence, so did the man. Wood cracked as his weight knocked the panels down. He tumbled through, down a shallow embankment on the other side, and disappeared from sight.

Ruth trampled her way through the netting. When she reached the gap in the now-broken fence, she saw the man jogging across a patch of partially cleared rubble that was turning to scrub. From the piles of bricks, it had been buildings once. Ahead was a factory that looked as if it had once been a school. Beyond that was the railway line. Ruth raised the revolver, but hesitated. The man was bobbing and weaving, but he was heading for the factory's brick wall. She launched herself down the embankment, skidding to the bottom of the slope in a spray of dirt and stones.

By the time she reached flat ground, the man was at the factory's wall, two hundred yards away from her. He'd stopped. He had his gun raised in his right hand. He lowered his weapon, and rubbed his shoulder. Was he surrendering?

Ruth took a step towards him. The man stuck his weapon into his belt, and took a step towards her. Ruth frowned. She took another step, and so did he. He raised his hands, not above his head, but stretched out in front.

Ruth took another cautious step, a sense of foreboding washing over her. She glanced around, left, right, then over her shoulder, and when she turned back to face the masked man, he'd turned around and was running for the wall.

"Stop!" Ruth yelled, uncertain whether she should fire. Before she'd made up her mind, he'd launched himself at the wall. He kicked his feet against the brick, reached up, grabbed the lip of the wall, hauled himself over, and dropped down into the factory beyond.

Ruth sprinted at the wall. Pumping her arms, she picked up speed. When she was three feet away, she launched herself at the wall. She pressed the toes of her boot against the brick, pushing herself upward. She stretched, reaching for the top of the wall, but her hand came up two inches too short. The rest of Ruth hit the wall. She slid to the ground, winded.

She picked herself up, and, with a slight limp, ran on, searching for a gate. She found it at the front of the factory. It was unlocked, and guarded by a sleeping sentry. She pushed her way through. Gun raised, she searched for the masked man. Twenty frantic, fruitless minutes later, she accepted that he'd escaped.

When she got back to Somerset Road, Ruth found that Isaac had vanished. Captain Mitchell stood outside 19B. A mixed squad of Marines, warders, and police officers were sealing off the street.

"He got away," Ruth said.

"Isaac said," Mitchell replied. "That's one more dead."

"No," Ruth said. "I mean the man escaped. I chased him, but he got away."

"The killer escaped," Mitchell said. "The victim is upstairs. Didn't you notice?" He led her back inside and upstairs. In the bedroom, lying in the bed, was a corpse. His throat had been slit. His thick black beard was now matted with blood.

"He didn't have a limp," Ruth said, only then realising. "The man I chased didn't have a limp."

"I think the victim is Mr Squires," Mitchell said. He glanced at the door, then took his tablet out of his pocket. He took a photograph of the victim's face. "I'll show this to Mrs Foster, see if she can make a positive I.D. Since he's lying in the bed, I think it's safe to assume he lived here. In which case, he's the barman from The White Hart. Do you recognise him?"

"I... I'm not sure."

"His name is Grenville Makepeace, according to Weaver. She was the one who interviewed him after your abduction."

"Then who did I chase?" Ruth asked, her eyes on the dead man's face.

"A good question," Mitchell said. "Search this place. See if you can find me an answer, or at least an answer as to why Mr Makepeace died tonight. Oh, and remember that you fired two shots in here."

"I don't think I did," Ruth said.

"Isaac was never here," Mitchell said. "It's simpler if his name stays out of the report. You came in alone, understand?" There was something in his tone, something she'd not heard before: disappointment.

"Yes, sir," she said.

She was glad when he'd left, and she could focus her mind on collecting evidence.

Mr Makepeace was well off. He had a three-room apartment on a nice street, ostensibly paid for on a barman's wage. Certainly, there was no immediately obvious clue that he had a second job. His rooms weren't particularly large, but they were well furnished, and the furnishings matched. Even in the small flat above the Dover police house, the furniture and crockery were all odd pieces, each salvaged individually from house-clearances and the National Store.

In the kitchen, she lifted the chair out from under the table, and then the other. Then she moved the table. She took out her tablet, turned on the light, and examined the polished floorboards. They were slightly discoloured underneath where the table leg stood, showing the table hadn't been moved in years. Owning furniture of a similar style was another sign of affluence, and the discolouration showed Makepeace had had that wealth for some time.

The living room contained a lot of books. At least two hundred by Ruth's quick count. They were mostly paperbacks, but they were there to be read rather than admired. The spines were cracked, and the tops had been dusted. All had a theme of war.

The room had a small two-seater sofa, but it was the chair by the window that was clearly used the most. She went into the kitchen to confirm her hunch. The man had a matching set of crockery, with enough plates and glasses to cater for four, but only the top-most plate looked well used. Similarly, the legs of one chair had marks on it that might have been caused by occasional knocking against a man's boots when he sat down. The other chair had no such marks, and the seat's padding felt less worn.

She ran a finger across the highest shelf she could reach, and then along the lip under the table. There was no dust. The man kept a clean home. He was solitary, though, and unused to having visitors. That didn't help reveal the identity of the masked man, nor why Makepeace had died.

The cupboards were well stocked, with enough food for at least two weeks, though the contents were unvaried. Tinned potatoes, peas, and cans of vitamin-enriched stewed apple that was primarily advertised as a supplement for children. There was half a loaf of bread, about two days old. Half a tin of unsweetened coffee, but no tea. A cold-box had been fitted to the exterior wall, but it was empty. She went back into the bedroom.

Perhaps Makepeace had been a go-between. The killer had hired Makepeace to rent the cottage, to collect the telegraph messages, and, presumably, a hundred and one other tasks. That way, the killer didn't care who could identify the barman since the killer always planned to murder him.

That theory lasted until she found the gun-case. It was concealed beneath a false panel at the bottom of the wardrobe. The case contained a dismantled rifle, an unloaded magazine, and four cartridges. There was a gap where a fifth was missing. They would have to do a ballistics test to confirm it, but it wasn't a great leap to assume this was the weapon with which Yanuck had been shot. That left two possibilities. Either the masked man was the sniper and Makepeace was storing his weapon. If so, then Makepeace was meant to take the fall for Yanuck's murder, and that was why he had died. Makepeace would be identified as Mr Squires, and they would stop looking for anyone else. The real killer would get away.

Ruth looked at the corpse. There was one colossal flaw in that theory. Makepeace's neck had been slit almost from ear to ear. There was no way anyone would think that was suicide or an accident. No, it was more likely that Makepeace *was* the sniper who'd killed Yanuck. In which case, who had killed Makepeace?

Chapter 17 - A Parting Gift
Twynham

Two hours later, Ruth regretted not having stopped for breakfast. She stepped out of Makepeace's bedroom and into the living room so the coroner's assistants could ease the stretcher around the landing and down the narrow stairs. Alone once more, Ruth sat on the small sofa.

The coroner had fingerprinted Makepeace's hand, and Ruth had compared that to the rifle's stock. It was a match. Of course, if Makepeace was being framed, then she would expect his prints to be on the weapon, but she was nearly certain that Makepeace was the sniper. The rifle would go into evidence, and someone else could dismantle it, searching for prints on the inside of the weapon.

Realising that sitting on the sofa, contaminating the crime scene, wasn't a good place to be found, she went back into the bedroom and collected the evidence bags. She was about to bring them downstairs, and then to Police House, when she heard footsteps that sounded as weary as her own. It was Captain Mitchell.

"Find anything?" he asked.

"A rifle," Ruth said, gesturing to the case.

"A Dragunov sniper rifle," Mitchell said as he pulled on his gloves. He picked up one of the cartridges. "That's the same calibre as the bullet that killed Yanuck. Different from the rifle Emmitt used, though."

"Dragunov? That sounds Russian."

"Only by original design," Mitchell said. "You could find a model similar to this in the armouries of Turkey, India, Ukraine, and a dozen other countries before the Blackout. Someone from the Naval Office will be able to give a more accurate assessment of which variant this weapon is. They think the ammunition we found when we arrested Adamovitch originally came from Bulgaria. I wouldn't be surprised if this came from the same stash, or one not a million miles from there. Hmmm. Yanuck was a smuggler, but his interest was in smuggling people into Britain and then blackmailing them while they were here. I'd assumed that the ammo had come from one of the groups now in Calais. What if it didn't? What if the motivation behind the attacks in Calais is to clear the continent of bandits? Get those thugs to charge westward, throwing themselves at our defences, destroying themselves and weakening us in the process?"

"I don't know," Ruth said, "but I think Makepeace was the sniper. His prints are on the weapon's stock. They could have been planted, but I don't think they were. I don't think his killer had the time."

Mitchell held the cartridge up to the light, then walked over to the window. "Do you remember me telling you about why I gave Riley the cottage?"

"You said it was to give Riley some space."

"It was," Mitchell said. "She needed room to become her own person since, in early adulthood, she was becoming too close a facsimile of myself. That was the reason, not the motivation. It's difficult being a father of a police officer. As a parent you want to keep your child safe. At the same time, you can't ask a copper not to go into danger. That doesn't mean you want to watch it. No, giving Riley some space was the right thing to do, but the reason I then left Twynham, the reason I then went to the continent, that was because I couldn't bear sitting in my room a few miles from her, not knowing if she'd made it home. There were more than a few nights when I'd take a midnight stroll just to check whether the lights were on in the cottage. Of course, who leaves the lights on when they've gone to bed? I couldn't knock on the door and check, since that would strip away the independence I wanted her to have. So, after the third night in a row when I'd waited from midnight to dawn to confirm she was safe, I went away. I had to accept there are some things I can't keep her safe from. Yes, it's difficult being the parent of a copper, though I dare say it's worse if your child is a soldier. Did you find anything else?"

"Um. No, not really," Ruth said. She wasn't sure whether he meant the story as an apology, or whether he expected her to apologise to him. She decided to focus on the investigation. "There was a handwritten ledger. It's got a lot of names and dates, then a list of numbers. Always one to ten, never anything higher. It was hidden behind the bookshelf. Some of the names appear quite often, others only once. I wondered if it might be gambling debts or something. Other than that, there's a weighted walking stick by the door, but there are no other weapons unless you count a clasp knife."

"What do you make of our victim?" Mitchell asked.

"My first impression? That he was living well beyond the means of a barman. These are nicer rooms than the apartment above the police station in Dover. Um, he read a lot. Mostly fiction, though he had some history books as well. All are about war. British wars, too. Mostly paperbacks, and mostly well read. There are no electronics. No tablets or computers. No secret hiding places, other than that false bottom to the wardrobe. Not that I've found yet, anyway."

"What about money?" Mitchell asked.

Ruth pointed to another evidence bag. "About fifty pounds."

"That's a lot, but not an unreasonable amount. Nothing that would tie him to any other part of the wider crime?"

"No."

"Hmm. Weaver interviewed him after your abduction. It was only a preliminary conversation. When you were found, our focus shifted to Longfield, and then to Emmitt. Grenville Makepeace was thirty-three years old, according to the information he gave Weaver. Orphaned by the Blackout, he drifted from place to place, doing the best he could. The mines, the railways, he even did a bit of fishing until he got the job in the pub five years ago. He was an assistant manager and worked there as often or as little as was needed. That's what he told Weaver. The question is how much of it we should believe. What she was able to confirm is that the pub is owned by the brewery, and that they only care about receipts. They have a regional manager for the entirety of Twynham, but otherwise Makepeace was left to run the pub in peace."

"He was thirteen during the Blackout," Ruth said. "Then he wasn't in the military, so how did he learn to shoot?"

"My money is on Emmitt," Mitchell said. "I know what he said, that if he'd known a sniper he wouldn't have shot the prime minister himself, but I don't believe him. Someone like Emmitt would want all the glory of that crime for themselves." He held the round up to the light. "Unless Emmitt no longer trusted him."

"It's always more questions, isn't it?" Ruth said.

"Always," Mitchell said. "But we're getting to the point where they turn into answers." He put the cartridge back into the rifle-case, and closed the lid. "I showed the photograph of his face to Mrs Foster. She confirmed that he was Mr Squires. Riley took the picture to the telegraph office and spoke to the clerk who'd seen the limping man loitering around. He remembered the small scar above his eye, the one that runs through his eyebrow. More importantly, another clerk recognised the photo as being the same man who sent the message to the warder last night. It's not exactly the official way to get a positive I.D., and it wouldn't stand up in court. By all accounts, the clerk almost had a heart attack when he saw the tablet. At any other time, we might get in trouble for that, but not today. No, not today."

"Has something else happened?" Ruth asked.

"A little after one o'clock this morning," Mitchell said, "the pirates in Calais launched an assault on our garrison. They were repulsed, but heavy casualties were taken on our side. You know how I feel about coincidences, and this doesn't feel like one of those. The fire-chief went into the courthouse. She was only able to give the briefest inspection. The fire wasn't completely out, and the lower levels are filled with smoke, but she confirmed that there was a body in Emmitt's cell. More importantly, the other cells were empty."

"You mean Adamovitch escaped?" Ruth asked.

"And an hour later, there was an attack in France. A few hours after that, Makepeace was murdered. There are many possible theories we can derive from that as to their future plans, but what seems clear is that the fire and the escape were timed to take place just as we were forced to commit more of our resources to holding the line in France. This had to have been planned long in advance. In fact, I'd say this attack was what Emmitt was waiting for. Perhaps he even planned the fire so that he could escape under its cover."

"But, instead, Adamovitch killed him," Ruth said. "This is why Yanuck was shot. Adamovitch wanted to be put in a cell opposite Emmitt just so he could make sure the man died."

"And then Adamovitch escaped, and did so after we had to commit even more of our finite resources to holding back the pirate onslaught. We *will* hold them back, and we *will* defeat them, but Calais will take priority over searching for a murderer."

Ruth frowned. "Makepeace shot Yanuck. That means he and Adamovitch were working together. I guess it was Adamovitch who killed Makepeace. That still leaves the question of who sent that cryptic telegram from Dover warning that Adamovitch was on the train."

"And we'll find out who sent it when we get to Dover," Mitchell said. "I asked Rebecca Cavendish to keep a train ready for us. At the same time, are we really likely to find this person still there?"

"True. Um… so Makepeace died because he was another loose end? At this rate, Adamovitch won't have many friends left." She looked around the room. "It really is a nice flat. I mean, *really* nice. I suppose he paid for it by being a killer for hire. In which case, why was he working in that pub if it wasn't for the money? It can't simply have been on the off-chance that they could set up the abduction of a police officer."

Mitchell's frown slid into a smile. "A very good point. Let's got and take a look at The White Hart."

The pub was shuttered. The doors were padlocked. A note pinned to the front said that the licence had been revoked and that a hearing would be held on the 9th January where evidence could be given in appeal.

"I didn't know they closed the pub," Ruth said.

"It was after the abduction," Mitchell said. "Weaver conducted the interviews, and spoke to everyone who worked here. She spoke to a few of the regulars, too. There was nothing obviously illegal going on, but I think she wanted a little retribution of her own." He pushed at the doors. "Seems secure." He fished in his pockets until he found a small bundle of keys.

"You have a key for this padlock?" Ruth asked.

"The government had them made in bulk, all to fit the same key. About six years ago, before we standardised the locks, we were locked out of one of the grain silos. You should ask Weaver about it."

"You mean she lost the key?"

"I didn't say that," Mitchell said. He frowned. "The key doesn't fit. Odd. Must be one of Weaver's. I suppose that makes sense, it wasn't as if we trusted our colleagues after your abduction." He put the key ring away and took out a small leather case of an identical style to that which Isaac had used when breaking into the barman's home. Five seconds later, the lock was open.

Inside, the air was stale, acrid with a sour tang. Mitchell pulled a compact flashlight out of his pocket and turned it on. Dust danced in the beam, and reflected off the grimy mirror behind the bar. Ruth's own torch was still in Dover. Instead, she took out the tablet, and turned on the light.

Mitchell raised an eyebrow. She shrugged. "It's the most useful thing on it," she said. "Makes for a great reading light."

An echo of a smile traced across his lips. "We can afford an hour looking here before we catch our train. Where would you start?"

"It's hard to say, isn't it?" Ruth said. "I mean, what are we actually looking for? Why would an assassin work in a pub?"

Mitchell shone the light at the door, then the walls. "The obvious reason is that he was using it to meet clients, but if he was a hitman, where are the bodies? The last few months aside, murder isn't so common we have a stack of cold cases waiting to be solved."

"There are casks behind the bar," Ruth said. "Eight wooden barrels and three square wooden boxes. It says Old Victory on this label. There's a hatch at the side. Ah, there's a metal barrel inside, stamped with the Eden Brewery."

"That's in Kent, near the border with Sussex," Mitchell said. "It's at the junction where the railway branches. One line heads to Hastings, another continues to Dover. There's not much there except the brewery, a few farms, and a repair yard for the Railway Company."

Ruth tapped the barrel. "It's still full. Okay, so what if Makepeace was a hitman, and the bodies were destroyed, or hidden in an old house somewhere?"

"He was a sniper," Mitchell said, as he lifted the dartboard from its nail. "The modus operandi is to kill people from such a distance that you can vanish before pursuit reaches you. If he aimed to hide the bodies, and thus the crime, he wouldn't shoot his victims. He'd trick them into coming to a secluded spot close to where he planned to hide the body. Why would someone hire a sniper to do that?"

"But just because he shot Yanuck doesn't mean that he always used a rifle," Ruth said.

"True, but we have to extrapolate from the evidence we have," Mitchell said, as he turned his attention to the chairs and tables.

"There's a few bottles behind the bar, and a few gaps in the dust," Ruth said. "I think someone helped themselves. Maybe that's why Weaver changed the padlock."

"Maybe. Any fingerprints?"

"Just smears," Ruth said.

"Well, whoever it was, they didn't sweep the floor," Mitchell said. "Check the register."

It was one of the new wooden tills with a cash-drawer. "It's unlocked, but there's money in it." She leafed through the notes and stamps. "Nearly forty pounds. Whoever took the bottles left the money. Or some of it. That's odd."

"Maybe a supplier who'd not been paid and saw taking the bottles as repossession. Most likely, whoever took the bottles was someone who didn't need the cash."

"Like Makepeace? So why did he come back here, because it can't just have been to get a free drink."

Mitchell crossed to the fireplace and peered up the chimney. "Nothing here. Anything under the bar? Behind the mugs? Any account books, order forms, anything like that?"

"A receipt book, a few delivery notices," Ruth said. "Nothing here that doesn't seem to belong, but it's hard to tell if anything's missing. Emmitt chose this pub for a reason, didn't he?"

"Did he?" Mitchell said, reaching up into the chimney. He pulled the lever that would close the hatch, sealing the flue. Soot cascaded down as he leapt backwards.

"Everything that happened was done for a purpose," Ruth said. "Or maybe it's better to say that Emmitt planned for everything to go wrong. Like, we were meant to find those counterfeiters, though perhaps not quite as soon as he thought. Commissioner Wallace was meant to be caught, but not in his house by us."

"And probably not alive," Mitchell said. "Go on."

"We were meant to find Ned Ludd. We weren't meant to capture Emmitt himself, but he'd already worked out his appeals in case we did. He had plans and backup plans and reasons for everything, so there had to be a reason that he chose this pub for that public meeting."

"Perhaps," Mitchell said, shining the light on the ceiling. "The meeting may have served another purpose, but it was primarily so that a police officer could be lured to a trap and abducted. Rupert Pine, the MP, was the one who told Riley about the meeting because Longfield was blackmailing him. In which case, yes, this pub was chosen as the location for a reason, and I wonder if it was because of Makepeace. Adamovitch wasn't important to Longfield. Remember how Emmitt described the butler?"

"A man who listened at keyholes."

"Exactly. Expendable, and perhaps Makepeace was the same, Emmitt no longer needed or trusted him. Perhaps Adamovitch learned of this by listening at one of Longfield's doors, and so he went to recruit Makepeace. They both knew that they would be discarded, arrested, or killed like so many of the other pawns in Emmitt's game. That is why they decided to act."

"If the plan was to abduct a police officer, Emmitt had to have known that, afterwards, you would tear down the city to look for... well, for me."

"And I was halfway through that job when I got word that Isaac had rescued you," Mitchell said. "We would have torn this pub apart. As it was, the investigation shifted. You led us to Simon Longfield, that led us to his mother, and that took us to the New Forest and to Emmitt. If we'd searched Makepeace's home, we'd have realised that he was up to something. But we didn't because the investigation had moved on."

"So Emmitt wanted us to arrest Makepeace?" Ruth asked.

"He had to," Mitchell said. "That public meeting could have been held anywhere. Well, I think we've found our motivation as to why Makepeace would work with Adamovitch to ensure that Emmitt died. We've got about forty minutes, let's try the kitchen."

Ruth followed him through the door and into the back room.

"I wouldn't want to eat anything cooked in here," she said. "The walls are practically shining with grease, except those that are covered in soot. I don't think they ever cleaned the saucepans." She opened a cupboard and quickly closed it again. "And they didn't even wash the bowls. Not properly."

Mitchell had his light fixed on the encrusted stove. "Why did Emmitt want us to search this place? What is it we're meant to find?"

Ruth shone the tablet's light around the kitchen, but nothing unusual jumped out at her. "The cellar, then?" she asked. "I mean, if I was hiding something, I wouldn't want it to be somewhere that a customer might stumble across it. On the other hand, someone came back to the pub after it was closed. How much do you want to bet that was Makepeace, and he was taking away whatever it is we're looking for?"

Mitchell checked his watch. "We'll check the cellar, and if we find nothing, we'll send for Weaver. She can get the cadets to take this place apart brick by brick while we go to Dover. Whatever it is, it might prove Makepeace was guilty of a crime, but it won't help us find Adamovitch."

Access to the cellar was through a hatch in the corridor between the kitchen and the bar. It led to steep stairs at the side of which were a pair of rails down which barrels could be rolled.

"There's a few inches of water at the bottom," Mitchell said, when he reached the bottom of the steps. "I *say* water. The smell tells me we're dealing with stale beer. That's the problem with these old pubs, there's no pump to drain the sump."

Ruth followed him down. The cellar extended beyond the front of the pub, to run for three feet under the pavement. Underneath the street was another hatch that was bolted from the inside. Like the stairs they'd just descended, there was a set of rails down which barrels could be rolled.

"That's odd," Ruth said. "Why do they need two ways to get barrels in and out? Why don't they just bring them in through the bar?"

Mitchell followed her light. "Why indeed," he said. He walked over to the hatch, and abruptly stopped underneath the pavement hatch.

"Don't move," he said.

"Why?"

"Just don't move," he said. Slowly he lowered the light to shine on his feet. There were three inches of mostly-water around his feet. Added to the angle from where Ruth stood near the stairs, she couldn't see what the light shone on.

"What is it?" she asked.

"What are you standing on?" he asked.

"Concrete, I suppose."

"Look down and check."

She shone the tablet's light at the murky water covering her feet. "It's hard to tell," she said.

"Then feel around with your hands," he said. "Do it carefully. Cautiously."

"Why?"

"Because," he said slowly and calmly, "I just stood on a metal plate. When I did, it clicked. Attached to the plate are two wires that run along the wall to somewhere over to the left. About twelve hours ago, someone burned down the courthouse with an incendiary. Now, what are you standing on?"

"Concrete," she said after a brief examination. "Just concrete."

"Okay. I want you to step back onto the stairs. Don't touch anything or step on anything that you didn't when coming down here, understand? Go upstairs. Go outside. Flag down a passer-by, and send them to get Weaver. Then clear the street. When she comes, send for… I don't know, but there has to be someone in the Navy or Marines who knows about explosives." Slowly, he fished out his tablet. "Damn, no answer. Are you still there?"

"What are you going to do?"

"Try to reach Isaac," Mitchell said.

"I'm not leaving," she said.

"Standing there isn't going to help the situation," Mitchell said. "Go and get Weaver."

Ruth ignored him. She shone the light around the room. "Can you shine your torch on the wires?"

"Ruth, leave," he said. "If this is a bomb, it didn't go off when I stepped on the plate, but it might be on a timer. Even if it's not, these wires run under three inches of stale beer and who knows what else but I'll bet it's corrosive. The circuit could break at any second."

"Right, so we don't have time to wait for Weaver. Besides, won't all the military personnel who know about explosives be in Calais? Shine your light on the wires. Find out where they go."

"If you're trying to make up for going after Makepeace alone, you don —"

"Sir, the light! Please!" Ruth said.

He shone his torch down, then up towards the left. "There are two wires," he said. "They disappear behind those metal barrels."

"Right," Ruth said. She crouched down, and stretched her hand out into the scummy water. She brushed her fingers along the ground until she was sure there was concrete beneath them. Hand extended in front of her, she sidled agonisingly slowly across the room. "It might help if you'd talk," she added.

"I'm standing on a pressure plate that's positioned beneath the hatch leading to the street," Mitchell said. "That suggests the bomb was set to go off when a delivery or collection was made. That's interesting and odd."

"I meant you should talk about something… well, distracting," she said. "I'm almost there. But, okay, why's it odd?"

"Well, because if the bomb was placed by Makepeace, then one of his co-workers would have set it off."

"Assuming it is a bomb," Ruth said. "Okay, I'm here." She'd reached the row of barrels behind which the two wires vanished. "There are lots of casks. Some wooden, some metal." She tapped one. It gonged. "It's empty."

"Just… Don't… just be careful," Mitchell said, and tried Isaac on the phone again. "No answer."

"The wires disappear behind this wooden cask."

"Behind or inside?" he asked.

"Behind," she lifted the barrel an inch. "Definitely behind."

"Don't—" Mitchell began through gritted teeth. "Look, but don't touch."

"Hard to see what I'm doing, then," she said. Carefully, she lifted the barrel up and placed it on the floor. The scum-covered water sploshed as it was displaced. "The wires go into the rack. No, into a box. Behind the box is a wall, but the bricks have been removed. I can't see anything except empty space behind it. The box is about two foot by one foot, and one foot tall. It's got a stencilled label that says it contains two-inch washers. Shall I open it?"

"No. Go outside, call for help."

"There's no time," she said. "I'll open it."

"Don't—"

"Done." She'd already lifted the lid. "What do explosives look like?"

"Depends on the kind," he said, slowly breathing out.

"It's a sort of greyish colour. Looks a little like clay."

"Plastic explosive," he said. "Maybe C4, maybe Semtex. Okay. Fine. Take a photo with your tablet."

She did.

"Show it to me."

She held it up.

"Okay, that looks like plastic. It's a little indistinct— No! Don't move. Do the wires go into the explosive?"

"No, into a metal cube, about six inches long, three inches wide. There's another wire going from that into something a bit like a metal pencil. It's sticking into the grey stuff."

"Right. Don't touch it. In fact, don't touch anything. We'll have that as a rule from now on. Quick question, did you move the box when you opened it?"

"A little, why?"

"Doesn't matter. How much is a little?"

"I picked it up."

"Right. Fine. That pencil thing is the detonator. Pull it out."

"Are you sure?"

"Positive," he said.

She did. Nothing happened.

"Now what?" she asked.

"Put the detonator down. Not on the explosives! Now, carefully, retracing your steps, go upstairs and outside."

"Is that it?"

"I think you've disarmed it, but the only way to be sure is for me to step off this pressure plate. I'm going to sprint for the stairs and then the front door. When I do that, I'd rather you weren't in the way. Go."

Ruth retraced her steps, upstairs, and then out onto the street.

She stood watching the door. A minute later, they opened. Mitchell pushed his way outside, then pushed her further down the street. They stopped twenty yards away. Another minute went by.

"I think we're okay," Mitchell said. He sat down on the kerb.

Ruth grinned. "That wasn't too bad."

Mitchell closed his eyes. "Usually, bombs like that would have some kind of anti-tamper device, maybe a primitive motion sensor. If the bomb is disturbed, the circuit is broken, the bomb is detonated. You could have set it off the moment you moved the box."

"Oh."

171

"But it didn't have one, and we're both still alive," he said. "You did good."

"Thanks. Um… how do you know about explosives?"

"I don't," he said. "What I know comes from Isaac, but that's a story for another day. Let me see your tablet, the photo you took."

"Um… sir, there are people, looking."

"Right now, I don't care."

She handed him the tablet.

"That's plastic explosive," he said. "You can shoot a bullet into it and it won't detonate. You can even set fire to it. I read about a war, once, when American soldiers would burn bricks of that stuff to boil water."

"Seriously?"

"It's ridiculously stable stuff," Mitchell said, handing the tablet back to her. "But I didn't think it had a shelf-life of over twenty years. That's something to look into."

"Did Makepeace set the bomb?" Ruth asked. "Why? Who was he trying to kill? If it was just one of his co-workers, why not shoot them? Unless he wanted the explosion to cover up something else."

"Good point," Mitchell said. He stood.

"Where are you going?"

"To find what Makepeace didn't want us to," he said. "This time, stay out here. Keep everyone back."

Onlookers were already gathering. When Ruth told them to step back, that only increased their curiosity. Ruth sent a pair of young children off to fetch Assistant Commissioner Weaver, but that further galvanised the crowd. Twenty minutes later, when Mitchell pushed the door open again, there were three-dozen people at either end of the street.

"Quite a crowd," Mitchell said. "Come inside a moment, I found an answer that satisfies many of our questions."

Ruth went back in, but Mitchell didn't go back down to the cellar. He'd brought up the metal box with the explosives, and placed it on a table. The trigger was on the bar. Next to the table was one of the metal casks.

"Here's what I think happened, and what was meant to happen," Mitchell said. "Adamovitch and Makepeace were small cogs in Longfield and Emmitt's machine. Adamovitch was going to take the fall for Longfield, and Makepeace was going to be set up by Emmitt. They both realised this, though I don't know which learned it first, or whether one told the other, or they both arrived at it separately. Together, they plotted to take over after Longfield died. Emmitt was the problem. After he wasn't immediately executed, they realised that he would escape. They probably knew exactly how and when because I think Makepeace helped construct the incendiary that destroyed the courthouse. The death of Yanuck, in that fashion, was designed to get Adamovitch into the cell close to Emmitt. I don't know how Adamovitch got out of his cell, but when he did, he prevented Emmitt from getting out of his. The fire was started, Adamovitch escaped. A few hours later, he killed Makepeace."

"Because there's no honour among thieves," Ruth said.

"And no loyalty among assassins. Makepeace, though, didn't suspect Adamovitch would betray him so quickly. The bomb was positioned so it would detonate when the brewery came to collect its barrels. Those are pricey things, barrels, and there are thirty of them here in the pub. An employee would be needed to open the hatch of course. The moment they stepped off the plate, there would be an explosion. The body would be obliterated. We would assume it was Makepeace. The brewery worker, safe outside, would even confirm that Makepeace had opened the pub. In reality, the body parts would belong to someone else. Maybe even Adamovitch. We would think Makepeace was dead, draw a line between the explosion and the fire in the courthouse, and double our efforts to find Adamovitch. I think that was Makepeace's plan. He was going to frame Adamovitch, but the butler killed the barman first."

"Is that why Makepeace killed the Luddites? He wanted Mrs Foster to give us a description of him?"

"I think so," Mitchell said.

"Okay but why did Emmitt wanted us to search the pub?"

"To shut down the smuggling ring," Mitchell said.

"What smuggling ring?" Ruth asked.

Mitchell tapped the metal barrel. "Take a look."

"Old Victory," Ruth said. She picked up the barrel. "It's empty."

"Take a closer look."

Ruth picked it up, examined the label, then turned the barrel upside down. "Can you just tell me what I'm looking for?"

"The base unscrews," Mitchell said. "Here." He showed her. The bottom five inches came away, leaving a small space inside.

"I don't get it," Ruth said. "What can you hide in there?"

"Yanuck was a smuggler," Mitchell said. "Of people, yes, but that wasn't all he was bringing in from Europe. It's ammunition, that's what they were bringing into the pub. Selling it on was Makepeace's real source of income."

"You mean the ammunition we found at that house where we arrested Adamovitch?"

"Some of it, at least," Mitchell said. "Ammunition is heavily taxed. A hunter gets ten rounds with their annual hunting licence. After that, a cartridge costs an hour's labour. The government-issued rounds won't fit in an old-world weapon, and there are plenty of those guns rusting away across the country. Thus there's a demand, and Makepeace met the supply."

"There can't have been much money in it, though," Ruth said. "I mean, you can only fit..." She turned the barrel over. "There's room for nine cartridges, maybe ten."

"I doubt Makepeace had to share it with anyone. Remember that Longfield and Emmitt's real currency was information with which they could blackmail people. It's a lot easier getting someone to commit a crime than trying to discover if they've broken the law in the past. They would know to whom the rounds had been sold, and so exactly where to apply pressure. I bet that book you found in Makepeace's flat was a list of his customers."

"And I suppose that they would need an alternative currency, I mean since the counterfeiting would have made the paper notes worthless."

"True, but at the same time, Longfield planned to take over the government. She wanted to create an insurrection, but would need to be able to control it, and ensure it fizzled out. What better way than to control the supply of ammunition? And what better way to ensure no more ammo entered the market than by having us come and close this pub? That's why Emmitt chose it for that meeting." He stood up. "We better go outside and keep an eye on that crowd until Weaver comes."

"And then Dover?" Ruth asked.

"All the clues lead back there," Mitchell said.

Ruth followed him outside. The crowd had drawn closer. Mitchell waved them back, but Ruth looked at the faces. It was supremely unlikely that Adamovitch would be here, but would he have returned to Dover?

"Sir, those pirates in Calais, they don't stand a chance, do they?" she asked.

"Not really, no," Mitchell said. "We'll take more casualties dislodging them, but we *will* manage it."

"And Emmitt would have known that, right? I mean, if he arranged for them to attack last night and on the fifth, he would have been aware we'd destroy them, right?"

"Of course. Longfield knew the strength of our forces."

"Then she and Emmitt would know that, once the bandits were defeated, we'd have to stay in Calais, and then move beyond?"

"As would anyone who's read a few history books," Mitchell said.

"What I mean is that it makes Yanuck useless," Ruth said.

"Ah, you mean he was another loose end that Longfield and Emmitt would want to tie up. Probably, and that's probably how Adamovitch enlisted his help."

"I'll be back in a moment," Ruth said.

"Where are you going?"

Ruth didn't answer, but ran back into the pub. She looked at the box, at the stencilled label on the front that claimed it contained washers. She peered closer until she was certain that she could make out the individual brush-strokes. She went back outside.

"I think I know who did it," she said.

"Who?"

"Mr Wilson was another loose end," Ruth said. "That's why he had to die. He worked in a place that repaired things, right? Metal things. He was a dab hand with a soldering iron, that's what Mr Watanabe said. I bet Mr Wilson could fix a false bottom to a metal cask. That box the bomb was in, the label looks like it's been stencilled, but it hasn't. You can see the brush marks. It's been perfectly painted on. I think it came from Sprocket and Sprung. Mr Wilson had to die because he created the barrels. He had to die because he'd finally accepted his family were gone. That's why he put their faces in that painting. Mr Wilson was willing to move on, and if he did, he might tell someone about the barrels and where they came from."

"Maybe," Mitchell said. "Maybe. There's Weaver. Let's tell her what we've found, then go to Dover and see if your theory is correct."

Chapter 18 - Travelling in Comfort
Twynham to Kent

As Mitchell and Ruth hurried away from the pub, a shadow detached itself from an alley. It was Isaac. He fell into step next to them.

"I tried to call you," Mitchell said.

"And here I am," Isaac said. "I saw Weaver, and decided to stay out of the way. You know how she gets. You've been sweating, Henry. Why so flustered?"

"There was a bomb," Ruth said.

"What?" Isaac asked.

Mitchell quickly explained.

"Yes, I would say the lesson there is not to play around with explosives," Isaac said. "Are we going to Dover, then?"

"You're meant to be keeping an eye on Riley," Mitchell said.

"She has two eyes of her own," Isaac said. "Besides, the last I saw of her, she and Maggie were going into Police House. That's one particular threshold I try not to cross, and lingering outside hardly seemed a good way of remaining inconspicuous."

"What about Ned Ludd and Mrs Foster?" Mitchell asked.

"Safe inside the convent with Mrs Zhang," Isaac said. "You know they won't let me inside. Kelly is on the roof, and she doesn't want anyone else that high, that way she'll know to shoot any shadow she sees. Loitering outside a convent would be more noticeable than the police station."

"The nuns let Ned Ludd inside," Ruth said. "Why not you?"

"Ah, it's not an issue of gender," Isaac said, sidestepping a barrow laden with wizened pears. "That's a tale that began when they required assistance mounting an expedition to Walsingham. Well, no, it began a few months before that when—"

"Not now, Isaac," Mitchell said.

"I'll tell you on the train," Isaac said to Ruth in a faux-conspiratorial whisper.

"You're coming with us?" Ruth asked.

"Of course," Isaac said. "But why is it only the two of you. Weaver seemed to have gathered a veritable army at that pub."

"There's a real army in Dover," Mitchell said. "We'll call out the Marines just as soon as we know where to deploy them."

"Wonderful," Isaac said. "I'd been planning to visit the city, but with the current restrictions, it's rather difficult."

"Restrictions?" Ruth asked. They came to a construction crew removing an old-world street light and laying a new one. There were only four workers on the project, but a crowd five times that size were eagerly offering destructive criticism. Ruth always found it surreal how life could continue, oblivious to the danger unfolding all about. "What restrictions?" she asked.

"You need a permit to travel to Kent," Mitchell said, "because of Calais."

"Oh. I didn't realise," she said.

"It's new," Mitchell said. "The paper only mentioned it on an inside page, but it'll get a more prominent coverage as soon as someone complains."

"A letter? What a splendid notion, Henry," Isaac said. "I'll jot down a few notes as we travel east. Now, tell me again about the explosive."

"Later," Mitchell said. They'd reached the station.

The terminus was bustling with goods wagons going north and coal coming south. So much coal, in fact, that four of the passenger platforms had been requisitioned for the transfer of the mineral. A thin cloud of black dust was drifting toward the long lines of passengers waiting to board the services for the Midlands, Wales, or the North. Mitchell pushed through the crowd, and through the barriers guarded by a pair of railway police, to the platforms reserved for the mail train and military services. There was only one train there, a locomotive pulling a single carriage.

"Where's the smoke stack?" Ruth asked.

"That's a diesel locomotive," Mitchell said. "It's Rebecca's new train."

Rebecca Cavendish herself was a little further down the platform, in deep discussion with a colonel of Marines. "Wait here," Mitchell added, and went to join the two women.

Ruth took in the locomotive. It was newly painted, mostly in off-white with a red cross and blue diagonals that, with a little imagination and a lot of squinting, almost looked like the Union Jack.

"Personally," Isaac said. "I'd have gone with camouflage."

"Hmm?" Ruth murmured. "Sorry?"

"For the train," Isaac said. "Rather than that red, white, and blue design. The train's going to France."

"It is?" Ruth asked.

"That's what I hear," Isaac said. "They'll use it to get troops ahead of the bandits once they've pushed them out of the city. They want that done before Christmas."

"How did you hear?" Ruth asked.

"By listening," Isaac said. Ruth didn't press. "Now, tell me again about this pub. Explain again why you were there."

So Ruth told him, though she kept her attention on the crowds on the other side of the barrier. Her impression of the station had always been that it was busy, but now it seemed frenetic, and it was only mid-afternoon.

Mitchell returned. The colonel continued her conversation with Rebecca Cavendish.

"We're going to catch a ride with Rebecca," Mitchell said. "She's taking her locomotive south in about twenty minutes. She'll collect a cargo of artillery shells from the depot near Horsham, and then take them through the Channel Tunnel. I'm going to send a telegram to Riley to let her know where we're going."

"You could call her," Isaac said. "I gave her a tablet."

"And I had to stop her from burying it in the garden," Mitchell said. "Last time I checked, it was at the back of the kitchen drawer." He walked off.

Ruth walked over to a bench and sat down. Isaac sat next to her.

"Riley doesn't trust you, does she?" Ruth said.

179

"She trusts me with Henry's life," Isaac said. "Though you're right, we have a complicated relationship."

"There was something I wanted to ask you about," Ruth said.

"About Riley? Or Mitchell? Or perhaps about that rather peculiar trip to Walsingham?"

"No. About Simon. Simon Longfield. What did you do with him? I mean, you said you sent him to Switzerland, but… well, I mean, is he dead?"

"Possibly."

"You don't know?" Ruth asked.

"I set him a task. A mission, if you like. An opportunity to redeem himself."

"In Switzerland?"

"It was an odd country," Isaac said. "You know that they had nuclear bunkers for every citizen, and that every citizen was meant to keep four months of supplies to hand in case of nuclear war? A product of being a small country surrounded by eternally belligerent neighbours."

"What's in Switzerland?" Ruth asked.

"Now? Probably nothing. Certainly not a functioning state."

"Then why did you send him?" she asked.

"It was a country once famous for many things, but perhaps most famous for its banks and its vaults."

"Ah." Ruth sensed she was getting close to the truth. "And there's something inside one of those?"

"That is what I'm not sure of," Isaac said. "There might be. There might not. If I were certain, I might have gone myself. But even if it is still there, I'm not sure it will help."

"Help who? Us, or you?"

"In the long run, both of us," Isaac said.

"This is about that artificial consciousness you created isn't it?" Ruth said. "And this phone network, that's not just so you can call Mister Mitchell, is it?"

"In a way, but only in the same way that everything is connected to the past and leading us towards the future," he said.

"After you... after you and Maggie started all of this, after you created that consciousness, after the world was destroyed, she worked in refugee camps and then she became a teacher. Whereas you... I don't know what you did, but you're not trying to redeem yourself, are you?"

"I've done nothing that would require redemption," Isaac said.

"What *are* you doing, Isaac? What are you up to?"

"A lot of things," Isaac said. "There is a lot of planning, a lot of talking, a lot of thinking here in Twynham. What's lacking are people who are actually *doing*."

"You won't tell me?"

"I'll tell you about Walsingham."

"No, don't bother," Ruth said. She remembered what Mitchell had said, and what Riley had once told her. She could only hope that, once this case was closed, the next one wouldn't involve Isaac.

When Mitchell returned he was grim-faced.

"What is it?" Isaac asked.

"I sent a message to Riley, and got one in reply," he said.

"What did she say?" Ruth asked.

Mitchell glanced around, taking in the crowd, and then the handful of workers moving towards the train. "Not here," he said. "I'll tell you when we're on the train."

The door was guarded by a burly man, six-feet-six, broad shouldered, with a tapered waist, and in a uniform that had to have been tailored for him. He saluted Captain Mitchell.

"Cooper Rehnquist," he said. "I'll show you aboard."

The carriage was different to those Ruth had previously travelled on. Those old-world passenger wagons had scratched windows, scuffed floors, and hastily re-upholstered seats. This carriage was immaculately clean and looked recently made. It was split into compartments, but with a wide aisle running down the platform-side. Running along the corridor, and underneath the exterior windows, was a polished-oak rail, positioned at the height a woman in a wheelchair could easily grab. Above the rail, the windows were clean and smear-free. Each had a set of heavy green curtains currently held back by a red braid rope. Not a single thread was hanging loose, nor was there a solitary speck of dirt on the floor, or smudge on the polished steel surrounding the compartment doors.

Judging by the discreet *unoccupied* sign above the lock, the first door belonged to a toilet. The door to the next was open. Inside was a storeroom and portable telegraph office. The third compartment contained a small galley. The one after that contained two rows of seats facing one another.

"This is you," Rehnquist said.

"How delightful," Isaac said. "Is the panelling oak?"

The guard frowned. "I… I dunno. Is it important?"

"Don't worry about him," Mitchell said. "Thank you."

They went inside and closed the door.

"Well, this *is* pleasant," Isaac said. "Though it's a little anachronistic, don't you think? Polished steel rather than chrome or brass, and it's a diesel locomotive rather than steam."

"What was in the message from Riley?" Ruth asked.

Mitchell took out the slip of yellow telegram paper. "Here."

"Ah, it's a puzzle," Isaac said. "Two words. *Arm, un-broken.* Or do you think the hyphen makes it three words?"

"What does it mean?" Ruth asked.

Before Mitchell could answer, Rebecca Cavendish opened the door.

"We're about to leave," she said. "The mail train and cargo services will be directed into sidings. It should take us two hours to reach the depot where we'll collect the artillery wagons. It'll take another two hours after that to reach Dover."

The train juddered. The carriage jolted. They began to move.

Cavendish took out a pocket watch. She smiled. "Right on time. Now, can you perhaps give me some more information on what this is about, Henry? You said you were chasing a killer. Is it connected with the fire at the courthouse?"

"It is," Mitchell said. "It's connected to a string of crimes, and they are connected to that business with Longfield."

"I heard the man you arrested in Dover escaped. Adamovitch, wasn't it? He's the one you're chasing?"

Mitchell pointed at the telegram. "It seems not. There was one corpse in the courthouse. The coroner has just completed an initial exam. The body was so badly burned we'll never be absolutely sure, but that message says the corpse's arm was un-broken. When Ruth stopped the assassination of the old prime minister, she shot Emmitt in the arm, breaking the bone. The man in the cells isn't Emmitt."

"It's Adamovitch?" Cavendish asked.

"Almost certainly," Mitchell said.

"Emmitt escaped?" Ruth asked. "He killed Adamovitch?"

"And you think he went to Dover?" Cavendish asked.

"I think so," Mitchell said. "I'd thought Adamovitch had escaped and was eliminating all the loose ends. I was wrong. Emmitt escaped, and he's seeking revenge. Someone in Dover sent that telegram warning the sniper that Adamovitch was on the train, and I can't think of anyone else Emmitt would want to kill."

"Then I'm glad this is your problem and I just have a war to fight," Cavendish said. "I'll send someone with some refreshments shortly."

She closed the door and wheeled her chair towards the engine.

"Emmitt's alive," Ruth murmured.

"It seems so," Mitchell said.

"Were we wrong about everything else?" Ruth asked.

"I don't think so," Mitchell said. "On balance, I'd say that our theory holds up to the point where the fire began. The incendiary was placed in the courthouse months ago. Possibly that was simply done in case Emmitt was arrested, perhaps there was another motive. Similarly, the assault on Calais was probably part of some other scheme. However, from the moment he was arrested, Emmitt planned to use the fire to mask his escape, and for that attack in France to tie up our resources so there would be few people to search for him. Adamovitch and Makepeace were trying to take over from Longfield and Emmitt. Adamovitch tried to murder Emmitt in those cells, but Emmitt is an assassin, Adamovitch was just a butler. He died. Emmitt escaped."

"And then Emmitt went after Makepeace," Ruth said. "I think that's who was in his room. I mean, that masked man didn't make much of an effort to kill me. The only person we know who might deliberately leave me alive is Emmitt."

"He killed Makepeace," Isaac said. "Presumably he then headed for Dover to kill… what did you say his name was?"

"Mr Watanabe," Ruth said. "He used to co-own that repair business, but sold his share so he could buy passage to Japan. Now he's just another employee. I guess he wants to return to his previous level of wealth."

"Let me see if I have this straight," Isaac said. "Yanuck ran a smuggling ring, bringing people and old-world weaponry into Britain. The ammunition was smuggled into Dover in the false bottoms of metal beer barrels that were made in this repair shop."

"By Mr Wilson, the painter and first victim," Ruth said.

"And under the instruction of Mr Watanabe," Isaac said. "Okay, these barrels went to Makepeace who sold the ammunition in Twynham. Yes?"

"And for Longfield and Emmitt, it was always more about blackmail than money," Ruth said. "Know who's committed a crime, and you can get them to commit another. But with Longfield dead, Adamovitch and Makepeace, and Watanabe, decided to take over."

"Take over what?" Isaac asked. "If the attacks on Calais were central to Emmitt's plans, and if those attacks were put in place months ago, then surely they knew that the smugglers would be useless the moment that the assault began. Emmitt wanted that smuggling ring shut down. That's why he picked the pub for that meeting. He and Longfield didn't want lots of ammunition on the streets, not long term, not when they planned to take over the government from the inside. While the authorities, namely Mitchell and as many Marines as he could muster, were chasing smugglers across Europe, those attacks on Calais would have occurred, yes? And then there would have been a regiment or two fewer to face them. Calais might have fallen, the Tunnel breached, and Dover besieged. That was Emmitt's plan. With that in tatters, what was it Adamovitch and Makepeace wanted? What did they think they'd gain? There's no more ammunition coming in from Europe. Neither of them can run for office, and that was how Longfield planned to seize power. Adamovitch was on the run. Makepeace intended to fake his own death. What I'm asking is what was their end game? Where, in all of this, did they see their victory, because the only ending I see for them is death?"

"Good point," Mitchell said. He closed his eyes, and leaned back. Ruth waited a moment to see if he'd offer an answer, then looked to Isaac to see if he'd suggest one.

Isaac shrugged. "It's a puzzle," he said. "I'm going to investigate that kitchen."

Ruth turned her eyes to the window, replaying the events, looking for the clue that she'd missed.

They sped through fields and forests, and then through ruins too fast for her to identify whether the people moving about were a work gang, scavengers, or looters.

Minutes turned to hours. Cooper Rehnquist opened the door to the compartment, informing them that they would be stopping soon to collect the cargo wagons for the garrison. By the time the wagons were attached and the train began the final leg of its journey towards Dover, Ruth realised that the only question that mattered was whether they would reach Dover before Emmitt wrought his revenge on Mr Watanabe.

Chapter 19 - Run
Dover

Rebecca Cavendish slid the door open. "We're nearing Dover, but since there's a spy there, I won't go into the city. I don't want them to know I'm shipping supplies through the Channel Tunnel."

"Spies and supplies for a war," Mitchell said as he stood. "It's everything we tried to avoid."

"And we managed it for twenty years, Henry," Cavendish said. "That's more than at anytime in recorded history."

"Only if you narrow your definition of a war," Isaac said, though only loud enough for Ruth to hear. He picked up his bag. "After you."

Ruth followed Mitchell and Cavendish to the rear of the train.

"When are you going through the Tunnel?" Henry asked.

"Tomorrow, an hour before dawn," Cavendish said. "Daylight doesn't matter underground, but we'll need it to unload the train. Electric lights would pinpoint our position, and the last thing we want is a mortar to hit the cargo wagons."

"They have mortars?" Ruth asked, as they reached the door at the rear of the train.

"Of course," Rebecca said, glancing around at her. "I thought you were stationed in Dover. Didn't you ever hear the barrages?"

"I thought those were our guns," Ruth said.

"Some of them," Cavendish said. "But they have mortars and rockets, as well as heavy machine guns. They are well armed, but they're running out of ammunition and have no means to get more."

"Good luck in Calais," Ruth said. The train began to slow.

"Luck has no place in war," Cavendish said. "Our lots were cast before the first trumpet blast, our fates decided before the bugle called. We're the cogs in the machine, waiting to break or be replaced. No, don't worry about me. After all, the last rumour I heard was that this would all be over by Christmas. This is as slow as we'll get. Jump."

Isaac leaped first, and landed nimbly. Mitchell went second, landing harder, and raised a hand to his side as he straightened. Ruth jumped, stumbled as her feet hit the ground, and almost fell.

The train sped up. Rebecca Cavendish, still by the door, raised a hand in farewell and salute. Ruth raised hers in return, and then turned to the captain.

"If Emmitt organised the pirates to attack on the fifth of November, and again the night of the fire, then do you think he also organised their supply of ammunition?"

"I think he might have controlled it," Mitchell said. "Through Yanuck or others. And with them gone, then, maybe, for once, this *will* be over by Christmas. Dover's that way."

They started walking.

"What I really meant," Ruth said, "was that Emmitt might try to escape to Calais."

"Unlikely," Mitchell said. "There's a garrison on this end of the Tunnel and an army at the other side. They've a ring of artillery around the city, with a naval blockade positioned off the coast. A narrow corridor has been left so the pirates can flee the city, but that's as much a trap as the siege is. No, Emmitt would know that, and would look for another way off this island."

"Assuming he wants to leave," Isaac said.

The sun began to set as they followed the railway towards Dover, though they didn't need daylight to spot the city. As day turned to night, and streetlights and searchlights came on, their orange glow was reflected off the heavy haze of coal smoke back onto the conurbation.

"Did you send a telegram ahead to get these suspects detained?" Isaac asked.

"No, it didn't seem wise," Mitchell said. "We might be wrong about Watanabe, and if we are, then the only suspect left is someone working in the telegraph office. The connection is tangential at best, but if I were planning to overthrow the government, the first thing I'd do seek to control the means of communication."

"More reason for me to extend the coverage of my network," Isaac said.

Ruth looked up, and almost tripped on a sleeper. "You mean the tablets, don't you? For the phone calls. Is that why you wanted come to Dover?"

"I've come to Dover to assist," Isaac said. "To assist and hopefully end something that should have been finished when the bombs fell twenty years ago."

"I told him about Emmitt," Mitchell said. "And the hotel."

"This is about me," Isaac said. "It always has been. That being said, I think it's time that Dover had its own radio station."

Ruth didn't reply.

"There's the railway gate up ahead," Mitchell said.

There were three gates in the city's walls. One to the north, one to the west, and one for the railway. The gate, like a large section of the wall, was made of sheet-steel salvaged from the hulls of ships that had run aground along the beaches near the city. The gate was now closed, though as they drew nearer, a light swung onto them. The gate clanged open, and a four-person squad ran outside.

"Halt! Advance and be recognised."

"I'm not sure that attitude will do much for the city's reputation as a tourist destination," Isaac said.

"Quiet," Mitchell said. They walked closer, stopping twenty yards from the sentries.

"I know you," the gate-captain said. "You're Constable Deering."

Ruth squinted ahead, but the glare of the spotlight made it impossible to make out his features. "I am," she said. "This is official police business."

Following a motioned instruction that Ruth couldn't see, the light swung away from them. She blinked, still blinded, but as her eyesight returned, she saw that the gate-captain was CPO Rubenstein, the senior NCO in the military police.

"I'm Captain Henry Mitchell. We're on the trail of a killer."

"Another one?" Rubenstein asked.

"It's the same case," Ruth said. "Mr Wilson's murder."

"Ah. I thought you'd arrested the people responsible," Rubenstein said.

"It's a long story," Ruth said.

"And one we don't have time for," Mitchell said. "Spread the word to the other gates, no one is to leave without my authorisation. Anyone who tries is to be detained. The same goes for anyone trying to get in."

"And what's *your* authorisation?" Rubenstein asked.

"The password of the day is Valencia," Mitchell said. He pulled a crumpled piece of paper from an inside pocket. "Here."

"Signed by the prime minister? That'll do," Rubenstein said.

"Good," Mitchell said. "Send a runner to the castle. Wake the admiral and call out the guard. We may have need of them tonight."

They left the gate and headed to the police station.

"That man is in the military police," Ruth said.

"So?" Isaac asked.

"I mean, the sentries are usually just ordinary Marines," Ruth said. "If CPO Rubenstein is doing that duty, then does that mean the Marines have been sent to France?"

"Probably," Mitchell said.

Ruth glanced back at the gate. "Sir, can we… I mean… Are you sure we're going to beat those pirates."

"Time will tell," Mitchell said.

Which wasn't the reassuring answer Ruth had hoped for.

Dusk had turned to night when they reached the police station. Sergeant Kettering was there alone, sitting behind the duty-desk with a stack of papers in front of her.

"Ruth? Captain Mitchell? You, sir, I don't know, but why are you all here? Is it a new case?" Kettering asked.

"It's more or less the same one," Mitchell said. "The murder of Mr Wilson. Those smugglers were sending bullets to Twynham where they'd be sold in a pub. The names of the purchasers were recorded so they could be blackmailed at a later date. Adamovitch is dead, as is Makepeace, the assassin who shot Yanuck. The man who killed them is Emmitt."

"The man who tried to shoot the prime minister?" Kettering said. "You think he came to Dover?"

"All things are possible," Mitchell said. "The final piece of the puzzle, the last suspect alive, is the person who sent the telegram from here warning Makepeace that Adamovitch and Yanuck were on that train."

"I followed that trail to a dead-end," Kettering said. "They've been trialling a new pre-payment scheme for short messages. You can buy the telegrams pre-stamped but with a blank message, then just drop them in a slot outside the office. I can say that the message was placed no more than thirty minutes before it was sent, but that's all I've found."

"We think it was Mr Watanabe," Ruth said. "And that Mr Wilson was the one who made the false bottoms for metal barrels, the ones they used to smuggle the bullets."

"Watanabe? Why?" Kettering asked.

"Money," Ruth said. "He was rich, now he's poor."

"Sadly, that's motive enough for most people," Kettering said.

"Do you know where he lives?" Mitchell asked.

"I've got it… somewhere… Ah, here," Kettering pulled a piece of paper from the pile. "But he'll be at work now. He supervises the late shift. Do you want backup? I can send for some sailors."

"Four of us should be enough," Mitchell said. "I'd rather do this quickly and quietly."

Twenty minutes later, the three officers and Isaac were in sight of the entrance to the Sprocket and Sprung workshop. The lights were on, but except for a streetlamp at the junction, the rest of the road was dark. Inside, a silhouetted figure moved across the wide windows of the workshop.

"No sentries," Isaac said. "How do you want to do this?"

"Properly," Mitchell said. "Isaac, take the back door. Mr Watanabe is our suspect. Others might be involved, or they all might be innocent. Sergeant Kettering and I will go in through the front, loud and fast.

Hopefully, the guilty will bolt. Deering, you come in right behind us and take up station by the front door. Remember, all of you," he added, though he looked at Isaac, "the gates are sealed, the coast is patrolled, there is no escape from Dover, and so there's no need to take any risks. Everyone clear? Everyone ready?"

"As always, Henry," Isaac said. "Give me three minutes." He eased himself backward, and jogged silently away down the street.

"He's an odd fish," Kettering said. "Where did you find him?"

"Out in the wilderness," Mitchell said. "We can trust him."

Kettering gave a noncommittal grunt but said no more. Ruth scanned the rooftops, but if Emmitt was up there, it was unlikely she'd spot him.

"It's time," Mitchell said.

He led the way, Kettering close behind, their weapons held tight in front. Ruth's own revolver was already a heavy weight in her hands. As their boots hit cracked concrete, they sounded as loud as a drum, but no one came to the warehouse door before they reached it.

Mitchell held up a hand with three fingers. Two. One. He pushed the door inward.

"Police!" he yelled, as he ran into the well-lit workspace. Kettering was two paces behind. Ruth sprinted in, revolver raised, and stopped just inside the door. She swung her weapon left and right, but there was no danger that she could see, only confused faces that were turning to fear as the guns were pointed at them. No one was running, not even Mr Watanabe. He sat at a workbench, one hand on a vice, the other holding a rasp, a heavy leather apron covering his clothes. There were five other workers in the room, all at similar workstations, holding similar tools, wearing similar expressions of shock.

Kettering made a beeline for Watanabe as Mitchell moved to the back of the room.

"Who else is here?" Kettering asked.

"No one," Watanabe said. "It's just us. Why? What's going on?"

"Ruth, go to the back," Mitchell said. "Check with Isaac whether anyone ran. Sergeant, watch them."

As Mitchell searched the rest of the workshop, Ruth went through the stockroom to the back door. It was unlocked. She pushed. There was no sign of Isaac. She took a step into the alley, thinking, for a moment, that he'd sped off in pursuit of someone.

"Is it over?" Isaac asked stepping out of the shadows.

Ruth nearly jumped. She lowered her gun. "Watanabe is inside. Did anyone run?"

"Not a soul," Isaac said.

They went back inside.

"There's no one else here," Mitchell said. "Sergeant, Isaac, watch these people. Mr Watanabe, I'd like a word, please."

Mitchell took Watanabe into Mrs Illyakov's office. Ruth followed.

The office had changed since she'd first seen it.

"What happened to the paintings?" Ruth asked, pointing at the blank wall."

"Your sergeant took them into evidence," Watanabe said. "What's going on? Why are you here?"

Mitchell looked around the office, then at Watanabe. "Do you know a man named Makepeace?"

"No," Watanabe said. "Should I?"

"What do you do here, Mr Watanabe?" Mitchell asked.

Ruth looked around the office. Without the paintings, the stark furnishings made it look utilitarian to the point of anonymous.

"We mend things," Watanabe said. "Repair things. Whatever people need."

"And who decides which of the staff work on which projects?" Mitchell asked.

"That depends on who is busy when the order comes in," Watanabe said. "Really, what's going on? We are very busy tonight. More so than usual, we received a shipment from the Navy this evening. Tools and equipment from Calais. It needs to be repaired and shipped out with the next group of reinforcements."

"If you're so busy, where's Mrs Illyakov?" Ruth asked.

"I don't know," Watanabe said. "And nor do I know where Jennings or Briars are."

"When did you last see her?" Mitchell asked.

"About two hours ago. No, a little longer. A telegram arrived. She disappeared."

"Along with two of your staff?" Mitchell asked.

"No," Watanabe said. "Their shifts hadn't started then. They should have begun work an hour ago."

Mitchell crossed to the desk. He checked the wastepaper bin, then the drawers. "No sign of a telegram. It arrived two hours ago?"

"Around then," Watanabe said.

Leaving Sergeant Kettering to guard the workshop and its employees, they went to the telegraph office. When messages came in, they were transcribed into a log-book. Mitchell ran his finger down the entries.

"It's one word," he said. "Run."

"Who sent it?" Ruth asked.

"Makepeace," Mitchell said. "It was sent two hours and…" Mitchell glanced at the clock. "Three hours and two minutes ago."

"Long after Makepeace was dead," Isaac said. "And while we were on our way here."

"Send a telegram to Twynham," Mitchell said to the operator. "Priority message to Sergeant Riley, Police House. Find out who sent the telegram to Illyakov. And I need a runner. You," he pointed at a woman, the youngest employee there. "Pen. Paper. Someone. Now!" He scrawled a note. "Take that to the admiral up at the castle. Go."

When she was gone, Mitchell led them outside, but only onto the street.

"Are we going to check Illyakov's home?" Ruth asked.

"If you were her, is that where you'd go?" Mitchell asked, watching the door.

"I suppose not," Ruth said. "Maybe to collect a few things, but then I'd leave the city. I don't know where I'd go, though."

"Right," Mitchell said. "Where is there to run to?"

"London," Isaac said. "If I were running from here, that's where I'd go. There's nothing but flooded streets and wild animals, but that makes it a good place to hide."

"London? Maybe," Mitchell said. He turned to Ruth. "If you were her, which way you go, which gate would you take?"

"Um… west, I suppose. The Marines and Navy have a training run to the north. Some go out at dawn, others at dusk. You have to get ten miles before you get some privacy. That's why they call the railway entrance The Lover's Door, but we'd have seen them if they went that way."

"The Lover's Door?" Isaac asked. "There's more to Dover than it would first appear. Westward, then?"

They jogged to the gate and reached it ten minutes later.

"Did a woman called Illyakov come through here?" Mitchell asked.

"About five-one, fifty-five years old. Petite, bony, but with broad shoulders. Has blonde-white hair," Ruth said.

"Probably travelling with two men," Isaac added.

"About an hour and a half ago," the gate-captain said. "That's pretty much all the traffic we've had."

"On foot, or on bikes?" Mitchell asked.

"On foot," the gate-captain said. "I reminded them that the gates would be closing. They said they weren't going out for long."

"Did they say where they were going, what they were doing?" Mitchell asked.

"She said something about a business decision to make. I didn't really ask."

"Were they carrying anything?" Isaac asked. "Were they armed?"

"Not that I could tell," the gate-captain said.

Mitchell scrawled a note. "Take that to the admiral," Mitchell said. "I want twenty Marines on our heels. Fully armed, and expecting trouble. The woman is suspected of working with the group in Calais. The prime minister wants them alive for questioning. And remember that we're ahead of you, so keep your fingers off triggers. Understand?"

"Yes, sir."

They borrowed three bicycles from the guards, and cycled along the dark road, away from the lights, not slowing until they reached the ruined lorry close to the cliff-top spot where Mr Wilson had drawn his inspiration. Mitchell slowed, dismounted, and leaned his bike against the lorry.

"It's too dark," Mitchell said. "On bikes, we're going to miss any trail they've left."

"You know, Henry," Isaac said, "I'm reminded that Emmitt used a truck to get away from the north after he ambushed that train. For Illyakov to have understood the full import of a one-word message, she had to have planned an escape. In which case, though they may have been on foot when they left Dover, I doubt they stayed that way for long."

"I hadn't thought of that," Ruth said. "And, because everyone goes back into the city at night, there won't be anyone to hear the sound of an engine."

"We'll walk this road until it curves to the north," Mitchell said. "We'll aim for the garrison around the Channel Tunnel. If we've found no sign of them by then, we'll detach as many sailors and Marines as can be spared and have them tear up the countryside until they find tyre marks. By now they'll be gone, of course."

"And you know where they'll have gone," Isaac said.

"London," Mitchell said. "I know. But there's no safety there. If that's where Illyakov has gone, there may be no need to go into the ruins to search for her."

"London's that bad?" Ruth asked.

"Not all of it," Mitchell said. "But you don't know which part will kill you until after it's happened. The streets are flooded. Half the buildings will collapse if you brush against them. Those that are still sound have become home to wild beasts long ago escaped from zoos. It's where the truly desperate run, and I've followed a few into its ancient streets, but there's no haven there. More pertinently, the Navy maintain a garrison on the Thames. Even if Illyakov escapes to that city, she won't escape from it."

Ruth glanced south, towards the inky blackness of the ocean's waves. She could hear them crashing against the beach, and she was reminded of one of her earlier suspicions, that of pirate raiders coming ashore. If Illyakov had planned an escape, wouldn't she have thought beyond simply getting away from Dover?"

"Ready?" Mitchell asked.

Ruth drew her revolver. Mitchell drew his sidearm. Isaac extracted his monstrous hand-cannon from the depths of his coat.

"If I'd known we were hunting bear, I'd have brought my bag of tricks. Here, a light to shine in the darkness." He passed Ruth a small flashlight. "After you, Henry."

They walked by moonlight, their torches mostly off, though occasionally flashing on when Isaac or Mitchell thought they spotted a trail. Ruth kept her eyes on the trees surrounding them. There was something familiar about the route. Obviously, it was the same one she'd walked with Mitchell when they were tracking Adamovitch only a few days before, but there was the vague shape of an older memory, too.

As they left Dover behind, the wind picked up, freshening the air. It was a chill wind, but it came from inland so didn't bring the sound of artillery from the continent. Ruth shivered at the thought, then turned her mind to the present, and her attention back to the woodland.

Mitchell paused, and raised a warning hand. Ruth and Isaac stopped. There was a flash of light as Mitchell switched on his torch. He washed the beam across the road, then turned it off, and moved to the right-hand verge. He waved them forward.

"The cottage where we found Adamovitch is a quarter mile over there," he whispered, pointing into the dense thicket of trees. "There are footprints. They're fresh."

"Going to Adamovitch's cottage?" Ruth asked.

"No," Mitchell said. "They're heading along the road. Three sets. *Only* three sets. One small, two large. I'm going to guess that's our quarry."

"You spotted those in the dark?" Ruth asked.

"Only because I was expecting them," Mitchell said. "I think I've worked it out. Up until now, we couldn't because we only had half the pieces. The other half can't be too far from here. Due west, more or less, is Folkestone and the garrison for the Channel Tunnel. Whether it was Yanuck, Emmitt, Illyakov, or Longfield, they didn't want everything hidden in one place. The second place can't be too close to the garrison, but it can't be too far from here."

It wasn't. Ruth spotted the light first, when they were another five hundred yards along the road. It came from deep inside the new-growth forest.

"There's no honest purpose for someone to be out in these woods after dark," Mitchell whispered.

"It might be pirate-raiders," Isaac said. "Come ashore to wreak havoc behind our lines." He jutted his head towards Ruth.

"The Marines can't be more than ten minutes behind us," Ruth said hurriedly. "Whether it's Illyakov or pirates, they'll run when they hear the troops coming along this road. We have to stop them."

"She's right," Mitchell said. "All we need to do is confirm the threat, and then pin them down. But remember the pub, remember the courthouse, there could be traps ahead."

"Then I'm in the lead," Isaac said, and moved into the forest before Mitchell could stop him.

Isaac moved nearly silently. Mitchell was just as quiet, speaking of both men's long experience of being pursuer or pursued out in the wilds of Britain and beyond. By comparison, and at least to her own ears, Ruth was like an elephant trampling through the undergrowth. The trees surrounding them were mostly deciduous, their leaves now dumped on the ground. Even so, little moon or star light reached the forest floor. She kept her eyes down, trying to spy the dry leaves and twigs before her feet found them. Whenever there was a particularly loud rustle or crack, she glanced ahead, but neither Isaac or Mitchell turned around, until, abruptly, they both stopped.

As the wind whipped the clouds eastward, moonlight bathed a large commercial plot. A ruined one-storey building, ringed by a car park, was situated a paved-track's length from a line of streetlamps that marked where the old road lay. Exotic vines trailed along the pocked tarmac, enveloping three rusting trucks in the car park and scaling the ruined building where a conifer's canopy jutted above the collapsed roof. Beyond the building, and either side of the paved track, were dense fields of shadowy overgrowth occasionally broken by a splinter of metal frame. There were no people, no lights, and no way for any of those three trucks to ever move again.

Ruth looked at Isaac, then at Mitchell. Both had their heads fixed towards the garden centre. Ruth turned her own towards it, trying to spot what they'd seen. There was a scrape of metal, and a shadow detached itself from a gaping hole to the left of a wall of ivy. The figure walked slowly across the car park, stopped, turned on a torch, and turned it off again, flashing the light six times in quick succession. The figure stood there, waiting for five minutes before they turned around. The figure walked to the wall of vines, and seemed to disappear into it. The vegetation had to be hanging over an old doorway.

"Isaac, take the back," Henry whispered. "I'll go in the front. Ruth, keep watch for anyone who makes it out through that wall, or who comes up that road."

"Yes, sir," Ruth said.

"It might not be Illyakov. Assume they're hostile," Mitchell said. "But let them run if they want to."

That contradictory instruction given, he tapped Isaac on the shoulder. Isaac crawled into the forest, vanishing within a few seconds. Ruth was about to ask what the signal would be when Mitchell edged forward to the screen of low bushes, then darted through them, sprinting in a crouch to the edge of the building.

Ruth re-gripped her revolver, uncertain what to do, though reasonably sure that Mitchell would be happy if she stayed exactly where she was. But she couldn't. Either she was a copper or she wasn't, and a copper's duty was to protect the innocent, and they were best served by bringing an end to the conspiracy.

She moved through the bushes until she felt broken tarmac beneath her knees. Looking at the building, she couldn't find Mitchell's shadow. Perhaps he was already inside. The nearest rusting truck was twenty yards away. She took a breath and sprinted for it.

Glass crunched loudly beneath her feet as she ducked behind the engine block. As she caught her breath and tried to quieten her beating heart, she listened for any sound from the building. Still there was nothing. She edged towards the side of the truck, shuffling her feet forward, but even so, more glass broke beneath them. She crouched down, trying to peer under the truck, but the trailing vines blocked her view.

She was about to run to the next truck, which had a clearer view of the front of the building, when there was a muffled shout from inside.

"Police!" Mitchell yelled. "Put the weapons down. You're surrounded!"

There was a shot from inside. A yell. Another shot, and then a barrage. The ivy curtain around the door flew apart as a figure ran through it.

Ruth stepped away from the truck, her revolver levelled. "Stop!" she yelled. "Police!"

It was Illyakov. She had a rifle in her hands, and she didn't stop. She swung the weapon up. Ruth fired.

Illyakov's gun went off. Bullets peppered the truck as Ruth ducked back behind its bulk, but the gunfire stopped almost as soon as it had begun. Cautiously, Ruth edged back around the truck. Illyakov was on the ground, the gun still in her grip. Just as cautiously, her revolver aimed at the woman, Ruth walked slowly towards her. Illyakov was dead. Ruth's bullet had taken her in the throat.

There was movement from the building, Ruth swung her weapon up, but it was only Isaac, though he was carrying an assault rifle in his hands.

"They're dead," he said.

"Mister Mitchell?" Ruth asked.

"Counting the evidence," Isaac said. "Is this her?"

"Yes," Ruth said. "Yes, this is Illyakov."

"Then we found her before Emmitt," Isaac said.

199

Chapter 20 - The Garrison
Folkestone

"There are no vehicles out back," Mitchell said when he finally came outside. "There's a little food and water, but only enough for the night. They weren't planning on staying here."

"The way that guy was signalling suggests they were waiting for someone," Isaac said.

Ruth bent down and searched Illyakov's corpse. "There's not much here. There's some spare ammunition. Oh, a book. I think it's in code."

"Let me see?" Isaac said. He took it. "Probably a simple cypher. Give me a few days and I'll crack it."

"Anything else?" Mitchell asked.

"Only this." Ruth shone her light on the piece of paper. "It's the telegram. One word, just like the log said. *Run.* Maybe they were waiting for the person who sent it."

"But who is that?" Isaac asked. "I thought, other than Emmitt, they're all dead or in jail."

"Sir, earlier, what did you mean by us not having half of the pieces?" Ruth asked.

"I meant the rest of the rifles and ammunition," Mitchell said. He flashed his light at the weapon still gripped in Illyakov's dead hand. "When we found Yanuck and Adamovitch there was one rifle and two thousand rounds. It's an odd number. More than a person than carry, but not more than a person could fire in a brief battle. Yet Yanuck was a smuggler, and there were three of them in that cottage. The weapons we found with Emmitt's people in those raids before we arrested him were SA80s, weapons used by the old British Army. These weapons are different, the ammunition a different calibre. We know, now, that the plan was always for Adamovitch to be arrested. It's a safe bet that Yanuck didn't know that he was destined to die in Twynham. In short, where were their weapons? Where was the rest of the ammunition?"

"It's inside?" Ruth asked.

"And there's a lot more than I was expecting," Mitchell said. "I thought there might be ten or twenty-thousand rounds and a dozen rifles."

"How much is there?"

"About a thousand AK-47 assault rifles, and around two-hundred thousand rounds of ammunition," Mitchell said. "That's not just enough to start a war. That's enough to win it."

"A thousand rifles? Who were they for?" Ruth asked.

"Albion, maybe?" Isaac suggested. "Those people up near Leicester might welcome the fire power."

"Hardly," Mitchell said. "It would bring a war that would guarantee they were wiped out. Besides, if Albion were the intended recipients, then Yanuck would have brought them ashore further north. The only way to move this quantity of weapons is by truck or—" He stopped.

"Sir?"

"You don't need to move the rifles if you can bring the people here," Mitchell said. He started walking towards the road. "Our Marines are in Calais. Our Navy is all at sea. If we were invaded, the pirates could rampage through the country for weeks before we were able to redeploy our people."

"The pirates in Calais?" Ruth asked.

"The entrance to the Channel Tunnel is only a few miles from here," Mitchell said. "They moved quickly across Europe to launch an attack on the garrison in Calais. When the garrison didn't collapse, why didn't they flee? Why did they dig in, and attack again? Sure, Emmitt might have threatened them, but they are as barbarous as he is. No, it wasn't out of fear, but because they thought they could pierce our defences. Having done so, they knew they would be able to resupply here, in Britain."

Ruth jogged to keep up. "If they made it through, they'd attack Dover, wouldn't they?"

"Some of them," Mitchell said. "They wouldn't take the castle. They probably wouldn't even take Dover, but they would cause more death and damage than we could afford. It would mean the end to any expeditions to

France for two years, maybe five. Long enough for those pirates to consolidate their grip. Long enough for a new political order to take root over here."

"But under whose leadership?" Ruth asked. "Not Emmitt's. Longfield's dead. So is Wallace. How does Illyakov benefit from continuing Longfield's scheme? She can't have thought she would run for government."

"No, and she didn't send that warning telegram to herself," Mitchell said. "Think about the time it was sent. Think about where we were."

"On the train," Ruth said.

"Yes, but more specifically we'd stopped to collect those cargo wagons. Illyakov had no food, no water, no truck in which to escape, and she wasn't running. No, she was waiting for someone, for something, but the only thing around here other than Dover is the Channel Tunnel."

"You mean someone on the train sent the message?" Ruth said. "They were going to smuggle her through to France?"

"Not exactly," Mitchell said. "For one thing, I think they'd have killed her."

"Who?"

"He means Rebecca Cavendish," Isaac said.

Hedges encroached on the road turning it into a narrow path only a few feet wide. Thorns and branches snagged at Ruth's clothing, but she didn't notice.

"Rebecca? But I thought she was your friend," Ruth said.

"So what?" Mitchell said. "The counterfeiting, the assassination, the sabotage, we were meant to discover all of those crimes. All of their plans were about sowing discord, confusion, and fear. The prize was Britain, won in an election. For it to work, the crimes had to be discovered. The clue was there from the beginning, from that first crime, the murder of Charles Carmichael. We found him in a field near a wrecked plane. And not just any plane, but one whose passengers I buried myself. One near a section of railway I helped to lay. There aren't many people who know that story, but Rebecca was one. I don't know if she was taunting me or giving me a clue. It hardly matters."

"The telegraph wires, they all run along train lines, don't they?" Ruth said. "And Emmitt knew which train Fairmont was on."

"And why were the other five Luddites killed?" Mitchell asked. "Because they knew something that we could never be told. Five telegraph wires were cut that day you stopped Ned Ludd from cutting a sixth, but who actually cut them? Who in Britain can announce their candidacy the day before the deadline and know they would win, and on winning, be selected as prime minister? Rebecca Cavendish."

"She has her own army, Henry. All those guards and railway police."

"Yes, but right now, she's surrounded by the garrison at the Channel Tunnel. We have to stop her getting to France. She knows too much. She knows everything, from where the munitions are kept to the disposition of every garrison."

They turned their run into a sprint.

The hedges vanished as they reached a section of road where vegetation had been cut back. After ten yards, that clearance extended far beyond the kerb. The fields either side had been emptied. A few solitary stumps marked where ancient trees had once stood, but even the trunks and had been taken away. The battered multi-arrowed road sign for the Channel Tunnel was redundant, because, ahead, were more lights than Ruth had seen outside of Twynham. There were even four suspended from a reconnaissance balloon a hundred metres up in the air, shining their spotlights down on the compass-point gates of the garrison. One of those lights abruptly changed direction, and came to cast a wide circle around the three of them, tracking them as they ran.

A minute and fifty metres closer, eight small lights appeared on the road, quickly getting brighter until they came to a halt at the edge of the searchlight's circle. It was eight Marines, each on a bicycle. They quickly dismounted, leaving their bikes propped on the road.

"Halt!" the sergeant yelled.

Mitchell raised his hands above his head, and slowed his run to a walk.

"I said halt!"

"Police! Police," Mitchell yelled, slowing fractionally more. "Has the train left? Is Cavendish still here?"

There was a clatter behind the Marines as a bike toppled over, knocking down the one next to it. Half the Marines swung around, two pivoted to the right, as they searched the darkness for some new threat. Only the Marine who'd spoken, and another next to her, kept their gaze on Mitchell, Isaac, and Ruth. They were older, Ruth realised. Rather, she realised just how young the rest of the patrol was. Recent recruits, she thought, just like Weaver had been using, though the reason was very different here.

"Eyes front!" the sergeant barked.

"We're police," Mitchell said. He reached a hand towards his pocket. At the sudden movement, one of the recruits swung his rifle up, aiming at Mitchell's face.

"Easy," the sergeant said, the words spoken both to her recruits and to the captain.

"Password of the day is Valencia, tomorrow's is Cadiz. My warrant," Mitchell said, taking out a folded piece of paper. "Signed by the prime minister. We're tracking a killer, one with a connection to Calais. Has the ammunition train left?"

The sergeant glanced at the letter. "The train's still here," she said.

"Good. Send three of your people south. There's an old garden centre about a mile from here. There's a body outside, and two corpses inside along with about a thousand assault rifles. There's a platoon coming from Dover, they should be there by now. Send three of your people to make sure the platoon's secured it. Send word back to Dover to expect an attack, then one of them is to return here and confirm the message has been received. We'll take their bikes."

While the sergeant was still issuing the command, Mitchell pushed his way through the group of Marines, grabbed a bicycle, and started cycling towards the lights. Ruth mounted a bike and followed the captain.

Half a mile further north, they came to the depot. Giant wire gates ran across the road. Set on rails embedded in concrete, they were closed.

Mitchell yelled at the figure in the watchtower, but it was only when the sergeant of Marines caught up with them and barked a command of her own that the gates were opened.

It was almost as bright as day inside the depot. Lights streamed from scores of log cabins and a handful of pre-Blackout brick structures. They shone inward from the gate tower and down from the balloon. Even the Channel Tunnel entrance was brightly lit. On the tracks in front of it was Cavendish's train. Around it were her railway guards, but nearby were scores of Marines.

"We need to get closer," Mitchell said. He turned to the sergeant. "Call out the guards. Call out the regiments. Call out everyone. On that train are people who are in league with the pirates in Calais. That train can't be allowed to leave, but the cargo wagons are full of artillery rounds. An unlucky bullet could destroy us all. Go!"

The sergeant sprinted away. Mitchell turned to the remainder of the Marine patrol that had followed them. He looked at each young face in turn. "Don't shoot unless you're sure of your target." He hesitated, shook his head, and cycled downhill, towards the train.

As the road curved away from the tracks, Mitchell jumped from his bike, skidding down an incline of gravel and sand. Ruth followed, her eyes fixed on Mitchell's back. She tried to keep one hand on her holstered revolver. She slipped, but there was an arm at her elbow, lifting her up.

"Watch your step," Isaac said.

Ruth nodded, turned her attention back to the train, and her focus to catching up with Mitchell.

They were four hundred yards from the train. Outside it were five people wearing the uniform of the Railway Company, but three wearing that of the Marines. On the platform, near a grey-clad building, were a score more, now watching the running figures.

Ruth wondered if Mitchell would shout a warning, or even shoot; he didn't. He just kept running.

One of the two railway guards at the back of the train saw them. He raised a shout. The guard at the middle of the train sprinted along the side of the cargo wagons. When she reached the carriages behind the locomotive, the guard jumped aboard. At the front, the two railway guards by the engine climbed on. The Marines they'd been talking to turned around, looking confused.

Five, Ruth thought, there were at least five. There were two more in railway-green on the platform, but they were acting as confused as the Marines. Perhaps that meant that not all the Railway Company were in league with Cavendish.

The two guards at the rear of the train climbed aboard. One stayed on the narrow platform at the rear of the wagon, the other went inside. A moment later, he came out carrying two rifles. He handed one to his comrade. He raised the other and fired a burst at Mitchell, Ruth, Isaac, and the running Marines.

A scream came from behind her, but Ruth didn't turn to look. Instead, she jinked left then right. The guard adjusted his sights and fired again. Dirt sprayed up in front of Ruth. The other guard brought his rifle to bear, and both of the weapons' barrels seemed to be pointing straight at her. There was another shot, but this one came from Ruth's left. One of the railway guards collapsed. The other edged backward into the doorway as Isaac, his rifle still held tight to his shoulder, ran past. Mitchell was already twenty yards ahead of Ruth, and fifty yards from the train. Fifty-one yards. The train was moving.

More shots came, but these weren't fired from the rear of the train, and they weren't aimed at Ruth, Isaac, or Mitchell. Most of the Marines on the platform, there to help load the trains, were unarmed. When the firing began, they'd grabbed shovels and picks, knifes and poles, and had charged at the train. They were cut down by machine-gun fire before they got close.

Screaming came from the platform. A yell of pain came from behind. Gunfire came from everywhere, and Ruth could no longer tell who was firing, or whether anyone was firing at her.

Mitchell was ten yards from the train, his hand already reaching out for the handrail by the ladder when the guard reappeared in the doorway. Before the guard could fire, Isaac did. The guard collapsed. Mitchell reached the train, and pulled himself aboard.

Isaac was ten paces behind. Eight. Six. Mitchell leaned out. Isaac let one hand fall from his rifle. He grabbed Mitchell's hand. Mitchell pulled him on board. Ruth was twenty paces away, and the train was accelerating.

Isaac gave Ruth a wave, and vanished inside the wagon. Mitchell gave her a nod of farewell and followed.

They were leaving her behind. She almost stopped, then. She almost let the train disappear into the Tunnel. Riley's words came back to her. Either she was a copper or she wasn't, and if she wasn't, what was she doing out here? Another memory of Riley came to her. Not of Riley in the wheelchair, but of the sergeant lying in the staircase of Longfield Hall, bleeding, close to death. Ruth sprinted the last ten yards, jumped, and grabbed the handrail. The metal was cold, damp, and she almost lost her grip. Her legs were pulled forwards, the tips of her right boot brushed against the wagon's spinning wheel. And then there was a hand at her wrist, pulling her up and onto the narrow platform.

"Just like Maggie," Isaac said. "You truly don't know when to quit."

Behind them, Ruth could see the Tunnel's entrance, and the Marines gathered there. Thankfully, they held their fire, but there had been no other train at the platform, there would be no help until they reached Calais.

The lights grew dimmer as the train sped away from the entrance, and deeper into the Channel Tunnel.

"We better join Henry," Isaac said.

They went inside.

Chapter 21 - The Front Line
Calais

The wagon was a pre-Blackout passenger carriage that had been re-purposed to carry cargo. The seats had been removed, and metal racks put in their place. Each of those contained a wooden box, though it was too dark to read the stencilling on the side. Two electric lanterns hung from the ceiling, but they were fitted with the recently manufactured bulbs whose dim illumination only added depth to the shadows. Metal sheets had been riveted over the windows, but they were already deep into the Channel Tunnel and beyond the lights around the entrance. Ruth had dropped her borrowed torch somewhere. There was a brief flash of humour when she imagined the consternation of the technophobic Marine who found it. That vanished when she saw the corpse.

A dark stain slowly spread from the three neat bullet holes across the woman's green railway company uniform. There was no weapon next to her, but Captain Mitchell had an assault rifle in one hand as he used the other to check the doors in the centre of the wagon.

"I think I saw her climbing into the carriage," Ruth said. "I counted five guards."

"Who were outside, yes," Mitchell said. "Plus someone who started the engine. That was probably Rebecca. There was no ramp leading from the train down to the platform, so she must have already been on board."

"Three dead, then," Isaac said. "And at least three more, still alive."

"The doors on either side are jammed closed," Mitchell said. "In the old world, there was an electric lock, but that was modified by a handle to manually open the mechanism. It's been broken."

"If the doors are sealed, how are they meant to unload the ammunition at the other end?" she asked.

"They're not," Isaac said. Rifle held low, he followed Mitchell towards the door at the end of the wagon that connected it with the next.

Ruth's mouth opened automatically to ask him what he meant, but then she understood. She checked her revolver was loaded, then followed the other two.

Mitchell reached the door, and pulled the handle down. The door swung open. There was a narrow gap between the two carriages, covered by three lengths of wooden panelling set on small turntables so that they moved with the motion of the train. The sides were covered in thick leather and loose chains. As Mitchell opened the door to the next carriage, a barrage of gunfire slammed into it, pushing it closed. One bullet went straight through, passing within an inch of Ruth's ear.

"Duck down," Mitchell hissed. "Aim high, Isaac."

"High it is," he said.

"One," Mitchell said and pushed the door open. He dived through as more gunfire came from ahead. Isaac had raised his gun and fired straight up at the roof. "Two," he muttered, and then, loud enough for his voice to be heard over the rattling wheels, he yelled "While it's unlikely a stray round will set off one of these shells, the chances increase with each shot you fire. Do you really want to die down here?"

There was a burst of gunfire from ahead. Rounds bit into the door and wagon's walls, others thudded into wooden crates.

"I guess he does." Isaac fired another shot at the roof.

There was a short burst from ahead.

"Clear!" Mitchell called.

Isaac pushed himself forward, sprinting down the carriage, rifle raised to his shoulder. Ruth followed.

Mitchell was bent over a man. "Dead," he said, his voice absent of emotion. "Did you see the wire?"

"In the connecting corridor, yes," Isaac said. "That confirms it."

"Taken with the doors, yes," Mitchell said.

"What wire?" Ruth asked.

"The entire train is one giant bomb," Mitchell said. "Missile might be a better word. When it reaches Calais, it'll detonate. It might be on a timer, it might be on a remote trigger. It might be set to a plate attached to the very front of the locomotive so that it explodes when it hits the first obstacle. I don't know. What I do know is that if this train explodes in Calais, it would rip a hole right through our lines. The pirates can attack, and they'll head through the Tunnel. They'd reach Folkestone and a garrison of recruits and walking wounded. And then they'd go looking for that garden centre with the stash of rifles and ammunition."

"But Cavendish will have to stop the train to get out, right?" Ruth asked.

"Assuming she hasn't decided to kill herself to complete the mission," Mitchell said. "Though that isn't like her. There are two rail tunnels connected by a service tunnel, though we only maintain one rail line. If she stops the train, she'll have to exit via the service tunnel, and that'll still bring her out in Folkestone or Calais. That's the good news. The bad news is that the Channel Tunnel's only thirty miles long. We're travelling at about forty-five miles an hour. We don't have long."

"And there are two hostiles left," Isaac said. "I say we go hard and fast through the last wagon, then her carriage, and to the locomotive. We'll detach it from the cargo wagons. If there is an explosion, it'll be in the Tunnel. The garrison will be safe."

Mitchell picked up the rifle next to the corpse. He held it out to Ruth. "You know how to fire this?"

"Sure. Kelly taught me. Well, it was something like this."

"This train *can't* reach Calais," Mitchell said. "If it does, thousands will die in the next few hours, tens of thousands more before the month is out. It can't reach Calais. Do you understand?"

"I do," Ruth said. She holstered her revolver and took the assault rifle. Kelly had showed her how an assault rifle worked. Although it would be more accurate to say she had given Ruth a lesson in how savage the recoil could be while Isaac had looked on, laughing.

"Be glad you're a copper," Mitchell said. "Sorry, Ruth." He ran to the connecting door, Isaac close on his heels. The captain threw the door open, and ran into the wagon. No shots came. The wagon was empty.

"Just the carriage, then the locomotive," Mitchell said, moving quickly past the racks of munitions. He pulled open the door connecting the wagon to Cavendish's carriage. "You see the wires?"

They were thick, and there were three of them, running through the wall of the cargo wagon, disappearing into a hole in the carriage wall.

"They had to have been installed after we got off the train," Mitchell said. "So it was done quickly, probably after we alighted and before they arrived in Folkestone. Isaac, if you can find the trigger, try to disarm it. I'll take the locomotive. Ruth, watch Isaac's back. Ready?" He pulled open the door. No shots came. The corridor running the length of the carriage was empty. The wire snaked along the polished wooden floor until it disappeared into a compartment near the front.

Mitchell bounded forward, sprinting for the far end of the carriage. Isaac stayed close behind. Ruth brought up the rear, her eyes on the dimly lit end of the corridor until she heard a sound behind her. As she turned around, she saw the door to a compartment open. The guard, Cooper Rehnquist, pushed himself outside. The giant man had a hatchet in his left hand, a hammer in the other. He snarled. He was four feet away. Ruth barely had time to bring the assault rifle up. Her first shot took him in the groin. The man screamed, doubling over as the recoil brought the gun up another inch. Ruth's finger hadn't left the trigger, and the gun was still set to fully automatic. Bullets thumped into the man as he fell. Into his stomach, his chest, his neck, his head. Blood and flesh sprayed the carriage walls. Bullets thumped into wall and the roof until the hammer clicked on an empty chamber.

"He's dead!" Isaac yelled. "Keep going, Henry."

Ruth turned around. Mitchell had disappeared. Ruth dropped the rifle, drew her revolver, and bounded past Isaac as he entered the cabin into which the wires ran. She reached the locomotive, just behind Mitchell.

There was a figure there, a woman, but she was standing by the engine's controls. The woman turned around, wildly firing a revolver. Ruth returned fire. So did Mitchell. The woman collapsed, and Ruth didn't know whether it was her bullet or the captain's that had killed her.

Mitchell slung his rifle, grabbed the bars either side of the short ladder, and climbed up into the locomotive's cab. Ruth followed.

"That's not Cavendish," Ruth said.

"No," Mitchell said. "That explains how she planned to escape. She was never on the train."

"Which is the brake?" Ruth asked.

"That is," Mitchell said, pointing to a long length of metal lying on the cab's floor. "Carrie was dismantling it."

"Carrie? That's her name?"

"She was with Cavendish from the start," Mitchell said. "Another rescued orphan, much like Riley."

"And she was going to kill herself for Cavendish?" Ruth asked, raising her voice as her words were whipped away by the wind.

"If things had worked out a little differently, I might have done the same myself," Mitchell said. "Loyalty's an odd thing. Now, let's see if we can stop the train."

The train rattled on. Ruth couldn't tell if it was picking up speed, and the instruments were no help. Some were covered in blood, others had been smashed by Carrie, others damaged by bullets. Those that were intact meant nothing to Ruth.

The door to the carriage opened, but before Ruth could raise her weapon, she saw it was Isaac.

"Did you dismantle it?" Mitchell asked.

"More or less," Isaac said. "It was on a one-minute timer that hadn't been activated. What was more interesting was who else was in that compartment."

"Who?" Ruth asked.

"I don't know her name," Isaac said, "but she was already dead and in a wheelchair. Not much of her would have been found when the bomb went off, but it might have been enough to make you think Cavendish was on the train. I take it she isn't?"

"No. It was just her," Mitchell said, pointing at the corpse. "She sabotaged the train before we got her. Do you think you can stop it?"

Isaac stepped up into the cab, and over the corpse. "Hmm… no. Maybe. Mechanical was never my interest. Digital, yes. Circuitry, to some extent. Mechanical, not so much."

"The train can't reach Calais," Mitchell said.

"I know," Isaac said.

"Won't they have sent a telegram from Folkestone?" Ruth asked.

"Perhaps, assuming the telegraph wasn't cut," Mitchell said. "But there's not much they can do at that end. Certainly not in time. We'll be there in about ten minutes. Fifteen at the outside."

"Then there are three options," Isaac said. "We can use a mortar shell to derail the locomotive, but that might set off the rest of the cargo. I don't know whether the Tunnel was built to withstand an explosion from the inside, but there would be smoke, there would be fire, and the Tunnel would be impassable until it's put out and any damage to the tracks and the air-circulation system repaired."

"What are the other two options?" Mitchell asked.

"Use a smaller explosive to destroy the coupling between the locomotive and the carriage." He pointed at the length of metal connecting the engine to the carriage. "The handle's been broken. We can't disconnect it, but we might be able to blow them apart. We're on an incline now, without forward motion, gravity will bring the carriages to a halt."

"Assuming that the wagons aren't derailed, and that the cargo doesn't explode," Mitchell said.

"Right, so that leaves option three," Isaac said. "As I say, we're on an incline. Gravity will act as a brake if we can shut down the locomotive."

"And that's what I was asking you," Mitchell said. "How do we stop the train?"

Isaac unslung his rifle "Shoot the damn thing and hope we hit something important."

The first three magazines did nothing but send ricochets pinging into the Tunnel's walls. The fourth magazine brought up a haze of smoke. Ruth was sent back into the carriage to collect ammo from the corpses. She found none on Rehnquist, so went back into the cargo wagons. She was on her way back to the front when the train began to slow. Thick smoke billowed from the engine, filling the corridor of the carriage.

"Will fire set off the cargo wagons?" she asked, coughing around the words.

"Almost certainly," Isaac said, taking the ammunition from her. "Still, the train *is* slowing. I think the garrison is safe."

"Not if the fire spreads," Mitchell said, pushing them back into the carriage. He shut the door. "How fast are we going? Too fast. If the cargo explodes, the Tunnel will be impassable, the garrison cut off."

"Other than saying a prayer to Isaac Newton, I'm not sure what else we can do," Isaac said.

The train continued to slow. Smoke crept around the door and into the carriage. Mitchell tried the door at the side. Like those in the cargo wagons, it was sealed. He raised his rifle, and fired at the window. Glass shattered. He peered outside. "Slow enough, and slower than a run. Ruth, I'm going to lower you outside. There's not much clearance, so be careful. Run ahead. Get to the garrison. Get fire extinguishers. Get cutting equipment. Get people."

"Get help. Got it," Ruth said.

Mitchell and Isaac lowered her outside. The train was barely moving, but the smoke was a thick blanket. Her left arm brushing against the Tunnel wall, she ran as smoke filled her lungs. She ran as flames licked at her coat. She ran as sparks landed in her hair. She ran past the burning locomotive, and kept running, towards the flickering lights at the end of the tunnel. Those lights were wrong. They were caused by open flame not electric lamps. As she outdistanced the train, the sound of metal grinding against metal was replaced with the dull crump and roar of artillery. That sound grew louder, all-encompassing, filling her world.

There was a sentry ahead, standing next to a pair of burning braziers. He stepped towards Ruth, the flames lit up his face and a thoroughly confused expression.

"Where'd you come from?" he asked. His hand was bandaged, his uniform torn and muddy, but his rifle was clean.

"The ammunition train. The locomotive. It's on fire!" Ruth gasped.

"Sarge! Sergeant!" the Marine barked.

A moment later, another figure appeared. This one was familiar, though it took Ruth a moment to place her.

"Corporal Lin?"

"Sergeant Lin, now," Lin said. "Ruth Deering, isn't it? Why's a copper come to France? Don't tell me they've run out of crimes in Britain?"

"The ammunition train, it was booby-trapped," Ruth said. "The locomotive is on fire. If it spreads—" But she didn't have a chance to finish. She didn't need to.

"On your feet, those of you who've still got 'em!" Lin yelled into the darkness. "The artillery train's on fire! Get the shells off. Get it into the service tunnel! Go!"

More orders were given, sending for a fire crew, for more Marines, for a general. As figures ran into the Channel Tunnel, Ruth stood, blinking, confused, disorientated by the constant barrage coming from the east.

"Talk to me while we run," Lin said, heading towards the train. "What's going on?"

"Sabotage," Ruth said. "The train was turned into a bomb."

"Sabotage?" Lin said. "That must be what happened to the lights."

"The lights?" Ruth asked.

"In the Channel Tunnel. Electricity comes from the power station in Dover. The lights went out about an hour ago. The cable must have been cut."

"What about the telegraph?" Ruth asked. "Is that intact?"

"No idea," Lin said. "The fans have stopped as well. Was that you?"

"Fans? What fans?"

"They have to circulate air through the Tunnel," Lin said. "It's why the smoke's not clearing."

If anything, the smoke grew thicker as they neared the locomotive.

"Down the sides!" Lin called. "And out through the service tunnels." She turned around, and grabbed the bandaged arm of the next Marine. The man winced. "Sorry. Go back up the tracks. Get everyone into the service tunnels. The shells go back that way, away from the locomotive. Everyone stays away from the fire!" She turned back to Ruth. "Everyone but us."

There were no flames, just thickly cloying smoke as they eased their way past the locomotive. Mitchell stood by the carriage.

"Lin? They sent you here?"

"It was my reward for going after Longfield," Lin said. "I've sent for the fire crew, and left someone up the track, they'll send everyone else through the service tunnel."

"Good," Mitchell said. "Because the wagon doors are—" He was interrupted by a loud creak, a rasp, a snap as metal was torn from its hinges. Ruth flinched, but it was only the first of the Marines. By bayonet and brute force, they'd levered the jammed doors apart.

Two minutes later, smoke now billowing freely from the locomotive, Ruth was one side of a crate, Lin the other, running through the cross-passage linking it with the service tunnel.

"You've been here since the first attack?" Ruth asked.

"On the fifth, yes," Lin said. "And before. I was here before they arrived. Not many of us left who were, not now."

Before Ruth could ask another question, they emerged from the cross-passage and into the access tunnel. Flickering candles and dim flashlights illuminated scores of stretchers laid end-to-end. Medics flitted from one to the next, sidestepping the hale and walking-wounded hauling crates towards the entrance.

"There are so many," Ruth murmured.

"They've been targeting our hospitals," Lin said. "That's who we're— Woah!" The sergeant slipped in a patch of viscous fluid. As she stood, for the first time, Ruth saw the stained bandage on Lin's leg.

"Are you okay?" Ruth asked.

"It's nothing but a scratch," Lin said, "and nothing compared to what these shells will do to the Cossacks."

They hurried on, though the sergeant was noticeably trying not to limp. As they neared the Tunnel's entrance, a squad of far-too-young but bandage-free Marines ran towards them. Some carried battered extinguishers, others axes and tools, and a few had buckets of sand.

"Where are the hoses?" Lin barked at the fire crew.

"There's no pressure," the fire-chief replied. "Not until they get the power line back up."

"Damn it," Lin muttered, leading Ruth towards a ruined building with bullet-flecked tricolour painted on the one remaining wall. They followed the other Marines down a narrow ramp and into the building's basement, adding their crate to the growing stack being opened and inspected by an older man with a week's worth of stubble.

Ruth took a step back, and then a look around. Few of the other men in the dimly lit basement were old enough to shave. The women were similarly young, too young. All, Ruth realised, the same age as her. New recruits, not old hands, yet even if the mud and grime was cleaned from their cheeks, they wouldn't be fresh faced underneath. There was a depth of experience in their eyes that spoke of the horrors they'd witnessed in the last few murderous days.

"General," Lin said.

Ruth turned around. The sergeant was speaking to one of the few other older people in the basement, a moustachioed man in his mid-fifties with sunken cheeks and wild eyes.

"General, it's the artillery train," Lin said. "The locomotive is on fire. We need to get it unloaded. We need those shells."

"On fire?" the general asked. "How?"

Lin shook her head. "Move, you lot!" she barked at the Marines. "If you've got two legs and at least one arm, get down that tunnel now, before the whole lot explodes!"

"Explodes?" The general said. "Then I should... I should contact high command."

"The telegraph is working, then?" Ruth asked.

"Who are you?" the general asked.

"Deering, police," Ruth said. "Is the telegraph working? We need to..." She hesitated, then decided a lie was better than the truth. "We need to report back to the prime minister immediately."

"What? You do? No. No, the telegraph stopped working when the power was cut. I... I should write my report. Yes. The prime minister will want it."

The general hurried away. Lin shook her head.

"General Stevens," Lin said. "It's not so much lions led by lambs as tigers commanded by a blind jellyfish." She winced, and looked down at her bandaged leg. "Back to it. We'll rest when we're dead."

They joined the crowd of Marines flowing into the service tunnel. As they threaded their way between the medics, the injured, and those bringing crates back down, Ruth lost sight of the sergeant. When she reached the train she ended up on one side of a crate with a turbaned man twice her size on the other.

"You're a copper," he said, in the soft burr of the Scottish lowlands.

"We were pursuing a criminal," Ruth said.

"Into a war zone? Talk about dedication," he said as they ran.

"Ruth Deering," Ruth said.

"Fazle Bhatt," he said. "Do you know when the reinforcements are going to arrive?"

"Sorry," Ruth said. "I'm just a constable."

"I know that story. They tell you nothing, nothing except hurry up and wait."

They ran through the lines of Marines streaming into and out of the service tunnel, and then past the growing pile of crates.

"We need to get these to my squad. You mind?" Bhatt asked.

"Sure," Ruth said. The box wasn't that heavy, but Bhatt's legs were far longer than hers. While he jogged easily along the side of the tracks she had to run just to avoid being dragged along. The railway tracks widened, branching and multiplying as they ran through the switching yard and toward the old terminal building where one wall appeared to be recently painted white.

"That was the hospital," Bhatt said. "We had a red cross on it at first, but that only gave them something to aim their mortars at."

"They targeted a hospital?" Ruth asked.

"Welcome to hell," Bhatt said.

Ruth had seen ruins before. She'd seen craters. She'd seen the glassy hole that marked where an atomic bomb had impacted. In Twynham, ruins had been levelled, repaired, or systematically dismantled for their component parts. Outside of Twynham, the ruins abandoned by humans had been occupied by flora, with wallflowers and weeds erupting from every crack in the mortar. This corner of France was infinitely worse. It was a place of mud and ice, of foetid water-filled shell craters, of scorched tree trunks absent of branches in a new growth forest that had spread across what must have been fields before the Blackout. Ruth reflexively ducked as shells whined and exploded, but Bhatt ran on, through the shattered woodland and into the ruined city of Calais, where the sea of mud was replaced by fractured bricks and broken concrete. The skyline, lit up by flares fired from the British lines, had been reduced to jagged splinters of brick in a landscape where no building remained whole.

"Incoming!" an unseen voice yelled.

Bhatt hauled the crate towards a shallow trench. As Ruth held the other end, she was dragged along and down into the dank, muddy interior. A moment later, there was a loud crump-crump-crump. The ground shook.

"Got to keep moving," Bhatt said, all good cheer gone from his voice. "Make a hole!" he barked at four walking wounded crouching to keep their heads below the parapet. Each Marine was bandaged, but each carried a rifle, and all were heading back towards the front line.

The trench took an abrupt right turn, then one to the left that ran through an old underground car park filled with smoke but few people. There were no signs, but Bhatt knew the way. The car park's wall had been breached. Beyond, a tunnel sloped upward into the basement of what had once been a home, then through another broken wall into the below-ground dining area of a restaurant. Ten Marines nervously adjusted straps while another four calmly played a hand of cards as they all waited for the order to attack.

Bhatt angled for the stairwell, then paused at its base. Ruth looked up and saw the ceiling turn orange. No, not the ceiling, she realised. It was the sky, illuminated by a flare. As she watched, the artillery barrage grew in intensity.

"We're returning fire," Bhatt said. He grinned. "Now we'll have them."

"You were that low on ammunition?" Ruth asked.

"The train was meant to arrive last night," Bhatt said. "They started attacking at sunset and never stopped."

Cavendish, Ruth thought. Or perhaps it was Emmitt, but someone had organised another co-ordinated attack, designed to push the infantry back towards the Channel Tunnel. Then, when the sabotaged train arrived, they would have been wiped out.

"Wait for the flare," Bhatt said as the orange glow began to subside. "Now."

He led her up the stairs, and then across a jumble of broken steel and brick towards the shattered plate glass window of a shop. A bullet whined past Ruth's ear. Against the background roar, she barely heard it. They ran through the shop, into a paved area that would once have been filled with chairs and tables. The tables were gone, and the paving slabs ripped up, added to the windows of a three-storey apartment building. From the bare girders, the building had once been taller, but only those three storeys remained.

"Preston!" Bhatt called. "Preston!"

"Weston!" a voice called back.

Bhatt led her through a narrow gap by a twisted girder.

"I got 'em, sir," Bhatt said.

Ruth blinked as a Marine turned on a torch and shone it on the crate.

"Perfect," he said. His accent was French, and though here were no badges of rank on his uniform, he was clearly an officer.

What Ruth had thought was an apartment block had really been a small hotel before the Blackout. There was a thin desk next to the stairs, with a row of pigeonholes behind it. There was a sign next to that, but it was in French, and she had no idea what it meant. Bhatt drew his bayonet, and levered the crate's lid open.

"Mortar rounds, yes?" the officer said. "*Now* we shall get them. In two days I shall take you to the chateaux. My grandfather may only have waited table, but we shall live there like kings!"

"I'll settle for a night's undisturbed sleep, sir," Bhatt said.

The light's face had been taped so as to restrict the beam, but there were only two other human-shaped shadows in the room. One was lying down. The other was kneeling over him.

"Hennessey!" the officer said. "He is dead, Hennessey." The officer said, this time more softly. "Martin is dead. You cannot help him, but you can avenge him. Come. Help Bhatt get the rounds to the team." Finally the officer looked at Ruth. "They are sending the police in as reinforcements?"

"No, ah, sir. I'm... we were chasing a murderer and I sort of ending up helping."

"Ah, you volunteered. Never volunteer," the officer said. "That is what my grandfather told me. Never volunteer, yet what did I do?"

"Volunteered to join the Marines," Bhatt said, as if it was a rhetorical question the officer had asked many times. The other Marine, Hennessey, detached himself from the shadows and walked over.

"Hennessey, good, listen. Four hundred metres east is the old radio transmitter. You can still see the spire. That spire is your marker, your guide. Fifty metres from here is a bakery. There is a wide strip of hideous orange plastic outside. You will see it when the flares go up. Go through the bakery to the buildings beyond. Johannes, Gopal, and Mathews have set up their position in those buildings. Take half the rounds. I'll take the other half to—"

"Grenade!" Bhatt bellowed pushing Hennessey and Ruth aside as he dived towards the stairwell. Ruth hadn't seen the object come down the stairs, but she heard the explosion though it was muffled by the bulk of Private Bhatt's body. Confused, she picked herself up as the officer drew his sidearm.

"They're above us!" he bellowed.

A figure appeared on the stairs. It was a man, bearded and blond, his arms bare despite the weather, his jacket festooned with sheathed knives. The officer fired. The pirate collapsed, but there was another behind him. That man, dressed in tattered muddy rags, carried a shotgun, and fired it before the officer could shoot. Hennessey screamed. Ruth had her revolver in her hand, though she didn't remember drawing it. She fired. Twice. The pirate collapsed.

The officer limped a pace towards the stairs.

"I think that's it."

"Are you all right, sir?" Ruth asked, as she crossed to Hennessey, but the man was dead.

"Fine," the officer said as he pulled a strip of cloth from a pouch and wrapped it around his calf. "You remember the route. Follow the spire. The bakery with the orange sign? Here." He unclipped the torch from Hennessey's webbing, picked up the canvas bag that Bhatt had half filled, and thrust both into her arms. "Go. I'll take the rest. Go!" He gestured at a dark gap behind the reception desk.

Ruth ran through, and found a heavy curtain blocking her path. She pushed her way through it, and then through another curtain, and then found herself outside.

She crouched by the wall, and looked up and down, left and right. There was nothing but darkness punctuated by the sound of artillery. She couldn't see the ground beneath her feet, let alone any orange sign. She fumbled her revolver's chamber open, and replaced the cartridges. She wished she'd kept the assault rifle that Isaac had given her, but wishes were dangerous, and making one would only lead to wishing that she was anywhere but here. That would lead to inaction, and right now, she had to act, she had to find that bakery.

There were a trio of flashes in the distance, but a roar of gunfire far closer. Then the sky was lit up by a flare. Ruth couldn't see a spire, but she saw an orange sign to her left, on the opposite side of the street. She ran.

After ten paces, there was a loud crack of fracturing stone. A splinter tore through her sleeve. She jinked right, running to the relative shelter of the buildings on the far side of the street, reaching them as a man staggered out into the road. Again he was blond, bearded, with a jacket covered in sheathed knives, except this man also carried a rifle in his hands. The man had the barrel pointing straight at Ruth, but when he pulled the trigger, nothing happened. Ruth screamed as she levelled her revolver, firing all six shots into the pirate's chest. The man collapsed, and Ruth took shelter in the doorway. Not a pirate, she thought, not really. What was it Lin had called them, Cossacks? This one looked more like a Viking, except for the rifle. That wasn't an AK-47 but one of the bull-pup designs that the British military used. She reloaded her revolver, holstered

222

it, and picked up the rifle. The safety was still on. At any other time that might have made her smile. She checked the magazine, slid the safety off, and ran once more, staying as close to the buildings as possible. Shells landed in the distance. Bullets hit brick, glass, and steel far closer. The flare finally went out. The road sank into darkness, but the gunfire didn't stop. Nor did Ruth.

She kept running until she reached a broken doorway that she thought, she hoped, was the bakery. She dived inside, and took cover.

There wasn't time to wait for the next flare. She took out the torch, shielded as much of it as she could with her hand, flashed it around the room, then turned it off. There were tables and chairs, a counter, a register, and a lot of grime. It didn't look like any bakery she knew, but there was a door behind the counter. Moving through buildings was going to be safer than the road, and she couldn't be more than a few dozen metres from where she needed to be.

Rifle raised, she crossed to the doorway. She turned the torch on again long enough to see there were no curtains, just a narrow hallway leading to a downward staircase filled with rubble fallen from the ceiling above. She looked at the hole in the ceiling. There was a depth to the darkness that suggested the hole extended to the roof.

"Do I go up?" she asked aloud.

"Identify yourself!" a woman called from above. The accent was English, but Ruth couldn't see who'd spoken.

"Um… Constable Deering. Police," she said.

"Who?" the voice asked, confused.

"Long story. Um… oh, Preston. Or is it Weston. I don't know the password, sorry."

A light came on, shining down into her eyes.

"I'll get the ladder," the woman said. It was made of rope, and it was dropped down the hole. "What are you doing here?"

"I was with Private Bhatt and…" Ruth hesitated. She'd never asked the officer's name.

"You've got the shells?" the woman asked.

"Um, yes. I think so."

"Then climb up. Quick. Up," the woman said. Ruth climbed.

The ladder led to a first floor. The speaker, a Marine corporal, turned her torch on again to inspect the bag's contents. By its light, Ruth could take in the room, though there wasn't much to see. There was a hole in the roof almost the width of the room, no glass in the windows, and no other people. Certainly there was no mortar team.

"Are you Gopal, Johannes, or Mathews?" Ruth asked.

"Corporal Joanna Johannes," she said. "We've been waiting for these all night. If we're lucky, it's not too late. Where's Fazle?"

"You mean Private Bhatt? He's dead. So is... so is Hennessey. I'm sorry."

Johannes sighed. "So it goes. Come on, it's not safe here."

The corporal took the bag and ran sure-footedly to the doorway on the other side of the room. Ruth followed, through the doorway, then across a wooden walkway that ran over a narrow alley. When she was halfway across, Ruth realised the walkway was really two doors, nailed together with floorboards covering the join. She focused on the Marine's back as Johannes disappeared into the building. Ruth followed her through and into what might once have been a child's bedroom, into a corridor, and up a narrow set of stairs into an attic. In one corner, a hole had been hacked in the roof. A mortar had been set up underneath. Two Marines stood near it.

"We've got the rounds," Johannes said.

"Who's this, Jo-Jo?" one of the Marines asked.

"Constable Deering, police," Ruth said. "Not a new recruit," she added. "I was chasing a criminal."

"Good enough," the other Marine said. "Mathews, get her lined up. Johannes, watch for the flare. A blue one, remember."

"Aye, Sarge," Johannes said, crossing to the mortar.

Ruth crossed to a battered chair and sat down.

"Don't make yourself too comfortable," Sergeant Gopal said. "We'll be moving out in a few minutes."

"Why? What's going on?" Ruth asked.

"We've got a bead on their supply dump," Gopal said. "They've been sloppy since they launched their attack at dusk. They had four of their supply trucks drive out, and one of the drivers used their lights."

"His lights," Johannes said. "Those thugs only have one use for women and we've no use for them."

"But now we know where their supply dump is," Gopal said. "More importantly, I think I know where the fuel store is."

"Wait," Ruth said. "They have trucks? You mean, like petrol vehicles?"

"Diesel, I think," Mathews chimed in. "It doesn't burn as well, but it does burn if we can drop a round on top of it. As long as we stop them using it, they can flee, but not very far."

"But the pirates *have* diesel?" Ruth asked. "I mean, we don't. Not really."

"Pirates?" Gopal said. "They ain't pirates. Pirates have gold teeth and treasure maps. Nah, this lot are the enemy. Cultists, I call 'em. Don't know where they got the fuel, mind, since most of them don't have a rifle to call their own."

"Cultists? You mean like a religion? The paper didn't print that."

"I mean like at least *three* religions," Gopal said. "Basically there are three main groups, but each of those is a collection of individual tribes more than it's a cohesive unit. Have you seen the thugs with all the knives? They're the Knights of St Sebastian. About ten years ago, they were laired up in the Wigierski National Park. Poland," he added. "The knives aren't exactly a stylistic choice. They didn't have any ammunition left. Anyway, we'd sent a convoy eastward, aiming for a failing village in Ukraine. These so-called knights attacked it, and killed half our people. The other half threw them out of the forest. Unfortunately, by the time our people made it to the Dnieper River, the knights had beaten us to it. We should have hunted them down, finished them then, but hindsight's a wonderful thing. They've been a nuisance in that part of the world for a decade. Always raiding villages, stealing livestock, but they rarely had any firearms, so we just had to supply the locals with enough ammunition to defend themselves, and with medicines to ensure there numbers grew—"

"Lights and movement, Sarge," Johannes whispered.

Gopal ran to the roof's edge, peering through the gap. "I make it four of 'em, on foot," he said. "When you see that flare, fire. Make sure you destroy the fuel tank, and then drop two incendiaries through the roof of the building next to it. *Through* the roof, remember."

"Aye, Sarge," Mathews said.

"Come on, copper," Gopal said. "Time to earn our crust."

Ruth fell in behind the sergeant, following him from the rooftop perch, back across the door-bridge, but not downstairs. He led her through the building's ruined rooms until they were at the far side of the row. Gopal crouched down by a shattered window, Ruth next to him. She said nothing, just gripped her rifle, and wished she'd not tried so hard to catch the train.

A flare lit up the sky to the north. It didn't light up the street below them, but cast deep shadows on the shattered piles of rubble. Four of those shadows were moving.

Gopal fired a single shot, then another. Ruth added a few shots of her own, but had no idea if they came close to the foe, let alone if she hit one of the attackers. Before the flare died, she caught sight of one of them. He didn't have a bandolier of knives or a leather jerkin. His clothing was mud-covered and tattered, clearly looted pre-Blackout wear of a plain, unadorned style. He clutched a rifle in his hands, at least until Gopal's bullet blew the back of his head off.

"Time to move," Gopal said.

"That was the flare, why didn't they fire the mortar."

"It didn't come over our position," Gopal said as he ran back through the ruined room. "We need a flare that'll light up their supply dump. We can't fire blind. This is our one chance to destroy them for good."

She followed him through gaping holes in walls, across landings strewn with bricks, and then down a narrow flight of stairs just as the building shook.

Gopal turned on his torch, and shone it around the hallway until it settled on a door that had a large B scored through the paintwork. Dust rained from above as Gopal crossed to the door. Just before he opened it, he turned the torch off. He swung the door open, and ran inside. Ruth followed. The room was empty.

It was the kitchen to a restaurant. A wide serving counter gave them a view of the dining area. Twenty years ago, it had been separated by a sheet of plate glass. Now that glass was gone, as were the windows that had looked out onto the street, giving them a clear view of the ruins outside.

"Now we watch," Gopal said. "They're firing at the window we were just in."

"I guessed," Ruth said. "They're going to send more people to attack?"

"They do the same thing every time," Gopal said. "In two minutes, they'll send over another ten mortar shells, then they'll attack."

Ruth propped her rifle on the counter, again wishing she hadn't come to France. "You mean that we're going to hold them here?" she asked.

"Pretty much," Gopal said. "At least until the flare comes. It won't be long."

"Right." The mortar fire had stopped now. An unnatural silence had settled over this corner of the battlefield, but explosions and gunfire reigned in the distance. "Those people, they weren't carrying knives."

"What, oh. Yeah, no, those are the Emir's people," Gopal said. "They're the very definition of generational fanatics. Don't ask who the Emir is, because it changes so often his followers rarely know. That's one of the few things they'll tell us when we take prisoners. Not that we ever take many."

"Who's the third group?"

"The Free Peoples' Democratic Army," Gopal said. "Though they change their name as often as the Emir is assassinated. The knights will torture you and then kill you. The Emir's lot will give you the chance to convert before they slit your throat. The Free Peoples will keep you alive, but make you wish that you were dead."

"They didn't print any of that in the papers."

"Yeah, well, up until a couple of years ago, they were just another bunch of marauding pirates," Gopal said. "The world was full of bands like theirs. Then something changed. Someone got them to work together. Don't know how. By rights they should be ripping each other's throat out.

Instead, they all came here. I reckon whoever managed that gave them their weapons, ammo, and fuel. Well, more fool them, because they're going to lose the lot as soon as that next flare is fired."

A mortar round hit the building above and ten feet to the left. The room shook. Dust fell. Ruth closed her eyes, but when she opened them, the street outside was as bright as day. In the distance, she saw figures running towards them. There were at least twenty, in a mixture of leather jerkins and grubby jackets.

"Here we go," Gopal said. "Short bursts. One magazine. Then you run, I'll cover you."

"Right," Ruth said. She doubted he was going to follow her, but she wasn't going to argue. And then there was a monstrous explosion that Ruth felt as much as she heard. The sky ahead lit up. The ground shook. The group on the road fell.

"That's their ammo dump!" Gopal said. "I knew it! I knew it!" And he spoke in a tone that suggested he'd only guessed it before. "I saw them bring their trucks in, and knew it had to be there." He fired, not aiming, but emptying his rifle at the group on the road. Ruth wasn't sure if she was meant to do the same, but before she could, Gopal stopped firing. "Time to go," he said.

He turned, and ran back to the doorway. Gopal turned the torch on, shining it down the dim corridor settling on one with an E hacked into the frame. "There."

Ruth followed him outside. They were in a narrow alley behind the buildings. There was movement to her left. She swung around. But it was only Johannes and Mathews. They had the mortar and ammo. Another flare lit up the sky, then a second.

"It's the counter attack," Gopal said. "I told 'em we'd find the supply dump!"

The moment of victory vanished with a gunshot's sharp retort. Corporal Johannes fell, clutching her leg. Ruth spun around. Her finger was already curling around the trigger before she even caught sight of the ragged figure at the other end of the alley. The man was fumbling with his rifle. Bullets from Ruth's weapon stitched a bloody line across his chest. The man fell, and Ruth's gun clicked on an empty chamber.

Gopal ran to the fallen corporal. "You all right, Jo-Jo?" the sergeant asked as he pulled a bandage from a pouch at his belt.

"Didn't hit an artery," she hissed. "Just damned painful."

"Constable, can you take her back to our lines. And pass on a message to whoever's in charge. Mathews, how many rounds do we have left?"

"Ten, Sarge."

"What's the message?" Ruth asked.

"Tell them to attack," Gopal said.

A moment later, Gopal and Mathews were sprinting down the alley, carrying the mortar and ammo, leaving Ruth alone with the injured corporal.

"Do you know the way back?" Ruth asked as she helped Johannes up.

"Sure, just head away from the gunfire," she said. "You should reload."

Ruth checked her pockets. "I don't have any more ammunition for the rifle."

"Me neither," Johannes said. "I've got a couple of grenades. Took them from one of the knights. You know how they work? Pull the pin and throw. Here."

Ruth dropped the rifle, took the grenade, but after the briefest hesitation, put it in her pocket and drew her revolver. With her other arm holding Johannes up, they limped away from the alley. Johannes pointed to a building with a letter M carved into the wood.

"Through there," Johannes said.

"The letters are a code?" Ruth asked.

"Yeah. Basically, letters are good. Letters with numbers are bad. Numbers on their own are very, very bad."

The door led into the almost intact ground floor of a small house. A hole had been hacked into the wall of a nearly immaculate living room, and that led to another home, another hole, and finally to a door that led outside, and almost straight into a mob.

"Password!" someone barked as rifles and lights were levelled.

"I've no idea," Johannes said. "But we've got them on the run."

The officer Ruth had met earlier stepped through the ragged line. "Corporal? Constable? You got the supply dump?" he asked.

"Aye, sir," Johannes said. "Has to be their principal artillery depot. I think we got the fuel store as well. Sergeant Gopal says you should attack."

"Good work," the officer said. "And you, Constable," he added. "Get back to our lines. We'll take it from here."

Flares and artillery arced up through the sky, turning night into day. No return fire came. At least, Ruth didn't think it did. The ground shook all around them as the enemy position was pounded into dust.

Just before they reached the British lines, a white flare, and then a blue one, arced up from close to the enemy position. The British artillery stopped firing, at least on that section of the front.

"Are they surrendering?" Ruth asked.

"No," Johannes said. "That means the infantry's about to go in."

Chapter 22 - The Home Front
15th November, Calais & Dover

"Put her here," a medic said gesturing at a cot.

"*She* can talk for herself," Johannes said as Ruth eased the corporal down onto the stretcher.

"Then you can't be too bad," the medic said, pulling a pair of surgical scissors from his pouch. A second later, the corporal's trouser leg and bandage had been cut free, the soiled cloth placed in a plant pot. The medic unclipped a battered metal bottle and poured a liberal dose of purple liquid over the wound. "You'll be fine," he said. A moment later, a new bandage had been slapped on the corporal's leg, and the medic vanished before he could be asked any questions.

"Is that it?" Ruth asked.

"The best healthcare in the world," Johannes said. She lay down on the stretcher.

"I'll see if I can find you a blanket or something," Ruth said. As she turned around, a familiar voice spoke.

"There you are," Captain Mitchell said. His uniform was covered in as much blood as Ruth's. "You've been helping with the wounded, too? Good, but we need to get back to Kent."

"This your boss?" Johannes asked.

"Captain Mitchell. Corporal Johannes," Ruth said.

"Corporal," Mitchell said. "You'll be here for a few more hours, I'm afraid. There's a bottleneck in the Tunnel, but we'll have you home soon. Ruth, we need to go."

"Thanks, copper," Johannes said. "See you back in Britain some day."

"Some day, Marine," Ruth said. "Some day."

Ruth fell into step next to Mitchell as they threaded their way past the stretchers. "Why aren't they taking them back to Britain?"

"There's no train," Mitchell said. "There should be two locomotives in reserve, ferrying the injured back and supplies forward, but Cavendish recalled them to England."

"She must have wanted a clean run for her train so it could plough straight into the garrison."

"I'd say so," Mitchell said. "Who knows where the trains are now, but they weren't in Folkestone. The general was told some story about diesel replacing steam, and he didn't question it. Idiot of a man. I'm not sure I've got the authority to remove him. Well, no, I *know* I don't have the authority to remove him, but I would have done if I knew how to run a battle. I doubt I could do it worse than him, but the Marines seem to have it hand despite his pusillanimous interference. We need to get back to Folkestone and get the admiral to come over here. She needs to take command, at least for now, and I need to get word of this to Atherton."

"I met him," Ruth said. "The general, I mean. Yeah, he didn't seem…" She trailed off and came to a halt as, on the stretcher ahead, a medic pulled a blanket over the face of a corpse.

"Why?" Ruth murmured.

Mitchell looked at her, and seemed to take in her stained uniform properly.

"You weren't simply helping with the wounded, were you?"

"I helped carry some mortar rounds."

"To the front?" he asked.

"I dunno. Where exactly is that?"

"Good question," Mitchell said. "I'm going back to Kent. I've got to get word to Atherton, and I've got to find Cavendish. You can stay here, if you want."

"You mean, to fight?"

"If you want to. Or just to help in anyway that's needed. My attempts to keep you out of danger have been a singular failure. If anything, they've got you into more trouble than if I'd left you alone."

"No," Ruth said. "It wasn't you. It was Emmitt. He thinks I'm this Sameen person. As long as he's alive, I'm not going to have a quiet life. But we need to stop Cavendish first."

Isaac was by the train. The locomotive was no longer smoking, and the ammunition had been unloaded.

"The fire's out," he said. He took in Ruth's uniform, but said nothing. "I've removed the bomb. It was a simple device. Nothing complex."

"Plastic explosives?" Mitchell asked.

"No, they'd used mortar rounds to create mines, and those were attached to the timer. They probably set it up in about ten minutes."

Ruth jumped as a length of metal was thrown out of the closest wagon to clang against the adjacent set of tracks.

"They're taking the metal racks out, converting the wagons to take stretchers," Isaac said. "As soon as we can get a locomotive up here, they'll take the wounded back. Do you know how many were seriously injured?"

"About two hundred in the last twenty-four hours," Mitchell said.

"How many dead?" Ruth asked.

"I'm not sure," Mitchell said. "Not yet. At least a hundred."

"They really threw everything into this attack, didn't they?" Isaac said.

"Because they were told that the British lines were going to be destroyed from the inside, and that there were small arms waiting for them in Kent," Mitchell said.

"You're going back?" Isaac asked.

"Yes," Ruth said. "We need to stop Cavendish. Justice needs to be done. Even now. *Especially* now."

There were bicycles in the access tunnel, piled near the furthest end of the aid-station beyond a cruder operating theatre than Ruth imagined could exist. The bicycles weren't being guarded. If they were there in case the Marines had to make a final, hasty retreat, Ruth was certain they would never be used.

The air in the Tunnel was stale, acrid, tinged with burning metal and oil. The pool of light from the torches cast weird shadows on the detritus littering the Tunnel's floor. At first it was pleasant, being alone in the dark with nothing but the back of Isaac's coat to look at. Soon, Ruth's mind returned to the bloody and confusing hours among the ruins of Calais.

The faces came back to her. Private Bhatt's, then Hennessey's, then the injured and dying Marines lining the service tunnel. Then came the face of the snarling blond cultists.

"Ruth?" Mitchell asked.

Ruth had stopped cycling. Her feet were on the ground, but her eyes were far away.

"It was different," Ruth said. "I shot Illyakov. I mean, she had a rifle, and I shot her, and I felt... not nothing, but she was a criminal. She was armed. She was going to shoot me. I don't know whether she killed anyone herself, but she caused Mr Wilson to be murdered and was complicit in the deaths of those five Luddites and whoever else. But those cultists... I mean, it's the same, but it's not. It's... one moment Private Bhatt and I were talking, and then next there was a grenade and he just jumped on top of it. He didn't think or hesitate or anything. He had to know he was going to die, but he did it anyway. I don't get it. I don't understand it. I don't understand *any* of it!"

"Me neither," Mitchell said. "And I've been doing this for twenty years. The good, the bad, they both still have the ability to surprise. I'm going on ahead. Isaac, stay with her."

But Ruth wasn't going to be left behind, not again.

The light at the end of the tunnel was a searchlight attached to a hasty barricade. Mitchell slowed, dismounted, and waved his empty hands above his head.

"British!" he called. Clearly thinking his American accent made that a dubious claim, he added "We're friendly. It's Captain Mitchell and Constable Deering."

They approached the barricade, and found the admiral herself commanding the detachment of Marines.

"Did you stop the train?" the admiral asked.

"Yes," Mitchell said. He took in the Marines. "Admiral, we need to talk. In private."

The two of them walked out of earshot, and that caused a barrage of questions from the Marines.

"Sorry," Ruth said. "I don't know anything. I really don't." She pushed her way through them and towards... daylight? Dawn was breaking over Kent.

"Was it still night in France?" she said to herself.

"More or less," Isaac said. He'd followed her outside. "There are still no trains here. Looks like they moved the dead, though."

Ruth had nothing to say. She looked up at the clouds, then at the trees, and then at a pair of blackbirds pecking at a gap between sleeper and rail. Next to the rails was a long platform dotted with small cranes and other machinery for the loading of heavy equipment. Everything seemed indecently peaceful.

On the platform was a small office with two Marines at attention outside. Next to them was a bench. Ruth climbed up onto the platform, and walked over to the bench.

The Marines eyed her, and her smoke-blackened, mud-stained, blood-soaked uniform.

"You were in Calais," one asked.

"I was."

"What's it like?" the other asked.

Ruth thought about it, then about the kind of answer she would want to hear if she was a newly recruited Marine only a few hours away from being sent to the frontline. "It's bad," she said, "but we're winning."

The two guards nodded. "Do you want to speak to him?"

"To whom?" she asked.

"The prisoner."

"You have a prisoner?"

Inside, handcuffed to a chair, guarded by another Marine, was a man wearing the uniform of the railway company.

"You worked for Cavendish?" Ruth asked.

The man glanced at Ruth, her uniform, and then at Isaac. "Don't I get a lawyer?"

"We'd have to arrest you first," Ruth said. She pulled out a chair from the table and sat down opposite him. "Do you know what was on that train?"

The man shook his head. Ruth wasn't sure if she believed him. She glanced at the Marine now standing by the door.

"That train was rigged with explosives," Ruth said. "When it reached the garrison in Calais, it was meant to detonate. It would have killed all of our people. A hole would have been ripped through our lines. Hundreds would have died, and the cultists would have poured down the Tunnel, and into Kent. Everyone here would die, and so would hundreds in Dover. More would have died in Sussex and beyond because most of our Marines would have been dead. Tens of thousands would have died before Britain was safe again. All because of you."

"Not me," the man said, shaking his head. "I don't know anything about that."

"What do you know?" Isaac asked.

"Just that we were told to make sure no one went onto that train," the man said. "We had to keep the Marines off it."

"Keep the Marines off? You mean that you had to shoot at them if they tried to board?" Ruth asked.

"No. I don't know. I mean Ms Cavendish gave the orders and we obeyed. We're soldiers, too, you know. What do you think we were doing when we laid track through the northeast, through Scotland? We fought and died to build this country."

"So why were you so happy to tear it apart?" Ruth asked.

"It wasn't like that," the man said.

"And you know what," Ruth said. "I don't care. Did Cavendish arrive on that train?"

"Maybe. Maybe not. What do I get if I tell you."

"Police protection," Mitchell said.

Ruth turned around. She hadn't realised he'd come in.

"If you talk, we'll arrest you," Mitchell said. "If you don't, we'll leave you here. They've telegraphed Dover, a locomotive will arrive in thirty minutes. How long will it take to get to Calais? Half an hour? An hour? Call it twenty minutes to load it with the wounded, and it'll be back here an hour after that. In three hours, hundreds of wounded will come through here. What do you think will happen to you then? You're not a criminal. You're not even an enemy combatant. You're a spy. A traitor."

"They'll rip me apart. That's murder. You're talking about murder!"

"Accidents happen," Mitchell said. "The admiral confirmed that Cavendish arrived on that train. Where did she go?"

"I don't know. I swear. I don't."

"How many with her?" Mitchell asked.

"Two, I think. I'm not sure."

"Anything else you want to ask?" Mitchell asked.

"No," Ruth said. "Not any more."

"The prime minister wants him alive," Mitchell said.

"Understood," the Marine said.

Mitchell led Isaac and Ruth outside, and around the building towards the rear. "Cavendish forged orders from Atherton himself," he said. "Trains were held in the depot in Sussex, and in Dover. Since yesterday evening, no train has come further east than Horsham."

"What's going to happen in Calais?" Ruth asked.

"The Dover train will be here in thirty minutes, give or take. The admiral is going to take all the troops in Folkestone through with her, and take over command in Calais, at least until someone else can be appointed. The wounded will be evacuated. The telegraph has to be repaired, as does the electrical supply. I don't know how long that'll take."

"It's not your problem, Henry," Isaac said. "The immediate crisis is over. All that's left is to find Cavendish."

"No, the crisis is only just beginning," Mitchell said. "The Railway Company, and their police, their guards, they're loyal to Cavendish. I don't know how loyal, but I can't risk sending a report to Atherton by telegram. I'll have to do it in person."

"We're not looking for Cavendish?" Ruth asked.

"We'll use that train from Dover to ferry the wounded out of Calais," Mitchell said. "We'll need a second locomotive to ferry them to Hastings or Twynham, and that's with whom I'll catch a ride, but it won't be for at least four hours, so we have time to search for her, but I doubt we'll find her, not now. The best we can do is work out which way she went."

They'd reached the rear of the buildings built next to the platform. Mitchell pointed to a shallow ramp that ran down to a gravel path. "Start looking for wheelchair marks," he said.

"The gravel looks new," Isaac said. "Remarkably new and clean."

They followed the path between two partially constructed sheds, both with roofs suspended on massive steel girders, but where no walls had been put in place. Ruth left the path, and walked around the handful of scattered boxes, crates, and stacked lengths of timber.

"What are you looking for?" Mitchell asked.

"They had trucks in Calais," Ruth said. "Maybe she drove away. I mean, she can't have walked."

"And she had a diesel locomotive," Isaac said. "She could have kept some of that fuel aside. Hmm. There was petrol in that old church where Ruth was taken after they abducted her. Perhaps the diesel came from the same place?"

"Smuggled from the U.S.? No, I don't think so," Mitchell said. "What I now wonder is whether the diesel in Calais actually came from here. A lot of effort was put into biodiesel, and that can run in a ship's engine as well as a locomotive or truck. If Cavendish's plan was to live, to escape, then perhaps she didn't go to London, but just to the coast."

"Well, there's no wheel marks here," Ruth said. "Not for a truck, not for a wheelchair."

Beyond the unfinished warehouses, gorse and bramble grew out of and around stubby concrete ruins. Beyond those was a new-growth forest. Mitchell left the path, stalking towards it. Ruth looked at Isaac. He shrugged and followed. Ruth glanced back towards the station. Her rage from earlier was fading, but so to was the fear that had welled up as they'd cycled through the Channel Tunnel. She didn't think Mitchell would really have thrown that prisoner to the Marines, or that the Marines would have harmed him. No, if their rage was anything like hers, they would want to see him tried and hanged.

"Here!" Isaac called. Ruth turned around. Isaac was pushing back a dense thicket of brambles. All of the suckers and tendrils had been carefully trimmed, so that, with only a few scratches from the longer thorns, a three-foot section could be rolled back. Underneath was a patch of muddy dirt, but in it were an unmistakable pair of wheel marks.

"I should have seen it before," Mitchell said. "But there are none so blind as those who don't want to see. There were tracks like this outside that church they held you prisoner, Ruth."

"Similar, maybe," Ruth said. She wasn't sure, and wasn't sure it mattered.

The trail continued intermittently until the track met an old road. There were a few moss-covered wrecks pushed into the ditch, but the road was otherwise clear. Remarkably clear, really, considering how impassable disused roads usually were. Had Cavendish done that to aid her escape?

"I've lost the trail," Mitchell said examining the verge either side. "But she would have gone north."

The wind picked up. Ruth raised her collar, and the movement cracked the mud crusted on her hands. As Mitchell and Isaac drew their weapons, she plunged her hands into her pockets. Her left hand found something hard. The grenade that Johannes had given her. She almost pulled it out, wanting to discard it, but she stopped herself. That wouldn't be safe for anyone else who ever came along this road. Instead, she left the grenade where it was, and let her hands fall to her sides.

The road ahead was bisected by a brook. The stream emerged from a shallow hill in a gentle trickle. Over the years, that had worn a path through the road, angling down to a lush grove of towering spruces. On the far side of the stream were four footprints, two pairs facing one another, as if two people had been carrying something over the gap.

"Two sets of footprints," Isaac said. "Two people carrying a wheelchair."

Mitchell glanced behind, then ahead. "If she'd come through here last night, before the train left, those would have dried by now."

"You mean she waited?" Ruth asked.

"I would have," Isaac said. "Somewhere close enough to the railway that she would know that her plan had worked."

"But how would she know?" Ruth asked. "How would she know if it failed?"

"By the sound of the artillery," Mitchell said. "But it's more likely she waited until first light so as to avoid having to use a torch whose light might have betrayed her presence to any patrols wandering the countryside. She didn't linger around here, though."

The road continued north, curving in and around thickets and groves that increasingly encroached on the battered tarmac. A seven-foot-wide path had been cut through them. From the discoloured stems discarded on the roadway, it had been done at least a week before, but nothing heavy had been ridden over them. Nothing heavier than a wheelchair. There were occasional wheel-marks visible in the damper patches of dirt.

Mitchell abruptly dropped to a crouch, and ran to the edge of the road and the cover of a rusting white van. The wheels had been removed, as had the lights, two of the doors, and all bar one of the seats, but the word 'Police' was still visible on the battered bonnet.

"Ahead," Mitchell whispered. "Do you see that house? There's a truck behind it. That's an old British Army truck."

"The one covered in leaves?" Isaac asked.

"Covered in branches," Mitchell said. "But there's no tree near them. That's hasty camouflage."

"You think they're in the house?" Isaac asked.

"Maybe."

The house was at the bottom of a dip in a road, a few yards south of a crossroads. On the far side, the road rose up a shallow hill disappearing behind a larger building with a sign affixed to the front. It was too far away to read the sign, but it had probably have been a pub, and it would have made a far better vantage point than the unremarkable detached house. The roof was moss-covered, but otherwise looked intact. The guttering hung loose, and at least one window was broken, but…

"Someone put boards over that window," Ruth whispered. "Someone tried to live here after the Blackout. No smoke, though. And I can't see anyone."

"What do you think, Henry?" Isaac asked.

"I think Cavendish cleared the road from here to the Tunnel's entrance. I think that crossroads marks a point where she could choose between heading towards London or going due north to somewhere she's concealed a boat. The question, then, is whether she had two trucks, and if not, why is she still here?"

"Here's hoping that her two compatriots decided to leave her behind," Isaac said, checking the magazine in his pistol. "How do you want to do this?"

"Quickly," Mitchell said, "because there's no way to do this circumspectly. Go through the trees. Get a bead on the back of the building. Stop them from driving away. Cavendish can't run, so if she can't drive, we've got her trapped. Anyone else who wants to run, let them."

"Just like old times," Isaac said. He jumped the ditch, pushed his way through the hedge, and disappeared into a forest that had once been a field.

Mitchell turned to Ruth. "We'll follow the hedge. Keep your head down. And..." He gave a rueful shrug. "And I don't have any more advice to give."

They were a hundred yards from the house when the first shot rang out. Ruth didn't see who fired it, though she was certain it came from ahead. Mitchell sped up, so Ruth did the same, running doubled-over along the ditch. Another shot came, and then a third, and then came a shout.

"There! By the road!" It was a man's voice and was followed by a staccato rat-a-tat of machine gun fire. Mitchell dived forward for the cover of a three-foot-high brick wall that separated the house from the fields around it. He fired blindly, emptying his pistol at the building as Ruth skidded into cover next to him.

"Aren't you meant to ask them to surrender?" Ruth asked.

"Good point," Mitchell muttered as he reloaded. "It's over, Rebecca!" he called out. A burst of gunfire came in reply. "Can you see the truck?" Mitchell asked. "Can they drive away?"

Ruth crawled along the edge of the wall to a section that had broken, spilling bricks and mortar down into the ditch. "I... no, there are branches in front of the engine. I don't think it can move."

Mitchell fired another two blind shots. The bullets hit stone. This time there was no return fire. Ruth rolled onto her side. She could see down the side of the wall to the rear of the property where a figure was running towards the woodland. Ruth raised her revolver, but before she could fire, the man collapsed. Isaac stepped out from behind a tree and ran towards the rear of the house.

"Isaac didn't let him run," Ruth said, heedless of the weapon in her own hand.

Mitchell didn't reply, but pushed himself up and over the wall, sprinting for the side of the house. He reached the wall by the window as the door opened and a figure ran out. Mitchell fired before the man had a chance to raise his rifle. He collapsed. Mitchell edged to the doorway.

The boards fell from the window next to him. A woman was there, an assault rifle in her hands. Not Cavendish, but someone younger. Someone not much older than Ruth. She barely registered that as she brought her revolver to bear, firing two shots into the window. The woman collapsed, slumping forward onto the frame.

"That just leaves you, doesn't it, Rebecca," Mitchell called out. "Two who helped you away from the garrison, but one who was already here, keeping an eye on your truck." He glanced at the corpse hanging from the window. "I remember her, I think. Another child you adopted. Another one who's dead. Did you really only save their lives in order that you could kill them later on?"

In a crouch, Ruth ran for the house. She reached the other side of the window.

Mitchell motioned toward the open window, and that she should fire two shots through it. Before Ruth could, there was a blast from a shotgun. The pellets shredded the doorway. Mitchell motioned for Ruth to stay where she was. He reached into his coat, took out his tablet, tapped at the screen, then put it on the ground.

"Rebecca," he called. "We disarmed the bomb on your train. The garrison in Calais is intact, and has been resupplied. The pirates have been repulsed. We're winning. It's over. There's no sanctuary for you in France. Not now."

"I... I see," Cavendish said. Her voice was clear, close. She couldn't be more than eight feet from the door. Ruth watched Mitchell, waiting for his signal.

"Why did you do it?" Mitchell asked.

"Do what?" Cavendish replied.

"Everything," Mitchell said. "You had weapons and ammunition stashed here in Kent for those pirates in Calais. You rigged an ammunition train to blow up the garrison in France. Before then you ordered the deaths of so many. You worked with Emmitt, didn't you?"

"What are you really asking, Henry?"

"You were never someone happy to take orders, Rebecca," Mitchell said.

"Ah, you mean was I behind this? Yes. Yes, I was. It was my plan."

"Your plan? Not Longfield's? Not Commissioner Wallace's?" Mitchell asked. Ruth frowned. The question seemed redundant. In fact, she couldn't think of any question that was pertinent other than whether the woman was going to surrender, and Ruth thought they already had the answer to that.

"The plan certainly wasn't Wallace's," Cavendish said. "That man was an idiot. A fool who lost an election yet still thought he could rule."

"When did the rot begin, Rebecca? When did you decide to betray us all?"

"I don't call it a betrayal," Cavendish said. "I would call it the opposite, but if I had to pick a time and a place, it was in the New Forest. Do you remember?"

"The New Forest? You mean when that wagon overturned, crushing your legs? I remember that."

"We had to lay track in the depths of winter," Cavendish said. "Laying it flat on the road because we couldn't spare the time to level the ground. If we hadn't linked our disparate communities, all would have been lost.

Of course it wasn't safe. Of course there were going to be accidents. I just didn't think I would be one of them. Who ever does?"

"That's when you concocted a plan for revenge, was it?" Mitchell asked.

"No," Cavendish said. "That was when I first saw we needed a different approach. The first journey I made in this cursed wheelchair was to our prime minister. I tried to propose a new plan. I was rebuffed, but I didn't give up. I proposed that plan time and time again, and time has proven I was correct. We had twenty years of the same ruler. Twenty years of the same policies. Twenty years of inaction. The result is that we have become prisoners on this island. We sent a few food parcels to a handful of coastal communities and told ourselves we were rebuilding the world. We said we didn't want war, so kept our military to a handful of ships and Marines, but they became our jailers. You've seen France. You've seen what lies beyond. Has ignoring the problem made it better?"

"Since you couldn't beat them, you co-ordinated those pirates and slavers. You arranged for them to attack us."

"Not exactly," Cavendish said. "That was Emmitt's plan. He wanted an eternal war, and through war we would rebuild the technologies that were lost. I planned to unite our enemies so that we could destroy them."

"Destroy them? By letting them maraud through Kent."

"Some people would die, yes," Cavendish said. "But their deaths would serve the greater good. When we were attacked, here on our own soil, people would finally see the truth. They would understand that evil has to be uprooted and destroyed. Whether it was the evil of the cultists, or the insanity of Emmitt and Longfield, or the narrow-minded bigotry of Wallace and his ilk, all would be brushed aside, replaced with a new order. There would be a generation of war, but then a century of peace."

"Yeah, you're not the first person to say that," Mitchell said. "The counterfeiting, the assassination, the destruction of the train, the sabotage, the murders, you facilitated it all?"

"There had to be a threat, Henry, and that threat had to be known. But how would people know they were under threat? How could we wake this nation from slumber?"

"How?" Mitchell said. "Through murder? Through chaos? Through fear? Why didn't you stand for office? You would have been elected. You could have become prime minister."

"I don't want power," Cavendish said. "I never have. I just want a future for our people. For all people."

"I don't buy it," Mitchell said. "Everything you've done ends with a new British Empire controlling almost the entire world."

"Really? I killed Yanuck, didn't I? That smuggler didn't know it, but I had already destroyed the rest of his people in the northeastern Mediterranean. There would be no more ammunition smuggled into Britain."

"Makepeace killed Yanuck," Mitchell said.

"Under my orders," Cavendish said.

"And did Emmitt shoot the prime minister under your orders?"

"Emmitt has never listened to me, though I like to think I was able to guide him, able to tame some of his wilder notions."

"What about those five Luddites, the saboteurs," Mitchell said. "You killed them, didn't you?"

"Makepeace did, but under my orders. It was cruel, yes, but it was a necessary cruelty. Emmitt wished for them to be captured, but in doing so, they would have revealed that they truly had nothing to do with the sabotage of the telegraph. Emmitt wished that my involvement was discovered, but I saw through his plans from the beginning."

"You plotted against him, while he plotted against you," Mitchell said. "And all the innocents died for your petty schemes which have come to naught. There was a vineyard in France. There was…" He stopped. "Villages and towns have been laid waste, thousands have died, because of your vanity."

"Not vanity, Henry. For the greater good. You have to see that, surely. You of all people have to understand the importance of that."

"I think we've got enough," Mitchell said, though this time far louder.

He picked up the tablet while, from inside there was a burst of footsteps, a thud, and a muffled yell.

"Got her, she's alone," Isaac called.

"Then it's over," Mitchell said. He pushed the wrecked door open and stood there, staring at the pitiful figure of Rebecca Cavendish. Once, she'd been a titan in Britain, a force of nature who had shaped the nation, whose name had been known and spoken in awe. Now, slumped in her chair, blood dripping from a gash in her face, clutching her bloody hand, she was a sad, miserable wretch.

Mitchell cuffed her hands together, around the arm of her wheelchair. "Bring her outside," he said. "It's time for you to face justice."

"I won't," Rebecca said, as Isaac pushed her chair towards the door. "Not the justice you mean. Certainly not the justice you want."

"You think no jury will dare find you guilty?" Mitchell said. "You think your people in the Railway Company will rescue you?" He took out the tablet. "I recorded our little chat. When everyone hears that, they'll know you really are."

"Oh, Henry, that will never be heard in court," Rebecca said.

Ruth stepped inside, away from the door so that Isaac had room to get her outside.

"It will," Mitchell said. "I think this particular case will establish a few new precedents."

"That wasn't what I meant," Cavendish said. The chair rocked, and she almost fell from it as Isaac pushed her down the worn step and onto the path outside. "Goodbye, Henry. I leave Britain to your—"

Blood sprayed from her head as a bullet slammed into her left temple, exiting the other side. Even as her head lolled forward, Isaac dragged the chair back into the room, but it was too late. She was dead.

Another shot came, the bullet thudding into and through one of the boarded-up windows.

"Emmitt?" Isaac asked, as he eased into the doorway. "It has to be, right?"

"It has to," Mitchell said. A bullet hit the door. "He's got us pinned down."

"State the obvious, Henry," Isaac said. "Though this explains why Cavendish didn't leave. She couldn't. Nor could her people. They were trapped, waiting to die."

"Then why didn't Emmitt kill them?" Ruth asked.

"A better question is why he's shooting at us," Isaac said. "I'm down to four bullets. How about you, Henry?"

"I've got six. Can you see him?"

"Not without giving him something to aim for," Isaac said. "But I think he's in that pub at the top of the hill. He's got a clear line of sight of the road, and of any help that might come from the garrison. What do you want to do? Toss a coin to see who plays decoy?"

"No. We'll wait until dark if we have to," Mitchell said. "Ruth, watch the door, Isaac, help me search this place. Let's see what weapons Cavendish's people have left behind."

As the two men began to search the ruined house, Ruth crossed to the door.

"Why hasn't Emmitt run?" she asked, but neither Mitchell nor Isaac heard her. "Why didn't he run after he shot Cavendish? He could have shot us when we were outside, but he didn't. He waited for us to confront her. He *wanted* us to confront her. He wanted us to hear what she had to say. But why hasn't he run?" She glanced around, but Mitchell had disappeared into the back, and she could hear Isaac upstairs.

Emmitt could have killed them before. He could have killed her a dozen times over. He hadn't. Perhaps he wouldn't kill her now. Her hand dropped to her pocket. Perhaps. The only thing she was certain of was that he had to be stopped.

She took a breath, and before doubt could set in, stepped out into the road. There was no shot. Perhaps he *had* gone, she thought as she took a step towards the pub at the top of the hill. He'd fired a few shots at them to buy himself a little more time. Maybe. Possibly. Probably. She walked up the hill, increasingly confident that she'd find the pub deserted until there was a shout from behind her.

"Ruth?" It was Mitchell. She turned around, and saw him in the doorway. And then there was a shot. Dirt sprayed from the ground two feet from the door. A fraction of a second later came another shot. This bullet thumped into the door's frame. Mitchell ducked back inside. Ruth turned her attention to the pub, and continued to walk up the hill.

When she was thirty feet from the pub, the clouds parted long enough for the sun to shine on the sign. For a fraction of a second, flaking gold paint reflected the morning's early gleam, and then the clouds returned, but she'd seen the pub's name. It was the Five Bells. That reminded her of something on the distant edge of memory. Just as the fragmentary images were resolving into a clear and understandable picture, there was another shot. This bullet came close to her, spraying dirt from the verge to her left.

"That's close enough, Sameen," Emmitt called. "I take it you want to talk?"

"I've questions," Ruth said.

"Of course you do, though I trust you won't ask whether I'm going to hand myself in?"

"No," Ruth said. "I know you won't."

"Then I'll give you a few minutes, but no more. Please put your gun on the ground."

Carefully, she bent, placing her revolver on the cracked tarmac. Then she took two steps away from it, and towards the pub. "Who's left, Emmitt?" she called out.

"Left? What do you mean, left?"

"How many of your confederates are still alive?" she asked.

"I could tell you none. I could tell you that they are legion. Would you believe me?"

"Where are you going now?" she asked.

"I could say that I'm staying in England. Or perhaps I have a boat waiting, twenty miles from here. You wouldn't believe that answer, either."

"No, I suppose not."

"So ask me something, the answer to which you know won't be a lie."

"Did you kill Makepeace?" she asked.

"I did," he said. "I'm surprised you didn't recognise me."

"Why did you kill Cavendish?"

"She betrayed me," Emmitt called back. "We had a deal, but she lacked faith. No doubt she thought, when captured, I would talk. But she sent a butler as an assassin. Killing her was a mercy, in many ways."

248

"The fire in the courthouse, that was you? That was your plan all along? A contingency in case you were captured?"

"More or less," Emmitt said. "I always have a contingency."

"Like in London?" Ruth asked. "In that university building?"

"Ah, Henry told you about that? I'm glad. Time is pressing, Sameen. This is your last question."

"I suppose I want to know why," she said. "But you're right; I won't believe anything you say, so I won't ask you a question. That's what you want, isn't it? That's why you didn't run the moment you were sure Cavendish was dead. You want me to ask you something about why or what next. Your reply will be another lie, one that will have us chasing our own tails, searching in Britain and beyond, distrusting our friends, suspicious of every shadow. Whatever you say, no matter how much truth is in it, or how much I want to believe that it's the truth, it will only serve yourself. So, no, I won't ask you a question. Instead, I'll tell you what I think. I think anyone who might help you is dead. Either you killed them, or Cavendish had them killed. I think you're alone, and your plans have failed. Everything you were working towards for the last twenty years is in ruins. None of it will come to pass, not now. It's over, Emmitt."

"We shall see," he said.

"Where are you going?" she asked. "Really?"

"I told you, that was your last question, and you squandered it."

"Fine. Take me with you," she said.

He laughed, a bitter, cruel bark completely absent of mirth. "Oh, yes, very good. I know Henry Mitchell's tricks, and he learned at least one of them from me. You have another gun concealed about your person."

That was the opening she had been waiting for.

"I don't," she said, as she unbuckled her belt and let her holster fall to the ground. She walked towards the pub. "No guns. No tricks. And no more lies from you. I just want an explanation. I want to *understand.*"

She undid her jacket and took it off, bundling it into a ball.

"See? No gun," she said. She slipped her hand into the jacket's pocket, and pulled the pin from the grenade Johannes had given her back in France. She threw the balled jacket through the pub's window.

"What!" Emmitt yelled, but more in confusion then fear.

Ruth dived forward, aiming for ditch on the other side of the road. As she rolled across the tarmac, gravel and grit, broken glass and jagged stone bit into and through her trousers and shirt. There was a long second of nothing, when she thought the grenade was a dud, and then it exploded.

The ground shook as her world filled with noise. Then it filled with wood, brick, and glass raining down on top of her. When it stopped, she picked herself up, and walked over to the fractured window.

Emmitt had made it halfway across the room before the grenade went off. Rather, most of him was now halfway across the room, but enough remained that Ruth was sure it was him, and she was sure that he was dead.

Mitchell and Isaac were already running up the hill. She sat at the side of the road, waiting for them, her eyes on the pub's sign, now swinging gently back and forth.

"That was—" Mitchell began, but Ruth didn't let him finish.

"It's over. Emmitt's dead," she said.

Isaac went over to the pub. "I'd have to agree with her," he said. "Was that a grenade?"

"From France," Ruth said.

"And you've—" Mitchell began, but stopped mid-sentence. "Did he say anything?"

"Mostly just taunts," Ruth said. "There might be a boat waiting for him twenty miles from here, but that might have been a lie. He admitted to killing Makepeace, and that he was working with Cavendish. Oh, and using the fire in the courthouse to escape was always part of his plan. He was one step ahead of us all the time."

"Until now," Mitchell said.

"Do you want to search the body?" Isaac asked.

"No," Mitchell said. "I want to go home and sleep, but there is the matter of the Railway Company still to be dealt with. Yes, the body needs to be searched. And this pub. And then the coast, twenty miles from here."

"I'll take care of that," Isaac said.

Mitchell hesitated.

"You're stretched beyond thin," Isaac said. "And I promise to share everything I find with you," he added.

"Fine," Mitchell said. "But make sure you do. Atherton needs to be informed about... about everything. Ruth, do you want to come back to Twynham with me?"

"What time is it?" she asked.

"A little after nine," Mitchell said.

"Then I should get back to Dover," she said. "After all, either I'm a copper or I'm not, and if I am, then I'm late for work." She stood up, and started down the hill, heading back towards Dover.

Epilogue 1 - Executive Decisions
16th November, Twynham

Prime Minister Atherton tapped at the tablet's screen, pausing the audio recording. "Damned by her own words," he said. "Cavendish knew that Emmitt was waiting to shoot her?"

"Almost certainly," Mitchell said. "The tyres on her getaway truck were slashed. She was trapped. I suspect the only reason her people didn't abandon her is that Emmitt was taking pot shots at them." He stretched out his legs, and briefly closed his eyes. It had been a frantic twenty-four hours, but so far there had been no new crisis in Britain, no more murders, and no insurrection.

"So that was Cavendish's death-bed confession," Atherton said. "The question is whether we can believe it."

"Yes," Mitchell said. "At least in broad strokes. It mostly confirms what the evidence has already proven."

"And Emmitt is dead?"

"You should have a report from the Dover coroner by tomorrow morning," Mitchell said. "But, yes. He's dead."

"You're sure."

"I am."

"Then that brings us to what we do next," Atherton said. He picked up his glass, and only then seemed to realise it was empty. He swivelled in his chair, turning to face the decanter by the door, and seemed to catch sight of the two portraits watching him. He sighed, and put the empty glass back on his desk. "What *do* we do? We can't use that recording in a trial."

"Since Cavendish is dead, there won't be trial," Mitchell said.

"Not of her, but what of her co-conspirators?"

"I doubt there are many," Mitchell said. "Not who knew what the woman really planned. Not who are still alive."

Atherton picked up a sheet of paper from the desk. "We've almost won a victory in Calais. That's what the admiral is calling it, though I don't know if I agree. She says that our objectives have been achieved now that the pirates have fled their positions."

"The Marines call them cultists," Mitchell said. "Personally, I'd prefer we just called them murderers, but I'm not I'm not the one putting my life on the line. Are they really retreating?"

"Some have fled," Atherton said. "But Calais is not yet entirely secure. There are…" He glanced at the sheet of paper again. "There are three groups who have gone to ground on the outskirts. One is in an old supermarket to the east, one group is in a church to the north, and the last is in a school three miles to the northeast of the city. Until they are dug out of their positions, we can't chase those who fled. Without pursuit, they'll have time to create a new bastion, this time further from our own supply lines. But our losses have been severe. Two hundred and seventeen are dead. At least four hundred will never return to frontline duty. A further eight hundred and ninety-two have been brought back to Britain for medical treatment."

"That many?" Mitchell said.

"Not from the battle, not directly," Atherton said. "Dysentery has swept through the ranks. This was our first major conflict and we were woefully unprepared. No, best we use the next few months to get ready, because this is only the beginning."

"It does seem that way," Mitchell said. "What are you doing about the Railway Company?"

"There I am on the horns of a dilemma," Atherton said. "The Railway Company directly employs thousands. Indirectly, it employs tens of thousands, and they all have families. They all have friends. And they all vote."

"You're worried about the election?" Mitchell asked.

"Since the conspiracy centred around placing a puppet in this chair, shouldn't I be? There are too many to lock-up. I can't conscript them, nor send them to one of our overseas outposts, as that would risk creating the insurrection that I am trying to stop. I *will* nationalise the railway, and bring it under direct control of the cabinet, but there is little else that can be done." Atherton fixed his eyes on the portraits that hung by the door. "Can one absolute good erase a lifetime of sin? We would not be here if it wasn't for Cavendish. The same can be said for many of her people."

"You want to hush this all up?" Mitchell half turned in his chair, and gestured at the paintings. "I bet Wilberforce once said something about how the motive didn't justify the ends. Either way, the truth will come out. Best to get ahead of it. Broadcast the recording. Let people decide for themselves."

"They tried to win power through disrupting the election, and though they are dead, they still might achieve that goal. My only true opponent is Alasdair McPherson, and he is a Luddite. Not like your deluded witness. I mean that McPherson is a genuine revolutionary, and is the only candidate I would even call a real politician. The others are venal, corrupt, and care for nothing but power. They are too busy fighting over which of them gets the right to call their party Conservative or Labour. No, they want to rule simply so that history can say that they did. They want their portrait on the wall, nothing more. There is even a growing movement that wants a monarch. Some of those say we should give the position to the King of Albion, mostly because the man knows how to sit on a horse."

"You mean you want to suppress this recording so as to guarantee your victory?" Mitchell asked.

"No. I want to impress upon you the delicate situation we are in," Atherton said. "I am not so naive as to assume that you haven't made copies of that recording. Nor do I forget that you believe yourself above the civil power."

"No," Mitchell said. "I believe that the law applies to the governors as much as the governed. You know what my father hated about politicians? They always thought that some policies were too complex for the average voter to understand. What you lot never grasped was that it was *you* who didn't understand what *we*, the electorate, actually wanted. After all, who is a newly elected politician but an elector a few hours after the last vote was cast?"

"Very pithy," Atherton said. He picked up a report from the desk. "We will take Calais and put a garrison in Boulogne, but we will need three months to resupply and retrain, and for our troops to recover. The offensive will start in March. The bodies will begin coming back in April, just in time for the election in May."

"Are you going to broadcast that recording?"

Atherton looked at the tablet. "If doing so has the opposite effect? If the nation falls apart?"

"Do you remember twenty years ago, when we first met?" Mitchell asked. "Do you remember that underground railway station?"

"Almost every night," Atherton said.

"And it's twenty years later, and we're still here," Mitchell said. "Have some faith in people, and they'll have faith in you."

"Hmm. Very well," Atherton said. "I will have it broadcast."

Mitchell stood. "I'll leave you that, too," he said, nodding at the tablet. "There's a few good books on there."

"Where are you going now? Home, or Dover?" Atherton asked.

"I was hoping to retire," Mitchell said. "I really was, but war will make bloody work for soldier and police officer alike. No, I'd like to retire, but I can't. I'm a copper, and I'm glad I'm not a soldier." He smiled. "But I'm even more glad I'm not a politician."

Epilogue 2 - Sameen
19th November, Dover

"Friends, comrades, we were betrayed," Alasdair McPherson yelled, though there was no need for him to raise his voice. The crowd gathered at Dover's dockside was small and they were hanging on the man's every word. "You heard that recording of Rebecca Cavendish, didn't you? You saw the words printed in the newspaper? Those we trusted to lead us have betrayed that trust. Cavendish. Wallace. Longfield. The industrialists, the politicians, the leaders who told us to trust *them* were motivated only by greed, by power. They wanted a return to the days of the one-percent, the days of exploitation, of unchecked capitalism at the expense of *our* labour and without consideration for the sweat of our brows. They want to bring back the old world. Well, some of us remember what the old world was *really* like. Inequality. Exploitation. Poverty. Working two jobs and still unable to feed your family. That was the old world. We were prisoners to technology in a world of distractions, told to be grateful that our lot was better than the starving millions in the nations we had destroyed. Bankrupt countries. Constant war. Constant terror. That was the old world. A dying world filled with corrupt autocrats who thought they were god. That is what they want to bring back. Is that what *you* want? Is it?"

The last demand was loud enough to cause a pair of sailors carrying shells onto the *HMS Resolve* to pause halfway up the gangplank.

"No lollygagging!" a bosun called out. "There are murderers, rapists, and cannibals in France waiting for a gift of those shells. Move it!"

The words were addressed solely to the two sailors, but yelled in a parade-ground bark loud enough to echo across the dockyard warehouses. The spell McPherson had been weaving was broken. A few near the rear of small crowd glanced towards the large clock on top of the shipping office, and drifted away.

Ruth checked the time herself. McPherson had another two minutes before he was breaking the law. He knew it, as did the woman with the angular nose standing next to the cart McPherson was using as a stage. Her eyes were glued to her pocket watch.

"No more, I say. No more," McPherson continued. "We must learn from the mistakes of the past. We must learn not to repeat them. There is a better way. A just way, a…"

Ruth tuned him out, and turned her attention to the crowd. It was four days since Cavendish and Emmitt had died. Three days since the radio broadcast of Mitchell's confrontation with the traitor, but McPherson had already been in Dover. Ruth wasn't sure why he was here, though it wasn't simply to protest the war. Not outright, anyway. Sergeant Kettering had said McPherson was simply trying to raise his profile before the election.

Ruth checked the time again. McPherson was allowed ten minutes before he could be charged with obstructing the military power. Exactly nine minutes after he began, he came to a finish.

"There is a better way than this," McPherson roared. "A better future for our children. It is not too late for us to change the course of history." And then he jumped down from the cart, grabbed one handle as the woman grabbed the other, and they pulled the cart away. A couple of people in the small crowd followed. Most turned around, heading back to work. There was a lot of work to be done.

Ruth, half turning around, paused as she saw a familiar face. Craddock, the pickpocket that they'd arrested the day Mr Wilson was murdered. She wondered what he was doing out of jail. The man hadn't noticed her in the shadows of the chandler's doorway. He was pushing his way through the crowd as if he was heading for the ship's gangway. As Craddock made his way around a middle-aged woman with a twice-broken nose and thrice-broken spectacles held together with wire, Ruth saw the thief's hand dip into the woman's pocket.

"Hoy! Stop!" she yelled, darting out from the shadows. "Stop! Thief!" The crowd stopped and turned to see who was shouting. Craddock didn't. As Ruth pushed and weaved her way towards him, the man dropped the woman's wallet and nimbly sidestepped his way through the crowd.

"Police! Move!" Ruth barked, and a few people did, but more got in her way as they turned around to see why she'd called out.

Craddock darted down the long alley that ran between two of the new-built warehouses storing replacement rope and timbers for the wood-and-steel ships. Ruth reached the back of the crowd and ran after him. Craddock reached a door halfway along. Ruth didn't stop running. She knew the doors were locked. Craddock gave them a pull, a shove, and realised it, too. He ran, but there was only twenty feet between them. Nineteen. Eighteen. Nineteen. He was faster than she, and the end of the alley was less than thirty feet away. If he reached it first, he could disappear into the warren of pubs and cafes that clustered around the docks. On the other hand, he wasn't going to get out of the city. Dover's gates were kept closed now even during daylight. The military police patrolled the city around the clock. The thief *would* be caught. But they were military and she was police. Craddock was a criminal, and he wasn't going to get away.

She found a last ounce of speed. The distance narrowed. The pickpocket drew nearer to the end of the alley as Ruth drew nearer to him. Craddock's left foot hit the pavement at the alley's end, and then a boathook hit him square in the shins.

Craddock tumbled out into the road, landing in a pile of recently deposited horse manure. Craddock made an attempt to stand up, but the boathook pushed him back down, a boathook held by Isaac.

"Seriously?" Ruth said.

"No thanks necessary," Isaac said. "I was simply doing my civic duty, assisting our gallant officers in the upholding of our laws."

"Yeah, but look at him," Ruth said. "He's covered in manure. It'll be hours before he's collected by the military police, during which time he'll stink up the station, and I've got to sleep there. Get up, you. And don't try to run."

"And that's the thanks an honest citizen gets for assisting the civil power," Isaac said.

"Don't start," Ruth said. "It's bad enough having you following me around without you spouting that kind of nonsense."

"In a bad mood today, are we, Ruth?" Isaac asked.

Ruth cuffed the thief, doing her best not to touch the man's manure-speckled coat. "Off to the police station," Ruth said to Craddock. "You know the way. On which note, how come you aren't in jail for robbing that master tailor?"

"The tailor didn't want to press charges," the thief said.

"Really? Why not?" she asked, but Craddock didn't reply. Nevertheless, Ruth's interest was piqued. Why would a master tailor not want to press charges? It was something to look into. There probably wasn't a crime at the bottom of it, but she was a copper, and it was something to investigate.

"Tell you what, Isaac," Ruth said. "Since you want to help, take him back to the cells. Give him a wash outside, a change of clothes, and," she added, slightly vindictively, "a hot cup of tea."

Three hours later, Ruth had spoken to the middle-aged woman whose pocket Craddock had picked, and discovered that she didn't want to press charges, either.

"An interesting business," Kettering said as she glanced through Ruth's notes. "Two victims of the same thief. One drops the charges, the other doesn't want them pressed, despite it being the definition of open and shut."

"Something is going on, isn't it?" Ruth said. "Something illegal. They don't want charges pressed because Craddock knows, and they know he'll tell."

"I would say so," Kettering said.

"Then I'm going to ask him," Ruth said.

"No, not yet," Kettering said. "Craddock isn't going anywhere, and this little piece of knowledge of his is clearly prized to him. He won't give it up so easily. No, let him sweat. Let's look into the victims first. But I can do that. It's getting on, there's only a few hours of daylight left if you still wanted to go out."

Ruth glanced at the clock. It was one thirty, still what she would call lunchtime, but Kettering was right. Night came early as the winter solstice neared. She almost said no. She almost said that she'd rather spend her time digging into this new mystery. And she *would* have preferred it, but there was an older mystery that she had to solve, one that would nag away at her until she did.

"I'll be back at five," Ruth said.

"As long as you're back by half past seven," Kettering said. "We're celebrating tonight."

"Celebrating what?" Ruth asked.

"Eloise has a new job. She's an apprentice to the coroner. It'll be months of moving corpses before she's even allowed to witness an autopsy, but it's still worth celebrating."

"It is?"

"She isn't joining the Marines," Kettering said. "I'd rather she dealt with dead bodies than became one."

Isaac was sitting by the front door of the police station, seemingly oblivious to the cold.

Ruth thrust her hands into her pockets. "How can you stand this weather?"

"I've lived through far worse," Isaac said. "The first year after the Blackout, I was certain the snow would never melt. The fire truly brought the ice. Before the Blackout, the data suggested nuclear winter was a myth. Perhaps it was. I have my own theory as to what brought the snow. I even wrote it up as a paper during one particularly icy spell. Not that I had it published. There was no university back then to review it, and no publication to print it. Perhaps I should dust it off, and see if the newspaper would be interested. Perhaps not. No, this is pleasant by comparison. Are we taking a stroll?"

"I don't suppose there's any point me telling you to stay behind?"

"Not really, no," he said, smiling.

"Have you heard from Mister Mitchell?" Ruth asked as they headed towards the western-gate.

"I was going to ask whether you had," Isaac said. "But no, I haven't."

"You can't call him?" she asked.

"Not unless we're both in Twynham," Isaac said.

Dover was bustling as ships arrived from the furthest corners of the world. Word had gone out to Africa, the Americas, and beyond, recalling all but the most essential of shipping. Marines and sailors were being reassigned, sent to stiffen the ranks of the newly recruited regiments. None of them looked happy about it.

They reached the gate and found it closed.

"Any business today?" Ruth asked.

"Only the official kind," the gate-captain asked. "You'll be back before nightfall?"

"Long before," Ruth said.

The postern gate was opened, and they were allowed through.

"Where are we looking today?" Isaac asked.

Ruth took out the map. "Square C4," she said. "And tomorrow we'll do C5."

It had begun with the pub from which Emmitt had shot Cavendish. The Five Bells, there was something about the name that had struck a chord with Ruth. It was so difficult to know what was true memory and what was overlaid fabrication based on recent observation, but that pub, at least its name, had resonated deep inside.

She'd found the map in the library and had divided up the area within five miles of the old Folkestone refugee camp. She was limiting her search to that which a small child could conceivably run. It would probably lead to nothing, but she had to search. She had to look, and make the effort simply so that she could tell herself she had.

"You know, I could install a map on your tablet," Isaac said.

"With McPherson in Dover, I think we'll avoid overt displays of technology for now," Ruth said. The newspaper hadn't printed anything about a surge in anti-technological sentiment, but she was increasingly suspicious that the paper was only printing what Atherton wanted the world to know. Certainly, the coverage of Cavendish's arrest had been... lacking. It had lacked in details, in names, and in condemnation of anyone other than Cavendish, Longfield, Wallace, and Fairmont. Emmitt's death had received only the briefest of mentions, with the paper implying that he'd just been another one of Cavendish's thugs. The article hadn't explicitly said that the crisis was over, though it had implied it, using soaring rhetoric exhorting all efforts now be directed into ridding Europe of the Knights of St Sebastian. They'd made no mention of the other two groups of cultists, but that, Ruth thought, was more because there was only so much room in the newspaper.

A letter had arrived that morning from Riley. She was working the investigation into the Railway Company. Five arrests had been made, and Riley expected to make at least five more, but not many more than that. The Railway Company had been nationalised, but nothing had obviously changed. The trains still ran on time. Telegrams were still delivered. The war in France continued.

"Life goes on," she said.

"It finds a way, doesn't it," Isaac said. "We're reaching the end of the road, at least as far as it runs in this square on your grid. Are we continuing, or going back?"

"No," Ruth said. "We'll go… that way." She pointed eastward, mostly because the ferns looked less dense than the bracken dotting the land to the west. "Are you going to build your antenna?" Ruth asked as she pushed a path through the damp fronds.

"*I* am not going to build it," Isaac said. "But a radio antenna is going to be built in the grounds of the castle."

"And you'll use it for your phone network?"

"I will."

"And who's going to have access to that?" Ruth asked.

"In time, everyone."

"How much time?" she asked.

"How swift does a river flow?" Isaac replied.

Ruth didn't press. Isaac was, for the most part, actually answering her questions. The answers weren't always complete, and they were rarely in depth, but they *were* answers.

The ferns thinned as the trees grew taller. They passed the remains of a wall, and then the ruin of a house. A fire had gutted it decades before, perhaps even before the Blackout. Ravens had taken nest therein, and they scattered as Ruth and Isaac approached, taking to the low branches of a towering oak. Beyond the house was a road, and beyond that was an old stone bridge that ran over a dry riverbed.

"That bridge," Ruth said. "That's familiar. Where are we?"

"The garden centre where we found Illyakov is about a quarter mile northwest of here," Isaac said.

"Did we come near here during the chase?"

"Here, no," Isaac said.

"So why is it familiar?" Ruth said.

"Perhaps it isn't," Isaac said. "I saw Marines practicing in the small-arms range with those AK-47s we found with Illyakov."

"You did?"

"It's a worrying development," Isaac said.

"Why?" Ruth asked. She crossed to the broken balustrade, and peered up and down the dry riverbed. "I mean, there's no point wasting that ammunition, is there?"

"It means we're so short of ammunition we have to take it from the enemy," Isaac said.

The riverbed was covered in shrubs and a few stubby saplings struggling to reach daylight under the shadow of the far larger trees on either side of the embankment.

"You have a store of ammunition, don't you?" Ruth said. "Maybe you should donate that to the cause." Hands grabbing for branches and roots, she slid down the embankment.

"And this was a new suit," Isaac muttered as he skidded down the bank after her. "I *do* have ammunition, but not enough to supply a war."

"Hmm. Is *this* familiar?" Ruth peered at cracked pillar supporting the bridge.

"You tell me," Isaac said.

"Probably not," Ruth said. "Which way is Dover? That way?" She set off along the riverbed. "What about your people, like Kelly and Mrs Zhang, why don't you get them to join the Marines?"

"They are not suited to taking orders," Isaac said, following her.

"They take orders from you," Ruth said.

"The people who… listen to me do so because I have offered them a refuge in a world where no other could be found. They are fighters, not soldiers."

Ruth let it go.

"I saw Mr Watanabe yesterday," she said. "There's nothing to charge him with. Not yet, anyway, but Sprocket and Sprung has been shut down while the Naval Intelligence Office and Commissioner Weaver battle over which one of them has the jurisdiction to continue the investigation."

"How is Mr Watanabe?" Isaac asked.

"Busy," Ruth said. "He's taken over a room near the railway station, him and the rest of his old co-workers. They're back to repairing everything that needs to be fixed. But you know what he said?"

"Tell me," Isaac said.

"That after the radio broadcast, after they said Cavendish's confession was recorded on a tablet, people have been coming in with battered phones and computers, asking if they can be repaired."

"Ah, so is that a case of the more things change the more they stay the same, or is it more an example of the wheel of time returning us to our—"

"What's that?" Ruth cut in, as she pushed through a dense patch of rhododendrons.

Ahead, covered in moss and ivy was a rusting truck. The doors at the back were open. The interior was empty except for a thin layer of mulch.

"How did they get it down here," Isaac said. "There must be a road or track up there. They can't have seen the gulch, and so drove right into it."

Ruth pushed her way along the vehicle, to the cab. The windows were smashed, the glass gone.

"Oh," she said, and took a step back.

"What?" Isaac said, coming up to join her.

"There are bones in here," Ruth said. "Pecked clean."

"By birds and foxes," Isaac said. "The drivers, I suppose."

"I suppose," Ruth said. She was getting that feeling of déjà-vu again. She gripped the grab-bar next to the cab. It came away in her hand along with a few inches of rusting metal around the bolts. Ruth tried the door. It was jammed shut.

"What are you trying to do?" Isaac asked.

"There's a… a wallet or something. It's on the floor, do you see, next to that skull."

"So?" Isaac asked.

"So this truck had to have come here after the Blackout, right? But we didn't have money until recently. Not money you could put in a wallet. So why is there one on the floor of the cab?"

"Hang on, then." Isaac pulled on the door, but it wouldn't budge. "We need Gregory for this," he said.

"How is he?" Ruth asked, as she braced her foot on the rotting rubber tyre and pulled herself onto the bonnet. The metal creaked, then dropped an inch.

"He's getting better," Isaac said. "Careful."

"I'm almost… there," Ruth said as she reached through the broken windscreen. "Got it," she said, as she grabbed the wallet. She jumped off the cab. "Oh, it's not a wallet. It's a photo album. There's an old couple in this picture, I think. And another in this one. Those are definitely pre-Blackout. And… oh. It's a family. A man, a woman, a girl. A young girl. I guess… I guess it's their daughter." The picture was faded, the features indistinct. She took the photograph out of the thin plastic sleeve. The paper felt brittle. She peered at the three people, then turned the picture over. "Oh," she said.

"What?" Isaac asked.

"Here," Ruth said. "There are three names on the back, and a date that's after the Blackout."

"Hassan, Saleema, Sameen," Isaac said. "Sameen. That girl in the picture is Sameen." He looked from the picture to Ruth. "There's no way of knowing that it's you."

"Isaac, I was here before," Ruth said. "I remember now. I *do*." She smiled. "I really do. I knew there was something familiar about this place. It's just… it's changed so much."

2019

Saleema Hafiz tried to move her head, but it felt like lead. It was hard to tell how long had passed since they'd taken shelter in the ruined truck. Minutes? Hours? She wasn't sure, but the rain had finally stopped. Hassan's eyes were open. His head was nodding back and forth as if he was trying to speak, but no words came out. Sameen's eyes were closed. She was twitching. Again, Saleema tried to move. Again, she found she couldn't.

There was a loud bang as of something hitting the cab. There was a rustle of leaves outside. Again, Saleema tried to move, tried to turn her head towards the feral animal that had found them and which would find them such easy prey. The cab door opened. It wasn't an animal. It was a girl, around Sameen's age and not too dissimilar in appearance. She had Sameen's bear in her hand.

"Get help," Saleema whispered.

The girl held the bear up towards Sameen.

"Go, girl, go! Get…. get help," Saleema said. "The… The Five Bells… Go there. Please."

Slowly, the girl lowered her hand, still holding the bear.

"Go. The Five Bells. There's a man," Saleema said. "He has… has medicine. Go. Please. Get… get help. The Five Bells… Five…" But the words were lost in a coughing fit.

Still clutching the bear, the girl turned, and ran away through the forest. Saleema tried to keep her eyes open, but couldn't. They slid closed. It didn't matter. She could rest now. The girl would get help. They would find Mr Emmitt, and arrest him. They would get the antidote and her family would be safe. They would reach Twynham, and then America. They would go to the wide plains. Their daughter would run barefoot through the waist high grass, knowing nothing but peace and love in a world without fear.

And then, like Hassan five minutes before, and her daughter a minute before that, Saleema Hafiz died.

"I was here before," Ruth said.

Isaac frowned. "I don't understand why you're smiling."

"It's not funny," Ruth said. "I mean, this is sad. It's *tragic*, but look. Look at that skull. It's not an adult's skull." She pointed through the window. "Look at the bones. There were two adults and a child who died in that cab." She held up the photograph. "Hassan, Saleema, and Sameen. The girl Emmitt was looking for, she died in this truck."

"You're not Sameen," Isaac said. "What else do you remember?"

"A woman telling me to go to the Five Bells," Ruth said. "No. No, I remember her saying The Five Bells. That's it, really. Then I remember running. Then… it's a blur, really. I remember Maggie. I remember, finally, feeling safe. That's all. I don't think it matters, not really, because I was just the person who found them. I went to get help, so I ran to the camp. There, Maggie found me, but no one found these people. Not until now. I'm *not* Sameen. The girl Emmitt was looking for is dead. It's over, Isaac. It really is. Come on, we need to follow this river bed and mark exactly where it is, because we'll need to find this truck again."

"We will?" Isaac asked.

"We have to bury the bodies," Ruth said. "But not here. And not at the old refugee camp. We should bury them at a cemetery in Dover where they *won't* be forgotten."

She trudged back along the riverbed, towards the city.

The war wouldn't be over by Christmas, but Christmas would come. 2039 would end, and a new year would begin. It would bring sadness and joy, work and pain, but she would face it as a new person. A great burden had been lifted from her, one she'd not realised she was carrying. For the first time in her life, she knew who she was. She was Ruth Deering. She was Maggie Deering's daughter. She was an officer in the British constabulary. Life goes on, and she felt like hers was about to begin.

The end.

27506415R00158

Printed in Great Britain
by Amazon